Praise for Award-Winning Author C. Hope Clark

Hope Clark's books have been honored as winners of the:

EPIC Award, Silver Falchion Award, Imadjinn Award,

and the

Daphne du Maurier Award.

"Another page turner."

—Brenda Burke, Amazon Vine Reviewer on *Edisto Bullet*

"A great series."

—Lynn Simmons, bookseller, Books-A-Million

"*Badge of Edisto* further establishes Clark's well-earned reputation as a master of the mystery genre."

—Jonathan Haupt, coeditor,
Our Prince of Scribes: Writers Remember Pat Conroy

The Novels of
C. Hope Clark

The Carolina Slade Mysteries

Lowcountry Bribe
Tidewater Murder
Palmetto Poison
Newberry Sin
Salkehatchie Secret
Lake Murray Money

The Edisto Island Mysteries

Murder on Edisto
Edisto Jinx
Echoes of Edisto
Edisto Stranger
Dying on Edisto
Edisto Tidings
Reunion on Edisto
Edisto Heat
Badge of Edisto
Edisto Bullet
Edge of Edisto
Edisto Storm
Hidden on Edisto

The Craven County Mysteries

Murdered in Craven
Burned in Craven
Craven County Line

Edge of Edisto

The Edisto Island Mysteries
Book 11

by

C. Hope Clark

Edisto Bridge Books

EDISTO
BRIDGE

Edisto Bridge Books
140A Amicks Ferry Road, PMB 4
Chapin, SC 29036
Print ISBN: 978-1-968423-20-9

Visit Hope at chopeclark.com

Cover design: Debra Dixon
Interior design: Hank Smith
Photo/Art credits:
(manipulated) © Eti Swinford | Dreamstime.com

:LEes:01:

Dedication

Dedicated to two special people:

First, I'd like to remember Lynn Zeluff, aka Zeller, who lived on Edisto until passing away in early 2024. She adored all that was Edisto and worked or volunteered at every venue in that beach town. She released this wonderful laugh and could tell tales I loved to listen to, and I snared a few snippets of her thoughts and inserted them into a few of my Edisto mysteries. She read everything I ever wrote about that island. Miss you, Zeller.

Next, I honor Henry Cheves, Edisto artist and watercolor painter extraordinaire. I miss his Facebook page depicting his latest design, the donations for his art going to charity. His cam footage showed us how Edisto beach looked in real time on any givenday, connecting us to the luscious reality he lived in and loved deeply,making the rest of us wish wewere like him. He had a wonderful, gifted eye for what Edisto meant not only to him but to everyone else.

Prologue

Lydia

IN SPITE OF THE rain, Lydia slipped to the porch, slinging her grandmother's antique embroidered shawl around her, staying far enough back not to let moisture ruin the velvet and silk. The shawl had been left to her instead of her mother, who'd OD'd when Lydia was a child, but it was all she owned of the women living under that roof. The slide of the material, the faded reds, the simple endurance of its age gave it wisdom. Wisdom over adversity. Not that she had unlocked the code to its insights. Still, each time she slung it around her shoulders, she felt... enabled.

Despite not holding many pleasant memories of either woman, she held better ones of Grandmother since she'd raised her, and, though feeble, the old woman had been a force to be reckoned with. Some days Lydia imagined being like her. She sure as hell didn't want to be like her mother, not that she remembered much of her.

Yet Lydia loved that shawl.

She was definitely moody this morning. And frustrated, and deeply introspective as to where her life was going. Hers and the others under her wing. Like she, maybe they, were on the edge of change.

Problems had piled up not even a week into their retreat from the real world—a trip and a time of year that she always looked forward to so much.

Instead she'd grown uneasy about the coastal weather, this house, and unfortunately, even the crew that vacationed with her. That had never been the case.

The perfect storm of disgruntlement.

What the hell had she been thinking letting Chiara bring a friend? There was needing sympathy, and then there was just plain needy, but Lydia was stuck with this friend now. Lydia gazed across the ocean with options pinging in her head and pondered what the hell to do now about the girl and what she'd done.

Son of a bitch.

She turned just to look at something different, putting her back to the gunmetal clouds and queasy sea to study... this place.

Regardless of what tourists thought, Edisto's appearances on "Best of" lists compiled by *Travel & Leisure* and *Southern Living* were not an accolade. Regulars and locals looked upon such recognition as a bane. The fresh attention was as welcome as bears to a campground picnic. The unexpected deluge of people from high-cost-of-living states only skyrocketed rental rates, ruining it for the regulars who used to call Edisto an affordable vacation.

Silly woman, believing what she paid last year would land them a similar quality address, and it was too late to demand a different house, one that at least had light bulbs in all the lamps. They'd make do. Christ, half the outlets didn't even work.

Three days in and they were still finding dead Palmetto bugs in closets and under furniture.

The kitchen held enough mismatched pots to cook for a football team but not a spatula in the place. No soap. Thank God she'd brought toilet paper. Many of the accommodations were minimal, just enough to check a box on the damn amenities list. Oh, for older times.

Enough stewing in your juices. She returned attention to the ocean, envisioning how the hell she would handle the issues heaped upon her, the house being the least of her worries.

Rain ran off the roof, landing muffled in the sand below, and a blue-gray haze coated St. Helena Sound. Nobody walked the waterline. The tide was muted, the landscape floating like a soft watercolor painting with the intricate details left out.

Choosing one of the slumped rattan chairs with its flattened, moldy cushions, she eased to sit. God help her. Breathing in slow, then slower, she closed her eyes and sought her Zen. Thank Jesus for salt water. It healed her each and every year.

But it might not be enough to fix this.

Toughen up.

The point was they were here for two weeks. Fourteen days away from the mundane and back into their altered lifestyle of being the women they felt they really were, doing what they desired, when they wanted, how they wanted. Their altered universe.

Gripping the shawl tighter, the seventy-five degrees chilly compared to the forthcoming ninety-degree day, the chair creaked, the seat sinking in spite of her recent ten-pound loss. The pounds had crept up on her after last summer, but strength training and high protein had allowed her to shed the weight in time for this arrival. She was still grateful for what she saw in the mirror. Sixty once felt an eternity away. The benchmark had come and gone three years ago. The rest of her time on earth would flash by like nothing.

Her ultimate goal was to live life to her demands, to her standards. Anyone who interfered were dealt with and deemed history. Life was too damn short.

Chill. Chill. You're here now. Not as planned, but you can handle this.

This. She hadn't handled something like *this* for decades, yet still, those emotions she'd thought calloused over currently bubbled beneath the surface, threatening to return.

Another deep breath, holding... then an exhale.

You don't have to do anything at the moment.

No. But she didn't have long. Right now, she was most grateful to have this late-morning moment to herself after such a long night. To regroup.

She woke up achy, partly due to the weather, partly a result of the worn mattress, making her wonder how much longer she would be coming back like this, in this capacity, playing the leading-lady role with the group. If she didn't get a grip fast, this would most certainly be her last.

Clouds hid the sun while haze hid Pine and Otter Islands which were normally easy to see. The morning was well on its way toward noon.

A gust hugged the house's corners then zipped around it, whistling, singing to announce another wave of rain. The snap of an American flag on a neighboring pole startled her to the right. Her line of vision suddenly caught sight of two doe and a fawn strolling through the tall dune grasses and the low hugging orange Carolina beach flowers. The animals grazed, oblivious of the drizzle, strolling through the very sand burrs that had taken residence on her slip-ons yesterday.

Her phone buzzed with a text, but she lolled her head back, the top of the chair hitting the nape of her neck, and she didn't answer.

God, give me another thirty minutes.

Wouldn't take long for the one text to turn into four, then five, then more, and the day would be filled with social obligations.

Her crew comprised five of the many recurring summer visitors on the beach, the ones who traditionally appeared year after year after year. Lydia considered her and her group regulars, not novice vacationers with their wagons of floats and towels and needy kids. Not a native, though, which one had to respect. Instead, they—or rather mostly she—belonged to a third class, well versed in the island, who still claimed Edisto as theirs. With a full understanding of the island, Lydia put her knowledge up against any of the natives. After all, she had been born there.

Thumps and low voices interrupted the rainy white noise. The house's residents stirred. Wouldn't be long before they laid out breakfast, ranging from Vivien's high-protein Greek yogurt to Robin's four scrambled eggs cooked only in extra-virgin olive oil. Chiara thrived on caffeine. Maddy ate whatever someone else offered to fix for her.

None married. No one wanting to be. Most had traveled that path already and deemed it unworthy of a repeat performance.

As orchestrator of this retreat and the eldest, Lydia snared the bedroom with the best view of the ocean, letting the others sort out who shared. As expected, the two youngest drew the short straws. Chiara was on the cusp of forty and oozed personality and had taken excellent care of herself. Quite a beauty, actually. Her maturity level had melded her with their older trio five years ago. Maddy, the newest, the one Lydia regretted bringing, was about the same age.

While the cadre was selective, the timing of Chiara's request to include Maddy was such that they had a moment's notice whether to adjust the number for the annual trek or hurt feelings. Banking on Chiara's inherent common sense, they gave the newest girl a go. After only three days, Lydia wished, way too late, that they hadn't.

The long-term unit of four—Lydia, Chiara, Vivien, and Robin—had an unspoken set of rules, and an unspoken method of learning them.

Vivien had been around as long as Lydia had, with Robin five years behind. Two and three decades each. Vivien held tight onto her decade at fifty-nine. They'd been a hard and fast trio until Chiara arrived, who rather accented them, Lydia thought. She made the team realize four worked best. Besides, everyone enjoyed mother-henning Chiara.

They planted their flag on Edisto Beach every year in June. Lydia sighed down to her navel but felt no release from the effort. One week into two weeks of bliss had gone to hell thanks to Maddy.

The drizzle turned to steady rain. The weather channel said the moisture might be gone by noon. She sure wished she'd grabbed her coffee before anchoring herself so comfortably in this porch spot.

"Lydia? When's our day going to start happening?" hollered Vivien from inside. "This week has been kinda slow." Lydia envisioned her licking her yogurt spoon. Three times on the front, three times on the back. Just like her attorney friend to act as if everything was fine.

"You see this weather?" Lydia hollered back.

"Nothing I want to do is outside," Vivien yelled back, laughing.

How the hell was she laughing? "Find a puzzle. It's early."

"I want people," she said. "Find us some friends. Where's our old buddies? Thought we had parties and a bit of fun lined up."

She feigned cabin fever, keeping up the charade in front of the others. "Give the world time to wake up," Lydia replied. "Impatience is never becoming on a lady."

Robin piped in. "You're so full of it, Lydia."

Yeah. They could think so, but Lydia made this group click. She'd give her crew a half hour more, then she'd start returning texts. As quiet as Vivien might make things appear, people were beginning to realize the women had arrived—certain people who'd come to expect every summer to seek out the ladies—and after thirty years, they had quite the list of friends. The group loved to socialize, and they each had the skills to make this summer fun.

"Where's Maddy?" Robin asked.

Chiara appeared from her bedroom, hair freshly blown dry. "Yeah, where is Maddy?"

"Didn't come in last night," Lydia said. "She checked in with me."

"Uh, oh," Robin teased. "She found her a live one. Good for her."

Chiara, however, didn't seem convinced. "Why didn't she text me?"

"Maybe she grew her own wings, honey." Robin pushed back Chiara more than the others. "Let it go. This evening, find your own."

Lydia left them to their banter. Maddy hadn't gone anywhere. She just wasn't right here... right now.

Chapter 1

Callie

EDISTO BEACH didn't owe its popularity solely to magazine features and blog lists of ten best places to do this or that. *People* drove Edisto's stellar reputation. The people behind the scenes—the cops, the shop owners, and the real estate agents—proved quite efficient at appeasing any discontented vacationers, while the town government banned the franchises that could ruin its "Edislow" image. The businesses bit their collective lips about the craziness of strangers throughout the summer. Edisto's community needed this horde of people—the nice and the polite, the rude and the demanding. The beach and much of the island gobbled up May-through-September money, smiling through the sweat and fifteen-hour days, knowing that January would be lean.

Police Chief Callie Jean Morgan's police department kept the community civil with its grand total of six officers, plus a deputy on loan from the county sheriff's department and the lone admin, Marie Gadson.

Of that line-up, Marie was the most important.

Lunch had come and gone unnoticed at the station. The June morning had brought rain, the wet forecast stretching into the early afternoon. Currently the humidity registered "thick as buttermilk through a straw."

Briny air wafted in whenever the disgruntled entered the building. Callie delegated two officers to patrol the streets while she managed the small storms that found their way to headquarters, tiny as it was.

Ten to one.

Those were the odds of a complaint needing serious attention. Marie kept the statistics. She kept all sorts of statistics to arm Callie in her monthly presentation to the town council. Marie always had a system for handling anything. Right now, six citizens waited in the lobby, nobody local, the air thick with the scents of body odor, deodorant, and assorted lotions.

Unaccustomed to a beach that didn't scream neon, motels, drive-throughs, and live music into the wee hours, many visitors wearied of the low-key environment by Thursday, which this day happened to be. That's when they most got into each other's hair. It was amazing at how many people couldn't stand being alone with themselves and their supposed loved ones. On Thursdays, the testiest flocked to the station wanting something fixed, changed, or done away with. As the chief of a very small department, Callie occupied the only private room in the station, meaning she took the loudest cases behind closed door. The rest faced Marie across the counter.

Callie had just escorted the third speeder of the day out of her office after listening to them rant about the heavy-handedness of one of her officers, which today would be either Thomas Gage or Annie Greer. Thomas hated writing tickets, and Annie let more than a few off with a warning. As a result, a complainant that came to Callie deserved whatever ticket they got, and each complainant usually left still in possession of said ticket and a deadline to pay the fine. Vacation rentals didn't come with permission to break the law.

Strategically, Marie handled the ones who fussed about not enough officers writing tickets. She allowed them to publicly air their grievance against dangerous speeders, allowed those words to hit their targets, aiming at those waiting in line to protest the ticket in their hand. One soul left on his own without being heard after ten minutes.

"I've been waiting here for an hour," shouted a man with an accent from at least five states away.

Callie eased up to Marie, putting her back to the crowd. "Is he next?"

Marie held her smile in place, nothing saccharin but enough to show the public she cared. Barely forty and a couple years younger than Callie, she'd done admin work for the Edisto PD since high school graduation.

She not only calmed the public but corralled the natives since they knew that she knew everyone's family secrets going back five generations or more. She appeared a tad older than her age, not attempting to cover the gray already taking residence in her once-blond hair. Her cut hadn't been altered in years, just long enough to pull back when the humidity was up, and her favorite uniform varied from jeans to loose shifts and mules, some days with floral peasant tops. Very much a mom look, an island look, a not-hunting-for-a-husband look, but the appearance made her homogenously safe to anyone, to include the rabble rousers who popped in during their seven-day stays.

"He's only been here twenty minutes," Marie uttered. "There are two ahead of him. Take the woman in blue."

Callie turned and motioned to the royal-and-aqua silk sarong wrapped around a late-thirty-something woman who wore it well. She stood out like a rose in a briar patch. The way she held arms around herself, Callie wanted to throw a sweater over her. "Ma'am? Care to come on back?"

"Wait, how do you know she's more important?" hollered the loud-mouth man.

But Marie addressed the man first. "Sir, has anyone died?"

He sputtered at the challenge. "Um, no."

"Anyone needing emergency medical attention?" Marie panned the room. "These questions apply to anyone here. Just trying to triage things."

Everyone shook their heads, the man's sunburned face taking on a deeper hue of red.

"Thank heavens for that, wouldn't y'all agree?" Marie said, to which all but the man nodded. "Then I thank you for your patience as we tend to each of your concerns. There's a drink machine if you want to exit and go around to the fire department. I promise I'll remember your place in line."

Wham, bam, the room quieted, Marie completely in control. The woman had managed this station through ten chiefs and double that in officers. There was a reason she'd outlasted everyone.

Callie motioned the sarong-clad woman to her office. She stood a good six inches over Callie, but then most people were taller than her five foot two.

"Now," Callie started, not writing, not recording, just being the ear most of these people needed for their crisis moment. "What can I do for you?"

The one-piece swimsuit beneath the wrap fit the woman like a second skin, muscles toned in her arms and legs, abs flat. Not a gym rat, but enough of a work-out enthusiast to maintain form. Yoga maybe. Callie's friend Sophie would approve.

The chill bumps on her arms said the air conditioner was a little much for this very pretty brunette. "My friend is missing," she said. "We came to the beach together, along with a group of girls, and she isn't answering her phone."

Many women's covens, multi-family collections, book clubs, and so on came to Edisto for retreats. In a crisis, they usually came to the police in a cluster, all a flutter. Callie's guess was this one hadn't broken the news to the others yet, hoping she didn't have to.

Callie held pen in hand. Missing person reports often turned into phones dying or being drowned, getting lost in the sand, or mistakenly dropped in the trash—any of which cut off the immediate contact the modern world had come to expect. People fell asleep in the sun or walked too far down the beach. Then there were the drunks.... But to the person unable to contact the one they loved, the possibilities were endless and all too scary. "Your name?"

"Chiara Hamilton."

"Can you spell that for me?" The hard K sound at the beginning of her first name threw Callie off.

The woman spelled out both names, neck muscles taut, eager to do this right to get someone to take her seriously.

"Where are you staying?" Callie asked.

"Time in a Bottle."

On the sound part of the beach, back facing the water. The white-siding house had a green roof versus the usual black and an extraordinarily large live oak with moss in the front yard—centered in the arc of a circular drive. The address was two-thirds the way down Palmetto Boulevard, close to Bailey Street. Not a higher-priced rental, at least fifty years old, with room for a dozen people if you filled all the bunks, doubles, and queens crammed into each bedroom, making it affordable for a group while enabling the owner to charge more.

"What is your friend's name?" Callie asked.

"Maddy Gillespie. She's in her late thirties, like me, only she's blond."

Chiara sat feet flat on the floor, palms on her thighs. While at first blush dressed for the water, she hadn't been in it. Her beach garb was for show, not swimming. She wore makeup. A dainty chain lay in the front valley of her neck, two rings on her hands, and earrings dangled from hooks in pierced ears, items easily lost in the surf. She hadn't been in the sun much. She wasn't tanned, red, or even pink around the edges. A social animal, which meant her girlfriend probably was as well.

They'd come to Edisto to party. Marie would agree.

But Callie also respected the fact that people—partiers or not—didn't come to police stations on whims. They came when their gut sensed the need and when their hearts worried what would happen if they didn't. She honored those feelings. She'd learned long ago to give them credence. Suffering fears about something you couldn't put a finger on had legitimate roots in DNA. Such feelings didn't have to make sense.

"What was she wearing?"

"A blue one-piece. They just work better after a certain age. It's all any of us wear."

Callie didn't interrupt, letting Chiara say whatever she felt like saying. Callie pointed to the necklace around her neck, then reached up and tapped her own ear, meaning earrings. "Jewelry?"

"Large gold hoops, but not too big. Two inches, maybe? A college ring. She's proud of that, having paid her way through four years. She's a middle-grade teacher, like me." Chiara smiled, proud on both their behalf. She seemed to reach inside herself, to remember more, then shrugged. "I think that's it... no, there was a necklace. A small gold circle with two tiny diamonds resting in the bottom of the circle. For her and her sister."

The room warmed like it usually did when Callie did a closed-door one-on-one, and whatever scent Chiara wore drifted to Callie's nose. Something light and almond. Callie bet Chiara wasn't cold any longer.

Callie used her soft yet firm voice, a balance she'd groomed years ago. "What makes you think she's missing?"

"She won't answer her phone. That's rule one in our group when we are out of sight of each other. If you can't answer right away, you must respond within thirty minutes." Chiara dipped her chin in emphasis. "Without question."

Not a bad rule. "Did you leave her messages?"

"Yes."

"Did you text?" Callie knew the answer but had to ask.

"Of course."

"How long has it been since you'd say she went past her... deadline?"

Chiara looked at her phone as Callie glanced up at her clock. Five twenty p.m.

"She left last night," she said. "On a date." Then before Callie could comment, she spilled out words Callie could've forecasted. "I know that doesn't sound worrisome. She's an adult, and no telling who she wound up talking to, or drinking with, or walking out of phone range with, but our rule is sacrosanct, Chief Morgan. She'd know to check her phone." The woman's green eyes all but bore a hole into Callie's. "Something is wrong."

"Who was her date?" Callie asked.

"I don't know."

"Yet y'all are close friends? Even coworkers?"

Chiara's antsiness increased, no doubt understanding how this sounded. While she believed the urgency real, that didn't necessarily make it so. "Did you check with the other ladies in your house? How many are there?"

"Three others... and no. I can't do that yet."

Most people exhausted everyone they knew before going to the authorities. Who didn't pray their missing someone was with someone familiar... and safe?

"Ms. Hamilton." Callie tried not to sound condescending, but Chiara had already tensed up in expectation. "I can tell you that the first thing we would do in hunting for your friend is touch base with everyone in your rental. If that fails, then we put out a BOLO—be on the lookout. But she isn't quite missing yet, is she? If she were a minor, that'd be another story, but she's, what, thirty?"

"Thirty-seven."

"That's a mighty social age around here. I can send a car to the house and have an officer talk to everyone and send a driver's license picture to my other officers, but there isn't much else we can do at the moment."

As happened half the time, tears spilled, and Callie moved the box of tissues closer. "I can see you care about Maddy. Is this her first time here?"

Chiara nodded, stemming her runny nose.

"Is this your group's first time coming to Edisto?"

The nose got another wipe before the woman shook her head. "Oh, no. I've been coming for five years. The other three have been coming for well over a decade, two of them closer to three. It's tradition. I replaced another woman five years ago, and I vouched for Maddy to come this time. She just joined."

The tears fell anew, with more passion, and her voice thickened. "You don't understand. We usually limit the group to four, but Maddy works with me and was so in need of a friend. She needed a trip to the beach as much or more than any of us, and she swore to me she'd fit in. She swore she'd follow the rules."

Maddy sounded like the thirteen-year-old being allowed at the adult table for Thanksgiving and spilling gravy all over the antique tablecloth.

The group sounded... strict. "What kind of group is this again?"

The tears stopped. "What do you mean?"

"You talk about rules and tradition. Sounds rather important. Almost legacy."

"Just ladies who meet for lunch once or twice a month then come to the beach for a few weeks in the summer. The older girls were very familiar with Edisto, so that's where we come."

"Where's home?" Callie asked, feeling a niggle she wished she didn't.

"Tampa," she replied, adding, "Florida," as if she had to.

A coastal city on the west side of the state, four hundred miles away, give or take. Funny how they left one beach for another. "How long are you staying?"

"Four weeks."

"Any chance Maddy went home? As the new kid on the block, has she had a falling out with the others?"

"No. I'm at her side all the time."

Apparently not.

Chiara collected herself. "What are we doing about Maddy?"

"Like I said, I'll send a car to the house, then if nobody's seen her, and she continues not to check in by tomorrow, we'll take it to another level."

Chiara deflated, and she'd fingered the tissue almost to shreds. Callie reached down and held out a small trash can, and the woman dropped the pieces in.

She might as well assign Officer Thomas Gage to run over there now and address this, before he went off shift. Ladies loved him. Maybe Officer Annie Greer could go with him. Both were closer to this woman's generation than any other officer, and they were the most handy.

She stood and escorted Chiara out, with repeated assurances someone would be over in an hour, giving her time to break the news to the other ladies. Chiara wasn't happy about the other women finding out but thanked Callie for letting her get to them first.

Marie sat at her desk, thirty minutes past quitting time. Only the loud-mouthed gentleman of earlier remained, seething on the community sofa against the wall. "He'll only speak to you," Marie said.

"Then I'll be happy to see him." Callie had replied loud enough for him to hear then lowered her voice. "Hey, would you mind radioing Thomas to go to *Time in a Bottle* and talk to those ladies? Apparently one of them hasn't reported in today. Might be good if he takes Annie with him."

"Got it," she said, then nodded to the waiting customer. "His name is Merrill Anders. Speeding ticket."

While Chiara had guarded her young skin from overexposure, this man had embraced the sun in spades. The leather texture and snow-white teeth of this fifty-something-year-old reminded her of the old actor George Hamilton, only no signs of St. Tropez bronzing mousse on this guy. His skin had been cooked via pure UV rays.

"About damn time," he muttered, staring down at her in passing as she motioned for him to enter her office.

She hadn't made it behind her desk before he launched into her.

"I wasn't going ten miles over the speed limit, Chief. I've seen others do more and not get the blue light. Your Officer Gage was out of line letting another car go past before pulling me."

Mr. Anders hadn't shown her the ticket, and this late in the day, she wasn't interested in seeing it. He'd said Thomas wrote the ticket, and that's all she had to hear. She hadn't a fairer officer on the force. She almost grinned at the word *force* for such a small cadre of uniforms. Guess the day had been long.

Strategically, she posed with elbows on her desk blotter, resting chin on knuckles. Once upon a time, she wouldn't have dreamed of exposing herself like this. She'd hardened these three years on the beach, and sometimes visitors just brought out the quirkiness in her.

"Where'd you get that?" he asked, pointing to the eight-inch ropey scar on Callie's forearm showing out from under roll-up sleeves. One couldn't miss it all bumpy, pinkish, and glaring.

"Oh, this? A burn scar," she said, looking down at it as if she'd forgotten she had it. "A few years ago I arrested the head of a mob, and one of his family burned my house down and murdered my husband. This thing on my arm came from flaming shrapnel."

His whole countenance slid like warm butter from irritation to dumbfoundedness, his suntan paling a bit. "Oh my God, I'm so sorry. What happened to the murderer?"

"I killed him."

She didn't have to say how, which had been with a broken beer bottle. She always felt that information over the top. "But hey, this is about you. I'm really sorry for your wait. Let's talk about this ticket."

His steam had left his engine.

"Ten miles over the speed limit... on which road was it?" she asked.

"Dock Site Road," he replied.

Oh wow. The road where Brice LeGrand used to live, where he pulled people for speeding in his stupid attempts to enforce the law. The town council still hadn't filled his slot, scheduling the special election in another week.

The memory almost knocked the steam out of her own engine.

"Mr. Anders," she said, righting herself. "Dock Site is thirty-five miles per hour. Ten miles over is forty-five, or thirty percent over the norm, and with you being written up for exactly ten miles over the limit tells me Officer Gage cut you some slack from the actual speed you were going. Since you had no recent tickets, he graciously wrote you a two-pointer instead of a four. Of course, I'll confirm all this with him. His radar will have to validate him, and we'd be happy to share that—"

"I didn't come to the beach for these kinds of nuisances."

"Agreed, and we relish those days of no such events," she replied.

"Bet you have quotas," he grumbled.

Brice used to actually ask for a quota system, feeling if the department didn't turn in a pile of tickets, they weren't covering their salaries. She'd informed him more than a few times that South Carolina Code Section 23-1-245 deemed police quotas unlawful. Citing that section to Anders, however, was a waste of breath. "No sir, we don't have quotas."

"Well," he said, then trailed off.

"Yep," she finished for him, remaining poised.

"I've got family waiting for me for dinner," he said, rising.

She respectfully stood. "And I hope it's a tasty one."

Anders left through the swinging door of the counter then straight out the station glass door. Marie stood, purse on her arm. "Another day..."

"Another ticket," Callie finished with a tired grin. "I'll lock up, Marie. Be safe going home."

Marie paused at the door. "By the way, I spoke with Thomas who'll contact Annie. Unless they turn up something, he said he'd fill you in tomorrow morning."

Marie left, Callie not far behind her. Two miles later, she parked the cruiser in the lot outside El Marko's, at the west end of a small strip mall on Jungle Road, a stone's throw from the grocery store and the causeway. Just under a mile from home.

The lot was full, but she had a reserved table. It might be small and next to the kitchen, but being the police chief who lived with the restaurant's owner came with perks.

A state agent retired after being shot in the leg, Mark Dupree was a Louisiana Cajun who wore Hawaiian shirts and ran a Mexican restaurant. He'd moved in with her two months prior, and she couldn't be happier. Their schedules didn't run much in sync, with his day ending around eleven p.m. and her alarm going off at six. They managed with her eating dinner where he worked, and him showering the food odors off at night, waking her up for cuddle time when he came to bed.

Her neighbor and buddy Sophie Bianchi greeted her inside. Yoga mistress by morning and El Marko's hostess by evening. Her fitness and the clothes she wore to accent them caught the eye of every man and woman who entered. Tonight was her red-and-orange theme. The nails she painted coral each and every morning blending perfectly.

"Your table awaits," Sophie said, sashaying as if she had to escort her friend, swinging a menu as if one was needed. At the table, she bent over and whispered, "Zeus is taking Buck and me deep-sea fishing on Saturday. You two want to come?"

Callie sat, knowing her presence would automatically generate one of three regular meals behind the swinging door. Sometimes Mark surprised her with how he arranged the food.

"Let me ask Mark," she said. "He'll need someone to cover, and with you on the boat, you won't be here either." Sophie ought to know this was the busy season, but Sophie did what Sophie wanted. It fell on Mark to take up the slack when one of her whims blew through.

"Sprite is coming home tonight," her friend said, glancing around the room to ensure she wasn't needed by a table or a new customer.

Callie checked her phone quickly. No messages from her son. "So, where's Jeb?"

"Sprite said he was spending the night with your mother." Sophie blinked. "He didn't tell you?"

Her son dated Sophie's daughter, and some days you couldn't slip a piece of paper between them. If they weren't both tackling degrees at the College of Charleston, Callie would worry about accidental grandchildren, because she and Sophie were just about convinced that day was inevitable.

"He'll let me know why when he wants to," Callie said, then pointed at the hostess station. "You've got business waiting."

"Oh." Soph jumped up as only her glutes and quads could do and scurried to do her job.

Callie's Blenheim ginger ale, as good a substitute for gin as she could muster, had found its way to a coaster to her left, and its first sparkling bite went down nicely.

She checked her messages once more, curious about Jeb in Middleton instead of here. Her mother Beverly was mayor of the small town, holding down a five-generation tradition Callie was supposed to have perpetuated but had refused. As Beverly's pride and joy, Jeb made impromptu visits to see his grandmother since she lived about thirty miles from his school and forty-five miles from Edisto. A nice little triangle that was close enough yet far enough.

The aromas hit her before she saw the plate, delivered by the hand of the chef.

"Your dinner, m'lady." Mark pulled out one of the two empty chairs and sat. "How was your day?" he said, setting the quilted mitt on the table. "Watch that plate. It's hot."

"Back-to-back complaints," she said, gingerly tasting the refried beans. "More than the usual tickets. Almost made me miss Brice." The mention of the recently deceased man, quite the nuisance when alive, made them both give a moment of silence. As many times as she'd bashed the man when he breathed, she couldn't make herself think too ill of him once he didn't.

"Anyway," she said. "Glad the day's over."

Her phone buzzed, lighting up on her left. Thomas. Mark automatically sat back, knowing she had to take the call. She held up a finger for Mark not to leave quite yet, wanting at least ten minutes with him if possible.

"Thomas?" she answered. He called on her phone versus the mic, knowing that this time of day she'd be amidst tourists and diners at El Marko's.

"Chief." He spoke low, and she could hear a few cicadas talking in the distance. He was outside. "Need you at *Time in a Bottle*, on the beach. We have a body, and from the reactions of these women you sent me to interview, it's likely to be one of them."

Callie stood, Mark taking the plate. Supper, like lunch, would come and go as well.

Chapter 2

CALLIE TOOK MARY Street to hit Palmetto Boulevard quickest, her blue light shooting her to the opposite side of the small beach in seconds. *Almost seven.* Daylight savings time gave them ample sunlight to address the scene, but that hour and a piece would go fast.

A small firetruck had already arrived, the station being closer to the scene, putting an EMT and firefighter on site. Thomas waited in the drive, opened Callie's door once she parked on the grounds, and escorted her beneath the house. Like all the others on the beach, *Time in a Bottle* rested on pylons for the passage of hurricane flood waters. They passed two rusted, well-used grills and assorted rope swings and chairs, and exited to a narrow boardwalk that carried them toward the water's edge. Gnats accosted them near the palmettos and dune grass but disappeared the closer they got to water.

Officer Annie Greer had staked off a sizeable area to keep people back, the EMT clearly in no hurry to save a life so clearly gone from this realm.

"Chief," he said. The other man, the firefighter, gave her a nod as well.

Callie gave a melancholy smile to acknowledge their words, but her focus rested on the dead girl. She began gathering her own impressions, but she wanted to hear the EMT's first. "What's your take on this, Buddy?"

"She was dead when we arrived," the middle-aged man said, putting his sunglasses back on to fight the evening sun. The sound being on the west of town, the water could amp up the glare. Buddy was a genuine guy, patient and slow-talking, and had been around enough years and dealt with enough beach issues to be respected. In this case, however, dead was clearly dead.

The woman lay on her back, arms and legs at odd angles like a tossed Raggedy Ann, the evening tide having nudged and nudged her until it could deposit her sufficiently in its retreat. No drag marks. Amazing how nobody had seen her until she'd beached on the sand. They didn't have many tourist deaths in the water on Edisto, but a season didn't go by without one. This was the first for this year.

The dead woman wore a one-piece, navy with a sculpted wrap across the front. Age mid-thirties, her dark-blond hair would've come down to her shoulder blades. Average weight and height. Callie's mind instantly pinged on the missing Maddy Gillespie, especially right outside the house where she stayed... minus the gold hoop earrings and the double diamond necklace. No sign of those.

A new spectator approached the tape, a couple others running toward it from down the beach. Word spread fast. "Oh my God, is she missing a hand?"

The deceased was indeed missing a hand. Her right. She was also missing the back of her left calf. Scrapes covered her legs, and she would've been bloodied up pretty good if she hadn't been washed clean by the tide well after her heart quit pumping.

No doubt a shark had bumped her a few times then taken a few tastes.

Not a *Jaws* sort of shark, but most any shark might take a nibble on something bobbing in the water. Whether on the southeast side of town—where the heavy wave action kept the beach continually churning, or on the sound—where waves were subtle and the water flatter, sharks thrived. Most visitors didn't realize they did. The natives were fully aware.

They weren't aggressive normally, using their teeth like humans used their hands, just to see what was what, only rarely with people. But whether hammerhead or bull, nurse shark or sand, they swam amongst everyone and everything else in these waters. Though a good swimmer, Callie wasn't a fan of occupying the same space as these creatures.

"What are you going to do about that shark, Chief?" asked a spectator.

Suddenly she was Chief Brody on Amity Island, only her shark hadn't eaten whole dogs or little boys. From the bite, it wasn't a fifth the size of the movie shark, either.

"Nothing to be done," she said. "These waters are their home, just like the dolphin and jellyfish."

That sparked rumblings amongst the gawkers. "We've got to swim with that maneater out there?"

Callie scanned the crowd, replying to the question while looking for Chiara. "Yes, ma'am. Just keep on respecting the ocean like always. No bounty offered to shark hunters today."

No sign of Chiara amongst the spectators.

The people stood solo and in couples, thank God no children, and thank goodness everyone hung back without being scolded. Some hunkered under their towels, a few others held arms crossed, some holding each other... as if this were November with a crisp breeze instead of June sticky and muggy.

"Anybody recognize this woman?" she asked.

More mumblings and lots of head shakes.

"Thomas?" she called, him instantly at her side, having hung back only ten feet away. "Where's the coroner?"

"On his way," he said. "Smith. Thirty minutes out. Twenty if someone else drove him."

Of course, it was Smith. Deputy Coroner Richard Smith, a sourpuss of a man a couple years younger than she was. Callie wasn't sure whether they'd given him this jurisdiction on purpose or to irritate her. The two didn't exactly get along, limiting their conversations to terse, minimal phrases, just enough to communicate and get the job done. He didn't seem to get law enforcement. She didn't seem to get him period.

In the meantime, Callie studied the body. The shark-bit hand hadn't totally disappeared but had been removed just behind the knuckles. A goose-egg of a lump stood out on her temple, her discoloring clearly visible with skin so pale. Callie'd wait for Smith's report once he carted the body back to Walterboro to see if he found water in her lungs—to see whether or not she'd been a drifting body when the shark took a nibble, or if she'd tried to fight it off, freaked, and drowned.

With the knot and the bruising, Callie rode the fence on a decision of accident or intentional. If there was foul play, she prayed skin and its DNA remained under her fingernails, at least those on the remaining hand, but that depended on how long this girl had been in the water. Callie's unofficial guess was not terribly long. Probably died that day if this was the missing girl reported by Chiara Hamilton and the timeline was correct as to time last seen.

No identification on her. No jewelry that might carry an inscription. If this wasn't their missing girl.... Edisto Beach wasn't big, and when this woman didn't appear home in the next few hours, someone would contact the station. Like Chiara had.

"Thomas?" she called again.

"Chief?" He instantly appeared. God, she loved this officer.

"You said these women in *Time in a Bottle* thought this might be their missing friend? Talk me through what was going on when this body showed up."

In other words, why the hell weren't they out here right now?

"I arrived at the house with Annie. There were four tenants, ranging in age from late thirties to sixties. They said the fifth member had gone out, gotten acquainted with someone, and hadn't been seen since yesterday. Only one is worried, though. The youngest said she was the one who reported her missing to you."

Callie nodded and waited, still discreetly scouting the crowd. "Go on."

"I heard a scream from the water, a tourist. Annie ran out first. I told the ladies in the house to stay put. We checked to ensure the girl on the beach was dead and called you, then the coroner. Annie and I ran a tape around the body, then I ran back to meet you at the road, and I barely made it when you pulled up. From the description those four ladies gave, this could be the missing friend. That'd be my bet considering the odds of this being someone else would be rather small."

Callie didn't place bets. She took one fact, one clue, one piece of evidence at a time to answer. It was time they confirmed if the woman belonged to *Time in a Bottle*. "Go bring at least one of them out here. We need to confirm if this is Maddy Gillespie since nobody else has called in a missing person."

He trotted off through the crowd filled with people hoping to witness another piece of the puzzle or hear some revelation they could take back to their house and spread. Annie attempted to shut down those tourists taking pictures. Tacky didn't begin to describe some people.

She watched Thomas climb the steps to the back porch, and it didn't take long for one woman to accompany him. Black-and-white-peppered hair in a colorful silk shawl, she was old enough to be Callie's mother.

They walked to the beach, in no hurry, but whether you knew the victim or not, who wanted to be in a hurry to see a dead body? You took the extra time of dragging your feet praying to the heavens this dead body wasn't one of yours, delaying reality as long as you could.

All heads turned, as if watching a couple walk down the aisle. Thomas took the woman's elbow as they approached.

Callie held out her hand, strategically placing herself between the woman's view and the body. "Ma'am. I'm Edisto Beach Police Chief Callie Morgan. I believe I spoke with Chiara Hamilton. She's staying in your house, am I right?"

The woman nodded. She had a fairly firm grip of herself. No shakes. No tears. Even wrapped in her shawl, she stood tall. Her long legs hid in a thin linen pair of teal-colored palazzo pants, accenting a swirl in the shawl. A tank top showed fit shoulders but also that the woman enjoyed the sun, her age evident from the skin damage.

Callie had met her partway for the introduction, so the body lay thirty feet behind her.

"Chief," Thomas said. "This is Lydia Barron. She coordinated their vacation. I believe you're somewhat in charge, ma'am?"

Lydia nodded.

"Sorry to meet you under these circumstances," Callie said.

"Thank you," Lydia said. "Yes, the five of us are friends, but guess you could say I run the club as its longest and oldest member."

"Thanks for that," Callie said. "Do you believe you're up to taking a look at this poor girl on the beach? It's not a pleasant experience, but if you can help us identify her, we'd sure appreciate it."

"I... I believe I can do that."

Opening then rewrapping the shawl around her, she used it like a hug. She waited for Thomas to touch her elbow again to take her closer, like an escort to royalty. Callie took a step to the side to allow them through, giving them a full view.

At the tape, Lydia halted. "Oh. Oh, my goodness."

Callie watched her gaze take in each injury first, before her attention settled on the head. Puffy but not obscenely so, the face should be recognizable to anyone who knew this woman.

Lydia released a deep sigh, her shoulders relaxing. "No, that's not Maddy."

Thomas glanced over at Callie. "You sure, Miss Lydia?" he asked.

"Positive," she said. "May I go now? So I can tell the others?"

"Sure," Callie said, studying Lydia for signs of a lie and seeing none.

Not that she wished this house to lose its friend, but identifying the body as Maddy would've made their problems easier. Now they had a dead woman with no one to claim her and concerned people who couldn't find their missing friend.

The crowd changed. Some left. Others appeared, each time Callie waiting for someone to scream and rush in to claim their loved one. Didn't happen.

Assistant Coroner Richard Smith arrived, as usual, having taken his time driving and now taking his time coming down the boardwalk.

They'd clashed before over her pilfering pockets for identification and touching the body for signs of criminal activity before he had a chance to do his thing, but this time she had no reason to, mainly because the body had no pockets, no jewelry, no nothing that wasn't out in the open evident.

"Chief," he said, not bothering to shake hands.

Callie was fine with that.

Didn't take him long to examine the body. Finally, he stood and faced her. "Got to get her to Walterboro before I can give you any answers."

This time Callie hadn't even asked about a guess as to cause of death. Felt odd to have someone so young and healthy, dressed like an upper-middle-class tourist, swept into their hands and their not having an open case to solve. Mystery women didn't wash up on her beach as a general rule. Yet they had nothing to go on, no urgent pleas from worried family members, and no timely guesses from the coroner. Still she would put her guys on it the best she could, without stirring the community into a frenzy. "I assumed you would have to take her to Walterboro for anything meaningful. The question is obvious, though. Did she drown or was she thrown in the water afterwards?"

He nodded, waiting for a clash.

Callie shrugged. "That's it, Richard. You do your thing and let me know."

He blinked a little fast, digesting the difference since the last time they'd share a crime scene. "Um, will do."

They soon had the victim bagged and gurneyed to the van. Annie disbursed the crowd, which didn't take much effort with the drama gone. Callie watched. Nobody looked out of place, out of sync, or suspicious.

She started toward the house, Thomas at her side. "From the description I received at the station from Chiara Hamilton, I was about convinced this was their missing Maddy. I'd like to talk to these ladies myself. You keep your ears open for any discrepancies in what you know."

"Would've been nice if she had been the missing——" He stopped and stutter-stepped as he realized what that sounded like. "Not what I meant..."

"No ears to hear, Thomas. Frankly, I agree with you. Now we have two cases to work."

He led Callie up the back stairs and to the porch. The weathered screen door sang a long creak as she entered. All four of the women tenants sat in worn-out rattan chairs, each with a drink in their hand. Callie bet alcohol laced all four.

Lydia stood and swept out a hand for Callie to find a chair and sit. Callie dragged a chair over, her back to the ocean, far enough distant to be able to judge each of their expressions.

"Y'all have had a hell of a day, haven't you?" she said, and received the appropriate eye rolling, sighs, and clinking of ice as they took another sip in toast of the understatement. Chiara appeared the most worried.

"Anyone heard from Maddy?" Callie asked, to head shakes all around. "Mind if I ask a question?"

Nobody moved, tensing at expectation.

"How much did this girl on the beach look like Maddy?"

The three turned to Lydia, the one who'd dared look at the dead body.

"It wasn't her, Chief Morgan. I believe I'd know."

Chiara chimed in, seemingly reluctant to challenge the boss. "Lydia, are you truly, really sure? I mean, she's my friend, and you haven't known her for long. Maybe I should have made the identification."

If Callie had known, she would've had Chiara do just that. Pictures would be available soon from the coroner of the body all cleaned up, but that would take time. Callie lifted her phone, having taken them of the scene herself. She found the best picture, head only, which wasn't terribly upsetting thanks to the water, and held it out toward Chiara.

She hesitated before scooting to the edge of her seat. Callie held onto the phone, not wanting Chiara to slide the screen to see the ones less palatable, like those of exposed calf muscle and bone.

Like Lydia had at the beach, Chiara deflated at the relief of not seeing her friend. "No, not her."

Lydia's glare at Callie was hard at first, probably for needing Chiara's second opinion about the body. But then, as if policing herself, she settled back in her chair.

This group's behavior felt odd to Callie. She could at least try to figure out why. "Miss Lydia."

Lydia perked at her name. "Yes?"

"What makes you the leader here?" A question that could be intimidating or simply answered, depending on the real answer.

"I've been coming here the longest," she said. "I make the rental arrangements, and I knew the people we socialize with from way back. Guess leadership sort of fell my way. No election. No ownership." She shrugged, glancing left to right at her girlfriends.

The one seated next to her laughed. "I'm Vivien Holden, by the way. I've been around the second longest. Anyway, with Lydia at the reins, my vacation becomes much easier. She tells me what to bring and when to come. Who has what party and what my share of the bill is. What's not to like?"

The next oldest spoke up, feeling the need to add her two cents. "I'm Robin Nilsson. I sure as hell don't want to plan this."

Then Chiara. "They'd been around forever by the time I came along. I wasn't about to change anything."

"There you go," Vivien said. "No science to it."

Thomas eyed each woman as he'd been instructed. He bobbled brows at Callie, as if saying, *no big deal.*

"And your rules?" Callie asked.

Lydia scratched her neck. "The rules. There really aren't that many. Don't leave us wondering where you are. Pay your bill. Rotate meal prep with a list on the fridge. I'm sure there are others, but I'm feeling rather... what's the word...?" She looked to Vivien.

"Flustered?" Vivien offered.

Robin pointed. "Caught off guard."

"Yeah," Chiara echoed.

Thomas made another facial shrug. He wasn't fazed.

All sorts vacationed at Edisto. Callie's gut, however, wasn't ready to treat this group as simple and innocent, and she couldn't say why.

"How long has Maddy been a member?" she asked, after noting the differences in how Lydia and Chiara acted about their missing friend. Chiara worked with Maddy and with them being of similar age, they'd be closer. Lydia claimed not to know the girl well. Was that all there was to it?

"She's still auditioning for a return visit, for lack of a better term," Lydia said, her stare at Chiara not unnoticed. "Chiara, you understand that."

Chiara just nodded. A sense of condescension hung on Lydia's words unless Callie had read them wrong.

Thomas couldn't resist. "Wait, how does that even work? She's temporary on probation?"

But Lydia was unfluffed. "We admit we are a clique, and we have been in existence for thirty years, Officer Gage." Her voice tensed. "We don't take new members lightly. At the last minute, Chiara was eager for

Maddy to tag along. She'd had personal issues and a ton of stress, and we chose to give her a chance. We're not totally heartless."

Callie put away her phone and took out her pocket notepad. "How's it going so far?"

Lydia gave an expression that tried to lessen the firm stance she'd taken. "Don't read too much into any of this, Chief. Like with any friends, the new girl takes some getting used to... and she has to feel she fits in. She's nice enough, but the jury's out whether she'll be long term."

"What's long term?"

Lydia motioned with her glass at her ladies.

Vivien took over. "There's no answer for that, and I'm not sure any of this matters since we don't know the dead girl."

Who auditioned for friendships? "And y'all always come to Edisto?"

"Have been for decades," Lydia replied. "We have lots of friends out here we come back and see each year."

A lot of people did that, the annual trek and hopeful reconnection with others doing the same. So why was Callie clueless to this group, or even any of these women?

"We're worried about Maddy," Chiara said, repeating her earlier concern.

Purposely, Callie looked over the line of women. "How about y'all call your regular friends, and ask them to call theirs, and see if anyone has seen her. I'd ask if this was unusual for her, but you're saying this is her first time out here."

"Correct, Chief," Lydia said. "And if she strolls back in sometime tonight or tomorrow without a damn good excuse, it'll be her last time coming. We don't come here for drama. We come here to leave the world behind, relax, and visit people. Trust me, when we find her we'll let you know, and you won't be worried with her again."

Which begged the question to Callie. Who would Maddy be off on her own visiting if this was her first time at Edisto and didn't know anyone? And second, why did she go off alone?

And why doesn't Chiara just walk up to the house of whomever Maddy was visiting to make sure she was still there. Unless Maddy had hitched a ride with this group and held an agenda all her own.

Chapter 3

Lydia

LYDIA WATCHED through the evening darkness from the side window of the front door. The two officers made their way to the remaining vehicle, the chief and the young man. The other, the young female officer, had driven off earlier in the other patrol car once the coroner left.

She was so damn mad she couldn't see straight.

Chiara... she knew better. They kept their profile extremely low, especially from the police. What the hell was she thinking of going to them before coming to her?

Vivien slid in beside her, close enough to whisper in her ear. She'd dressed in a bathing suit right after breakfast that morning—like everyone else—to avoid suspicion, but she hadn't left the house. Robin and Chiara had. Robin had a date. Chiara was supposed to have one. As the person in charge of the schedule, Lydia would have to check to see if Chiara had stood him up in her wild-hair decision to go to the authorities. "This... is going to ruin us." Then she turned to Vivien. "That sounded horrible. Sorry."

"Sounded realistic," Vivien replied, rubbing her arm. "That's why you're in charge."

Vivien was ever the steady one, though Lydia ran the show. She wasn't sure how she'd have lasted this long without her best friend, but it had truly been Vivien who suggested the two of them come to Edisto the first time, which easily evolved into every summer. She understood what it meant to Lydia.

Friends didn't come any tighter.

"Maddy shouldn't even be here," Lydia mumbled, keeping the conversation low and between them. They thought so much alike, having finished each other's sentences for three decades.

Lydia's best friend in the world was four years younger but had always carried an old soul. She embraced her gray and wore her hair long, even going so much as to highlight it lighter and whiter. Its striking thickness hung straight, pushed from her face with assorted headbands. She ran on the thin side, but not unhealthy, her skin carefully maintained— pale and satin smooth due to expensive treatments Lydia regularly kidded her about. Her effort paid off. She was beautiful.

They were all handsome, each in her own way.

The two senior women had clicked from the second they'd met at a bar in Atlanta. That night both experienced blind dates that had soured in minutes, but having dressed for a night on the town, finding themselves with time on their hands and nobody expecting them at home, they made the most of the evening. With Lydia single and lonely without a roommate, and Vivien barely meeting expenses after a nasty divorce, they combined resources into Lydia's apartment not long after. A few months later, Lydia's date backhanded her, splitting a lip. Then Vivien's ex decided she must be gay to leave him and move in with another woman, and he started stalking her.

The events only united the two women, convincing them there was safety in numbers. Even with Vivien being a real estate and sometimes civil attorney and Lydia a voice narrator by day and part-time night club singer and waitress in the evenings at a venue that paid more than the average bachelor's degree opportunity, they clicked—two women miles apart in experiences—and the stalking incident became the final straw. They pulled up roots and disappeared. Out of all the no-income-tax states, Florida beckoned most.

Vivien's ex made some noise about the move, but Lydia had lived a childhood that had forced her to think in adult ways, and she hired someone to visit him during his downtown, swanky lunch one day to convince him to move on. Chasing Vivien could do nothing but hurt his future... and his health.

Vivien tugged on Lydia's shawl. "Maybe you saw something in Maddy of ourselves, like the rest of us did. She's young. She's scared. We had to scramble and fight our way to where we are. She's just getting started. We can be there for her." She kissed her on the ear, making her crack a smile.

Officially, Lydia hadn't actually cast her preference for Maddy's inclusion, because the other three voted yes first, negating the need for the fourth. Maybe she could've changed their minds. Maybe she should've challenged them, but instead the count was in, and she caved, seeing no need for argument. Chiara had been so adamant, so sweet, and so willing to take responsibility for this girl who had a not-too-distant rough experience with an ex-boyfriend. If they wanted to give Maddy Gillespie a chance, who was she to try to overthrow the result? Hadn't they all a hard-luck story they tried to shed, using Edisto to pretend it didn't exist?

"We normally vet these ladies way more than this, Vivian." Lydia took a light hold of her friend's hand. "But Chiara brings in a lost puppy and everyone goes soft and willing to take her in."

Vivien let Lydia loose and brushed her palm over the shawl. She loved that shawl, having borrowed it a time or two. "You went all soft with Robin once upon a time and look how long she's been with us. Loyal and trusting. She loves us, and we love her. She was a mess, remember?"

Damn her. She usually caved when Vivien reasoned with her, but on the other hand, Vivien didn't like conflict. Strange for an attorney. Probably why she handled real estate instead of criminal cases. They often joked at how much stronger one's backbone was than the other. Emergencies, however, fell into Lydia's lap.

But then, Lydia practically raised herself. Even Vivien didn't have a clear handle on her best friend's youth, which they'd decided to leave in the past, like the bedroom abuse by Vivien's ex. Leaving Atlanta had served them well, and they'd managed quite well in Tampa. If they had to, they'd move again. Thank God they hadn't seen the need.

Each time they arrived in Edisto, however, Lydia chose a different rental, not repeating an address in thirty years with more than enough houses to choose from. Safer that way. Always the practical one, Vivien suggested they buy an Edisto house ten years ago, not necessarily on the beach, but something they could rely upon each summer. No surprises of missing spatulas or too few lightbulbs, but Lydia had no inclination of putting down roots that anyone else would recognize. Taxes, utilities, homeowner's associations were all ties with identities attached. Only a handful of the natives associated Lydia with the girl she used to be. She avoided them to keep that history dusty and forgotten.

Hearing Brice LeGrand had died only a month before they arrived, however, had kicked her in the gut. No wonder he hadn't answered calls. He'd been first on her list to see this week. But who did she expect to notify her of his passing if she never let anyone know of her existence outside of dates and parties during the group's summer vacation?

The news put an even wetter blanket feel on the trip than Maddy had, leaving her nerves unsettled.

Keep your head.

No matter what happened, who happened, or why, Edisto was a magnet, a magic draw, and she'd developed a skill in maintaining that wall between who she'd been on the island in her youth and who she'd become as a woman. Unfortunately, she was being forced to draw upon all her skills, to include those ancient-history ones.

This was not going to be the usual summer of old partners, sweet easy earnings, and the beach. "Call a meeting," she said low to her Viv.

"Sure. Let's air this out... properly." Vivien patted her shoulder before retreating to the other two on the porch.

Lydia gave her a minute before joining them.

Seeing the need to improve the ambience after such a harsh and dark evening, the two other ladies, minus Maddy, had already prepared platters to nosh on, a hodge podge of cheeses, fruit and nuts they'd brought with them, using each lady's favorite. Vivien's Turkish figs, Robin's butter olives, Chiara's herbed Brie, and Lydia's organic eighty-five-percent dark chocolate. Robin could make a charcuterie board like nobody's business, often adding shrimp from Flowers Seafood to the mix, but they hadn't made it there yet.

Nothing represented Maddy's tastes.

They were going to ask about her absence. A full day was a long time. And what about tonight...?

Lydia assumed her previous seat. "Ladies. We have to consider damage control. Let's get our stories straight."

Chiara almost spit out her cracker and cheese. "What stories? What damage? Open up to us, Lydia. We're not stupid."

Unsurprisingly, she would be the most obstinate, especially with her being on the defensive about her friend. Lydia lifted a glass, appreciating the refill someone had provided, and took a swallow of the vodka tonic.

"But Maddy was," she said, setting the glass down. "All it takes is one screw-up. It's why we test-drive and scrutinize, Chiara. We are done with Maddy. When she shows back up, she packs and leaves. We can't get involved with the boyfriend she fought with, the job she struggles with, or the landlord she can't get along with." Chiara had used all three to plead for Maddy to come. *The poor girl had so much on her plate these days.*

"Um," Chiara said. "She's been working in the same school with me for five years, Lydia. I can't ignore those things. Especially the boyfriend. He's dangerous."

This was so damn hard. Lydia had spoken long and hard with Maddy, offered advice, calmed her, offered her a bottle of Valium. "Chiara, what part of *we don't care* don't you understand?" she made herself say.

Jesus, this was hard.

Chiara went silent.

"So, what do we do?" Robin asked, voice low and stable. "Lay low or business as usual? Are we just waiting for Maddy to come back?"

Lydia broke off a small piece of chocolate, giving herself an extra few seconds of silence to think. "We do what we came here for."

Chiara stared, then broke off to stare at Vivien. Then Robin. "You act like you just crossed her name off a list. She hasn't come back. I reported her missing. We can't pretend nothing's wrong."

This time Vivien took charge, in her softer voice. "In essence we did cross her off, honey, but that's about future vacations. For now, we give her space. We've spoken to her date, and he says she left there healthy, but she wasn't into having much... *fun*, shall we say? So when she left, his date unfulfilled, he called Lydia."

Everyone stilled. They never had unhappy friends.

Chiara came back to life first. "Why didn't she call me?"

"I don't know," Lydia said. "Did y'all have a falling out?"

"No. Well, not really."

Vivien peered at her, head tilted. "Which means what?"

"She didn't like who we were," Chiara said.

Vivien shrugged. "We gave her shelter and protection and shoulders to cry on. We of all people understand what she's going through with that idiot she was fighting to get rid of. Who is she to judge?"

"Who is she to turn her back on us?" Lydia added.

Chiara gasped, mouth gaping twice in search of what to say. "We don't care what happened to her because she broke our rules? Shouldn't I inform her sister?" She leaped to her feet, her knees knocking the short table, making Robin grab a glass before it spilled. "For God's sake, she didn't run to the store for tampons. She's missing. She doesn't answer her phone, and nobody's seen her."

"She called me," Lydia said, when in fact, in a way, she seriously did. "She needs space. I wish you hadn't gone to the police, Chiara. We should be talking about you and your actions as much as Maddy's."

Chiara stood there in the middle of the porch, her angry gaze bouncing from one woman to the other.

"Sit down. Maddy asked me to keep a confidence," Lydia said, fighting to be the boss they expected her to be. "We've crossed the big bridge, people. On Edisto, people try to forget what they left behind for the time they are here. It's what the place is known for. Nobody cares what anyone is doing. The cops aren't even worried about her. People sleep on the beach, shack up with new acquaintances, get passed-out drunk, and go swimming when and where they shouldn't. They show back up. If they don't, it's because they were stupid. I can't say it any clearer than that. Maddy asked that we give her space. Our lifestyle sort of... threw her for a loop."

Chiara sank to the cushion, stunned at the frankness. "A girl just died in the ocean. That could've been Maddy. If she were one of us, you'd care. Shouldn't I call her sister in Tampa?"

"And tell her what?"

"Um, that Maddy is missing?"

Vivien again. "It's only been a few hours, hon, and Maddy told us to give her room. How many times do we have to tell you that? Don't upset the sister. Don't make her think she has to come down only for Maddy to reappear once the sister is halfway here."

"Besides," Lydia added. "Who of you hasn't made a last-minute decision to spend the whole night with a man instead of coming home?"

Chiara looked lost, and her voice went thin. "Not seeing her doing that. She was afraid of doing what we do." She was groping for answers.

Lydia remained firm. The group expected her to. "You do your thing and let her do hers."

Everyone went silent. Nobody could argue. Vivien first, then Lydia, each took a bite of something on the tray. Robin stared off into the dark, toward the sounds of the night sea. "What now?"

Lydia slipped one more crumble of chocolate, taking time to let it disappear. "I have texts from our friends, asking when we're coming over. I say..." She looked over at Vivien.

"Business as usual," Vivien finished.

They needed attention taken off of them. They'd spent too many years taking their leisure to this level to let one last-minute addition ruin it all. This was the only chance for Lydia to revisit her Edisto each year, and this glitch wasn't doing that in.

"Chiara, steer clear of the Chief," she said. "If she contacts you, which I doubt, tell her we're sorry for the disruption, but we aren't Maddy's keeper. We aren't upset so she shouldn't be."

She glared as if Lydia had lost her mind. "I can't do that."

"What would you have us do?" Lydia asked when the silence just hung and hung.

"I... I don't know."

"Exactly," she said. "You don't know." She polished off her vodka tonic and rose to pour another.

Good God Almighty. I can't trust Maddy as far as I can throw her, but she's taken care of for now. And Chiara... shit. This whole mess is a tiger by the tail.

Back in the kitchen she downed the fresh drink and poured another. In spite of the mistake she'd made, she was committed now. To what end, she had no clue. Not yet.

Chapter 4

BY THE TIME Callie and Thomas left *Time in a Bottle*, it was close to ten, though a full moon and its reflection off the waters surrounding the community made it feel earlier.

She waited until they reached the cars before speaking to her officer. "Nobody's reported a missing family member," she said. "By now someone should be frantic. It's not like she washed over from Beaufort. She came from Edisto."

"True that." He got in the car, waiting for Callie to slide into the driver's seat before saying more. "You never heard of these women before?" he asked, as she buckled in. "I mean, thirty years of summers ought to put them on the map, don't you think? Practically a damn legacy."

She started the engine and eased out south on Palmetto. "I was about to ask you the same thing. They are foreign to me, but I've been here full-time for only three years, Thomas. You've been here longer."

"But I'm young. What about your mother? Wouldn't she know?"

Callie glanced over at him, impressed. "She just might. Smart man. I need to check in with her anyway. What other nuggets of revelation are you keeping in that head of yours?"

"This," he said, pulling out a business card and holding it out for her to see.

She was unable to make it out in the dark. "They have a business card? That's odd."

"This isn't theirs, Chief. This is Sophie's yoga card."

Just what Callie needed to hear. "Yeah, Soph!"

Sophie had feelers everywhere, and if she'd been courting this group for yoga classes, all the better. Though too late to approach her tonight, she'd be the first person Callie greeted when the sun came up.

The dead girl looking like the missing one was rather creepy, but then neither was unique in appearance, both consisting of similar traits that made up a certain thirty-ish stereotype. Average coloring for a blonde, average height and weight, no tattoos or scars. The visuals of the two women seemed no more than coincidental.

Callie didn't believe in coincidences, but this one had merit. There was nothing of substance to connect these two women.

Pulling up under the police station streetlights, their glow confined by the oak trees and moss around the government complex, she dropped Thomas off at his faded pickup, waved goodbye, and went home. She held onto the business card.

She was grateful he was on duty tomorrow with a body on the agenda.

Only two miles away *Chelsea Morning* waited. She welcomed returning home these days—home being a rebuilt house on Jungle Road that still smelled of fresh paint and stained wood. In that short drive, however, she continued being intrigued about a thirty-year-old ladies' club. This type of Edistonian was a different breed than the short-term native, the long-term native, and the occasional visitor. While she didn't actually need to delve into them, she remained curious about the club. Sophie, Marie, Beverly, and the town's mastermind real estate broker Janet Wainwright might be familiar. Brice had been around longer than anyone she knew, and for the third time today, Callie thought about going to him before remembering she couldn't.

She didn't really understand the how and why of missing an old archnemesis, but clearly she did.

As for the dead girl, she'd talk with Mark, Sophie, and Janet. Mark might have seen her dine at El Marko's. Since the girl was fit, she might've stretched in one of Sophie's classes, or again, been hosted by her at the restaurant. And, of course, Janet might recognize a renter.

Odds were, however, the station would receive a call in the morning from someone hunting their girlfriend, wife, sister, or child. She sure hoped so.

Chelsea Morning rose up on her left, and her heart swelled. She'd almost not rebuilt the place after the fire last year. So much baggage came with that address but so did a lot of memories. Not rebuilding felt like lopping off her arm, losing a permanent part of herself.

One hold-a-breath moment, on a particularly low evening when she wasn't sure she even wanted to be law enforcement anymore much less live on a beach that had tried to fire her, kill her, and ostracize her, she'd come close to agreeing to sell the level, scorched piece of land.

Janet Wainwright, real estate broker extraordinaire, was highly intelligent and incredibly savvy in maneuvering people. She could talk most anyone into buying, selling, or renting. Who knew a retired Marine drill sergeant could possess such a perfect balance of ordering, coaxing, and stroking to get people to sign on the dotted line?

Janet badgered her about the empty lot a half-dozen times, usually catching her off balance at the restaurant, at the station, even at a parade so that Callie wasn't so focused. Planting seeds. Ultimately, Callie visited the broker's office on Jungle Road one winter day when she knew she wouldn't be interrupted and the public wouldn't hear.

"What's it worth?" Callie had asked, seated across the desk from the older Marine.

"The question is what's it worth to you?" Janet said. "The market is hot, and in two to three months, will be on fire, pardon the pun. You've cleared the fire debris, so it's prime to sell."

It already had septic and water. Callie wasn't sure how complicated a contractor would find installing new pillars for building over flood waters with the roots of the old ones still embedded twenty feet in the ground.

"Not your problem," Janet had explained.

Then Mark knocked on Janet's office door, not waiting for the okay to come in. As was the norm with him, he carried a paper bag filled with treats from El Marko's and hesitated not two seconds spreading the contents on two plates before Janet on the desk. Opening the three bottled waters he snared from Janet's own refrigerator in an alcove off her outer office, he finished serving, then planted himself in the chair next to Callie.

"What are we talking about?" he'd said, though Callie guessed he already knew.

"Numbers," she said.

"None of your business," Janet added.

He'd laid a hand over his heart. "I'm crushed, Janet." Then he'd turned to Callie. "And I'm worried about you. You are not in a state to sign a listing agreement." He quickly turned to Janet. "Not that that's what you're attempting to do."

Janet puffed up, snatching a cinnamon churro from a plate.

He said no more, having said enough to disrupt the flow and make Callie think twice.

She had eaten a couple items, then switched the conversation to tourist issues, petty theft of rentals, and the depth in which Airbnb messed with the bottom line of the island's property management agencies. Then she'd gone home to her temporary residence on Palmetto and counted herself blessed in dodging a bullet.

Janet could be a sneaky witch at times.

Edisto was home, in spite of her losses. Three of Edisto's civil servants had died on Callie's watch. Officer Francis Dickens, Officer Michael Seabrook, and Town Councilman Brice LeGrand. She'd caught blowback on the first two, especially Seabrook's death with him being a favored son, and she'd expected even more so when Brice was murdered, yet the town folk hadn't held her accountable for him. The poor dunce had pulled a speeder one night, to generate fines for the town's coffers all the while attempting to prove he could do Callie's job as well as she could. Silly, stupid.... The speeder turned out to be a dangerous evader with Callie in hot pursuit on his tail. The culprit had shot Brice center-mass dead.

The town mourned the guy properly, actually missing the dufus while also appreciating her for taking down the shooter. They loved her in their assorted weird ways, and she loved them back. Both sides had grown so much these last three years.

And she'd found solace and love in the new resident and owner of El Marko's. Come to think of it, Mark Dupree ought to be locking up and coming home about now.

Home. She loved how he called her place home. He'd danced around the we/us feel of things since they'd moved in a month ago. She liked things as they were, frankly, but was that saying she wasn't willing to take them further if he asked?

Her phone rang, and a little shock coursed through her at the interruption, then again at the caller ID.

Jeb.

"Anything wrong?" she answered knowing he was in Middleton with Beverly, and it was awful late to be calling.

"Had to wait until she was in bed," he said, the gut-throat noises of frogs in the background. Having grown up in that house, she recognized the sounds of the back courtyard. She'd have called from the front yard herself because Beverly's bedroom was on the backside of the house. Just because she had imbibed plenty of evening gin didn't mean she couldn't hear. Callie's mother was the most functioning alcoholic she'd ever known.

"Did she call you to come to Middleton, or did you call her and got reeled in for a visit?" The former meant his grandmother was in a worse place than average because she never reached out to people. People had to come to her. It was just her way.

"I called and told her I was headed to Edisto but was willing to come have dinner since our last visit was two months ago. She had dinner delivered here, and we ate Italian on china and silver."

Eating in so she could drink and not be judged while at the same time attempting to impress. Callie'd been there. Such evenings had gone far in instilling her own drinking habits. Having moved home after her husband was murdered in Boston, Callie'd taken her drinking skills to higher levels of tolerance under that roof, or so she told herself those mornings she couldn't wake until noon.

She sure hoped Beverly was a better grandmother than a mother. Jeb didn't spill what was said and what went on when he spent nights in Middleton. He was the best caregiver in the family, to be honest. Callie should know. He'd waited a year to go to college, the interim used to nurse her back to sanity, health, and less booze. Callie hoped to God he wasn't being sucked into doing the same with his grandmother.

"So how is she?" she asked.

"Sad," he said. "Like she was when Grandpa died."

Callie's father had died three years ago this month, exactly two days ago. Callie had called Beverly on the anniversary date, but her mother had donned the stiff upper lip. She never showed weakness to her daughter. The thing was, Callie missed Lawton as well and had hoped they could push aside their disagreements in the name of their mutual loss. Having also been a bit melancholy that day, Callie'd wanted to remember him with her mother, but Beverly had shifted conversation to town politics instead, then queries about Jeb's academics. Thinking back, the whole phone call had been rather weird. Maybe that's what grief did... made things weird.

"Well, I'm proud of you being there with her," she said. "I called, but she didn't want to talk about it. I suspect this month is hard for her."

"Um, Mom, it's not about Grandpa."

How could Beverly's glum not be about Lawton? "What else could it be?"

"She says she doesn't ever want to come to Edisto again."

That was new. Beverly originally built *Chelsea Morning,* a year before Callie was born, subsequently spending many a weekend and summer there. Then once Callie grew up and assumed the house, Beverly made impromptu monthly drop-ins.

Mother and daughter were polar opposites. The whole world recognized the lack of synchronicity between them, which made Beverly testy and Callie impatient, but they were family, nonetheless.

Callie used to write it off to mother-daughter power struggles, something Callie labeled stereotypical, until she learned Beverly had adopted her, and Lawton's long-time mistress Sarah was her biological mom. The two mothers had informed Callie together, in a united front. At forty, Callie had felt herself too old to get bent out of shape about it... after a couple days of emotional acclimation.

She learned to really like Sarah, though, who lived most of the time on the beach, one door down from Sophie. But Callie continued her relationship with Beverly, business as usual, which didn't mean smooth sailing. They'd never been in the same room for more than an hour without some rub, plus Beverly was the queen of sarcasm.

"Did she say why she hated Edisto? She gets along with Sarah. The house burning down last year set her back, I'm sure, but I'd have thought she got over that by now."

"Mom," he said. "Come on. Think about it. What's changed recently?"

She thought, at first lost as to what affected her mother that was tied to Edisto. Then her jaw dropped.

Surely not. Callie thought that was ancient history. Like the beau who dropped you in eleventh grade, the experience might've been heart wrenching at the time, but not enough to replay to your grandkids.

"Brice?" she asked.

"Yes," he replied, soft, but in a tone that said she should've known better. "She cried, Mom. Not sloppy crying, but softly, like tears rolling down while she talked. I don't think I've ever seen her cry before. Not even at Grandpa's funeral."

Callie laid her forehead on the steering wheel. Should she have known? She felt she should have, but Beverly had given no indication to her whatsoever of still carrying a torch for Brice. The thought almost nauseated her, but in a weird way made sense for no other reason than Brice represented an era when Beverly was loose and young and dating a man almost considered an Edisto prince.

She felt like a heel, but whether due to lack of DNA or an inability to mesh, Beverly hadn't confided in her daughter, instead unloading on their sweet boy.

"Thank you, son," she finally said, sighing at the end. "Not sure how much she told you about Brice..."

"She's never spoken to me about him," he said. "But surely you knew. Seriously, Mom, she's downright morose."

Callie listened to her own frogs in the marsh, unsure what to say. Unsure whether Jeb was scolding her.

Aware that Brice had dated Beverly in their teens, then early twenties, back in the, what... seventies, Callie'd never known much more than they had been an item on the beach. Beverly hadn't entertained Brice once she married Lawton, to Callie's knowledge, despite Lawton's continued liaisons with Sarah.

Brice, however, had almost hated Callie for simply existing. Some said it was because Callie was the daughter of the woman he had let get away. Even after it came out that Sarah was the real mother, Brice didn't change his attitude. Simply put, Callie was part of Beverly's world that Brice had missed out on. Elder Edisto social circles believed he never got over her, and Callie's presence only rubbed salt in his wounded memory.

"Do I need to come there?" She could leave Thomas in charge of the two cases, guide him via texts or calls to follow up on the slim-to-nothing leads they had. Even so, her leaving for a visit with her mother while the department dealt with a missing person and an unidentified body wouldn't be a "good look" for Edisto's chief. But if Callie gave her mother a few hours' attention, the effort might do them both good.

"No, let's wait on that," Jeb said, spoken so grown up. "We'll talk once I'm back on Edisto. Just felt you needed to hear it from me, since..."

Since he wasn't sure Beverly would tell her own daughter.

Callie wasn't sure what she was supposed to feel. She never expected Brice's death to send her mother spiraling. Beverly hadn't attended the funeral, which felt odd, but not overly so. But for her never to want to return to Edisto? That vow meant not coming to see her daughter.

Jeb might not have said the words aloud, but Callie was sure he thought them.

"When are you coming here?" she asked, trying not to sound as needy as her mother. "Sprite probably misses you," she tagged on, wincing at taking the cheap shot to draw her son home.

"Sprite is fine," he said. "Sophie will keep her plenty occupied, I'm sure. But I'll leave some time tomorrow. Can't say when. Depends on Grandma."

"Of course," Callie said. "Well, I'll be here. Love you, son."

"Love you, too, Mom."

She hung up, the silence outside settling over her like a light blanket. She worried about Beverly. And she worried about her son worrying too much about his mother and his grandmother. The kid hated law enforcement but said he understood her need to wear the badge. That difference laid guilt on her at times, but both had learned a long time ago, she in her way and he in his, that she was a cop and ever would be.

A scurrying in the brush snared her attention, and she caught the tail-end of a raccoon disappearing under some myrtle shrubs. Gosh, how long had she been sitting here? Her phone flashed almost eleven. She locked up the cruiser and took the two levels of stairs fourteen feet up to her porch, admiring the house as each motion sensor light came on to show the way.

Beverly had built the original house using the infamous pastels of the time, inside and out. So after Callie decided to keep the place, ghosts and all, she staked her claim with nautical navy for the siding, and white trim accented in red to integrate the red porch swing from *Windswept*, Seabrook's old house on Palmetto.

That swing. A lot of tears, hugs, arguments, and philosophizing advice lived in those weathered boards, along with a few risky bouts of sex.

That's where Mark found her, still in uniform, when he arrived a half hour later.

"Good. You're still awake," he said from the landing halfway up the steps. Unless he'd been on his feet all day, like today, one didn't notice his limp, remnant of a bullet in his thigh when he was active as a state agent. Tonight the limp showed, especially with nobody but her around to see it.

She knew better than to assist, stopping the swing to show she waited for him. He set the signature paper bag between them before easing down to sit.

"Hurt much?" she asked, pilfering through the bag.

"Nothing out of the norm," he replied, a soft grin showing how much he loved her loving his take-home pleasures. "Sorry those aren't hot. Ought to still be warm, though."

"I'd eat them ice-cold," she said, half a quesadilla in her mouth. "Give me a sec," she added, moaning after a swallow, having forgotten that the last food she'd eaten had been a granola bar for breakfast, found in the reaches of her desk drawer.

She'd tuck a leg up under her except she still wore her utility belt. The swing wasn't squeaking like it had at the other house. Something told her Mark had made sure of that in the installation. "You hear about the body washed up on the sound?" she finally asked.

"Yep."

Of course, he had. Edisto was two and a half square miles of ears and whispers.

"No identification. No reports of her being lost, though get this... we have another report of another girl who looks like her, who hasn't reported back to her group's beach house. We had the latter group make sure the body wasn't their missing acquaintance."

"People tend to show up the next day," he said, understanding the social antics of beach visitors who forgot the rules and mores of the mainland, thinking life was looser and rather unrestrictive on vacay.

"Jeb called about fifteen minutes before you got home."

"Everything all right?" he asked, pinching off a piece of a churro.

"He's fine, but he says Beverly's depressed."

He sighed and patted her on the leg. "Can't help you there. I've met her maybe five times, each time for not much longer than a meal. Even Christmas was rather brief. She seems a very professionally driven woman."

He was fully aware of Callie's small but dysfunctional family. He'd even mentioned being rather satisfied with his lack of one. No living parents. No siblings. No ex and no kids. One could be sad or happy about that. Mark chose the second.

She put her foot down, slowing the swing. "Jeb will be in sometime tomorrow, plus I will have two cases to jump on. But before bed you need a shower. I smell my dinner on your shirt."

"Care to join me?" he asked.

"You're tired," she said.

"You are, too, but we both could use soap."

She stood. "Suits me, but something tells me we need shut-eye tonight. No telling what tomorrow will bring."

He grabbed the bag. "It's why we live for the moment, Sunshine. And get what we can while the getting is good."

Inside, he threw away the remnants while she shed the cop gear and uniform, turned on the water and tried to put aside all the names in her head. Tomorrow meant talks with Beverly, Sarah, Sophie, and/or Marie, not to mention constant checking in with Thomas. Hunting for Maddy maybe. More conversation with Chiara if Maddy hadn't shown. She halfway expected that situation to solve itself. She hoped so, anyway.

And none of her enumerated "to-do" list accounted for time spent with her son.

The arm sliding around her ribs brought her back to the present, and regardless of what they'd said earlier about it being late, they took their time ensuring each other was clean.

Chapter 5

AS USUAL, MARK slept in while Callie rose at dawn. They'd drifted off to sleep half past twelve or so, and while it took an alarm to awaken her most mornings, just past five her brain had engaged. She'd lain there sorting where to start. This wouldn't be an air-conditioned-office day like the one before.

Last night's retreat with Mark merited another shower this morning, but she made it an in-and-out affair.

Toweling off, she decided to tackle Sophie first. She would be a double tap. She was familiar with any Edisto traditions and long-time repeat visitors—like Lydia claimed to be—plus there was no telling what Jeb told Sprite who then told Sophie about Callie's mother. Then there was the business card. Sophie might even have met Maddy. Triple tap. She might recognize the dead girl. Everyone sooner or later in their vacation stopped in El Marko's where, as hostess, Sophie eyed every diner.

A lot of material to cover but maybe not as much physical ground as she thought.

The problem with missing tourists is that they had no roots. During their brief getaway to the sea, they had no obligations, functioned on no schedules, and did what they wanted. Such behavior made for a good number of tickets some days, but it also made it difficult to judge who was really missing versus who didn't want to be found. Maddy sort of fell in that last realm. Lydia wasn't disturbed in the least and seemed the more level-headed when judged against Chiara. So how was Callie supposed to be concerned?

The body would take priority, of course. but she had no leads until the coroner came through. Or until someone finally decided the poor young woman was missing. Surely someone important existed in her life.

Callie left Mark snoring and slipped out to find Sophie, which made her think of grabbing a banana on her way out, one of Sophie's favorite foods. All Callie had to do was walk next door to run the yoga maven down. Her five-days-a-week class didn't start until nine. She'd still be home.

Callie hadn't knocked twice before the door swung open as if Sophie had stood waiting behind it. "Come in," she said, scouting carefully outside before stepping back.

"What's up?" Callie couldn't resist a look over her shoulder.

"Just checking to see if Jeb was with you." As usual, Sophie had managed to inject drama into the morning. "Sprite's been talking to me."

"Is your yoga still at nine today?" Callie asked, hunting for the trashcan to discard the banana peel, unwilling to encourage Sophie. Her life was a continual jumping-bean ordeal, and you learned to wait before leaping aboard. "Wanted to use your infinite knowledge on a few topics, if you don't mind, Soph."

"Wait," her neighbor said, almost breathless, running to the stairs, disappearing in tippy-toe fashion up toward the second floor. She reappeared as if she'd pivoted quickly and come back down. "Good, good," she said, waving Callie to the kitchen.

"What are you—?"

"Shhh, keep it down. Sprite's still sleeping, and I don't want her involved. I was coming to see you this morning because I felt you needed to hear this. So glad you came by."

Callie eased herself into a kitchen chair, now curious as to what was so critical. If it involved Sprite, then it likely involved Jeb. She preferred hearing about a crisis from her own son, thank you very much, but she took information however she could get it, if it involved him. "I'm listening."

"Beverly is having a nervous breakdown. Jeb is afraid to leave her. He might leave school to take care of her, and Sprite is worried he'll screw up his degree."

Her heart taking a flip, Callie willed it to chill out. This was Sophie. This was Sprite, who didn't possess quite the flamboyance of her mother but had the capacity to get excited before grasping all the facts. Just like Jeb—taking a page from Callie's book—chose not to spread magpie hearsay, but then, that also meant he kept many things to himself.

She wondered about a lifetime of this... drama... with grandchildren in the middle.

Then Callie shook off those thoughts and tuned in, all ears, wondering what Jeb hadn't told her last night, wondering which of what she was hearing now was fluff and fancy.

"I just spoke to Beverly not that long ago," Callie said, not wanting to admit they hadn't exactly connected well. "Three days ago was the two-year anniversary of my father's murder. She's down, but she's a strong woman." No point bringing up Beverly's ancient history with Brice.

"So why is Jeb over there on an emergency call?" Sophie asked, hip cocked, never fond of being on the misunderstood side of gossip.

"Because Beverly adores her grandson. He called to check on her; she saw the opportunity to have him over, and voila... we have Jeb taking care of his grandmother. They have a vibe, and I'm rather proud of him for tending to her. She could use some attention living in that big rambling house, but it's not like she wants a nursemaid. She's not that kind of woman."

Sophie had used the word *breakdown*, which had a myriad of interpretations, especially with Beverly, who hadn't even broken down when Lawton died, for God's sake. That funeral for Middleton's well-loved mayor had been a landmark event, and she'd hosted the lieutenant governor and two senators that day, not to mention three-hundred-plus others. It had been a blur for Callie, her focus on Jeb, yet Beverly ran the show like an emcee.

This wasn't about Lawton, though she sadly wished it was. Her father may have had his mistress, but he'd done so with Beverly's approval, giving her the right to do the same. She just hadn't. Callie was beginning to wish she had. Brice clearly meant way more to Beverly than she'd imagined. Not that anyone had the right to pass judgment on who was attracted to whom, but Callie's stomach lurched at the thought of her family in bed with his, literally.

Then a different slant of reality hit her. No wonder Jeb found her short-sighted. Beverly had to feel alone with both of the men in her life deceased. On the backside of her sixties, there had to be a slight sense of mortality rearing its head.

But Sophie's message still needed clarification. "What do you mean Jeb is thinking of dropping out of school?"

Sophie lowered her voice. "Sprite said he was worried enough to take a break. Maybe move in with her. Needless to say, that's not setting well with Sprite, but, hey, that's your son. He likes to fix things, like his mother. I can see where that would drive Sprite crazy. Not sure how that's going to work long term between them."

"Jesus H. Christ, Mother, that's not anywhere near what I said." Sprite strolled in, her eyes thick from sleep, her long thick, jet-black waves disheveled. The effect only gave her an Italian bombshell look.

She was a beautiful girl with a strong heart, and Jeb adored her. Like her mother, however, she loved attention.

"Then what did I get wrong, oh daughter of mine?" Unable to help herself, Sophie pushed lush locks of hair away from her child's eyes. Sprite let her, acting as if she had to, then went to the refrigerator, pulling out, surprise, some of her mother's carrot juice.

In boy-short underwear and a tee that Callie recognized as Jeb's, Sprite plopped at the kitchen table and snared a banana from the center bowl. "I said that Jeb felt sorry for his grandmother being alone, and he wished he could do something. I told him not to skip school, because nobody, including his grandmother, wanted that."

Sophie popped her perky little nose up. "Then I was right."

"On what planet?" Sprite pointed the banana at Callie. "I won't let him drop out of school, Ms. Morgan."

Amazingly, the assurance of a somewhat spoiled little twenty-year-old mitigated Callie's concern over the matter. "Thanks," she said. "Jeb's good for her, but there's also the saying about *too much of a good thing*."

"But he says your mother has secrets even you don't know about," the girl continued.

Callie stilled. The problem wasn't her surprise. The problem was what those secrets were. She'd been blindsided about who her mother was two years ago. She didn't relish another such shock... like Brice might be her father or some such absurdity.

Hell, now she wished she hadn't had that thought.

"Is Jeb coming home today?" Callie asked, trying not to sound needy.

"That's what he said. But he plans to visit weekly to make sure she's good."

Again, her son doing the grown-ups' jobs.

Damn, families were complicated.

The girl rose and strode past her mother back toward the stairs, pausing with a hand on the banister. "Anything else you need me to clear up? Mother can turn a one-car parade into a traffic pile-up."

"Just—" Callie started, then almost changed her mind. Anything she said to Sprite would get to Jeb, but in this case, what would it hurt? "If he gives the least hint about choosing his grandmother over school, please tell me. His education is important."

Sprite gave her head a jerk. "Trust me, Ms. Morgan. What he decides impacts me, and if he tries to go off the rails, I'll tell you. And I'll tell him that I'm doing it. The last thing he wants to do is upset you." She padded her bare feet up the steps.

Sophie kept staring up. Callie tried to rethink what had been said. The shower turned on upstairs.

"We've got some crazy kids," Sophie said under her breath.

Callie checked the seashell clock on the wall. Going on eight. Sophie would have to get ready to leave soon for yoga. "That wasn't what I came for," she said.

Sophie spun. "Is it case stuff? I love it when you need me for your cases. Is it about a case?"

"It is. Have you done a yoga class for a group of women at *Time in a Bottle*?"

Sophie clasped her hands. "Yes! I'm signed up to give them a class a week for four weeks. We had one on Tuesday. A couple of them were quite good at it. They're in decent shape. Even the older ones."

Callie had moved around to one of the bar stools where she could lean elbows on the counter that allowed one to look through a cutout into the kitchen. The spot was the most popular when people came over, with a wider view of both the kitchen and living room. Sophie came over and joined her.

Tuesday was two days ago and the day before Maddy disappeared. "How many were in your class?"

"Five," she said. "We held it on the beach outside their place. It's flat, and we met at seven, before my nine o'clock class at the Pavilion. They aren't morning ladies, but we got past that. A pleasant bunch."

Callie could count on Sophie's honesty. She just had to control the questions she asked to ensure she got facts, not embellishments. "Is this the first time you've dealt with them?"

Sophie parked a foot up on the bar stool. She could pose in the most incredible angles, which she often bragged played well in the bedroom, too. "Oh, no, honey. I see them every summer. As long as I've been teaching yoga out here, they've been on my calendar. They're probably the private class I've taught the most."

"Same women?" Callie asked.

From her expression, Sophie just now wondered why her yoga class was now part of an investigation. She loved the detective side of Callie and was ever curious... to a point. She wanted no part of danger after having had a brush or two with it from being too nosy before.

"Four of them were repeats from last year, yes," she said, pausing. "I guess for four or five years once I think about it. They're a blast. We do, or rather they do, mimosas after each session." She thought harder.

"Lydia, Vivien, and Robin have been around as long as I've been teaching classes."

Mimosas after each session. Sophie rarely drank, and when she did, she nursed one. On yoga days, however, she abstained. Except for the occasional joint, Sophie's body was her temple. She kept her stash under Sprite's bathroom sink, not that Callie cared.

"Do you know them well?" Callie said. "Do you keep up with them other than when they come to Edisto?"

Sophie shook her head. "I can barely keep up with people living on the island, much less renters. I just see them when they come to town. I've become rather accustomed to their expected little income each June, though."

"Tell me more about them," Callie said, opening the proverbial door.

But Sophie had turned suspicious. "Which one's in trouble?"

"Nobody's in trouble."

"Then what's the case?"

This was the point at which Sophie didn't divulge information until you released some of your own.

"One of them is missing," she said.

"Which one?"

"I need to hear you describe them first. She might not even have been there."

Hesitating, Sophie seemed to deem that fair. "Like I said, there were five. So, is that right?"

"Just talk to me, Soph. Keep going." She was right, though.

"Well," she said, doing a side-to-side bobble-headed move. "The leader is Lydia Barron. She's the oldest. Her moves are pretty slick, if you ask me, and I would be the one to know. Guessing she's close to Social Security. I don't get into age, very much."

Bullshit you don't, but age was not an issue here. "Next?"

She described them from the eldest to the youngest, and Callie let her do so covering whatever she felt was worthy of note.

"Vivien is my favorite. She has her act together, I'm telling you. She lets Lydia be the boss, but, honey, this lady is the calm amidst all that estrogen. She doesn't show up Lydia on the mat, but between you and me, she's the fittest. Age? A little younger than Lydia."

So far, they agreed on these women, though Callie might take a harder look at Vivien. She seemed harmless, but in hindsight, she might have a deeper level to her. She didn't seem too disturbed that Maddy was gone either, and something about that school of thought still niggled Callie.

She'd risen this morning wanting to call the women, asking if Maddy came home. She hoped they'd have called her or the department if the prodigal girl returned, but they hadn't, and with vacationers being late risers just because they could, Callie tended to wait until after nine in the morning to make calls.

Sophie was now prattling on about Robin. The good thing about Sophie was she was more than nosy. She retained details like names, where people were from, and who their family members were. What they drank and how badly they sunburned. Sometimes little things like their jewelry. Sometimes details Callie could use.

"Robin is sweet. She struggled with going from downward dog into seal, but she has T-Rex arms. She's the follower in the group. The not-make-waves person." Sophie winked. "She's like me. Lives on healthy alimony from an ex who has plenty, but she sort of blends into the carpet, you know what I mean?"

Nice job, Sophie.

"I don't have to work, you know," she continued. "I just do it for fun."

"You'd be bored to pieces otherwise."

She made a silly face in agreement. "Then comes Chiara. I love her name. It means light or clear, meaning she loves the brighter side of life. Which also means she doesn't like lies. They make her nervous. She's got great balance. You can tell she works on it. Handsome glutes."

"Was she nervous the day of your class?"

Sophie had to ponder that question. "Not really. She seemed to be treating Maddy as a protégé." Her nose wrinkled. "Then there's Maddy. She's a mess if you ask me. Not the favorite for sure. She screwed up her poses and battled following direction. There we were, chimes in the background, and she was grunting and stumbling." A polished nail on a pointed finger went up. "And I'll tell you this about her. Her aura ran orange on Tuesday. Those people tend to learn lessons the hard way. Just like she couldn't follow yoga instructions, chances are she doesn't follow life's instructions any better." After a moment of thought, she shook her head. "She didn't belong there. I doubt she'll be back. These ladies are serious about their leisure time. I mean, four weeks. What does that tell you?"

Again, why did they let Maddy come along?

"So," Sophie said. "Is she the one missing?"

Callie nodded. "She is. You aren't surprised."

Unwrapping herself from her stool, Sophie stood. "She's the newest, the biggest mess, the least conforming, and the most likely to make mistakes. How long has she been gone?"

"Since lunch yesterday. They haven't called me today to say she came home."

Sophie's carefully plucked brows raised high. "They hope she doesn't come back."

"That's rather harsh."

But the yoga mistress shrugged her shoulders. "That's what my senses tell me. I told you she didn't fit in. If they didn't kill her, how is any of this their fault?"

Callie scoffed. "Damn, Sophie. That's downright cold."

"Just reading people, girlfriend. Can you hold them accountable?"

Callie shrugged.

"Exactly." Sophie ran to the hall closet and grabbed her special mat. She stored the everyday ones at the Pavilion for those who forgot theirs. "I take it you aren't working out with me in that garb, so I need to send you packing. I like being there at least twenty minutes early."

"Darn, I wanted to ask you about the dead girl. I'd bet anyone a hundred dollars you won't want to be teaching yoga on that beach outside their house where we found the body."

Sophie dropped the yoga mat. "Thanks for the warning. God, no!" She mumbled, "Not sure I want to go over there next week, or the weeks after. Guess I have to. Four weeks of a private class is a solid gig."

Callie just waited for the soliloquy to end.

Sophie came closer, as if she avoided neighboring ears, possibly Sprite's upstairs. "Did a shark really eat a whole leg?"

Typical. "No. Most of one hand and the back of her calf. Not nearly as disgusting as the rumor mill says, huh?"

Thoughts wrinkled up Sophie's mouth, her eyes squinting. "Not sure any of that matters if she's dead."

"Correct," Callie said, pulling out her phone. "Now, the picture I have is of her dead, Soph, but nothing nasty. Would you look at it for me? Tell me if you've seen her?"

There was some hesitation, but curiosity got the better of her. "Um, sure."

Callie made Sophie sit back on the bar stool then pulled up the picture on her phone.

"Oh, oh, oh…" Sophie reared back at first, putting distance between her and unpleasantry. Then she settled and studied closer, even pinching the picture to see it better. "Saw her at the grocery store," she said.

"Did you speak?"

"No."

"Did she have someone with her?"

"No."

"Did she have a conversation with anyone?"

"No."

"Did you see what she drove?"

"Nope. Sorry. But she bought mixers, chips, blue cheese, dish soap, and eggs."

Details. Sophie could note the oddest details.

Callie put the photo away just as a revelation spread across Sophie's face, as if the whole room had shifted. "Oh God, oh God!" She leapt from her stool. "Callie! You made me look at something revolting in my house! Sprite!"

Callie took her hand, the one waving toward the stairs. "Don't involve her, Sophie. There's no need to upset her."

"No, no, she's got to sage the house while I'm at yoga! We've talked about too much bad not to deep clean at least the downstairs. Oh my God, I can't believe I let you talk to me about such atrocities, much less show pictures."

One picture, but Sophie was already texting a message to her daughter, then pulling a sage stick from a credenza drawer and setting it on an abalone shell bowl. "I wish I could do it, but she can handle herself," she grumbled.

Sophie could be such a hypocrite, begging to hear the juicy stuff from Callie's days then fussing about any of it ruining her home's *Chi*.

Callie followed Sophie to the door, then through to the porch, and noted how, as always, she didn't lock her door. "Your daughter's in there, naked in the shower, with all that bad energy we left, and you leave the door unlocked?"

"How many times do I have to say it, Miss Police Chief. You plan for bad things to happen, and they gravitate to you. Lock up your house and you attract negative energy. Don't make things any worse than they are, Callie!"

Callie'd heard that mantra a hundred times and never understood it, but this was Sophie's house. The officers were aware she didn't lock up, and they kept an eye on it a little harder than most.

She had planned to go see Sarah next, owing her biological mother a visit. She might have insight on Beverly. She'd also been around the island longer than Sophie and might have some read on Lydia's crew.

Sarah, however, wasn't an early riser, and from her vantage on the porch, Callie couldn't see a light on or movement at the place next door to Sophie's.

She'd catch her later. And she figured instead of calling Lydia, she'd just mosey over to *Time in a Bottle* in person. Their friend having been gone almost twenty hours had to have altered their feelings from yesterday, and she wanted to judge their behaviors when she asked why nobody seemed to care.

Unless Maddy had come home. That would be wonderful considering all else on her agenda for the day.

Chapter 6

Lydia

THAT'S JUST GREAT.

A patrol car waited outside, not in the drive, but along Palmetto Road, acting as if the driver watched traffic while probably studying the beach house. *Time in a Bottle* sat too far back for someone inside to really tell. That huge oak tree hindered much of the view. Lydia hoped it was the young male officer versus the chief. She was nosy. He was a treat to look at.

She also hoped this was nothing more than traffic control.

Vivien slipped up behind her. "Whatcha looking at?"

"That." Lydia pointed toward the street with her cup, the coffee still hot enough to fog up the glass.

"Oh." With her nose pressed against the glass on the other side of the door, Vivien took a harder study. "They work around the clock, I guess. Glad they're watching for speeders." She went back to the kitchen. Robin had taken over the stove, eggs at the ready. Chiara, however, remained in her room.

Whoever this was wasn't watching traffic. Traffic wasn't much of an issue this far down Palmetto, particularly this early. Whoever this was waited for those inside to be up and dressed before coming to call.

Damn it, she needed to check on Maddy but not with a cop in her lap. After the girl took a triple dose of Valium last night, Lydia confiscated the bottle. What she took shouldn't have done real harm, but her slick trick to put things out of her head meant she could do it again and miscalculate. At least she should still be doped up and unaware.

Vivien had only echoed Lydia's thoughts earlier that morning... don't tell the other two women. Don't tell the cops. Don't tell anyone... yet.

But wouldn't that make matters worse? There really wasn't a right answer here.

In the meantime, Lydia doled out medication, made sure the girl was fed and hydrated... and kept hidden. She hated leaving the girl downstairs, but the weather wasn't terrible, the concrete floor cool in the storage room. Thank God she had the only key. If she brought out Maddy, the girl would lose her mind and give everything away.

No, for now, this was for her own good.

But four weeks. Jesus, they had more like a day or two, max, before something accidental turned totally criminal.

Chiara... damn her. There was no way to tell her Maddy was okay without their whole world going to hell.

A tiger by the tail.

Chiara entertained one of their regular friends last night, at his place, a man she'd socialized with last year and the year before. They'd urged her to go out rather than mope around the house, she and Vivien assuring her that Maddy was still fine. She went begrudgingly, returning in slightly better spirits. However, once in the room she shared with Maddy, with all of Maddy's things around her, she fell back into a mood.

God, she'd even texted herself from Maddy's phone twice, showing the two brief messages to Chiara. *Give me time to think.* Then hours later, *I'm better. The beach is helping. Sort of made a friend. I'll be in touch.*

She showed them to Chiara before her date, to demonstrate she wasn't as hardened a group leader as Chiara might think. The fact Maddy texted Lydia instead of her left Chiara in a quandary, but she had to admit Maddy wasn't in dire straits. Later, she showed the texts to Robin. Bases covered, for now.

Yes, Maddy was irresponsible. Yesterday Lydia halfway expected that body on the beach to be hers, fearing she'd gotten loose from the storage room in a Valium stupor and drowned herself. For an ugly, ugly second, she wished it true.

Some might consider that attitude harsh, but she'd lived long enough and experienced enough to be pragmatic. Call it a certain level of upbringing. Call it genes. Vivien understood. The ladies' club was designed to represent only independent sorts who were tired of being a victim. As long as they kept things between the rails, all was fair in love and war.

Lydia might have admired Maddy the other night, considered her a true-blue member if she hadn't gone berserk. Her wounds still raw from her issues in Florida likely robbed her of her senses.

A car door slammed, and Lydia scooted sideways, to avoid being seen. A quick glance told her the chief was gracing them with her presence again, which meant she had more questions... or suspicions.

Shit, shit, shit. Her story had to be enough to satisfy the badge while not giving anything away to Robin and Chiara. She didn't want them involved.

By the time the chief knocked, Robin had eggs on her plate, and Lydia took over the skillet. Not that eggs were her thing, but she'd do anything to look busy and make the chief feel like she was an inconvenience in a typical beach house rental.

Vivien answered the door. "Why hello, Chief Morgan. Mighty early for a social call, or is this professional? Be happy to whip up some breakfast for you. I make avocado toast to die for." She waved the chief in.

Of course, Chief Morgan declined to eat, graciously telling everyone else to go ahead. She was a tiny little thing. Without all that belt and uniform, she couldn't weigh much more than a hundred and twenty.

But it didn't take size for her to stand to the side and analyze. "Since there have been no calls, I came by to see if Maddy had reappeared by any chance," she said, looking around the big kitchen/living room area as if Maddy might be sitting somewhere with her coffee and toast.

Vivien fixed the visitor a cup of coffee to her liking and sat alongside Robin at the long table. Built for twelve to accommodate those families who crammed every cousin and uncle in a rental, the oak table consumed an enormous amount of space giving the area a cavernous feel. The chief sat across from Robin, giving Lydia the choice to sit next to Robin, at the opposite empty end, or next to the guest. She chose Robin.

"Where's Chiara this morning?" the chief asked.

"Still in bed," Vivien said. "She came in late and hasn't decided to join us yet. Vacation rules, you know. We don't wake anyone before noon, especially if they've been out."

The chief took that in, giving them a few breaths of silence. Lydia felt tactics at play.

"Anyone heard anything from Maddy?" she asked, though surely, she'd figured no one had. She was testing them.

All heads shook. If only they'd had a briefing on how to behave before the chief got here, because this visit had been inevitable.

"Don't you find that rather... irregular?" she asked. "Come lunch it'll be twenty-four hours."

"It's how we roll," Robin said, not sounding nearly as firm as she intended. How could she? She sat there in a vintage Spider Man tee that puddled around her. When she stood, it came down to her knees.

"No, not what I understood," the chief said. "Per Chiara you have this engraved-in-stone rule about check-ins. Seemed to have Chiara rather disturbed yesterday." She made a conscious glance toward Chiara's bedroom, where she was told the woman slept.

"Maddy is green," Lydia said, before anyone else spoke. "She's trying to get over an old boyfriend, and we felt sorry for her. She clearly didn't grasp how strongly we feel about keeping each other apprised of our whereabouts, but in hindsight, she evidently was so hungry to carve out a fresh life that she leaped. She's our hardest drinker, too." She pulled out her phone. "She sent me two texts thus far. Care to see them?"

"Yes, I would."

Trying not to appear reluctant, Lydia passed over the phone to the chief who read them and handed it back. "Mind sending those to me?"

"Not at all."

The chief took the table in, observing quietly as she panned from person to person, face-to-face. "Sounds like—like you said—she wasn't a good fit."

Vivien softly shook her head, agreeing.

"Quite a slip from the norm for such a well-formed group. What, thirty years, you said?"

"Yes, at least for Vivien and me." Lydia didn't care to fill in anything she wasn't specifically asked and kicked herself for saying more than *yes*.

"With Robin number three, for over a decade, right?" She looked to Robin instead of Lydia.

"Yes," Lydia replied anyway. The chief needed to realize who was in charge.

"May I see Maddy's room?"

That caught Lydia off guard, and she wasn't sure why. Why couldn't she see it? "Why?" she still asked. *Damn. Did that sound like a cover-up?*

"That's deflection," the chief said. "But to answer your question, I'd like to see for myself if she took things with her that might indicate she wasn't coming back."

"She hasn't."

"Mind if I look for myself?"

Cops. You could afford their irritation, but you best beware their suspicion. "Chiara is still sleeping."

"I'll do my best not to wake her. Promise."

Now what was she supposed to say? Vivien and Robin had long conceded the conversation. The chief was on a mission, and she wasn't leaving without addressing her list of questions. To deter her or attempt to misdirect her would only dig her in deeper, keep her there longer, make her confront each of them until they got so nervous one of them said too much, like they worried too about Maddy being gone. How nobody had talked to her but Lydia, who might be the last person she'd reach out to.

"Go ahead," Lydia said, standing to escort the chief to the bedroom, the others remaining at the table.

At the entrance, she eased the bedroom door open. Chiara lifted her head. "Is she back yet?"

The chief moved past into the room. Chiara sat straight up, covering herself, then touched her hair as if feeling to see what a mess she might be.

"No, Maddy's not back," the chief said, entering the room. She wasn't commandeering, just observing, drawn to the other side of the room where Maddy would have slept. Clothes remained on the bed where she'd struggled with what to wear. In the bathroom, her makeup bag was gone along with her toothbrush and other toiletries since the shared bath only held one set of everything now.

The chief turned to Lydia. "Does she normally pack for a sleepover when she goes on a date?"

Lydia held up hands. "Not sure what her normal is, remember? Guess she does. She's rebounding after a bad relationship, so... maybe she decided to go for the gusto? On the other hand, she could've been too embarrassed to tell us she went back to the boyfriend. We don't know her so we can't really answer very well, can we?"

The chief gave the room one more look. "Sorry to wake you," she said to Chiara, "but would you check your phone, in case Maddy's called or texted?"

Chiara dropped the covers and retrieved her phone, eager to do just as asked. One could see her wilt at finding nothing.

"That a no?" the chief asked.

Chiara shook her head, a fresh waterfall of concern so evident after the reprieve of a few hours' sleep and no worry.

"You seem more upset than the others," the chief said, easing to the side of the bed. "Explain that for me."

"We work together in the Pinellas County School District, at a magnet middle school. She teaches accelerated math, and I teach honors English. We've known each other for five years. I've listened to her talk about her relationship for months, and I was the one who suggested she come with us. Suggested it to her then suggested it to the club." Her eyes had already filled with tears, and the explanation only made them spill.

"Does she have family?" came the next question.

Chiara nodded. "A sister in Florida. I started to call her..." but she stopped, with a glance to Lydia.

"Go on," the chief said. "You started to call the sister... and what?"

"Um, I decided not to scare her. Not if Maddy was just playing around, or spent the night somewhere, or... whatever. Just felt an extreme thing to do right now since she... texted Lydia."

Good job, hon. Almost perfect.

"Care to give me the sister's number?" Chief Morgan asked.

Instinctively going to her contacts list on her phone, Chiara stopped. "Um, I don't have it. Maybe I could call our HR department at work. Surely, she's Maddy's emergency contact. I... I never thought about needing it. I mean, I haven't given Lydia an emergency contact for me."

Excellent again.

"Well, when you get a chance," the chief said, without missing a beat, "how about calling your HR and retrieving that for me." She reached into a pocket and removed a business card. "And call me when you have it."

Chiara reached up and took the card, reading it like she'd never seen one before.

"Why don't you go ahead and get dressed, Chi," Lydia said, holding out her arm to show the chief the way to leave. "I'll get Vivien to fix you something to eat."

Chief Morgan kept walking, and surprisingly, she actually continued straight to the front door, but before taking the knob in her hand, before any of them could be fully relieved at her leaving so soon, she turned, speaking loud enough for all but Chiara to hear. "I've got to be honest, ladies. I'm not sure what's going on here. Granted, we don't have a body, so we're not talking worst-case scenario. At least not yet. But not contacting her best friend who is clearly distraught... to find someplace else to lay her head when she'd never been here before... just concerns me."

Lydia awaited the accusation she'd be forced to deny. She prayed Chiara stayed in her room. Miss Pressure Cooker might say anything without much push.

Vivien and Robin looked to their leader.

The chief continued. "You see? I'm all but hearing your unspoken words, wishing each other to remain quiet, wondering what I know. Wondering when I'll uncover what I don't. Just wanting me gone."

She let her thoughts settle over the three, indoctrinating them, but the other ladies had relied on Lydia for too long through too many situations not to let her handle controversy. They remained quiet, though Robin's eyes were wide as saucers.

"Listen." Chief Morgan took her tone down. "Help me find Maddy, and we're good, ladies. I don't go looking for trouble on Edisto Beach. Especially not from people who come one day and are gone the next. But I don't run from it either. And I don't ignore the obvious. You've got something going on, and now you've got a kink in the works with Maddy's disappearance. Find her, my friends, or you're going to be seeing a lot more of me in your business."

Lydia mentally accepted the dare. The chief might think she was all that, but she couldn't do a damn thing to them about Maddy. Without a body or a crime scene, all she had was a quasi-missing person nobody was concerned was missing.

But without a doubt, she could harass them to pieces if she had a mind to. And knowing this chief, at least knowing her lineage like Lydia did, she would be well capable of doing exactly that.

But finding Maddy wasn't the real issue. Frankly, that was the least of their problems.

Chapter 7

JUST FOR GOOD measure, and to irritate the ladies she left in the house, Callie remained seated in her car, pretending to look down taking notes, appearing chilled.

But she was pissed as hell.

Common sense told her to be patient, but her gut said she had every right to be disturbed. The nonchalance under that roof angered her. The disrespect for the uniform got under her skin. The indifference concerned her so much that she had no idea whether Maddy was in trouble. The average cop would move on. She, however, would feel better if she laid eyes on the woman, just to put her mind at ease.

Chiara, the girl most familiar with Maddy, seemed the most worried. The others seemed little more than burdened, their summer holiday inconvenienced by a silly, stupid girl.

Callie went back to scanning the road, trying to decide which person on her list to question next about the dead woman, the priority. She wished the coroner would call sooner than later. The most her people could do right now was go door to door with the photo of a dead girl, and that wasn't going to make any of them very popular. Not in this season. As for Maddy, regardless of the *Time in a Bottle* clique not wanting to make a big to-do about her, Callie'd have Marie shoot out a photo of her to all uniforms, too, and have them query commercial venues throughout their day... just for the hell of it. If the girl had simply fallen out with her gal friends, then so be it. No harm done.

A Hyundai took the rounded curve from the Villas, spotted her marked unit, and almost stood on its headlights braking to the speed limit. She held her stare as the driver crept by, pretending she wasn't there, staring at the road ahead as if his life depended on it.

Good, he'd never take that curve like that again, and hopefully he'd be gone by the weekend.

With the forecast in the eighties today, folks would pack the beach and keep the roads busy. She almost called in another officer to cover but didn't. The department wasn't big enough for such luxury. She would remain active, as backup, hoping that's all she was needed for. She could, however, earnestly hope the coroner identified the body somehow and that Maddy reappeared in a hungover stupor, putting Edisto back to right.

She hated this limbo on the dead woman, though. Was a killer out there or had the girl screwed up by swimming alone at night?

It was going on ten. She lifted her radio. "All good, Marie?"

"All good, Chief." The morning was quiet, nothing on the horizon, but to say too much aloud only invited trouble. The ritual of *less said the better* was the sort of thing Sophie would agree with.

Callie heard the phone in the background.

"Uh oh," Marie said. "You shouldn't have radioed. Hold on a sec."

"No problem."

Didn't take long for Marie to return. "Chief?"

"Yep."

"That was Zeller. Says a car's been parked outside the Pavilion since noon yesterday, right in front of the stairs. Normally she wouldn't care, but with that girl being found dead yesterday and nobody knowing who she is, she thought she ought to tell you."

Bravo for the Edisto regulars. "Thanks. On it."

"Oh, and Raysor's back."

Some peace fell over her. "Thought he wasn't coming back until tomorrow."

"He said he missed us. How about that?"

Callie laughed, enjoying the change in mood and very grateful for the return of the seasoned deputy. Deputy Don Raysor belonged to Colleton County Sheriff's Department, not Edisto Beach PD, but he'd been on loan to the town of Edisto Beach for half his career. Thank goodness Colleton paid his salary.

Edisto Beach had limited funds for employment, but the county appreciated the huge tax base that came from the coastal town, so it seemed a decent trade-off. She didn't care that his patrol car and uniform were tan and brown, unlike the navy and black of Edisto. He was experienced and familiar with every inlet, road, and family in the region, loosely kin to at least ten percent of the county's population.

Lately, he'd been working more for the county in Walterboro, having been called in due to a huge trial gone national in scope. With national media like CNN, FOX, and MSNBC, atop the locals of WCBD, WLTX, WIS, and more, the small town had converted into a madhouse of journalists, the curious, and the amateur wannabes seeing themselves becoming wealthy via podcasts and future books.

With the small county courthouse now empty and exhausted from the intense attention, the murderer in jail, and the traffic back to normal, Raysor could return. Edisto was practically his home. Like Marie, his inherent knowledge carried a lot of weight... matching his girth.

"Just put the son of a gun to work," Callie said, still smiling. They'd missed the old cuss.

"He put himself to work," Marie replied. "Just thought you'd like to know."

"Thanks. I'll be on the lookout for him. I'm headed to the Pavilion."

"Zeller said she'd be waiting for you. Over and out."

Zeller worked at a local boutique just off the causeway and would have to pass that way coming and going to her job. She must've been headed to work. She'd lived on the beach for ages, and like Sophie, kept an eye on the comings and goings of regulars. Another person to ask about Lydia and her group if the opportunity arose.

With no need for a light, Callie pulled a U-turn to take Palmetto all the way to the other end of town.

Even with *Time in a Bottle* gone from her rearview mirror, she couldn't push Lydia out of her mind. The woman's attitude clung to her like mold on a rock. She was the dynamic one in the lot, and people gravitated to certain personalities like hers to make the decisions. Every beach group had one. These leaders loved taking charge, and the others appreciated not being bothered, but Lydia seemed more than just the unspoken temporary leader. Either she really hated Maddy and honestly didn't give a damn, or she knew more than she was saying. Callie sensed she called the shots outside of Edisto as well. All of them appeared to be from the Tampa area.

Chiara seemed on the outs with the group over the Maddy situation, maybe jeopardizing her own right to return next year to whatever this pilgrimage was. This morning as she lay sequestered in her bedroom depressed, the others went about their day. Callie got the vibe of involuntary restraint. She'd changed her mind about speaking up... started then stopped, because Lydia was in the room. That concerned Callie greatly.

But there was professional concern and then there was just letting someone rub you wrong, and Callie had to be sure she managed the two appropriately. Truth was, if the parties responsible for Maddy weren't upset, she couldn't force them to be. After all, she'd never met the woman. Just because Callie didn't trust Lydia didn't mean she was guilty of something.

But she wasn't going to one hundred percent buy into their viewpoint that no one needed to give a damn, either.

At the Pavilion, Zeller waited outside the car, apparently having run back over from her job to personally address her concern once Marie told her Callie was on the way. In her early seventies, Zeller had held every seasonal job on the island from food prep at the restaurants to, like this season, managing sales at a gift shop. People liked her. Callie read her as an old hippie. Her name was a homemade, easy-to-remember spin-off of her difficult-to-remember last name that began with a Z. Callie wouldn't be able to spell it if she had to.

"You didn't have to wait for me," Callie said, stepping out of her car.

Cropped white hair accented by a years-old tan from enjoying the outdoors and wearing Birkenstocks on her feet, Zeller sported khaki shorts and a crisp button-up shirt. "Don't like secondhand messages myself," she said loud enough to be heard over the wind and the tide, "and I thought you'd be the same. Especially with a dead girl on your plate."

First-hand was always better. Zeller was no dummy.

"Appreciate it," Callie said, walking around the car. "When did you notice it yesterday?"

Zeller put on her shades. The sun was in its full glory today, heating up the beach. "About this time. Wouldn't have remembered it except for the tag. I love personalized tags, and out here you see some doozies. Haven't seen a one I couldn't solve."

The sun's reflection off the white Explorer almost blinded them because the SUV had been well maintained and not long ago washed. The car not more than two years old, the tag was in-state and read RN4KIDS. Neatly placed stickers on the bumper and in the windshield showed parking garage numbers for Middleton Medical Center and Boeing Industries, both North Charleston employers.

The doors were locked with no purse or personal items out for display in the front seat other than a pen and a small tumbler, probably coffee. The back doors and the hatch door were tinted so dark she could hardly see in.

No probable cause to force access. She could get a search warrant once she could make some sort of connection to the deceased or her family, but she had to be careful notifying family too soon, too. A husband or other close kin could easily be a person of interest.

She peered up and looked across the street for a cam at the gas station, knowing full well the Pavilion had none facing this direction. She couldn't tell from here the angle of the gas station cam, which meant the lens was far enough away that clearly identifying the driver would be difficult if not impossible.

2Beach was Edisto Beach. With no defined parking lot, only sand surrounded the Pavilion. Sand and water. The venue catered to the day-trippers as much or more than the regulars, with the typical shells, floaters, tee-shirt souvenirs, and other tourist sundries inside. You could tell they catered to anyone and everyone by the ramp aiding the disabled and elderly—an expensive ramp as long as the building and a clear contrast to the rental properties that stood two stories off the ground. No elevator in site. Insurance companies frowned upon elevators. They were considered channels for storm water, and since elevators weren't generally required in rental houses of less than three stories, few owners bothered to jump through the hurdles of having one approved.

The breezes and periodic gusts off the water not fifty feet away right now had drifted sand against the two tires on the west side of the auto and hidden the human tracks of the driver, enough to show the car hadn't moved in a while.

Seeing the police car, then the uniform, people slowed—some upstairs shoppers peering down, others easing over from the water. A worker from the Pavilion stuck his head out the door. "What's up, Zeller?"

"Bob, didn't you notice this car out here all night?"

The guy grimaced with a hard sarcasm. "You're kidding, right?"

"Might belong to that dead girl," she hollered over the wind.

Callie really wished Zeller hadn't said that because the words set the handful of tourists buzzing. A couple got on their phone. Others snapped pictures. Callie looked up at the worker. "Any chance you saw who the driver was?"

He shook his head. No surprise there.

She might as well turn to the gathering. "Any of y'all familiar with the driver of this car?"

But nobody was, most of them day visitors, the others not paying attention to who drove what car. Nobody cared. Nobody came on vacation to care about much of anything.

Murmurs picked up, though, much as it had with the onlookers on the sound where they found the dead girl. The word *shark* kept reaching Callie's ears.

A mom dared wander over with two kids in tow. "Is it true what they are saying? That a shark killed that woman?"

"Coroner hasn't made a determination yet," Callie replied, watching what she said and how she said it in front of what looked like an eight- and a ten-year-old.

"So what are we supposed to do?" the mom said, drawing the youngest to her.

"Your call, ma'am. Sharks are always out there. Use your best judgment when and where you swim. Avoid swimming where people are cast fishing, and sharks are more common in the evening. Wherever anything is feeding, whether fish, gulls, pelicans, or dolphin, expect shark to be around, too."

The woman gasped, most likely remembering how she'd violated one, if not all the informal guidelines.

It never failed to amaze Callie how people body surfed the waves not thirty feet from where a man cast a serious hook with serious bait on the end, meaning he fished for serious-sized fish. Sometimes on an incoming tide one might catch sea bass or croaker, but other times a ray or a shark.

A middle-aged man came up, his accent from nowhere near South Carolina. "Why don't you people have shark towers here? Where I'm from, we take care of people swimming."

You people. The condescension grated on her like sand on an open blister. Locals didn't like it either, often telling visitors to take their suggestions back home with them, but Callie pushed through a smile. "We don't have enough shark issues nor the staffing."

His sneer wasn't flattering. "You ought to with all the damn money we pay for these places." Yet he paid half here what he'd have had to pay up north or out west.

Shark towers were originally nothing more than lifeguard stands, overlooking surfers and swimmers on bigger, more turbulent coasts than this one. Though common on bigger beach areas with bigger police departments and bigger budgets which enabled the locale to employ enough folks, the towers were a pain to build, maintain, and staff.

If you go in salt water, you meet saltwater creatures, she wanted to say.

"One life is worth the cost, Chief," mouthed off a woman somewhere behind the man. "You should at least have a vigilant beach patrol. You might not have lost that woman like you did, if you had."

Sure, let's put a shark tower, say, every thousand feet. Even that would be considered too far apart by many people's standards. That would be two dozen towers, two dozen guards, times at least two to allow people to go home, eat, be sick, have holidays, and take vacations of their own. Just have them eight months out of the year, too, with time off when the beaches were bare. At least thirty people.

She didn't bother calculating the dollars. Towers weren't happening.

This week the topic was towers. Last week, there were complaints about not having rip-tide sirens when every single beach access had signs describing them and warning beachcombers of their existence. Some tourists loved arriving, loudly voicing opinions on perceived needed improvements, then leaving, tsking themselves all the way home. Those were the ones Edisto prayed wouldn't return.

God, she tired of people becoming instant experts about what the Edisto Beach PD ought to be doing. If the news got out about murder, somebody would go all profound with unlimited foresight in stating if the police did their jobs properly, nobody would be killed.

So many people didn't want the police until they needed them, and then they'd question the manner in which the police helped. The job had become more thankless in the last five years. She couldn't fathom working on her old stomping grounds in Boston these days. Or would that atmosphere be better than this tiny piece of ground where anyone had direct access to each and every officer, including the chief?

"Y'all," Zeller said, shouting out to the crowd that had grown fatter than Callie preferred. Zeller had climbed up a half-dozen steps to be seen better. Her gravelly voice from years of cigarettes resonated across the audience.

"We on Edisto love our police department, and especially Chief Morgan. She's taken down the type culprit that would keep you awake at night, and not just one or two, either. She's our guardian angel out here. She's golden. She knows what the hell she's doing, so how about letting her do her job instead of giving her shit. This isn't *Jaws*. This is real life, people. Just go on your way and let her be. Appreciate it." She came back down, like the meeting was adjourned.

Wow. Um, thanks?

Zeller returned. "How was that?"

No wonder Zeller was friends with Sophie. They were two peas in a pod in a way. "Whatever works."

"Girl, I'm tight with Sophie, and I'm aware of the shit this place has put you through."

She reads minds, too.

"People's eyes have been opened, and you are our lady, you hear?" Zeller almost commanded.

"Um, yes. Thanks again." Callie turned to study the vehicle, a hint of embarrassment still on her cheeks, hoping that by doing her job and not entertaining questions, people would fade away.

"What else?" Zeller asked. "Want me to wave off people pulling in here? I can maintain a crime scene for you."

Callie shook her head. "All's good, Zeller," but then caught herself. "Maybe I do have a question for you."

About that time, a familiar brown cruiser pulled in. The driver's door opened, and the car dipped as Deputy Don Raysor pushed out. That only drew more attention, as if this new cop brought fresh, groundbreaking news, especially one from another jurisdiction. Those who'd moved off tried to slip back closer.

Raysor noticed, scoffed, and came over to Callie, arms out. "I'm baaaack."

Chapter 8

CALLIE GAVE RAYSOR his hug, her almost smothered from sight in his embrace. "Glad you're here, big guy."

The deputy let loose and turned to Zeller. "You want to hug me, too?"

"I'll pass," she said. "A little late to the show, aren't you?"

"Hell, I've been hobnobbing with celebrities, or didn't you know?" He dropped the smile act. "I can't tell you how damn glad I am to be back here on planet Earth. Famous people are pains in the ass, and don't get me started on attorneys and their demands. For a month there, Walterboro thought it was Hollywood, with all the locals losing their damn minds trying to collect autographs and snap pictures. They had a damn lottery to be allowed inside to watch the trial. Can you believe that crap?" He shook his head, as if he needed to chase those experiences away in order to come back to reality. "Anything going on around here?"

Callie was more than eager to fill him in, but doing so in front of Zeller wasn't appropriate.

"They found a woman's body is what happened," Zeller spilled before Callie could say a word. "Washed up half eaten by sharks."

A woman in the crowd about ten feet away gasped, hand over her mouth.

"Zeller," Callie said, pulling her further away. "Raysor and I can handle things from here."

Then she stopped herself. Callie had enough people to catch up with over the next couple of days, and she didn't want to add Zeller to the list. She moved out further, Zeller and Raysor following.

"Let me ask you one more thing," she said low, reaching for her phone, opening it to the photos. She tapped the pic of Maddy Gillespie and aimed it toward her eager novice assistant. "Know her by any chance?"

Zeller eased out readers and propped them on her nose, then bent over like a pup sniffing without getting too close. "Nope. Haven't seen her before."

Callie didn't ask Raysor, and he didn't offer, figuring he'd be enlightened once Zeller left. Besides, he'd just returned to the beach. Maddy had disappeared before he'd had a chance to see her.

"Ever heard of the name Lydia Barron?" Callie then asked. "She comes with a group of women every year, she says. Has been for thirty years."

Not having a photo to look at, Zeller removed her lenses and slid them in her breast pocket, looking at Callie hard. She squinted. "Anyone been around that long, I would know her. Barron, you say? She's lying or that ain't her name. Nobody's been around this town for that long without me, Sophie, Janet..." She began a list of old residents, stumbling when she almost mentioned Brice. "Sorry about that. Keep forgetting he's gone. But this guy—" She lightly backhanded Raysor's hefty arm. "He ought to be familiar as much as anyone."

Everything Zeller said had already crossed Callie's thoughts. "Just think of the name Lydia, then, and not the last name. These women seem to enjoy gadding about socializing, meeting friends from years past. They stay here a whole month partying."

After thinking a moment, Zeller raised her brows, chuckling in that raspy way of hers. She nudged Raysor, like he ought to be reading her mind.

Callie waited to hear what was so funny. Raysor wore a quizzical look.

"What's so special about this Maddy girl?" Zeller asked.

"She's missing."

"Belongs to that group of women you're talking about?"

"Her first summer." Callie waited.

"You know, a lot of lady groups reappear each summer."

Callie sighed. "I'm aware. There are three book clubs that I know of. There are three teachers' groups. There are at least fifty reunions. Never saw any of these women before though."

Zeller chuckled again. Callie was about to get perturbed at being left out of the joke. "Thanks for the help, Zeller. Now, if you don't mind, Raysor and I need to move on with our work."

Still with a sparkle in her eye, Zeller leaned in, lowering her voice from the people still hanging around. "Hookers, honey. They're probably hookers, or so the rumor says. With me never having been invited I can't confirm, but they walk amongst us for sure. Probably why you haven't heard of them. They fly under the radar, so to speak."

Her smirk wasn't fun anymore.

Callie blew off the thought... then didn't. While Zeller's suggestion was little more than that, a suggestion, maybe more like gossip, she guessed the possibility existed. Hard to hang that label around these ladies' necks without more proof than they were a bunch who enjoyed Edisto, though. Based on that vague definition, the beach would be half red-light district during prime months of the season. She'd never caught the first whiff of hookers, frankly. More like ladies kicking up their heels, making acquaintances at the beginning of a week, and telling them goodbye the next weekend.

"Brice would've been able to tell you," Zeller tacked on. "I heard he hooked up with one particular lady of the evening every summer. I never met her. Couldn't describe her. His ex, whom you know, was too dense or didn't care, but of course, we sure learned why she wasn't looking very hard, didn't we?"

Now Raysor chuckled, and Callie couldn't help but grin at that image. Brice would've been too cheap to pay enough for a decent hooker, which conjured all sorts of mental images, and Zeller's recollection of Brice's marital history held merit. His ex-wife had been caught with his best friend about eighteen months ago, and after a Twitter war of accusations, he'd narrowly avoided jail time for threatening her, gun in hand. He'd been an idiot. The wife had been an idiot. The whole island had enjoyed the gossip for months.

"But you don't know the name Lydia?" Callie asked again, pulling the talk back around, not wanting to go down a rabbit hole of tales and blather.

"No. Feel like I should if she's been around this long. Especially if they... you know."

She still stuck to that presumption. Even so, an alias was not unusual nor illegal if you wanted to present yourself as someone different during your vacation, but none of that mattered. Finding Maddy was the point of concern regarding *Time in a Bottle* and its tenants' activities. But right now, standing outside the Pavilion, the focus should be on the dead woman.

"Don't let me hold you up from work."

"I'm good. The store won't be busy this time of day."

Callie doubted that. They were drifting into the lunch hour, when people came in from the sun and did touristy things. "No, seriously," Callie said. "Thanks. You've been great."

She stood still, not making any more conversation, hoping Zeller read it was time to leave. Sweet of the woman to be so helpful, but Callie didn't need a groupie or arm-chair detective any longer.

Zeller tipped her head with a one-finger salute then struck out for her own vehicle, and they watched her drive toward work. When she left, gawkers thinned, realizing nothing earth-shattering was happening, and there were shells and shark's teeth to find.

Raysor sat against the hood of Callie's car. "She's right about the rumor."

She gave him a wry look.

He held up his palms, eyebrows arched high. "I cannot confirm nor deny."

Callie finished filling him in on Maddy then told him to put that topic aside so she could inform him of the dead woman's case. She described where, when, and how she was found. The coroner's preliminary report. The fact it was a questionable death.

He went to the white Explorer, attempting to see inside. "It used to be easy slipping into cars before everything got computerized," he grumbled, taking in the vehicle from every angle.

Callie took a picture of the VIN and the tag, then inside her cruiser, pulled up the program with the state's transportation department. The car came back registered to Nolan and Elizabeth Brown. Registration led to an address in Charleston. A driver's license check confirmed the same address, and that Elizabeth Brown was the same age as Nolan.

That license confirmation made her about the same age as Maddy Gillespie, the picture showing a grinning girl who could be her sister.

But unless this woman had a twin, the driver's license pic versus the beach photo of the deceased confirmed her as Elizabeth Brown.

One step closer.

Callie trotted upstairs to the store and asked them to tolerate the car remaining parked for the time being. They obliged. She didn't bother asking for a copy of the cam footage after glancing at it and finding angles wrong and resolution grainy and nothing showing when the white car arrived much less who drove it there. Their best cam faced the one hundred block of the beach, showing Facebook users the weather and surf quality twenty-four-seven.

"When are you telling the husband?" Raysor asked.

"Once I talk to the coroner."

She really didn't want to contact Mr. Brown yet, much preferring to have more on Mrs. Brown before Mr. Brown shot a myriad of questions at her that she couldn't answer.

"Let me get a warrant to search this car first. There's not even a missing-person notice for her. Maybe she was on some sort of sabbatical, but I just want to know more. Besides, if he's worried, wouldn't he have contacted us?"

Like Maddy, it was as if nobody cared she was lost. That made Callie wonder about Nolan's whereabouts these last few days.

Maybe he was on a business trip. Maybe he had died some time ago and Elizabeth was a widow. Maybe the wife came out on a whim and hadn't told her husband or came to meet some *other* significant other.

One baby step at a time, but Callie'd get there. The only real fact she did have was that the girl wasn't coming home.

Callie hoped that wasn't the case for Maddy.

"In your patrolling, how about keeping an eye on this car, okay? I'll call when we have a warrant to search it. Touch base with Thomas. He and Annie are on duty today."

Raysor winked.

"Hey," she said, as he got in his cruiser. "Great to have you back."

He blew her an awkward kiss and laughed.

"We've gotta beat that Hollywood out of you," she yelled, as he closed the door laughing.

His taillights disappeared down Palmetto. It was after eleven and Callie breathed easier having the extra body on duty. She pondered which person on her list she wanted to brain pick next. Wainwright rental sign on a structure a hundred feet away caught her eye. Janet's office wasn't but a block and a half from the Pavilion as the crow flew. She'd drop in afterward to El Marko's right across the street.

In seconds, she rounded the east end of Palmetto and continued past the grocery store, recently changed to Food Lion from Pig-Lo, which had been BI-LO and Piggly Wiggly before that. No nicknames for the latest switch that she'd heard.

Turning left onto Jungle Road, the second favorite street in town after Palmetto, she passed McConkey's and the strip mall, turning right into Wainwright Realty's gravel lot.

The lantana shrubs had popped into their brightest gold, accented by red rosebuds on the verge of opening. Janet Wainwright, retired Marine, flaunted the Corp's colors any way she could. As Callie reached the top of the porch steps to go inside, she admired red geraniums against yellow siding, which reinforced Janet's salute to the Corp.

A couple waited in the lobby, eying framed photos of various houses Janet had resold a dozen times. The receptionist, dressed in a gold sundress and red earrings, froze at the sight of the police. "Um, she's with a client, Chief Morgan."

Callie understood what that meant. If the receptionist interrupted her hard-nosed boss, her job was toast. Janet played no games.

Instead, Callie held out the driver's license photo of Elizabeth Brown. "Is this a recent client of yours?"

"Renter, buyer, or seller?" the twenty-something asked.

"Any of the above." Callie held it closer.

The girl gave it a hard look, but Callie read the lack of connection in the girl's expression before the receptionist had a chance to deny affiliation.

"How long before those clients in there will be done?" she asked, noticing that the ones wandering around had taken notice of the uniform. For the sake of the receptionist, she didn't want these customers to bail.

"What about Arthur?" she asked, reminding herself that the Wainwright nephew and heir had graduated with his business degree, obtained his real estate license, and become Janet's full-time minion. "Is he in?"

"He's showing a house, Chief. I'm really, really sorry."

Poor girl was nervous at being unable to please, so Callie did something else before this girl was reduced to tears. Callie'd saved Janet's private cell during a holiday case when she'd helped salvage the nephew's ass from a jail term. So she texted the driver's license photo to Janet, including the fact she waited outside her door for a reply which validated that the receptionist had done a fine job not interrupting Janet who had clients inside her office and outside.

Didn't take a full minute before Janet replied.

Sold that couple their condo five years ago. On Wyndham. Would have to research the name. I'm busy.

Callie snorted a soft laugh, making the receptionist ease her shoulders a smidge.

Another text came through, and Callie expected another smart-ass retort from the Marine. With the grin still on her face, she read her phone.

Not Janet.

The assistant coroner.

No sign of water in lungs. Call me.

Chapter 9

OUTSIDE WAINWRIGHT Realty, Callie called the assistant coroner from her car, for both air conditioning and privacy's sake. "Richard? Callie."

"No water in her lungs," he said. "And the head injury was enough to kill her."

"The head injury—" she started.

"Caused by an irregularly shaped object that I'd be inclined to say was something like an everyday rock."

A rock was a murder weapon next to impossible to identify. A damn rock could be anywhere. Being on a beach meant anywhere encompassed literal miles of water and marsh.

"She wasn't bound, but I can't tell you if she fell or was hit on the head."

"You haven't identified a struggle, and you can't tell if murder or accident?"

"Right. Whether an accident or someone shoved her or bashed her or simply didn't stop her fall is anyone's guess. But I don't guess. That's your job."

Look at Mr. Assistant Coroner taking a jab! She almost liked him better this way. More human than Dr. Frankenstein.

"How long had she been dead?"

"Twelve hours, give or take."

Which would mean she fell off a boat or was washed out with the tide then brought back in... who knew... but it was at night, pre-dawn. If anyone dumped her, they should've taken her out further, though. Many didn't appreciate the power of tidal action, which made a lot of difference whether body disposal remained a mystery or came back to haunt you. Also, sharks didn't gobble up people whole, either, or gnaw away at a corpse until it was gone. If there was a culprit here, they appeared to be someone who didn't understand the coast.

And that person wouldn't be anybody local.

"Blood alcohol?" she asked.

"Point zero four."

Elizabeth—funny how *the dead girl* now had a name—had a buzz, nothing more. A DUI would measure over twice that.

"Sexual violation?"

"No."

Richard hung up, after confirming he wasn't done and a tox screen would be forthcoming in a day or two.

Callie was grateful the man had called her back so promptly with at least this much information. Richard loved his work, but he seemed bothered by everyone, mostly police, asking him when and how to do his job. However, the man was in the right job. Though far from a social butterfly, he was thorough in his work. She often wondered why he chose Walterboro and not Savannah or Charleston where the reputable, well-funded, and more sophisticated forensic departments had all the fancy tools, but then, those places might warrant more people skills.

Elizabeth died before going into the water. Not while swimming, and probably not falling off a boat, thus, the lack of water in the lungs. Well, she could've fallen off a jetty or dock and hit her head, and in that split second died before hitting the water, but what were the odds? That made Callie lean toward someone either murdering her or disposing of her body after an accident. Either of those was an illegal act.

Callie always hated to hear officers say an assailant was probably the spouse or boyfriend, because that could alter their effort to investigate impartially, without bias, but, in fact, those were the odds.

As soon as she could get back to the office, she would hunt for the correct Wyndham address for Elizabeth Brown and add that to the vehicle warrant she'd request from the magistrate. Shouldn't take an hour or two for the warrant, then she'd search both car and rental property. After that, she'd locate Nolan Brown and ask him to account for his whereabouts these last couple of days.

She headed back to the station.

No lunch today. No seeing Mark till dark either. Still, she took the same route by the restaurant and glanced over to see how crowded the parking was. Almost noon. The lot wasn't dinner full, but not far from it. Good. Maybe it was best she not interrupt him. She loved how successful he'd become out here and how smartly he continued to run El Marko's. Who didn't like Mexican? Who didn't like it any time of the year?

Who didn't like Mark Dupree?

Taking Jungle Road, she drove carefully, an ample number of cyclists and golf-cart folks out and about, some waving as she passed. The route took her by her own home, giving her a chance to admire her paint choices again. Damn how that white trim popped against the nautical blue, and the red door and swing…. She'd put up the sign *Chelsea Morning* two weeks ago, the custom sweep of words in blues, both dark and light tints, so striking hanging from the base of her porch for all passersby to see.

Jeb hadn't arrived home yet. His car wasn't at Sophie's next door either. No telling how long Beverly would keep him, but sooner or later her mayoral duties would draw enough attention that Jeb could escape, particularly this being a weekday. Callie halfway expected Jeb to head to Edisto once he had lunch with Beverly. God, he was a good kid. She worried more about him over-extending himself to deal with everyone else's issues than about him ever getting into trouble.

She also wasn't stupid. When Beverly couldn't get Callie to consider a future in politics by agreeing to run one day for mayor, she threatened to groom Jeb. Their adversarial views on that subject were such that they rarely talked about it anymore. Neither did Jeb discuss it much with Callie. She held no doubt, however, that Beverly continued to entertain Jeb as her successor. Neither she nor Callie had an idea how seriously Jeb would take the political future he'd been offered.

That had to gall Beverly. She prided herself on knowing absolutely everything worth knowing. That brought Callie back to thinking about work. She did expect Beverly to have heard of Lydia's club. And she might have to call whether or not she wanted to.

The next house in her view was Sarah's. She was home, and if Callie hadn't an urgent need to get that warrant on its way and contact Nolan Brown, she'd stop in. She'd known this particular mother for two years now. Way gentler than Beverly and way less competitive, she displayed more of what Callie considered a maternal instinct. Sarah had disappeared for the major part of last year after losing her husband, but she was back on the island now, and Callie tried to stop in at least once a week for mother-daughter conversation. They had a lot of time to catch up on.

Sarah had lived on Edisto for more than forty years. She also might be aware of Lydia's group.

Beverly, Janet, and Sarah. Boy, if that wasn't a line of diverse characters, but they were on her to-do list, if not today, then tomorrow. If not in person, preferable, then by phone. (*Hello, Beverly*). If in person, Beverly's interview would have to be a lunch appointment so that it had an ending time, the logic being both women were civil servants with schedules.

To each of these women, Callie would present Lydia at face value, much as she had introduced herself, along with Vivien and Robin, the old-timers in the group. But Lydia might not be well known if she changed names each time she came. If they limited themselves to socializing with only particular transients each year, who would know?

But thirty years was a long time. Facial recognition alone should identify her, and the rentals would have a history of her comings and goings. Thirty years ago, one might get along with fake identification, but today's property managers wanted the face to match the identity. You could call yourself another name to anyone else, but a four-week rental meant the renter would have to present photo ID.

Lydia's suspicious behavior triggered Callie's sixth sense.

Had she similarly triggered Janet Wainwright? The reason to chat with Janet was that *Time in a Bottle* was a Wainwright rental. The odds were good that much of Lydia's renting over the years might have been through Janet's agency. Folks tended to stay with an agent they trusted rather than switching to Airbnb or VRBO. Then there was the fact that once Janet got a grip into you, she didn't readily let go. Hopefully, that meant Janet required identification to rent a place she was responsible for managing. That chat merited way more than a text.

For grins and giggles, she ought to ask Janet how long she'd been aiding and abetting a whore house. Seeing her cheeks turn Marine Corps red against that white hair would be entertaining.

Thanks for the humor, Zeller. Good ol' Zeller. Her joke about Brice's affiliation with hookers was worth the chuckle. Edisto PD would be familiar with such an enterprise several years in the making, she'd think. Brice, for example. He'd never been one to keep a confidence, his or anyone else's. Zeller's claiming knowledge of such behavior was probably no more than Brice's attempt to raise his level of studsmanship in the community. She almost wished him alive just so they could have such a humorous, embarrassing conversation.

Oh Brice. Gone in body but not out of mind. Thinking about him made her circle around to ponder Beverly again. Why after all these years was her mother so upset at Brice's demise? Some sort of guilt at play? Maybe she *should* ask her mother to lunch tomorrow, especially after Jeb's call today.

Despondency was not in Beverly's vocabulary. Beverly hadn't come to Brice's funeral, claiming a critical town issue made the trip impossible.

Callie had never seen a Middleton event Beverly could not stall or reschedule. She also hadn't been to Edisto since Brice's death, though, so there might be substance to Jeb's concerns.

Back at the station, she had Marie draw up the warrant.

Callie called Janet again using the personal number.

"Chief," Janet answered.

"About that Wyndham condo. The couple's names are Nolan and Elizabeth Brown. Can you tell me the condo address?"

"I looked it up after you left. Number 27F Sea Oaks."

"Do they rent it when not using it?"

"Yes, they do."

She never made a conversation easy. "Do you happen to have a key?" Callie asked.

Janet's efficiency of speech made her an irritation sometimes.

"Of course I have the key," she said. "Are you getting a warrant?"

Of course she would require that, too.

"On its way."

"Then a key you shall have. Clients await, Chief." Janet hung up.

Damn it! She'd wanted to set up a time to talk about Lydia.

She'd call back later. Elizabeth Nolan took precedence, and Callie had necessary case tasks calling her name. A husband might wonder why his wife hadn't called, or a child could be missing their mom.

She printed off the picture from Elizabeth Brown's DL for Marie, then had her send it to all the officers, on duty and off, for them to query the beach's restaurants, particularly those that served alcohol. She added age and a description of the bathing suit and a note of instruction to downplay the shark business. She gave the condo's address and the make and model of the car.

She'd already ignored five calls and seven texts from Charleston reporters, which prompted her to contact the mayor and brief him about the updates, because they'd be calling him, too. He'd, however, be forced to offer responses, because Callie sure as hell wasn't.

She despised paparazzi about as much as she did organized crime. Pure leeches of human suffering. If the powers that be on Edisto Beach expected the press to be catered to, they'd have to do it. Since the leading citizens preferred disseminating good news over the bad, they'd stall as long as they could, though. They'd prefer to keep Edisto as close to a fictitious Brigadoon as one could ask for, which made them perfect for managing, dismissing, or cold-shouldering the press.

The mayor would pull out half his hair in the meantime attempting to handle the inquiries. Hurricanes, press, the obnoxious side of the nastier tourists, and the demanding side of the natives meant most mayors lasted no more than two terms. The ones who lasted longest truly loved the beach and fought to keep it secure, its secrets not broadcast to the mainland. The current one had one term under his belt, and the jury was out on whether he'd run again.

Voices drifted back to Callie's ear. Marie had people backing up in reception but nothing adversarial. Callie would leave things to her office manager unless she called for help, at least for a few more moments. Callie wanted to look up more about Nolan Brown, to have a better feel for him before delivering the message his wife was dead, which needed to be done today.

Records, website, and social media had him still living in Charleston, at the address on the driver's licenses. He was an engineer for Boeing per LinkedIn and had been since he'd graduated Clemson University in mechanical engineering. You had to love social media and the people who loved posting their lives for all to see.

He saltwater fished. He golfed. He wore a lot of khakis and polo shirts. He was a walking, talking cliché of an almost-forty Lowcountry man. He had a couple hundred friends, which meant links to their pages... and Elizabeth's.

Clicking over, there was Elizabeth. Elizabeth laughing. Elizabeth with her Boston terrier. Elizabeth with her sister. Elizabeth in a huddle with other pediatric nurses where she worked at Middleton Medical Center.

No sign of children, thank goodness, but also no Elizabeth with Nolan short of their wedding picture which appeared to be maybe a decade old. A few group shots of barbecues and work gatherings, but none of the pictures paired the two in any sort of amorous pose. Trouble in paradise? No evidence of that other than the lack of romantic public display.

But couples hid so much, and social media had become a venue to tell the world all was fine behind those doors.

Neither of them had a criminal record. Neither had as much as a ticket.

She didn't have much to work with. Boy, would she love to find a phone in that car.

She'd get her ducks in a row first and stall this death notification as long as she could. At least after she had a chance to go through the condo and vehicle. Tonight maybe, after Nolan got home from work.

She heard a raised voice in the outer office. While she waited for the magistrate to answer, she could at least lend her support in processing complaints and issues, working alongside Marie. For fifteen minutes Callie handled another disgruntled speeder, again tagged by Thomas—caught blowing into town across the causeway, fifteen miles over the speed limit, straight into the part of town with the highest odds of a pedestrian casualty. She had a zero tolerance for speeding in that spot, and her officers knew it. The speeder understood as well by the time he left.

Another visitor came in asking about electric cars, while another claimed someone stole their rods and reels from beneath their rental. Marie took care of them. Fishing poles left beneath the houses disappeared like pumpkin pie on Thanksgiving, with visitors stealing from each other, which was easy with unmarked poles. That type of theft used to be uncommon, but this season it had tripled in frequency.

She calmed one concerned citizen, angry that a golf cart driven by two pre-teens had scratched his Lexus parked on the street. Callie agreed to assign the case to Annie.

Two people were left. She let Marie choose, and then she escorted the other to her office.

"Welcome to Edisto Police Department," she said to the man in his early- to mid-twenties. "What can we do for you?"

He slapped a familiar paper on her desk. "Do you know what that is?" He didn't yell, but his anger came through.

She slid the ticket toward her, turning it around to read better. He'd not introduced himself, but the ticket gave his name. Mr. Drew Holmes. He was staying at a beachfront rental on the 400 block of Palmetto.

"A ticket," she said. "Is there a problem with it?"

"Damn straight there is," the young man said. "Some neighbor or walker or whoever, complained we had our porch lights on too late."

She already recognized what the problem possibly was, but she let him spill it... so he could back himself into a corner.

When she didn't immediately answer, he continued unchecked as if this one point would make everything clear, "A ticket for damn turtles!"

"There is an ordinance for the sea turtles, Mr. Holmes, and I could probably guess correctly that the rental owner gave you information about the rules. This isn't just Edisto, mind you. There are local, state, and federal laws protecting these animals."

The ticket addressed lighting on the backside of the rental, and open drapes exposing lots of additional lighting.

"Why is the ticket inappropriate?" she asked.

"We did not plan for a turtle nest right outside our place on the beach. I could toss a rock and hit the thing. At night, all these gawkers gather around it with their little red lights. We've been here since Saturday, paid a helluva lot of money to be in the house we're in, and we get the damn turtle patrol each and every night while being forced to live in the dark."

Guess he wasn't a nature fan. Callie waited for the rest of the story.

"Someone has knocked on our door each and every night. Here we are sitting on the porch, trying to enjoy the view, attempting to take shots of the Milky Way on some very expensive cameras, by the way, when strangers become Karens, telling us to shut down our lights and close our curtains. Some tell us how the house ought to be this or that when it isn't even our damn house!"

There it was. The EBLTP had gotten involved. The Edisto Beach Loggerhead Turtle Project was a well-orchestrated nonprofit that protected these turtles, and they canvassed the beach each and every night in search of new nests and signs of a nest hatching. Hoards could gather when a turtle *boil* took place, the babies scrambling up out of the sand to find the ocean.

They didn't often have to call the police with problems about a visitor who failed to follow the law, because they and the renting public policed the nests and knocked on doors, requesting compliance. These turtles had a serious following, with supporters from most of the fifty states.

And Mr. Holmes had just admitted he'd violated the lighting ordinance not once but several times.

"The ticket sticks, Mr. Holmes. We take turtles seriously out here."

He jerked to the edge of his chair. "But why me?"

"Is the lease in your name?"

"Yes, but everyone chipped in."

"But you're responsible for the rental, sir." Callie's personal phone rang. Caller ID Jeb.

"I just signed the paper. There are twenty of us," he continued.

She held up her phone, but he kept going. "This stains my record, not theirs."

Callie could tell him to read his lease, but she'd waste her breath. "Sir, I'm sorry, but I must take this."

She put the phone to her ear. "Give me a moment, please." Then to her office guest, she delivered the verdict. "I'm afraid the ticket stands."

"See if I come to this damn island again," he said, snatching the paper, the backs of his knees scooting the chair with a pitchy scrape.

She didn't bother telling him there was a waiting list this time of year for houses fronting the beach, in view of the ocean... and the turtle nests. Sometimes you enjoyed hearing a tourist profess never to spend his dollars in your community again.

He yanked the door open, and as tiny as her office was, she reached an arm out to catch it before it banged against the wall. Then she returned attention to her phone. "Hello, son. How're things with you and your grandmother?"

"I'm in the ER, Mom. I brought her in. They just took her back."

Marie appeared in her doorway, waving a piece of paper. The warrant had come through.

Chapter 10

Lydia

CHIARA HAD MIRED herself in a quilt with a fixed gaze on the ocean. Lydia had taken four calls and assorted texts from their annual friends asking why she wasn't available. She assured them she'd be in touch. Chiara just had a small bug, that's all.

She tired of this damn crap. Between Chiara and Maddy, the group couldn't even bring friends over, and a few were asking when they were having their annual get-together. What were they supposed to do, lock Chiara in the bedroom and pretend she didn't exist?

To be honest, what was the difference in Chiara hiding upstairs and Maddy downstairs?

Lydia released an angry grunt.

"What?" Chiara asked, annoyed, as if the grunt was directed at her.

But Lydia said nothing, turning away. Things could not continue like this.

As always, Lydia had footed the bill for the beach house. No rental agency signed with five parties, five signatures, and five methods of payment. Who would want that headache? How many people came and how many paid was not their problem, and whoever didn't like the one-renter-one-payment method could be passed over for another group just as eager to spend time at Edisto Beach. One person had to be responsible, and Lydia assumed that role each year.

Four weeks meant a sixteen-grand fee, payable up front. She had expected the price, which was within a thousand of last year's cost, but she had expected equivalent if not more quality in the house. A worn-out rental was the first negative of this year's trek. That meant next year could easily scrape twenty thousand dollars out of their pockets just to maintain this standard.

These damn property managers. Vultures, all of them. Four-week rentals for them meant three weeks without having to pay a cleaning crew or assorted other week-to-week costs. They were a primo gig, for

God's sake. That damn crazy Marine woman. She'd probably negotiate with the devil for a better seat in Hell.

But that was the least of their problems. And the accumulation of all these problems made any issue seem bigger than it was. The biggest problem was indeed bigger than anyone imagined.

Still... she had to be here, and she had to fix this. This beach, this island... they were in her DNA. So many people on social media said that, how Edisto was their annual fix, their vacay crack, so to speak, but she meant it. She'd been born here. You weren't dropped into this world on this island without the salt water forever running in your veins. Then there were the people you left behind... the people you missed.

She wished she'd never left.

No, she didn't. She'd had to. For others' sake as well as hers.

She'd die if she couldn't keep coming back, though, and this new problem held the potential of sabotaging those returns.

Shit, shit, shit.

Chiara opened the quilt and resorted herself in the creaky rattan seat, snagging Lydia's attention back to the present.

Seriously? It was over eighty degrees out there. Chiara had parked herself in front of the open sliding doors—the air conditioning at her back and the muggy humidity to her front in some sort of improbable hope to balance the temperature.

Vivien and Robin were long gone, meeting friends. Lydia stayed behind because of Chiara, rescheduling a lunch date with a man she hadn't seen since last year. Griffin McCants. A lovely man her age. One year they almost courted the thought of a long-term relationship, but then decided that their summer visits kept the magic more alive. Besides, he was married.

But he continued to be a dear friend... and this bitch on the back porch was keeping them from having a pleasant afternoon.

Lydia couldn't leave her alone in the house. Guests might appear. Maddy might make herself known, and that was a confrontation Lydia definitely had to be here for.

This situation wasn't working, and when Vivien returned, they needed a meeting, just the two of them. To study the legalities. To ponder how to weather this incredible ordeal with the power to ruin them all.

She continued to send herself texts as if from Maddy. One said she couldn't show her face yet, and another touted she might just go on home. But she couldn't keep doing this either.

Vivien had offered to stay behind, and right now Lydia almost wished she had, but they couldn't shy away from all their friends. They held a long reputation of seeing these people, having these dates, offering enjoyment, and having Chiara sidelined was bad enough. Besides, Vivien held a decades-long history with some of these folks. No, Lydia wouldn't hear of Vivien canceling her day. Robin didn't offer, but it wasn't her place to babysit Chiara. It was the leader's role.

All these changes and needs for adjustments were beginning to mount, with a conclusion nowhere in sight. Chiara couldn't be allowed to sit here all month. Lydia couldn't tend to her all that time, either. Then there was Maddy....

Chiara sighed long and hard from the porch, like she needed Lydia to hear.

"That's it," Lydia said, loud enough for her to hear.

Chiara peered over her shoulder. "Why should you be bothered? You don't even like her. There's something wrong with her not calling me..." And she started crying.

Damn it to hell. This was enough. "Shut *up*, Chiara."

She turned in her seat, eyes wide. "What's your problem, Lydia?"

Damn her all to hell. "Shut the fuck up with your whining."

Chiara clammed up... for a moment. But then like a flip of a switch, she tossed the blanket to the floor and stood, fists clenched. "You do not get to talk to me like that. I don't give a damn if you're a hundred years old and been in charge the whole time."

That was it. This limbo was over. She wanted to be part of the problem, then damn it, she'd just bought membership in this shit storm that was her damn doing for inviting Maddy to Edisto to begin with.

"Stay right there," Lydia said, teeth clenched.

"I don't have to—"

Lydia jabbed the air with a finger. "This time you do. Shut up. I'll be right back. You want answers? Then you're about to get them, and you might just wish you hadn't asked for the privilege."

That stopped Chiara cold.

"You've crossed the line this time, girl." Lydia strode into her bedroom and grabbed the storage room key, shaking it at Chiara as she made her way past her on the porch to take the stairs to ground level. "So help me, if you leave this spot I'll pack your bags and kick you to the curb myself then sue you for the rent."

Trying not to make noise though her heart pounding sounded like it would wake the dead, she reminded herself she still had to remain clandestine. Peering around, ensuring nobody could see from the beach or from the rental on either side, she inserted the key so as not to be heard, and entered the storage room.

Maddy lay dozing on a pile of blankets, three pillows under and around her. She didn't look quite as comatose as she had yesterday after her overdose, but she wasn't lovely to look at, either. No bath in going on three days, her hair an absolute spider web of abuse from her tossing, turning, crying, and distress. Pale. Even asleep, the girl still appeared in shock.

Damn. Lydia wasn't sure Maddy was up to going up the stairs, much less meeting Chiara. As far as Maddy knew, Lydia was her only confidante. No telling how Maddy would behave if she learned that Chiara, Vivien, and the rest of the world started learning about what had happened the other night.

Lydia stooped down. The Valium wasn't just to keep Maddy calm but to keep her quiet. Keep the shock at bay long enough for the group to figure this out.

Lydia touched her shoulder. "Maddy? Honey?"

Maddy groaned, unwilling to comply, half rolling in a sluggish manner to put space between her dreams and whoever this was interrupting them.

She'd wet the bed.

"What the hell... Maddy!"

Lydia whipped around as Chiara ran in, sliding to her knees beside the pile of blankets cradling her friend. Only took a couple seconds for her to turn to Lydia, her mouth open to launch into a scalding censure, but Lydia slapped one hand over her face, the other behind her head as firm leverage, then gave all a quick shake for emphasis.

"Hush," Lydia whispered. "She's fine. She's just on Valium. She's been on it for two days." Mashing her palm harder in front, the one behind Chiara's head tightened. "Can I trust you to stay quiet? This is for Maddy's sake more than yours or mine. Do you hear me?"

Chiara wasn't quick to catch on, but when Lydia refused to let her loose, she glanced at her friend then back at the woman holding her and nodded.

"Promise?"

She nodded again.

Lydia lightened her grip but didn't let go. "If the police find Maddy, she's done for," she explained. "Also, I'm done for. Vivien's done for. And now you. You wanted to know where Maddy was, well now you do, which makes you culpable to everything else."

Frozen in place, Chiara's expression showed she clearly fought to understand what that meant, then when she immediately couldn't, she returned to dote on her best friend.

Lydia sat back on the cool concrete floor and watched, not relaxed, but just tense enough, in case one or the other of them decided to make noise.

God, to think her worst thought about Maddy going off rogue was how the bill would be paid. The other ladies repaid her weekly from their beach earnings. That had always been the deal, and they'd never failed to come through. At first that was her biggest concern about Maddy coming, Lydia even studying how to file for compensation from the magistrate's court. She'd even researched whether she had to do so in South Carolina or once they returned to Florida. The latter, she'd hoped. The magistrate and she were really good friends.

"Sit up," she said.

Chiara ignored her.

So help her, Lydia wanted to yell, "Sit the hell up or get the hell out of this house," but the need to be clandestine remained paramount. Their troubles couldn't withstand this childish headbutting. These times were serious and required working together, not disagreeing about how they got there and who was responsible. They were well beyond that.

Chiara turned, a scowl broadcasting pure hatred for her.

"We're not going to endure this without cooperation. We'll all go down if we don't create a united front. This,"—and Lydia motioned to Maddy—"was her doing. She ran to me for help. I offered. Now, listen to me."

Chiara didn't indicate whether she'd heard, her anger so intense. Clearly, she wanted to heap all that was wrong on Lydia's head.

"Going to the police forced Maddy into hiding," Lydia said.

Chiara stiffened. "It's not my fault. Nobody told me—"

"Stop with the blame. We're together in this or totally fucked. Is that much clear to you?"

"I don't give a shit about you, Lydia. You've shown a side that appalls me. You've displayed a cold, cold manner that almost makes me want to throw up."

Lydia reached out to show she cared, but Chiara flinched back. "Hate me all you like," she said. "Just understand that I'm leading us out of this mess, but all it takes is for one of us to stray again... like you going to the cops... and we all are done for."

"I don't even know what that means," Chiara said in a pout, attention back on Maddy.

She still wasn't grasping the seriousness. Guess she wouldn't unless she had all the facts. As much as Lydia hadn't wanted to suck in Robin and Chiara about the night before last, she had to.

This would either unite the ladies... or render them apart forever.

"Then let me enlighten you," Lydia said, not with animus but with the sound of a mother craving for her daughter to grasp hold of what might change her life forever. A mother choosing to make her child grow up sooner than she really wished she had to, in order to protect her. Innocence be damned.

Lydia hadn't had a mother like that. And she hadn't had the opportunity to be the sort of mother she'd hoped to be.

She took Chiara's hand, and when the woman tried to retract, Lydia held firm, gaze fixed on the eyes of this girl she was responsible for... whether the girl realized it or not.

Then Lydia told her the event of the other night, the details, and the intricacies of what she'd had to do. What Maddy had done... and been unable to do. No punches pulled.

Chiara sank onto the floor, legs out, then felt the need to slide herself against the wall, a hand still resting on her friend. "Jesus, Lydia." No anger. No tears. Just utter amazement and a lack of speech for a minute or two. Finally, she managed to ask, "What do we do now?"

"Keep Maddy settled until a plan comes together... or we leave the island. The problem is, if we leave early, we look guilty. If we show Maddy, the chief will want to ask her what happened. The chief does not need to know what happened, Chiara. Please tell me you understand that."

"Yes, ma'am," she replied, and Lydia fully felt the girl meant it.

Thank God.

She gave Chiara a moment since Maddy appeared to be anchored deep in her chemical sleep. Chiara was young still. Maybe they needed a minimum age for the group... assuming the group lived through this.

For the last five years, Chiara had been a decent fit with the group. Inviting Maddy had knocked Chiara out of her orbit, and Lydia wondered if Maddy was more than a friend to Chiara, not that sexual orientation mattered to any of them. Some of them weren't foreign to the experience.

She dared again to touch Chiara's dark hair, and this time she let her. "Why don't you call Mr. Warrick back," Lydia said. "You like him.

He's called me once and texted twice, asking how you were doing."

"Now? With all this hanging over us?"

"What's more questionable than us being reclusive and not doing what we came to do... what quite a few people expect of us. That leads to talk. Talk that can reach the wrong ears. This beach isn't that big, hon."

Chiara stroked Maddy's arm.

"She'll be fine," Lydia said.

Hank Warrick was a likeable guy. A dentist. Blond hair and blue eyes and single to boot. Low key and one of those willing to just languish in the sun or on the back porch of his rental, facing the water. If one was in the market for a mate, he'd be high on Lydia's list... if she were his age, meaning Chiara's age. Chiara saw him several times last summer. Like once- or twice-a-week times. He seemed to just come to see her.

Chiara tried to take that in. "He's a nice guy, but look at us, Lydia. How are we to act like nothing's wrong?"

"Have a couple of drinks as soon as you meet him. He's keeping his day open for you," Lydia added.

"This is... sick," she said.

"Do you have a solution?"

Chiara stood. "No, I don't. But does she have to stay down here? If we all know the story..."

She had a valid point. "I'll bring her upstairs and put her to bed. How's that? You go get ready."

Lydia watched her leave, uncomfortable with how her world had shifted on its axis but accepting of her role in it. Now all she had to do was tell Robin.

They hadn't solved a damn thing, but somehow the juggling act took on a different style. She guessed that was good. As long as the chief stayed in the dark.

She needed Vivien. The plans they'd stalled in making needed to be made now.

Chapter 11

CALLIE FROZE IN her chair listening to a nervous Jeb on the phone. Marie stood in the door with a warrant hot off the press and ready to be served, grinning at the efficiency of it arriving so quickly.

"Say that again?" Callie said to her son.

Marie wilted, lowered the paper, and watched to see what emergency might need her assistance.

It's Jeb, Callie mouthed to her, to buy privacy and return the office manager to her work.

Marie tipped her head in knowing acknowledgement and disappeared. The front doorbell sounded as another civilian entered the station.

"I had to take Grandma to the emergency room," he said. "She said she was lightheaded, Mom, then complained about her arm, then got winded. I just couldn't take a chance. When she agreed for me to take her, I really felt something was up."

Jeb had handled enough trauma in his day not to lose his mind over such an event, but he had reason to be a little freaked out—this was his grandmother. Add to that Beverly didn't do medical environments very well. She hated white coats. She thought she would live forever, not that her parents had. They'd made money from real estate and died in their sixties from drinking and cigarettes and as rich a Southern palate as one could enjoy, like Beverly, thinking they'd live decades longer. She was now their age. Beverly avoided doctors, with Callie suspecting her mother didn't want to hear she should lay off the gin and improve her diet. At least she didn't smoke.

This sounded like what most people tried to excuse away... a heart issue. But Callie seriously doubted that Beverly had heart issues. Some people wondered if she had a heart.

Callie started to ask if Jeb felt she ought to come, but thought better of asking her son to make a decision she should damn well make herself. What she wanted was someone to give her permission to get back to work.

Son of a bitch. Callie wanted to be the one going through the car and the condo. Her officers were good people, but they didn't have enough time on the job and were not investigators. She'd been one for fifteen years in a city that threw enough challenges at you to keep you at your peak or get shot.

"Mom?"

"Just a second, Jeb."

The other most experienced investigators on the beach were retired. Mark, via the State Law Enforcement Division, and Stan Waltham, her old boss from Boston PD. Mark had his hands full at the restaurant. She couldn't ask him to choose crime solving over a packed house of diners. Stan, however, drooled for opportunities such as this, but she couldn't make a case in court if she put a civilian in charge of the investigation. Chain of evidence meant everything, and there was no telling what they'd find in the car and condo. Raysor was a beat cop, and while he'd know more than Thomas, he wouldn't know as much as Stan.

Damn it, Beverly.

If Callie got to the hospital and this was nothing... no, she couldn't think like that. She hoped it was nothing.

"Mom!"

"I'm juggling a murder investigation and a missing person, Jeb. Let me think."

"You have to think about it?" The screech in his voice reminded her of his puberty years.

"Sorry! It's the job talking. I'm trying to juggle too many balls, Jeb. Of course I'll leave right away. Middleton Medical Center?"

"Yes, ma'am."

She hung up. She should've just immediately said she'd be there. There was a reason divorce rates were high in law enforcement, but there were no statistics about parents and their children.

As usual she called her best uniform. Thomas was most familiar with the case... cases. "Hey, I've got to rush to Middleton. Something about my mother. I need you to pick up the warrant that lets you search both the car and condo that belongs to the dead girl. Her name is Elizabeth Brown. The vehicle is parked outside the Pavilion. The condo key is with Janet Wainwright, who already said she needs to see the warrant first."

"You know we don't need her approval, Chief."

"Yeah, but we have to live in this town with her, so we give her this."

"Fine. What else?"

"The co-owner is Nolan Brown. I suspect husband. Confirm that for me, please. Search every inch of both the condo and the car," she said. "Get prints. Elizabeth Nolan was found on the opposite side of the island from the car, but then, that's where the condo is. Would be nice to find a reason why her car wasn't. Check her console, glove box, over the visor—"

"I know. On it, Chief. Do this alone or take Annie?"

Somebody had to be free for other potential problems. "No, leave her on patrol. Instead, I'm sending Raysor."

"Good. So glad he's back."

"I'm also sending Stan, just in case."

Silence on the phone. "In case of what?"

While Thomas loved Stan, having spent many social events with the man, he recognized this for what it was. "He's babysitting me?"

"He's seasoned at this stuff. The girl didn't have water in her lungs, Thomas. This is a potential homicide investigation, the likes of which you've never done. At a minimum, it's a body disposal by someone panicking, now with something to hide. Stan has done many of these. How many have you investigated?"

He sighed but not in a resigned way.

"Are you pouting on me?" she asked, her impatience rising. She needed to get on the road. "I would do it myself but... Can I trust you or not? I can just give it to Raysor and Stan."

She didn't readily scold this officer, and he knew it. She was handing him an opportunity. "No, no, I got it, Chief. Sorry to add more on your plate." He was smart enough to wonder why she wasn't doing this herself but not quite smart enough to puzzle it out sooner. "May I ask why you aren't doing this?"

There he was. "My mother was rushed to the ER."

"Oh, sorry. Keep you apprised or give you space?"

"Keep me apprised. I appreciate your concern. I'll touch base with you later."

She hung up and called Stan. Glassware clinked in the background and voices murmured. Clearly at El Marko's, her old boss was probably finishing up his lunch. That put him two blocks from the vehicle, where she told Thomas to start, and almost across the street from Wainwright Realty where Thomas was to pick up the condo key. She explained the case. He'd heard of the body but hadn't bothered her with questions, understanding she'd fill him in at some point.

"I'll keep an eye on them, Chicklet."

"Let them lead, okay? Just be there for questions or nudges."

"I get it. What's so urgent that you aren't involved?"

She took out her keys. "Hold on a sec, if you don't mind. I'm trying to leave the station." She muted the phone, informed Marie about Thomas, Stan, and Raysor acting on the warrant, Annie remaining on patrol, and that Thomas would be there any moment to pick up the warrant.

Marie nodded, studying her boss. "What in the world is wrong?"

"Mother's in the hospital. Jeb rushed her there." Callie headed to the door, not wanting to discuss it.

"I hope everything's okay," Marie hollered as Callie left the building.

Returning to Stan on hold, she explained Jeb's call.

"Chicklet, don't you worry. I'll take care of things. Family comes first. Have you told Mark?"

She hadn't. She hadn't even thought about him. That didn't make her feel any better either. "No. But I'll—"

"You drive and take care of business. I'll tell Mark. Check in with us when you have news, okay?"

He'd been her anchor going back for decades now. She thanked the heavens for the umpteenth time for putting Stan in her orbit.

She took her cruiser without thinking about the potential appearance of impropriety then didn't care. She needed to get there, analyze the situation, and if possible, get back to Edisto ASAP.

She drove faster than the speed limit, but nothing ridiculously so. Not on Highway 174. Those oaks didn't bend regardless of how fast the car that ran into them, as several people a year found out. With both hands on the wheel and her focus on the road, she had fifty miles ahead of her. Shades lessened the flickering of evening sun through the oak canopy overhead.

Letting the cases fill her mind, she rethought the details of both Maddy and Elizabeth, hoping Elizabeth was an accident, hoping Maddy was a woman who'd pouted and gone home. But by the time she reached the McKinley Bridge, taking her over the Dawhoo River and delivering her off the island to the mainland, her thoughts bounced back to Beverly.

God, she had so many mixed feelings about her mother being hospitalized. She shouldn't. Beverly had family with her and more family coming. Family was important. She was seeing to her responsibilities, and yet, the farther she drove from Edisto, the guiltier she felt about handing over her police work to others, which in turn made her feel guilty for thinking even for a moment that work took priority over family.

Didn't take her long on the roller coaster of emotions to conclude that she preferred bodies to facing Beverly. Especially now. Approaching Beverly at a weak moment would inevitably put her in a bitch of a mood at appearing vulnerable. Tables would turn on her that Jeb had to be the one Beverly had been forced turned to, her hinting at the message that he cared more.

Callie would become the child again. The child who couldn't wait to grow up and get the hell out of Middleton to escape the mind games and dominance of her parents.

But what if this event turned into a crossroads for her mother, her health, and her career as mayor? If Beverly wasn't mayor, she'd disintegrate. Garden clubs and lunch-bunch meetings wouldn't sustain this woman in the least. Retirement wasn't in her vocabulary.

Was this the start of Beverly becoming a senior needing constant care? God, Callie just couldn't see that happening to such a rock-hard persona. She'd always envisioned Beverly dying in full action, commanding a town meeting, lighting the town Christmas tree, hosting a gala attended by state celebrities who'd attempt to impress her more than she cared to impress them.

Not as an old woman limited by her failing body... or, God forbid, her mind.

Their mother-daughter relationship was convoluted and far from Hallmark potential. Callie often envied daughters who shared secrets with their moms, calling them every other day to share what the kids said, how the world was treating them, what to bring to the next Sunday dinner.

But while envying such families, Callie held no pretense that she evolved from such stock. Not a soul in the family fit the Hallmark stereotype. Lawton came the closest, the glue in the family, but even he kept his secrets—from his long-time courtesan to his backdoor deals and obligations as mayor that he loved so. As a result of her parents' time being so occupied in politics and social demands, Callie had been taught to be independent, and independent she was. Almost too much so, which meant empathy was rarely practiced in the Cantrell/Morgan clan. A major reason she adhered to weekly visits with Sarah was to see if she could absorb some of her biological mother's sweetness. So far she hadn't felt all that successful.

Jeb was the best balanced, put-together adult of the whole bloody lot of them. Beverly filled their lives with drama. Callie still judged Beverly, having switched to her adoptive instead of her biological mother. All of these emotions bubbled and frothed right now. If the worst happened, if she lost Beverly.... Damn it, she had no idea how to feel about that.

She returned her attention to the road, forcing herself out of her feelings. Once past Adams Run, she flipped her lights and mashed the gas heading toward Middleton. She kept telling herself the sooner she arrived and got to the bottom of this, the quicker she could retreat back across the bridge to the island that made her as close to whole as anything else.

On Alternate Highway 17, she zigzagged around the outskirts of Middleton to a state highway that took her straight to the hospital parking lot. The cruiser's markings gave her easy access to parking, and she trotted into the emergency room, people parting way for the running officer.

Some would criticize the perks the uniform gave her, but right now she couldn't care less. A saccharin receptionist took her partway in and gave directions to Beverly's curtained location, since this ER didn't come with rooms.

"Mother?" she said, pushing aside the curtain, slinging it closed behind her.

Jeb sat in an uncomfortable plastic chair against the wall and rose. Beverly lay propped up in bed, attached to monitors that blinked, blipped, and whooshed, the last happening right as Callie reached the bedside.

She waited for the blood pressure reading to finalize. One thirty over eighty.

"That's pretty normal," she said, focusing back on Beverly.

"Oh, it's probably nothing," Beverly said, reaching down to straighten her sheet. "Jeb insisted."

Callie fought not to judge the situation, though instinct told her there might have been a taste of theater involved in the episode, pushing Jeb to err on the side of caution.

He'd never tell her that, and Callie didn't need to jump to conclusions. "What did the doctor say?"

"She's a resident, not a doctor," Jeb said.

"A resident is a doctor, sweet boy," Beverly corrected, like only a grandmother could. Then to Callie, "She said they'd run tests and see what they see. They drew blood already." She held up her band-aided arm as proof. "But they have to rule out the bad stuff first. I believe they're just being overly cautious because... of who I am."

Callie contained her sarcasm. This was not the time nor place for it. "Let me see what answers I can get for you." To Jeb, she added, "You okay sitting with her while I'm gone?"

"You're the person who just got here."

Okay, he wasn't happy with her, probably because of the delayed response on the phone. Sometimes she wondered if Jeb and Beverly discussed her in her absence.

Of course they did.

She walked around the bed to his side, holding out her arms to hug him. He obliged, and the squeeze felt legitimate. "Thanks so much for taking care of her, son. If anyone had to take charge, frankly, I'm glad it was you."

Jeb gave her another squeeze and released her, turning to reclaim his chair, not letting her see the emotion in his eyes.

She eased through the curtain, keeping in mind that anything said was in earshot of Beverly's ER stall. There was nothing wrong with her mother's hearing.

Leaning over the central station, uncertain who was nurse, intern, or doctor, she said loud enough for several of them to hear, the uniform making them do a double take,

"I'm looking for the doctor tending to Beverly Cantrell. I'm her daughter, Callie Morgan."

A couple of people looked at each other. A couple returned to their computer screens. One lab coat of substantial size came around the counter, and when she did, Callie motioned for her to follow her to a corner.

"Didn't want her to hear," Callie said, lowering her voice, having to peer up to a woman who had seventy pounds on her and eight inches of height, dark blond hair swept back into a braid so tight her forehead couldn't wrinkle if it wanted to. The whiteness of the coat added points to an intimidating appearance.

"Why not? She seems an intelligent enough woman, as does her grandson."

For the life of her, Callie couldn't describe why she didn't want Beverly to hear. One for the doc.

"I'm the resident on duty tonight," the coat continued. "Doctor Peyton Winter. I'm afraid we don't have much to tell you yet."

"I'm sure you examined her when she came in, though," Callie said, wanting to hear everything from the moment Beverly arrived, only not from Beverly.

The doctor didn't try to hide her suspicion of Callie's motives, or that's how Callie felt. She wasn't in the mood to dance, though.

"Listen," Callie said, her back to anyone who might overhear. No telling who in that ER was familiar with the town mayor, and the last thing Beverly wanted was to show weakness to anyone who might use it against her. That much Callie understood and understood well, and Beverly would expect her to protect her almighty image. "She thinks she's invincible, Dr. Winter. As mayor of Middleton—"

"That doesn't factor in when it comes to medical treatment," the doctor popped back.

"It does factor into her well-being. She's a politician, and whether you voted for her is beyond the point. You are right in vowing to give the best medical treatment to anyone and everyone, but slinging her name around for all to hear doesn't need to happen. I'm her daughter. And her healthcare power of attorney. Now," she said, taking a slight pause to segue into the intended purpose. "What have you done and what do you suspect and how long before we know anything else?"

She leaned over the counter and pulled a chart from the carousel. She flipped a few pages, nodded her head, and began. "She came in complaining of pain in her arm, and she demonstrated a lot of anxiety and some shortness of breath," the doc said. "Her heart rate was elevated, and in light of those symptoms, her family history, and her age, we considered heart issues first. The EKG looked reasonable. We took blood and urine. I don't immediately see anything to be concerned about, but that's why we have tests. With it being in the evening, some of these tests won't be back until the morning, and since we aren't sure she needs a room, she'll be kept comfortable here, under close supervision, until we know more."

The doctor stopped. "That about cover it for you? It's the same information we told your mother."

Doctor Winter was in no short supply of confidence, but in Callie's experience, when it came to medical treatment, and coroners like Richard Smith, you overlooked personality and appreciated the skills. These were early times in the ER, but Callie'd give this Amazonian doctor the benefit of the doubt. You wanted to land on the good side of doctors, or you risked landing on the bottom of their list for appointments, feedback, and exams.

"I greatly appreciate what you're doing," Callie said. "You don't mind someone staying with her throughout, do you?"

"Not at all. Anything to keep the patient settled. Speaking of settled, the relaxant we gave her ought to have kicked in. Doesn't knock her out, but it takes an edge off that anxiety. No point her staying up all night worrying." She smiled, and Callie wasn't sure how genuine it was. "After all, worrying is your job, isn't it?"

The doctor turned and left.

Callie told herself again not to take issue with personality. Skill mattered most.

When she returned, Beverly was nodding. She jerked herself awake when Callie entered the room. "They aren't overly worried, but are not confident enough to send you home, Mother. Some of the tests won't be back until morning, so you're stuck here for the night. Did you get a chance to eat anything before you came in?"

"We had Oscar's deliver at home earlier," Beverly said.

Oscar's was her favorite eatery in Middleton, having been in existence for as long as Callie could remember. They could do upscale burgers—with sauces and additions like avocado or Gouda or pimento cheese from scratch—on yeast buns baked onsite. Or they could provide omelet a la Oscar with a crab sauce, tuna tartar, or prime rib as rare as you'd like. Callie recalled having birthdays there, whether she wanted them there or not, because Oscar's relished Mayor Lawton Cantrell making a splash for all to see.

"And you kept dinner down? It didn't upset your stomach?" Callie asked.

"Washed it down with a light martini," her mother replied. "In honor of Jeb being there."

More like she ate because Jeb was there, foregoing the standard triple dose of drinks.

Callie smiled, not feeling this the time or place or the right person to remind her mother that she'd feel better without booze. "Well, they say you're supposed to sleep as much as you can," she said, then peered over at Jeb. He smiled, but she saw the tiredness in his eyes as he looked up from his phone, most likely chatting with Sprite.

"You want to go to Edisto, and I'll take over here?" she asked him.

"No, I'm good. Sprite's good. I'll wait. It'll be morning before they tell us anything, huh?"

"Afraid so, Son. And they don't wheel in beds for us. Sleep in the car if you like."

"For now, I'll sit here."

She assumed her position in the matching chair next to his. "How's town council treating you these days?" she asked her mother, choosing the question that most assured a response because there was always a head-butting going on amongst its members and the rest of town hall's powers that be.

But, surprisingly, her mother the mayor wasn't so keen for the topic. "Let me just rest here a little, dear."

Callie could definitely live with that.

Within ten minutes, Beverly snored, her lip-sticked mouth agape.

Callie turned to Jeb to tell him she'd be out in the hall, checking on the station, but he'd nodded off, his phone still in both hands, resting in his lap.

Sliding out of her seat, she went through the double doors and around the corner to call Thomas. He said he'd keep her apprised, but she'd heard nothing back. While she'd had an hour's drive and an hour at the ER—where time passed at a snail's pace, she had sense enough to realize that in that short length of real time he hadn't had the opportunity to complete much of a search of both car and condo. She hung up the call. She didn't want to nag the man, and she had Stan and Raysor there to keep anything from going awry.

Damn, this would be a long night.

Unless....

She did a map search for a particular address, and to her amazement, she found the street wasn't five miles from the hospital. Rush hour was long past. Reaching a North Charleston address wouldn't take her fifteen minutes even if she caught all the lights.

First, she went back to check on Beverly. She'd turned on her side, curtailing her snoring but embracing a much deeper sleep. Jeb had put his phone aside, crossed his arms, and slumped into a nap of his own.

"I'm running out," she told the nurse at the center station, and pulled out a business card, her gold shield bright and obvious on it. "This is my number. Call me if there's any development on Beverly Cantrell, please."

The nurse took the card, a bit stunned at the authority of it.

"Anything at all," Callie repeated, imagining papers covering the card before she got out the door.

"We will," the girl said, and Callie exited, hoping that Nolan Brown wasn't working overtime at Boeing this evening. While some might wonder why it took her so long to tell one spouse about the death of another, she had to make sure of the identity. She'd done about the best she could do. Waiting longer would be cruel. Now was a good a time as any to make the death notification and read him as to whether he cared or not.

Chapter 12

CALLIE TROTTED out of the ER, doing a double take at the clock. Just after eight in the evening. The time would be in her favor. Surely Nolan Brown was home from Boeing where he supposedly worked as an engineer per his LinkedIn account.

Ten miles to Boeing and five miles to the Brown house. She'd try the house first. She hated speaking to anyone at their place of business where there was too much opportunity for coworkers to read intentions wrong and sully careers.

Dusk had triggered the ambient lighting at the entrance to Live Oak Farms, an upper-middle-class neighborhood with an upper-middle-class price range just under a million dollars, from her observation and semi-informed guess. Beach property was priced much differently than inland subdivisions, but this was still the Lowcountry, and quality went for prime dollar wherever you were.

She stopped at the entrance, away from the signage and lighting, and checked for texts. Thomas still hadn't called, but with Stan and Raysor there, he might've not needed to. They also might've told him to let her be for the time being so she could concentrate on her mother.

Poor Thomas. Two papa bears overseeing him, and a mother hen who could swoop in at any moment.

There were a few texts, one ending with a quoted admonition from Stan for her not to come home any time soon. *We got this.*

He threw in snippets of updates. Elizabeth's purse was found locked in the glove box. A key ring was in the purse but not the car keys nor the condo key. There was no phone.

Callie needed a better update, more than Stan and his slow, clunky fingers could manage in texts.

He answered in one ring. "We've got this," he mumbled, telling her others were within earshot.

"I need more than you're willing to type," she said. "Update me."

She heard the sliding-glass door squeal open then shut, then frogs in the background. He opened up to her, and she could ask questions.

At the condo, a studio-sized affair, they found a suitcase unpacked in the closet, her clothes in a dresser. Her toiletries remained in the bathroom. No food wrappers. No souvenirs. Five books consisting of mystery fiction on an end table with sticky notes on them, indicating the order in which to read them, a popular series well known on the island by a South Carolina author. A receipt from The Edisto Bookstore was found just inside the cover of book one, ironically titled *Murder on Edisto*. No other receipts in the car to trace other activities, but in the condo trash they discovered a myriad of meal orders, all deliveries.

They were dusting for prints, a tedious task, and she imagined both Raysor and Stan sitting back watching Thomas do the deed. The report thus far was that the place had already shown itself to be pretty clean short of one main set of prints, assumed to be Elizabeth's mostly per their locations on her possessions, the toilet, handles, etc. Two others were conducive to cleaning staff, but Janet would be pretty cooperative in confirming those.

No letters, no sticky notes, no jotted messages on menus. A simple loner from all appearances. Very neat. Bed made. They had called in Raysor's people from the sheriff's department to assist in obtaining prints in the car, but they wouldn't arrive until morning. Thomas would continue with the condo into the night. None of the neighbors had seen Elizabeth's coming or going for more than a day. Nobody had seen the car.

Callie thanked Stan, told him to do the same to Thomas, and chose to hang up and go see Mr. Brown.

Like most subdivisions in the Lowcountry, the street names were derived from clichés of the area. GPS took her past Plantation, Palmetto, Egret, Whitetail, and Bohicket streets. The community consisted of several hundred homes with an established community center including a pool and meeting house. Probably a gym. No house less than three thousand square feet, no sign of vinyl siding, and landscaping flaunted fine specimens she doubted the residents understood how to plant.

After one wrong turn and a cul-de-sac, she landed in the drive of 204 Indigo Trail. Gratefully, dark had fallen. The neighbors would be at dinner, in the midst of their nightly streaming-channel routine, and readying children for bed. No cars in the driveway, but the house sported a two-car garage and a third bay for a boat. Lights shown downstairs.

A man answered quickly, as if expecting somebody else.

"Mr. Nolan Brown?" Callie introduced herself in title and location and waited for his response.

He seemed stunned. She gave him an easier question to answer. "Do you own a condominium on Edisto Beach? At 27F Sea Oats?"

"Um, yes."

"You are Nolan Brown, I assume? Employed at Boeing Industries in North Charleston?"

It was as if a bubble popped. "Oh, yes, yes. Sorry. I am Nolan Brown, and yes, that's where I work. Would you like to come... wait, what's wrong? You mentioned Edisto. Is this about my wife?"

"Sir, mind if we discuss this inside instead of on your front porch for all your neighbors to see and hear?"

One of several cliché sentences she hated saying, because the recipients instantly expected the worst.

"Of course, come on in. Would you like anything to drink? A Coke or juice? Water, perhaps? I assume you have to say no to beer." His voice held a slight quiver to it.

The beer remark drew a forced smile from her, which in turn lightened things up with him. "Water is good," she said, because she seriously was thirsty. She couldn't remember having anything since coffee at the station.

He still wore khakis, loafers, his button-up Oxford shirt tucked in with a leather belt. He hadn't been home long, or he lived more uptight than most.

Or he remained dressed expecting someone, her first impression when he answered her knock too expectantly.

He took her to the living room, the formal one in lieu of the family room with the sixty-inch screen over the fireplace, and motioned toward the sofa while he left for their drinks. Quickly returning, just short of a trot, he set her water on a coaster before her, so as not to mar the cherry coffee table. The dark-maroon, leather sofa was buttery soft to the touch. He took the wraparound upholstered chair at an angle to her. He'd helped himself to a beer.

"What's this about?" he asked again.

She'd waited for him to do just that. Letting them go first often made interviewees find an internal place to feel comfortable, their question also a sign of their ability to converse.

She took a deep pull on the water to moisten her mouth, set it back on the coaster, and pulled out a notepad, not bothering to ask if she could record the exchange. Too early in the game for that. "Mr. Brown, we found a white Explorer parked outside of the Pavilion on Edisto

Beach, apparently left there for quite a while from the way the sand was blown against the tires."

She let that sink in.

He nodded, brows coming together, him trying not to rock. He gripped the beer bottle tighter, now with both hands, letting it sink between his knees.

He didn't ask so she did. "Sir, is Elizabeth Brown your wife?"

He nodded again, then feeling he was supposed to talk, said, "Yes. She is my wife."

"What do you do at Boeing?"

"I'm an industrial engineer." Everyone understood Boeing hired mainly engineers.

"And your wife?"

"She's a nurse."

"What kind of nurse, and where does she work?"

"Oh, sorry. She works at Middleton just up the road. Pediatric floor. Night shift mostly. She says the kids are *more precious*, as she puts it, when the families aren't there. God, she loves that job."

He made her sound almost saintly. That was the price one paid investigating deaths like this. The more you learned about them, the more human they became, and ultimately, the more deeply their passing impacted you.

He couldn't stop rolling the bottle between his fingers. She halfway expected him to start peeling off the label.

"When did you last see her?" Callie asked, wanting to keep him together before breaking the news.

"Why?"

People asked why for a myriad of reasons, the most common being their earnest need to get to the point... to hear why a cop had to show up on one's doorstep. But those people still could be innocent or guilty. "We're trying to build a timeline based upon who has seen her. Since the car looked almost abandoned, we started with the owner of it... you."

She hadn't fully answered his question, but she'd made it sound more logical.

"She's missing?" he asked.

She continued leading him, speaking calmly. "Mr. Brown, just tell me when you last saw her, and we'll take it from there."

"No! Is she missing, I said. Is she... dead?"

But Callie instead sat waiting, her not answering basically a repeat of her request to him.

As if he sensed he had to answer the question to get his answer, he obliged. "She left here five days ago, at the end of her shift. She had her suitcase in her car and left from work." He looked at Callie as if waiting to hear if he'd answered correctly.

"Does she normally go stay at Edisto alone? Y'all share the title, so I'd think it would make for a nice getaway for a couple." She paused for him to see where she was going. "In other words, why didn't you go with her?"

He sighed in frustration. "I would love to, but she's turned that place into her retreat. She needs to change her damn job." Those last words came out with spit. He wiped his mouth. "Sorry. I really don't mean that because she loves her work, but it takes a toll on her."

"Go on," Callie said.

He shook his head with a breath pushed out for emphasis. "The sick babies upset her, which to her is any kid five and under. They're all her babies. She lost two last week, one who she fussed over for the last five months. Sometimes she has to disappear to the beach to get over the trauma of those kids. How she loves the job is beyond me. When things get rough, and this last week was a zinger, she heads to the beach where she shuts off all screens, reads her books, has meals delivered, and goes swimming at night. Her private escape from reality."

Why wasn't the husband a part of that reality?

And God, swimming at night? Could this case get any closer to the movie *Jaws*?

"Why swim in the dark?" she asked.

"She's a night nurse. She likes to stay on her schedule so it's not so difficult reacclimating when she returns to her shift."

Nodding, Callie made note of that. She understood it, but she didn't approve. No one watched her when she swam? What if she ran into trouble in the water with a cramp or a riptide? What if she ran into someone spotting opportunity to mess with a lone, pretty female victim at two in the morning?

"Please tell me what's going on." he said. "I've answered your questions, now you answer mine. What the hell brings the Edisto Beach police chief to my doorstep asking questions about my wife?"

"Mr. Brown," she started, pushing her water away, slipping her notepad back in her pocket. "As I said, we found the white Explorer at the Pavilion where it had sat overnight, at least twenty-four hours to the best of our knowledge."

A pileup of emotion splashed across his face. "You haven't said anything about a search. Have you conducted a search? Maybe she was ill. Maybe she drank herself silly and fell asleep at the condo." Tears he probably didn't even realize he shed started, always the hard part for her. His voice thickened. "Why aren't you back on your beach hunting for where she could be?"

"Our officers are going over the condo as we speak. They'll study both the car and the condo again in the morning."

He wanted to look away, but he couldn't, a few tears having found their way down to drip off his chin. He didn't bother wiping them.

He clung to an unvoiced hope but clearly bracing for that ultimate notice.

Callie took a breath. "We discovered a woman's body washed up on the sound side of the beach yesterday morning. She had no identification. It wasn't until someone reported the car that we put two and two together."

"No, no, that cannot be her," he said, groping for the phone in his pocket. He set the beer bottle on the carpet propped against his foot as he dialed. The call went to voicemail. He tried again, this time leaving a message. "Hon? This is me. Please call as soon as you get this. Please, please call me." Then, to Callie, "She's not going to call, is she?" He burst into sobs, the beer bottle falling over, spilling into the carpet. He didn't bother picking it up, his hands needed to cover his grief.

This was the incredibly difficult part, watching the notified family as their internal mechanisms fought not to believe what they knew was the truth. The desire to hug them was strong at times, but the formality of studying the person, noting whether they go into shock, faint, or lose control and throw things, even taking swings at the uniform delivering the message, was more important. Grief messages dove deep into a person, and reactions were unpredictable. She had no choice but to maintain that observation from enough distance to be able to manage the reaction.

This was also when she judged whether the death really mattered. That initial, instant response that most people can't feign. Sometimes that reaction seemed not enough. Sometimes overkill. It all factored into the investigation.

In this case, Mr. Brown simply melted into the upholstered chair, sobbing, lost to all time and space.

Pretty legitimate.

"How did she die?" he managed between sobs.

"Blow to the head. She did not drown. There was no sexual abuse."

One could see him attempting to categorize the facts. "Murdered?" he asked, his frown so hard and intense it pained her to watch.

"We don't know yet," she said.

After a few minutes, when his tears ebbed, she continued. "Mr. Brown, when you greeted me at the door, you seemed to be expecting someone else. Care to share who that might be?"

"Liz," he said. "I expected it to be Liz, trying to surprise me. I'd been praying she'd come home early."

That news took her by surprise. "Why would you think that?"

He released one more sob, a very resigned one, then took in some shaky breaths. "Because I didn't last see her five days ago, Chief Morgan. I saw her the afternoon of the day before yesterday. I went to Edisto to console her, asking her to let me stay with her, to convince her that she didn't have to hurt alone. I hate it when she locks up all those feelings. It's not healthy, I keep telling her. Not healthy at all."

Callie pulled out her notebook again and flipped pages to where she left off. "Do you mind explaining why you lied to me?"

"I went to Edisto feeling like I wasn't doing enough for her, and when she wouldn't let me stay, I returned feeling even more negligent. An Edisto cop shows up on my doorstep, with what can't be good news, and I'm supposed to volunteer that... that... I'm a shitty husband?"

Maybe it was that simple. "Okay, Mr. Brown, let's start over. When did she leave home? When did you last talk to her? And when did you last see her face-to-face?"

He nodded in jerky movements.

She walked him through it all again. The results were little more than he drove to Edisto midday, ate dinner with his wife on the beach, listened to her mourn her babies, and begged her to let him into her world so he could help support her through this fresh level of heartache. They talked for hours, but she still preferred the solitude to collect herself. He left around eight in the evening. She promised to consider coming home early, assuring him that he'd really helped, but to give her space for the night. And maybe the next day.

"I hated her walking the beach at night. I started to stay behind and, you know, follow her. Make sure she was fine, but I knew how mad that would make her if I invaded her space." He gave a sad, melancholy, slow laugh. "She loves her space."

"Mr. Brown," she said, easing into this question. "Can you account for your whereabouts for the last week? Up to and including yesterday?"

He stiffened. "Am I a suspect now?"

"A formality. With your wife's strange comings and goings, we need to confirm where everyone in her life was for these days. Surely you understand."

His nod was positive, but he carried an uncertainty about him now. She didn't blame him. He was stupid if he didn't see he was a suspect.

"Are you okay?" she asked, making sure he wasn't changing behaviors or tactics on her with this being dropped in his lap.

"I'm good. I understand."

"Good, because I have one additional request."

Wiping his cheeks, rubbing one eye as if it had something in it, he said, "Anything. I promise I didn't kill my wife."

To that, Callie didn't respond. "I know this will be difficult, but would you meet me in Walterboro tomorrow, say, around noon? We need you to identify the body."

Chapter 13

CALLIE LEFT NOLAN Brown's house around eleven, after staying with him until a friend arrived, a friend who stared her down as if she'd accosted Nolan, but nothing Callie hadn't experienced before. Nolan was devastated, no pretense in his coming apart about his wife's demise.

But then she'd seen killers rue the killing they'd done, too.

He'd originally lied about having been on Edisto. Though he hadn't been difficult to bring around in the admission, he'd still hidden that fact. He could be devastated at having done the deed as deeply or more than if a stranger had. Absolutely. It was a matter of proving where he was from the time he said he left Edisto, around eight in the evening, to the following dawn when the coroner stated she died.

She'd obtained the make and model of his car, already having Elizabeth's, as well as the tag. Tomorrow Marie could scan the causeway's cam for the time period in question. A time-consuming process, but one Marie could start and stop between other duties, and if anyone could spot a tag, it was Marie. She loved cam work.

On television, producers showed law enforcement tapping the computer brains on modern makes and models of cars, narrowing down where a car had been, but she didn't have those tools. She hated the idea of turning this over to SLED because they didn't have enough manpower for their own heavy caseload, much less one of hers, and even they weren't CSI Las Vegas. Murder fell into a whole other category of crime, and most tiny towns like hers fell short of resources, but she had more experience investigating murder than most small towns.

Besides, unlike the complex case Raysor had just assisted in for the Colleton Sheriff's Office—deep financial fraud, a double murder, and layer after layer of public corruption—this was a limited scenario case. The woman had either died at the hand of her husband in a one-off crisis, had been the victim of a pure accident in which someone panicked and dumped her out to sea, or had been killed by a stranger who capitalized on a moment. Those were the first-level options she was running at the moment. Anything else would be some version of those three.

She was most concerned about someone in her town hunting for vulnerable women. That scared her, because Maddy could just as well be one of those vulnerable women, whom they just hadn't found yet. She could be the body dumped in the ocean that successfully disappeared.

Callie pulled into a shopping area with three fast-food selections. Tacos, burgers, or fried chicken. Nothing healthy

Texting Jeb to ask his preference, she held her breath waiting for a reply that demanded where she'd been and informing her she'd missed the doctor. Instead, he replied. *Burger with fries and a shake.*

Your grandmother? she texted back.

Same, he typed.

The fact Beverly would eat any of that food was a surprise. Plus, she'd already eaten something earlier in the evening. Beverly must feel better.

Callie had one more task to accomplish before entering the drive-through, though. She called Mark. He'd be arriving home about now, and she hated not being there when he did. That was their time when the world was still, and nobody needed them. Tonight would be the first evening they'd missed those hours since they'd moved into the new house.

"I was hoping you'd call," he answered. "I was afraid I'd interrupt if I did. Tell me what happened and how's she doing."

Hearing him transported her back home, into the bed, relaxed and grateful it was just the two of them. She sank into her seat, closed her eyes, and took in his words. "Oh, you don't know how good it is to hear your voice."

But her need for him only amped his concern. "Is it serious?"

"To tell you the truth, I don't think so?" She said it like a question, because that's where her thoughts hovered right now... between the not knowing and the infamous Beverly milk-the-spotlight show. She just couldn't tell. "She looks good, acts good, and so far, they've found nothing, though quite a few tests haven't come back. But who knows with her? I'm scared not to be worried, if that makes sense."

He'd met Beverly a half-dozen times, and after said acclimation, he had chosen to remain in the background. He didn't care to give the potential mother-in-law anything to work with or against, not wishing to make Callie's relationship with Beverly any more caustic.

"Sure it makes sense," he said. "She's enjoying this attention to a point. A lot of people do that in hospitals. And she's probably more dramatic the more anxious she is. How're you doing? Or should I ask how she is treating you?"

"I'm being good. No fussing. Patient. I'm letting her be her. Besides, she has Jeb to fuss over, spoil, coddle, and he's letting her for fear she is really ill. I couldn't stand sitting around with both of them nodding off, so I ran down the husband of the dead woman and made the death notification."

"How'd that go?" He hadn't done much of that, but he fully understood the importance of the moment from the view of an investigator.

She explained the evening including some preamble about Elizabeth Nolan that she hadn't had a chance to brief him on yet. Just a light dusting of an overview since Stan would catch him up. "The husband lied to me about seeing his wife at Edisto. Claims he was worried and went to check on her. She sent him home, promising to return early. Probably on the up and up, but I'm not giving him a pass quite yet."

Mark waited for more, and she appreciated that he was giving her room to vent, but she didn't need it. Not yet. She was an expert at compartmentalizing. The seriously ill Beverly scenario had been parked in a far back closet during the Nolan Brown interview. Now it was time to open one door and close the other.

"Well, call me if you hear something," Mark said. "No matter the time."

She wanted to delve more deeply into Elizabeth and Nolan Brown with him, but Mark needed his sleep, and she was still piecing things together about the Brown family universe, so she let him go. The car echoed a white-noise loneliness once she hung up.

After filling dinner orders, reaching the hospital again didn't take long with traffic so thin, and she soon passed out bags in the ER, having also bought a sack of tacos for the nurses behind the central station. It never hurt to feed your medical providers.

"Any news?" she asked, taking her seat once Jeb and Beverly were set up with laps of napkins and food.

"Everything's normal," Beverly said.

"No," Jeb said. "A couple of tests were normal, but there are several more we won't know about until the morning, so nothing much has changed."

Beverly chowed down on the burger, not her normal food of

choice, and not her normal dainty eating habits she displayed with guests at working lunches. All of her lunches were working lunches with conservative nibbles of non-dripping, non-complex meal choices. Callie rarely managed lunch alone with her mother without her squeezing in some businessperson or political peer for part of the meal. Despite her mother's indecorous manners tonight, however, Callie noticed she still sported diamond studs, her wedding ring with another gem or two, and pearls around her neck. Even in the hospital she reigned in style, probably telling nurses that her baubles and gems were staying on and don't try to take them off. Callie could hear Beverly thinking, *no telling who might cross my path while I'm in here.*

Jeb made quick work of the burger and balled up the wrapper to toss it across the cramped room into the waste basket. "She's been on the phone for an hour running the town. Waking people up."

Guess their naps had energized them.

He sounded rather proud of his grandmother being able to keep Middleton on its toes. "She wants to fire one guy but said she couldn't since he was in an elected position." He looked at her admirably. "But I think she's got some sort of plan to backdoor him in the next election." Raising his fist, he waited for Beverly to bump him back. She did.

Callie took her time eating her burger. She'd passed on the fries. With the greasy, cheesy, calorie-infused sandwich her focus of attention, she pretended she didn't spot the inconsistency of Jeb fussing at her for policing Edisto while admiring his grandmother mayoring Middleton. Both did so above and beyond the nine-to-five. During holidays, interrupting dinners... during health crises.

Since when did Beverly learn how to bump fists?

Family comes second to the public good. That had been beaten into her head for as long as Callie could remember. Beverly ranted until it felt cliché: *the need of all outweighs the need of the one.*

Where did Jeb think Callie got her work ethic?

Though Callie could cite a long list of negatives when it came to her parents' child rearing, teaching public service wasn't one of them. From interrupted Christmases, missed birthday parties, or forgotten school presentations, the family understood that a greater good existed over personal accomplishments, and thinking otherwise was pure selfishness.

Beverly's service meant long hours, which hopefully converted to more votes come reelection so that she could continue serving others. A noble cycle.

Callie's service, however, could get you killed, had gotten Jeb's father and grandfather killed, both times someone getting even with Callie.

Beverly motioned for someone to come take the finished meal from her lap, and Jeb jumped up to oblige. "He's been the most delicious company, Callie," she said. "He's managed my iPad, my phone, even taken calls for me, taking notes in this app on his phone. He's been trying to teach me how to do it." She pointed at her phone. "That would be incredible."

Clearly she was grooming him to follow in her footsteps. No, ma'am, there were no bones about it.

Callie tried to share a look with Jeb, but he consciously avoided her gaze. That only meant one thing. He was enjoying this camaraderie, this taste of the political world. She could even go so far as to believe he was entertaining the idea of one day doing just what Beverly wanted him to do. All he had to do was graduate in two more years with his business degree. That could explain why he stayed longer than the norm this time. If Beverly was indeed ill, though, Callie was grateful the fates had intervened to keep Jeb at her side until he could rush her to the hospital.

Town government was not Callie's choice for her son, but putting a badge on him didn't sit well with her even more. He wasn't quite aware of how cutthroat politics could be regardless of how altruistic you thought you were. There was something about that climate that sullied you to one degree or another. Period.

"Callie," her mother said, once her lap was clean. "Can you give Jeb and me a moment? I've been teaching him a thing or two about some issues we have with town council, and he showed quite the keen interest. Unfortunately, this hospital diversion interrupted us, but I've had a few calls since then that shed new light on these matters. I'd like his youthful take on two of them, from an outsider's view since he doesn't live in Middleton."

"You're asking *me* to leave?" she asked, wanting to hear her mother distill her verbosity into something more direct. She wanted Jeb to hear it.

Beverly painted on a smile. *The* smile. "I mean, no point in you sitting around while we discuss affairs of state. Jeb shows an interest, and God knows you don't. You've made that fact abundantly clear over the years."

To think Callie was about to tell Jeb he could drive on to Edisto and meet Sprite, while Callie assumed the family caregiving role. "Um, how much time do you need for this executive session, Madam Mayor. A half hour? An hour?"

Beverly couldn't hide condescension if she had to. "An hour would be nice. Don't go far."

Don't go far. Where the hell was she supposed to go? And to order both Callie's departure and request to stay close? She wasn't a damn bungee cord.

Callie shook her head, stood, and let her mother have the final word. To Jeb, she said, "Text me if there's any news or any change. You hear? And don't ask her if you need to. Just do it."

Beverly felt no heat from Callie's flare, propped comfortably under clean sheets, her two pillows fluffed, her calm in place.

"Yes, ma'am," he said, tense—avoiding a crossfire he had no way of exiting unscathed. Callie doubted he registered at all the contrast in how she had been ousted now after earlier having been scolded for taking a couple of extra minutes to delegate a damn murder investigation in order to break her neck getting there.

She didn't just step outside the room. She strode, marching outside the ER to the main lobby where she aimed to sit off in a corner and study her phone to kill time, but in a quick reverse decision, she decided to pace, get in her steps. She couldn't stand being still. God, she hadn't run in a week, and she needed to work off steam. Her steam took her up a hall. She had no idea where it went. *Who cared.*

Callie couldn't be mad at Jeb. She could rarely be angry at that child. He strove to do the right thing. That attribute she credited to herself and her deceased husband, *thank you very much*, despite the fact the boy rebuked her at every turn doing "too much" of the right thing when she let law enforcement needs dictate her time. For goodness' sake, Jeb hadn't even been around Beverly for his first fifteen years, except for the customary annual visit, and look at them now. One would think Callie had been the one out of touch for fifteen years.

Well, she sort of was, but.... She wasn't sure how to end that sentence.

Maybe that was what grandparents were for? Unconditional friends to their grandchildren? But how would Callie know how normal grandparents behaved? Her mother was a chip off the old block. Callie's maternal grandparents worked their real estate business in a furious frenzy, as if five minutes of downtime lost them hundreds of thousands. Ever committed with a deal, always in a sales process that couldn't wait, they used to stop off an hour, tops, to her birthday celebrations to drop off cash tucked inside a custom card that invariably out-wowed any other, the sum of money out-wowing the gifts as well.

Buying loyalty.

Her paternal grandparents died when Callie was in elementary school. That grandfather had been mayor of Middleton, thus explaining her father's work ethic, which her mother fought to perpetuate now having stepped into his shoes upon his death.

Callie made a turn, then another, noting passing nurses who smiled back, seeing only the cop uniform that enabled Callie to walk without being questioned as to where she was going and why. Soon finding herself at the elevators, she pondered whether to take yet another benign hallway on this floor or check out something else. It was late, and she didn't want to wake anyone—*Wait.*

Studying the elevator marquee, she found the floor that piqued her interest. She punched the button, and the elevator soon arrived, unencumbered by the daytime crowds. She punched another button and the doors closed.

With no one else calling for a ride, the elevator took her straight to level five. She exited, the halls tomb-like, but the sign overhead identified her destination. Pediatrics.

Elizabeth Brown worked nights in this hospital, on this floor. One nurse sat behind the counter, and she spotted another move from one room to another about five doors down. She went to the nurses' station and waited for the woman to look up.

The nurse looked seasoned, in her forties, in soft lavender scrubs, her black hair cropped short with enough length on top to give her bangs across her forehead. Efficient yet snazzy. She looked up, noted Callie's name plate and patch on her sleeve before connecting eye to eye. "Yes?"

Callie liked the nurse looking for identification, sizing up the speaker before responding.

"Does Elizabeth Brown work here?"

"Normally she does, but she's off tonight. May I help you?" Curt but professional.

Callie introduced herself. "Mind if I ask a few questions about her?"

The tag on the lavender top read Macie Gibbons, RN. Glancing around, as if she measured whether or not to say how busy she was, she returned her attention to the officer not three feet from her nose. "You're from Edisto Beach, huh? Something wrong?"

"Are you her supervisor?"

"I'm the charge nurse, so yes."

"Well, Ms. Gibbons, mind if I ask you a few questions? I've got time to wait if you get called."

"I'm not fueling anything against one of my nurses, mind you. Is something wrong with Lizzie?"

Callie didn't care to pronounce Elizabeth dead to her coworkers yet, not when the husband was still in shock from just learning himself.

"Her husband's worried about her," was the compromise Callie was willing to make.

"Then I would've thought he'd have called himself instead of sending the cops."

Sending the cops. Here was a woman with a burr under her saddle about law enforcement.

"He told me she worked here. I have a family member in the ER, and I thought I'd fill in the waiting time by checking out her place of employment. Nothing critical."

"Humph," came the reply.

"Lizzie stays on my beach," Callie said, softening her voice, reminding herself where she stood, surrounded by sick people who didn't need to hear this in the middle of the night. Especially children. "We have some concerns about her safety."

"Not sure I want to get involved." Macie clicked a couple keys on her computer, rose and walked away, disappearing into a glassed-off room. She gave Callie a hard glance, then turned her back.

Chapter 14

CALLIE HAD BEEN shot down twice in one night by the stethoscope crowd, the resident and now this charge nurse on the pediatric floor. One would think being a female in uniform would slide her right through to cooperation from two female medical professionals. With the doctor Callie had to assume the uniform challenged her authority somehow. That or her mother the mayor had already tarnished that relationship before Callie reached the hospital.

This nurse, however, had snubbed her, sassed her, turned her back on her, and moved to a glass-walled office to be out of reach.

Callie mentally replayed her introduction, her questions, and for the life of her, couldn't see where she'd erred. *Let's try this again.*

"Ma'am?" she called, trying not too loud but just enough to carry the distance through the opening to that back office.

Did she just sneak a look up at me?

Callie's normal method of connecting began with letting the person know she expected results and had all the patience in the world and would be willing to bend to their schedule. That hadn't worked here despite most of the children asleep for the night, their needy parents gone or chilling in a recliner.

Callie rounded the counter to its opening and zigzagged her way past stations to the glass office. "Ms. Gibbons," she said, foregoing the first name Macie in deference to her role. "May I please have a few minutes? Like I said, Elizabeth's husband is concerned, and I'm trying to backtrack as to what, if anything, may be wrong."

"You serving papers?"

That caught Callie off guard. "No. Not serving papers. Just asking questions about who Lizzie is."

"I've been conned at work before. About my son, my staff... my ex. Cops at work are never a good thing."

Callie held palms up. "No papers, and I'm not trying to jam you up." She thought she caught signs of the nurse's shoulders dropping a notch. Then they snapped back up.

"Please?"

Chin up, the nurse scooted past Callie in the doorway, returning to her station. "I need to be on duty. There are only two of us tonight. I'll give you a few minutes, and I reserve the option to refuse any questions I don't feel comfortable answering."

"Fair enough," Callie said, following, returning to her place on the other side of the counter to salvage some of the nurse's respect.

Macie Gibbons laid down her pen and sat back in her chair, arms crossed. Not the best attitude but better.

"Ms. Gibbons, what are Elizabeth's... Lizzie, I believe you called her... what are her normal hours?"

"Nights, seven to seven, three to four days a week. She works overtime a lot."

Callie didn't pull out her notebook or her recorder. With this air of distrust, her memory would suffice for now. "Does her husband mind about the overtime?"

"No, because Boeing works him just as hard, just as long. Lizzie leaves herself open for fill-in. The children love her. She's a natural with the bitty ones."

Indeed, Lizzie was fast becoming a saint, and Callie'd heard enough to hate that the beaten, shark-bitten body belonged to such a good soul, assuming all this was solid. "Does she retreat to Edisto often?"

The nurse gave a light shrug from behind those crossed arms. "She tries to go at least once a month. She really had to get away this week, though. I mean, really, really had to."

"Lucky her husband could get away with her with his hours and all."

"Oh,"—and Macie cocked her brows up into her bangs— "he didn't go with her. She usually goes alone. Most of the time she flies solo down there."

"What makes this instance of her taking off different than any other?" Callie asked. "And if this was such a different situation, why didn't he go with her?"

A lifestyle had begun to take shape. The husband worked maybe too much. The wife poured herself into her own job, and with no children at home, she used the ones in the hospital as surrogates, her love for them making overtime easier. But then, he could be working overtime because his wife was never at home.

Macie gave the question about Nolan a moment's thought, as if she second-guessed whether Callie would understand. "Her husband rarely gets off, so she has to go alone. Based on history and this spell being particularly tough, I'm not sure she even asked him. Went on a day's notice and left straight from work. She'd had a terribly rough couple of weeks."

"So the last time you saw her was..."

"She worked Saturday night then left straight from here."

Talking about work seemed to open Macie up. Callie leaned on the counter, showing keen interest.

Macie's arms uncrossed. "Two of the littlest ones succumbed within two days of each other, while another was touch and go. He's better, mind you, but not out of the woods. If that poor baby makes it, though, he'll go home with problems." With a pitiful, empathetic sigh, she displayed the horribleness of it all. "Lizzie's normally a tough nut, but those cases... especially this time..." She faded into an *um, um, um,* letting Callie's imagination complete the thought.

"Not sure I could do this job," Callie said, meaning it.

"Humph," said Macie. "I damn sure know I couldn't do yours."

Callie didn't know what rubbed Macie wrong about police, but now was not the moment to inquire. Callie smiled at the shared appreciation for their first-responder roles. She'd broken through.

"How long have you known Lizzie?" she asked. "You sound close, or is that just because you work as a team here?"

"No, we're close, honey. Known her since she started here, maybe ten years? Wait, no, probably going on twelve, now. She started when they returned from their honeymoon."

"So you do know Nolan," Callie said, using his name. Speaking in the more familiar could lower Macie's guard... though she was softening up quite nicely as it was.

"Yeah. He's agreeable enough."

Callie heard the *but* without the nurse manager saying it and waited to see if Macie could tack on something else.

Which she did. "They're both workaholics. Not having children is an issue, but nothing bad enough to tear apart their marriage. It's just sad, is all. Some women were made to be mothers. Lizzie's one of them. But she and Nolan still adore each other, even if they couldn't have children of their own."

Good heavens, everything about this case was sad. Callie noticed that same nurse she'd seen from the elevator now crossing from one room to another, stealing a look toward the uniform at the front desk as she did.

"Thanks for your time. I was hoping to speak to Lizzie, but I'd best get back to my family," Callie said. "You know how it is sitting around with nothing to do."

Macie returned a big nod. "Makes people crotchety. A hospital is where you need patience the most, but unfortunately, it's also where some have it in short supply. Even nurses have to yell into a towel some days." She squinted. "Not sure how long your relative will be stuck in this place, but Lizzie reports back for tomorrow night's shift. You might be able to catch her then."

Lizzie had been dead for a day and a half, yet Macie hadn't wondered about a lack of texts, emails, or calls. Callie guessed they weren't *that* close.

"I appreciate the chat," Callie said, pushing away from the counter. "You keep tending those babies like you do."

Macie finally grinned. "Sure will. Take care out there."

Callie tipped her chin and strolled off, as if she needed to stretch her legs, just killing hours because waiting for people to heal was a long, slow game. Macie's head went back down to tend her duties.

The evening dimming lights had kicked in, making everything sound quieter and feel calmer. Callie was certain there was a science to all of this. Time stood still. It also made her feel more alone.

The lights over the doors indicated the room where a nurse, a doctor, or an aide tended a patient, making it easy for staff to find each other. Callie walked to the end of the hall, peered out the window to the street below, stretched, then turned to mosey her way back. Slowing, then slowing more, she ducked into a room.

A child of three or four slept the deep sleep only such an age could own. Eyelids motionless, mouth slightly agape, tresses of dark hair slightly sweaty against her temples, the girl was sweet enough to steal your breath. The innocence made Callie wonder what ailed her, then she didn't want to know.

The nurse turned, jerked as though startled, but didn't release a peep or any other sign of noise, her professional instincts telling her not to awaken the patient. Her finger went up over her lips, silently shushing Callie, then she gave a dismissive wave inviting Callie to exit the room.

But when Callie started to leave, the nurse unexpectedly caught her sleeve, parked her at the door, then motioned Callie to wait. Sliding out the door first, the nurse disappeared into the room to the right, further away from the nurse's station. Callie could only assume she was to do the same. So she did.

The room had no patient, and Callie softly shut the door.

"I heard you asking about Lizzie?" said the nurse. "I'm Dawn. Dawn Meyer. Don't listen to Macie. I'm way closer to Lizzie, and something's not right."

Callie slid her a business card. Dawn tucked it away without reading it, attention still on the door.

"Have you heard from her?" Callie asked, hoping to cut to the chase since they were being so clandestine. Callie wasn't about to play Macie for a fool quite yet. Nurse managers tended to have their ducks in a row.

"No, and I should've heard something. She isn't even texting me back."

This was more like it. "Maybe she's having too good a trip," Callie offered, but Dawn shook her head before Callie finished the sentence.

"She and Nolan have been having problems."

"I thought the sick children sort of sent her over the edge, pushing her to take a break," Callie suggested.

"Oh, now, well, yes, that was horrid. One baby she held to the end because the parents had gone to dinner and didn't get back before the child slid away."

Jesus, how did a parent live with that?

A hand went over the nurse's mouth as she composed herself for a second. Then she pulled it away, waving the air as if it would flush away the thought. "Anyway, she left to get her head right, to cry, to consider her marriage, the whole mess. When one gets sucker punched by the loss of a child, you tend to look at the futility of everything else in your life. It's why she runs away like she does. I just go home and binge on ice cream and Hallmark movies and cry into my cat's fur."

"Oh," Callie said, acting ignorant and stunned, which wasn't far from the truth.

"Her sorry husband doesn't deserve her. Engineers... all brain, no soul."

Okay, now she had the opposite here. Macie protected Lizzie, singing the song that all was good other than the bane of employment and the sweat of a young couple earning a living. Dawn, on the other hand, unloaded all that was wrong in Lizzie's life, presenting her as burdened and overwhelmed in her efforts to be an angel.

"Is she missing?" Dawn asked.

"She hasn't responded to her husband." Again, you didn't

broadcast a death until the body was formally identified, which wouldn't happen until tomorrow.

"It's usually the husband or boyfriend," Dawn said.

"Their relationship was that eroded?" Then Callie added, "Does he abuse her?"

Dawn did a little uptick thing with her nose. "Let's just say Lizzie talked to an attorney."

The door pushed open. It was too heavy to sling open with any effect, but if she could have, Macie would have slung it. "What nonsense has she been telling you?"

"It's not nonsense," Dawn said.

But Macie turned on Callie instead. "Something told me not to talk to you. Something told me that inviting the police was a mistake. Get off this floor before I call security."

"You know as well as I do something's amiss with Lizzie," Dawn professed. "You're just too concerned about anything making you or your floor look short of perfection. You don't know Lizzie like I do. I haven't heard from her in over a day. That's not like her."

"I haven't heard from her either," Macie said, her jaw tense.

Leaning in, Dawn directed a challenging stare at her supervisor. "She wouldn't tell you anything if it didn't involve the damn employee handbook." She pointed at Macie for Callie's sake. "No more heart in that one than in Nolan Brown."

Macie looked about to explode. "Don't you have work to do? Or is this your break? Of course, I could call it AWOL."

Dawn gave Macie a double dose of it before marching back into the hallway.

"Off my floor," Macie said, pointing toward where Dawn went, "or I will indeed call security."

Callie didn't explain to Macie how that threat might fall short or how she might be contacted again about Elizabeth's employment habits and her familiarity with Nolan. It was late. Kids were sleeping. Callie had heard enough for now. The employment was confirmed, and there were signs of smoke in the Brown marriage.

"Thank you for talking to me," she said, leaving past the nurse.

"Wish I hadn't," Macie replied.

Callie wondered which one of them would call Nolan first.

Took her longer than she remembered to find her way back to the ER, but once she arrived, she found Beverly sleeping. Callie woke Jeb and told him to go sleep in his car if he wasn't willing to grab some shut-eye at his grandmother's house. He accepted the car. Callie replaced him in the plastic chair against the wall, grateful the chair didn't have arms, allowing her utility belt to rest easy as she propped up her feet on the bed's mechanics, crossed her arms, and closed her eyes. As the hubbub of gurneys, spongey sneakers, dings and beeps of the ER faded into the background, her last thought before dozing off was the slim chance that hospital security would come looking for her.

THE CURTAIN OF Beverly's bay area slung back, jolting Callie awake. Beverly exclaimed, groping around for something she wasn't finding. "My brush, my mirror… oh my gosh, my mints." Each word screeched a little higher.

Callie blinked hard, stood, and found Beverly's purse on the corner counter, and laid it in her mother's lap, moving in slow motion in an attempt to collect her wits. What she didn't have to think twice about was that first impressions were as important to her mother as the right hairdresser.

Jeb came rushing in, and Callie motioned for him to close the curtain and remain on that side of the room, doing a zipper movement across her mouth.

"Get out until I'm ready," Beverly instructed the elderly doctor standing at the foot of her bed. "How dare you barge in like this without seeing if I'm decent."

The white-coated man stood five foot six at best, his age a few years older than Beverly. His thick hair held waves that beckoned someone's fingers, even as snow white as the tresses were.

"I've seen you undone before, Beverly. And you deserve to have had to spend the night here, though it's a sin that these doctors and nurses had to put up with you. Madam, they can't treat you without a decent, honest history, but never fear. I've educated them. I've seen all the tests they've done to be on the safe side, and, frankly, you ought to be ashamed of yourself."

Beverly frantically attempted to preen with a compact mirror in one hand, a hair pick with another, her lipstick, concealer, and pressed powder strewn across the covers. "Shut up, you old duck." She winced once at the movement of her left arm.

"Hello, Callie," the doctor said, a smirk remaining on his lips at the patient.

"Hey, Doctor McCain. What's the real story here, if you don't mind my asking, because I'll never get it from her."

Doctor Benedict McCain had served as the family doctor back to her grandparents on Beverly's side. He could've retired, and had attempted to twice, but came back to tend to the old-school families who weren't interested in change. He represented one of a very small few who wielded power over Beverly.

He turned to his patient. "Mind if I tell your daughter the truth?"

Callie's blood froze, in spite of the old man's grin. Doctors could smile through anything. What he classified as normal, everyday medical jargon could be frightening to her or Jeb. For sure, Beverly hadn't been so up close and sharing with Jeb over her health.

"Tell her what?" Beverly spouted, having moved on to her lips.

The doctor smacked his hand on the metal bed rail, his wedding ring pinging like a Methodist bell ringer. "Pay attention, Beverly. I'm talking about your health, and these two people in this room are your closest kin and are in need of understanding your maladies. They'll be the ones picking up your pieces when your time comes."

Beverly stopped her primping, covered the lipstick, closed the compact, and dropped everything into her lap. "You're scaring them, you old fool."

"Yeah," Jeb said from behind the man. "You sort of are."

All the doctor did was cock his white fluffy brows, clearly having succeeded in soliciting a certain concern.

Callie leaned over the railing, wanting to fuss hard, real hard, but remembering there was sickness and tragedy outside that curtain. The real kind of tragedy, not this theatrical shit going down here. "Tell him he can tell us," she told her mother.

"Callie..."

"Tell him!"

Chapter 15

Lydia

CHIEF MORGAN had been outspoken enough yesterday. In so many words the ladies at *Time in a Bottle* better find Maddy or they'd be on her shit list.

Well, they had Maddy, but Chiara had messed everything up informing the police, damn her.

Lydia had set her head on straight, though. At least she thought she had. She'd school Robin as soon as she got in, and they'd be on a united front. Yes, this would be much better. Lydia didn't see herself as heartless as others thought, especially the chief of police. Whatever she did she did for the greater good of the crew.

So quit second-guessing yourself. Nobody else would've handled Maddy this well.

After Lydia had sent Chiara to Mr. Warrick's house and maneuvered Maddy into her real bed upstairs, her own Mr. Griffin had called back, and they'd spoken for two hours, planning something later that night... maybe.

He'd sooth her, making her feel needed and missed.... No, that just wasn't right.

An hour after nightfall, Vivien arrived, having cut her own date short, worried about Lydia being left alone with Chiara.

"Where'd she go?" she asked, coming in the door.

"I told her," Lydia said.

Vivien froze mid-step, then eased her belongings onto the bar. "Told who what exactly?"

"I had to, Viv. Chiara was having a fit, and we couldn't leave Maddy downstairs any longer."

Her head tilted up, Vivien took that in, no judgment in her eyes, "You told her some of it, or you—"

"I took her downstairs, told her most of the story, then sent her on a Warrick date. I assured her I'd bring Maddy up and make her comfortable, but she had to keep her mouth shut about any and all of it or the world would crash down on all our heads."

"True that," she replied. "What about Robin?"

"We tell her, too."

With a sigh, Vivien thought a second, then made her way to the kitchen. "I need a drink."

She poured a wine then strode to the bedroom, peering in to make sure Maddy was really in there.

"She ought to be up any time," Lydia said. "I quit medicating her."

Pulling the door closed, Vivien made her way through the living room to the porch, a location fast becoming their routine spot for all things leisure... and lately for all things needing serious discussion.

"You're taking a chance," she said in that sultry low voice of hers as Lydia assumed the seat beside her.

"Better me than Maddy."

Vivien couldn't argue with that. "You trust Robin?"

"Better than the other two. We still can't let the chief know Maddy's here. Not yet. Maddy's a wreck and might still talk."

Vivien sighed, staring out toward the water. "But the longer she's *missing*, the more questionable it becomes as to why."

"We need time to groom her," Lydia said, then tacked on, "as well as the other two."

Vivien had already downed half her glass of wine, and sat there with an arm across her body, holding up the elbow of the other arm that held her drink.

Lydia could read the thoughts in her best friend's head. She wished they had just let Maddy go on the record for that night, instead of Lydia taking her in and hiding her. None of the rest would've been dragged into it. In hindsight... the best logic. But that's not what took place. That wasn't Lydia.

"She came to me asking for help, Viv. It was my place to be there for her."

Vivien scoffed. "Not sure our unofficial rules go to that extreme, girl. Face it. You just reacted." She let that sink in, then added, "You acted on instinct... you acted on—"

"Experience," Lydia said.

"Yes."

Some time went by. Robin and Chiara weren't expected back soon, maybe not till the morning. Scenarios played through Lydia's head. What if Maddy wasn't consolable? How and when could they present Maddy to the chief without looking incredibly orchestrated... and without the chief asking where Maddy had been?

Chiara was almost as big a problem. What would she say about Maddy? What would Maddy say about her? Why had this been such a huge mishap of communication if nothing was wrong?

Lydia felt the hand on her knee before she heard Vivien's voice. "Lydia, you there?"

With a smile, she laid her hand over Vivien's. "Yes, sorry. Too deep in thought as to the plan."

"What plan?"

"Exactly."

"Listen to me," her friend said. "Go see your delicious Mr. Griffin."

"Now?"

"You sent Chiara to Mr. Warrick's, no doubt to relax her and get herself out of her own head. Admit it."

Lydia could only give a slight, melancholy chuckle to the positive, and the drifting in of thoughts from mention of the man could be described as nothing short of palliative.

Before all of this Maddy business, three days ago, Lydia had visited the man for a long afternoon that turned into a complete night. He'd provided a wonderful evening. They sat and listened to seventies music on a porch overlooking the marsh, sharing grapefruit margaritas laced with colorful cocktail sugar, a recipe he'd acquired during one of his twice-a-year jaunts to Scottsdale in his business as a corporate broker. He bought and sold failing businesses. Apparently, there was good money in it.

He'd asked her to accompany him on the next trip planned for October, painting such beautiful pictures of what she would see in the desert and the surrounding purple hills, promising her silver and turquoise jewelry. Mexican food like she'd never tasted, he said.

Lydia almost said yes. On the other hand, she also hadn't said no. There were three weeks left in this trip. Plenty of time to get reacquainted and see if the cards were still playing in their favor when it came time to leave.

The married part is what tugged on her when it really shouldn't. Griffin and wife no longer shared a bed and rarely shared the same house. He owned three with her favorite being in Washington DC, and his being the lovely cream-and-white two-story with a marsh view on Dock Site Road, Edisto. It was how he could stay here so long, and whenever he liked. He'd even offered it to her if he wasn't using it, but no way she could risk the wife learning of her husband's *other* Edisto pastime. However, she hadn't given him an absolute no on that offer yet, either.

Regardless of how loose a marriage he claimed he practiced, regardless of how armor-plated he avowed his life was from scandal, however, she and the group didn't need the theater. She argued with herself that she also didn't need the commitment. Promising him that he was her top social priority whenever he arrived in Edisto was about as committed as she cared to be. She learned a long time ago that money wasn't the best glue for a relationship. Her not caring, however, only seemed to make him love her more.

Which made her likewise worry if he'd feel differently if she asked him to give up his wife and accept her full-time. Her gut, however, told her not to go down that road.

"Go," Vivien said, nudging her with the hand holding her glass, bringing Lydia back from her thoughts. "I'll handle Maddy when she wakes up. I'll handle the other two if they show, which they shouldn't."

Lydia smiled at her friend. Lifting her phone in her habit of watching for queries and requests, schedules, and suggestions, she spotted Griffin's brief text.

Drinks?

Was she capable of an evening with a gentleman after what she'd had to do with and for Maddy? She was quite capable of managing the wiles, drama, and inconveniences of women and their dates, and those things she could compartmentalize, but the other night... that had dredged up her old self. All that she had overcome. All that had kept her from living on Edisto. All that she had sacrificed.

But just as she'd explained to Chiara that she was expected to perform business as usual because people would be watching, expecting the norm, wondering why if they weren't... Lydia held the same responsibility. One might say even more of a duty with her being the figurehead of the group.

Rattan creaking, she rose from her chair, in acceptance of Viv's suggestion. They didn't exchange words. On one hand it felt wrong to go out, but on the other it felt necessary. Either way, Vivien remained stable behind her as support, which made her friend her biggest blessing. With her, all things were possible.

Griffin accepted.

I'll take whatever minutes I can get, Sweetness.

By the time she reached his house, barely a mile around the tip of the beach and past the marina, he'd had dinner delivered. Taking their enjoyment to the dock, they watched the moon come and go, then had nightcaps, the lap of high tide against the piers below.

Meaning to leave around midnight, she conceded and stayed the night, needing so much to be held... someone else being the protector. His bedroom faced the marsh, a large picture window with an arced top allowing her to watch the ink-black sky turn navy, then the assorted pastel purples and pinks of dawn. She slipped out just past six, her trademark left on the pillow... a maroon velvet rose trimmed in sepia-colored tulle, like her shawl.

The silence outside removed any sense of immediacy, and she sat in her car a moment, appreciating the sky's changing colors, the water reflective of it. Finally, she pulled out, heading south to wrap around where the road turned into Palmetto, but she didn't drive far.

Brice's address was also on Dock Site Road. She hadn't thought twice about passing it last night with so much on her mind... what she left at *Time in a Bottle* versus the man she needed to appreciate ahead on the marsh.

Brice's house still stood dark and unused in the half-light dawn. No for-sale sign in the yard, the residence appeared to have slipped into a coma. Guess two months after his death was too soon to expect someone to liquidate assets. He'd divorced his wife and had no kids, which could mean probate keeping this baby empty for one or two years.

In a last-minute tug of affectionate memory, she couldn't help but pull into the drive. She shut off the engine, killed the lights, and tried to replay last summer.

He preferred evenings most days. Being head of town council put him somewhat in the spotlight, and the way this beach turned in and shut down around nine gave him the discretion he needed. Last summer he'd finally ditched his wife, free of all tethers since she'd been the one caught screwing his best friend and had bragged to the world about it on Twitter. He even took Lydia out fishing once, in broad daylight, the bold move gripping her heart. She'd never seen him happier.

What were the chances the house might be... open?

Getting out of the car, she held the door to a soft shut, then took the stairs up to the door. Locked. She trotted back down to ground level and ventured around to the back, taking those stairs to the porch overlooking the deeper part of Big Bay Creek.

Her heart caught. Nothing had changed. Even the chaise was in the same spot, facing northwest to catch the evening sun, or like now, the slow awakening of an early morn.

She'd dozed in that chaise a few times, letting the sun warm her into the cool evening... to the time when a starry sky could reflect on the still water, or when a moonless heaven amplified the invisible splashes of wildlife.

Leaning on the railing, eyes closed, she eased back into one of those past summer nights with its warm breeze coming in gentle off the bay, enveloping and soothing. Brice's arms slipping up behind her, her lids shut, letting the temperate sensation of the air partner with his breath on the back of her neck.

Oh my. She stared across the water, hand on her chest, feeling the thuds of her heart, just like back then.

Tears pooled. *No, no, this wasn't allowed.* She widened her eyes, to enable the breeze to evaporate the moisture. She didn't cry. Lydia Barron didn't do regrets. Blinking, she overcame. With a sigh, she contained herself.

No, she wouldn't cry. She could, however, miss a friend.

Blowing out a deep breath, she turned to give the back door a try. It was locked as well, only this time, after glancing at both sides for the neighbors, she let herself in.

Nobody knew she had this key but Brice.

Discovery wasn't smart, especially with the chief not all that keen on them of late, so she left the lights off.

Walking through the sitting area that overlooked the water, she started to just take a rest at the window seat. She could still smell him, and she drank in his scent. He wasn't a looker, and he wasn't necessarily a charmer, but they'd thoroughly enjoyed each other's company for reasons that made little sense and didn't have to.

Instead of sitting, she wandered through the kitchen, curious to see if much had changed, hoping it hadn't so she could recall how he turned off that lamp, set a coaster on that table for her vodka, and turned back the covers on his bed.

Pausing to recall the last time she'd been here, it took her a second, a challenge on whether she wanted to remember hard enough to risk pining again. The decorative lures framed on one wall reminded her. He'd been fishing earlier that day and had fried up the catch with coleslaw of his own recipe and served it with beer in frozen mugs. Then he'd surprised her with lemon icebox pie. Homemade. Was it a hard pie to fix? No. The directions were on the back of the condensed milk can, but he did it just for her.

Still fingering the key, she realized she'd held a key to his place for five years now, having never used it. The night he gave it to her had been sweet and knowing she really didn't need access to his place if he wasn't there to let her in, she accepted. Like a promise ring or a high school ring on a chain around a girl's neck, it was symbolic.

Even when he was still married to Aberdeen, he would call when she'd be gone for a day. These people and their marriages that they regretted having but didn't seem to have the gumption to dissolve. They talked about that a time or two. He said he'd divorce her for Lydia.

She told him he had to divorce her for himself.

He tried to explain why he had to have a person to run to, but the more he tried to mold his thoughts into words, the weaker the explanation. He just couldn't admit that he couldn't stand being single. That meant being alone, which he wasn't good at. A lot of men were like that.

Lydia never told him there was no husband in her future. That always scared dates who temporarily fell in love. These poor gentlemen wanted that option to be there, somewhere... just in case they made that leap that she knew would never happen. It was a game. Not to them, but it was. Just a game of living a temporary world of wants and wishes and empty of regrets.

Not wanting to see the bedroom for fear of melancholy destroying the memories, she returned to the porch and took a nautical cushion from the window seat so tastefully upholstered to match the curtains and assumed her spot back outside on that chaise. The pillow clutched across her belly, she leaned back and breathed steadily, listening for the night noises of creatures along Big Bay Creek.

I'll miss you, Brice.

A half hour passed. Enough for her to hear traffic in the distance and the sun to be up. Finally, she rose and took the steps down, keeping the pillow. At the base, she strolled past the storage room that most ocean homes built around the pillars holding the ground floor up off the ground and out of the way of a storm surge.

Time to scurry before someone noticed a stranger at the empty house, a house every resident knew belonged to Brice. But instead, she placed a hand on the storage doorknob, wanting to see what of his remained down there that they'd used together. His tackle boxes... she could grab one of his fishing lures and it would never be missed.

A car ventured up Dock Site Road before she was half inside the storage, and she made the mistake of taking a second to see what kind of driver might be out this early.

Shit. An Edisto Beach Police Department cruiser.

The young lady officer made eye contact with her and slowed, then moved to park behind Lydia's car.

Lydia slipped the pillow into the storage room and nudged the door closed. Then she walked to the front to meet the blond officer who had just been at her house the other night... when they found the dead girl.

"Morning, Officer."

"Ma'am."

"Sorry to appear like I'm snooping, but I guess I kinda am. There wasn't a rental sign, but it was empty. I'm not happy with our rental and thought I'd walk around and see if this one might be available. You know, a sign on the back facing the water or on the porch..." She cocked her head. "We've met, haven't we?"

Lydia played the scene by instinct. If you're somewhere you're not supposed to be, just act like you are.

"Yes, ma'am. You're at *Time in a Bottle*. I'm Annie Greer. I was one of the officers on the scene when they found the girl."

Lydia did a double take at the phrase *found the girl*. Her initial thought was of Maddy, being so obsessed with dealing with her, but then she caught herself. This was about the girl on the beach. "Oh, yes, that's right. Horrible thing that poor dear they found washed up."

"But you were missing a friend, if I remember," Annie said, going to the storage room and trying the door. It opened. She peered inside then pushed it back shut.

"We are. I mean, she had checked in by phone, but she hasn't returned. She's been having horrible boyfriend problems, and we're chalking it up to that." Close enough to the truth.

"If she returns, we're supposed to contact the chief, which we will definitely be doing. No point in her worrying about us when she has the whole beach to tend to."

Annie held up a finger for Lydia to remain in place, then she went up the back porch stairs. Finding the door locked, she soon returned and went up the front stairs to check that entrance. Satisfied, she returned. "The house isn't available," she said. "Probably won't be for a while."

Lydia started to ask why, to further the pretense of someone ignorant to the real estate market, but figured she'd pushed far enough.

"Well, sorry if I've violated some rule. I just love being out this early in the morning, and the house caught my eye." Then she stood, poised, as though ignorantly waiting for the cop to write her a ticket, behaving deprecating enough that the officer might give her a pass.

"No harm done. I just don't advise you to trespass on property. Someone could've been asleep in there and thought you were a burglar. No telling how that might've turned out."

"Yes, you're absolutely right." She waited.

"I'll wait for you to get into your car, ma'am," Annie said.

Lydia hopped to it, and once she was behind the wheel, Annie got in her own. She backed away, letting Lydia pull out before her, and watched as Lydia drove toward Palmetto as she'd been doing so before. She kept an eye on her rearview mirror.

The cruiser followed her.

Lydia had no choice but to head toward home, where she was expected to be, where the officer would probably leave her be and move on to the rest of her day. But her heart drummed in her chest.

What if Annie had seen the pillow slung into the storage room, finding it on the floor when she peered in and wondered how and why? What if the officer called in to the chief, telling her about the happenstance meeting? What if this stupid little incident prompted the chief to return today?

As expected, and as she'd hoped, Annie drove past when Lydia pulled into the drive, with one last glance at Lydia in case she looked in her mirror... which she had.

She put a hand on her chest, feeling her pulse still at a run. Today. No doubt today her group of ladies had to get their affairs in order, their scripts memorized, their details straight. Maddy had to come home, and the chief had to be told.

Hopefully, she'd take a simple phone call and be done with it.

She sat a few minutes more, her heartbeat back to normal, her thinking more controlled.

Chances were the officer went on, checking the rest of the beach, assured Lydia was home. She'd never expect Lydia to go back and retrieve that pillow, nor one of those fishing lures she hoped were still kept in that green-and-red tackle box above the freezer in that storage room.

Chapter 16

AMIDST HER SMOOTHED out, snow-white sheets, Beverly's face drew up like a wrinkle, embarrassed. One would think the town council watched on a camera the way this doctor had a rein on her. "Say whatever you like, Benny," she said. "But it's nothing, and you know it."

She didn't act as if her health malady was nothing, and Callie stood stiff waiting for whatever this blast of news would mean for Beverly, and ultimately herself and Jeb. If her condition was nothing, then why the hell had they been in the emergency room for twelve hours?

White-haired Doctor Gadsden smiled deeply and turned his focus on Callie. "She has gout."

That news took a second to sink in. No heart disease? No cancer? *Seriously? Gout?*

"Let me get this straight," Callie said to the doc, giving Beverly the meagerest, briefest glance. "Mother complains about her arm, shortness of breath, and dizziness only for it to be gout? Is this something relatively new?" She held out her palms, like a scale on either side of herself. "How is gout..." She wiggled one hand. "And heart problems..." She wiggled the other. "Alike in any possible way?"

"Humph," came from the propped-up pillow behind her, and Callie ignored whatever indignity Beverly imagined she experienced right now.

"Fatigue, swelling of legs and feet, and shortness of breath can account for any of a dozen things," the doctor said. "Gout can be quite painful and falls in that category. She gets it in her right big toe and her left elbow on occasion."

Beverly had winced at using her elbow to freshen her makeup.

"How long has this been going on?" Callie asked, daring to glance around hard at her mother.

"Five years... six," said the doctor.

Jeb had gone from stunned to searching his phone for the dangers and symptoms of his grandmother's ailment. He'd eventually see what Callie already knew, which was that Beverly's drinking and irregular eating habits didn't help. Especially the drinking part.

"The gin?" Callie asked, not completing the sentence.

"Yes, the gin," the doctor said.

She didn't know what to say, nor if this was the right place to say it. Her own blood pressure had spiked at the fact she'd had no idea about the gout, more so that her mother felt her gout flare worthy of confiscating her grandson, and eventually her daughter. While she wasn't venting in front of all these people, her insides boiled.

This escapade was worthy of a royal one-on-one with Beverly. The kind that both she and her mother avoided, which meant she wasn't about to drive back to Edisto now, then have to deal with her mother dodging phone calls for the next few months. No. This was happening today.

"Go ahead," she said to Doctor Gadsden. "Deal with her." Callie sat back in her seat. Jeb could do what he wanted... stand there and listen or leave. He needed to experience his grandmother's ways on his own and come to his own conclusions. She was struggling hard enough to deal with her own anger at Beverly's disregard for the time and lives of others.

The doctor went over the tests, none indicting heart issues, several underlining the need for her to get her diet and drinking under control. Her cholesterol was up, her kidneys weren't exactly a hundred percent, and she bordered on being anemic. Callie wouldn't have been surprised in the least if he'd mentioned cirrhosis, but he didn't.

Beverly took everything in without as much as a blink. In the end, all she had to say was, "May I go home now?"

The doctor agreed, and a nurse came in to free her from the equipment so she could get dressed. The ER needed the bed. The doctor had patients waiting at his practice. Callie had a dead body and a person still missing.

Son of a bitch, Mother!

Callie escorted Jeb out to the lobby while nurses took care of paperwork and Beverly fixed herself up proper enough to leave in public.

"You head back to Edisto," she told her son. "Go see Sprite, maybe catch a real nap. I'll get your grandmother home after I feed her breakfast somewhere." *And have a hard chat.*

He didn't argue. "She likes the restaurant Sweetwater, on Richardson Avenue. Opens at ten."

Callie looked at her watch to hide her surprise at Jeb knowing this and not her. Nine twenty-five.

Jeb seemed to be the collector of all things positive about his grandmother. Callie appeared to collect the negative.

"You have two years until you graduate," she said. A totally out-of-the-blue remark, but in her mind the leapfrog to the topic felt necessary. Beverly had reined in Jeb longer than usual this time.

"I'm not running for office any time soon, Mom."

"So she has discussed it with you."

He looked tired after last night—and at his young age—which meant she had to look somewhere between tired and dead. His laugh even sounded weary.

"Of course she has, Mom. Especially once she has a couple of drinks. It's funny listening to her invent the future. I just decided if the dream makes her happy, fine, I'll listen. With me having no idea what I'll be doing in two years, what can it hurt?"

This was the line they both walked. Him giving Beverly all the leeway in the world, and Callie drawing upon forty-plus years of her mother's *politics* to see the woman coming for him with a single-minded purpose that would not be denied.

Beverly and Lawton had attempted to groom Callie from the time she entered tenth grade. It had taken her moving to Boston and marrying a Yankee for them to sense she wasn't playing their sport. Politics was a long-tail game, though, and the two of them had been damn good at it. If Beverly wanted Jeb to run for office one day, this calling and beckoning, the coddling and spoiling, wouldn't end anytime soon. She hoped Jeb understood that.

"You can't run for mayor until you're thirty anyway," he tacked on.

Bam, right between the eyes. He'd pondered the thought long enough to at least look up the requirements. *God, Beverly.* The kid had ten years to go, yet here she was messing with his head, planting seeds, stroking his ego to coax him to enter public service with her, once again serving as the mastermind behind the campaign... like she'd done Lawton.

The problem was she was damn good at king-making. Her first time running for mayor after Lawton died, she ran unopposed. The community knew better than to defy the dynasty. They'd part the sea for Jeb, too. Beverly would make sure of it.

"Just promise me you'll look at all your options," she said. Saying more would only push him toward Beverly.

He hugged her. *Oh, glory days*, he hugged her, and she hugged him back so hard. The sun even shone brighter. She pulled away enjoying that she had to look up oh so high at him. "Let me go take care of your grandmother, and you go get some sleep."

"You need some, too," he said, and gave her another abbreviated hug before going to his car. But he halted halfway. "Wait, I haven't told her I'm leaving."

"I'll tell her. She'll understand. Go."

Inside, she reached the stall to find Beverly almost ready, the paperwork having been shot through amazingly fast to enable a quick release. She sat in that horrible plastic chair, an aide accommodatingly poofing up Beverly's hair.

"Let's go to breakfast," Callie said.

"Give me five minutes," Beverly said. "Isn't she good at this? I told her she ought to be a hairdresser instead of an aide."

Of course, they didn't leave for fifteen minutes, but Beverly eventually let them wheel her to the exit, and Callie pulled up in the patrol car. At the sight of the vehicle, Beverly almost refused to get out of the wheelchair.

"It's me or Uber," Callie said, holding open the door.

"Where's Jeb again?"

"On his way to his girlfriend at the beach. Afraid you're stuck with me, but I believe buying you breakfast might help make things more palatable."

"By now it's brunch," she said reaching out for Callie to take her hand, ever with a corrective remark.

With rush hour come and gone, the seven-mile drive took fifteen minutes, the car and its precious cargo earning them a free parking space at a meter, something Beverly was quite accustomed to.

Sweetwater had a delectable brunch menu. Callie didn't realize Beverly had gravitated to loving the place, but, hey, nice to know. Who didn't love omelets?

Callie reminded her mother to avoid the sauces and meats and go with something veggie. She suggested Beverly go more with straight fruit without the eggs, the recommendation punting the mayor back to spinach on her omelet. Coffee with no sugar. Whole wheat toast.

"Jeb wouldn't have pushed me so much—"

"Which is why I'm the one taking you home." Callie leaned in. "Gout? The first thing they tell you to avoid is alcohol." She didn't ask why her mother hadn't ceased drinking. Instead, she asked, "How the hell are you going to stop drinking living alone?"

Beverly unfolded the napkin instead of popping it open for her lap.

"I can do whatever I put my mind to do. I can taper off, if need be."

"You can indeed, Mother, and while you are stubborn as hell, people don't taper off booze. You quit cold turkey and suffer the results. Drinking—"

"Says the pot to the kettle." Beverly's stare came with one highly arched, well-manicured, tinted brow.

"Says someone who has stopped drinking."

But Beverly only grinned deeper. "How long since the last one?"

Callie almost said a couple years, referencing the rough patch after Seabrook died, but she sort of slipped off the wagon six months ago during her self-imposed sabbatical. When she regained her badge, she quit cold turkey. The return had meant that much to her.

She understood as much as anyone how difficult it was to quit. The trouble was her mother had been at it for as long as Callie had been alive, a lot deeper habit to discard.

"I'll email you a diet," Callie said. "But I doubt it will look much different than the one Doctor Gadsden already gave you." She didn't state the fact she'd be calling Beverly inquiring how she's doing, what she's eating, and how much she's drinking, hoping she wouldn't be wasting her time. Beverly had to want this, or it wouldn't happen.

No response, at least not to Callie. Beverly gave a saccharin grin to someone she recognized and returned interest to her coffee. She smiled up again at the mention of her name three booths down.

With all these familiars in the room, Callie leaned over to softly say, "And quit sucking in Jeb to run for office."

That grabbed her mother's attention. "I'm not."

"You are."

"He's practically an adult."

"He's twenty and practically a child. Give him a chance to graduate and make choices before you attempt to rein him in. You've planted your seed, he's aware, now give him space. I don't want to fight you on this, because he'll wind up disgruntled with both of us. He loves you, and he's proud of you. No doubt your not-so-subtle suggestions as to his future are logged into his head. How about trying to be just a spoiling grandmother? Show him your human side."

That speech landed Callie a *tsk* and an eye roll.

Okay, message delivered. Time to move on to the next topic. "What's this about you never wanting to come to Edisto again?"

This time the gaze in her coffee cup darted straight to meet with Callie's. "I'd had a drink when I said that."

Or two, or three... doubles. Drunk or not, she'd meant what she said. Beverly was a highly functioning alcoholic.

"Listen, Mother," and Callie leaned in tighter, her tone fainter. "I know you miss Brice. You might not believe this, but we all do. He was such a strong piece of Edisto, and nobody doubted his devotion to the beach."

"I didn't say that because of Brice." She took a sip of coffee to pause. "I... just don't seem to have the time, nor a place to stay anymore. I mean, you just built your new house, and you have your new man."

"Mark."

"Yes, Mark. The Cajun."

Callie let that stab roll off. "We welcome you to come stay any time you like. The floor plan is your old floor plan, as a matter of fact. I did that for you, and I think you'll like it."

Beverly acted as if she didn't know what to do with the hospitable gesture. The two women were more natural at being adversarial. They had been since Callie had hit puberty.

Their food arrived around ten twenty. Callie still had an appointment in Walterboro around noon to meet Nolan Brown to identify Elizabeth's body.

She let her mother eat, recognize passersby, and enjoy no obligations for ten or fifteen more minutes, then asked, "You aren't going in to work today, are you?"

"Haven't quite decided."

Beverly was probably working up the excuses and diagnoses to spin for her people so that it erred on the side of her being stronger, not debilitated. Never show weakness. She might not even tell them about the hospital, writing up her illness this morning to a sinus headache. The problem was, no telling who at the medical center had recognized the mayor.

"I have to be in Walterboro at noon, Mother." Best to let her know now so they didn't dally. "While I've got you, I'd like to pick your brain, if you don't mind."

Beverly gave her an expectant look and continued with her omelet.

"Are you familiar with the name Lydia Barron?"

"Should I be?" Fishing with a question, a trait of hers.

"The woman and her lady friends have come to Edisto Beach for thirty years, or so the story goes. I met her this week. One of her lady friends is missing, and for some reason she isn't too disturbed about the disappearance." She waited, hoping Beverly was taking her seriously and searching her mental data banks. "She just comes in the summers for about a month. That can't be too many people to choose from."

Beverly finished a bite, her tongue moving around inside over her teeth, hunting for pieces of spinach. A sip of coffee finished the job. "The name? Not familiar. And lots of people come back every summer."

"Not like this," Callie said, watching her closely, leaving off the part *and you know it.*

"I have heard of a group like that. Don't know them personally, though. Brice told me that he and Aberdeen had disagreements over them. Word was she, meaning Aberdeen, couldn't... *satisfy* him..." It was like she suddenly realized this was her daughter across the table. "He said... he said he..."

"I'm forty-three, Mother. I've heard and seen a lot more than you might imagine."

Just a hint of a raise of her mother's brow. "You were just out of college, still taking finals, had just told us you were marrying a Boston Yankee and leaving the state. It was about that time, if I recall, that Brice told your father about his *testosterone outlet.* Like Lawton needed that sort of thing." Beverly poo-poo'd the thought with a wave of the hand not holding her coffee cup. "Aberdeen's gone anyway, and Brice wouldn't—"

The reality of what she was about to say stopped her cold. Aberdeen had moved away after the divorce last year. Brice, however, wouldn't be around any longer to bitch about his ex.

"Mother," Callie said, actually reaching across the table to lay a hand on her mother's. "You miss him. He was a big part of your life once upon a time, and he was a piece of your life for all the years since. It's okay."

Her mother blushed. *Blushed!* But the cracked façade cracked further as the stoic, unflappable Beverly Cantrell blinked away moisture in her eyes and took back her hand. All Callie could think to do was pretend she didn't see the humanity that rarely saw the light of day.

"You were saying?" Callie asked after a moment. "He couldn't satisfy her so he... what?"

With a quick, discreet sniffle, Beverly proceeded. "He made friends with *The Summer Ladies.*"

"Meaning, he found himself a hooker?"

"Yes."

"That he nicknamed *The Summer Ladies?*"

"Oh, he didn't nickname them."

"Who did?"

"No idea, but the men around there, at least the ones who grew up there, understand exactly who that is, I dare say. I don't ask questions. Nobody does. Some of the wives were rather relieved when they came around, to be honest. Their husbands left them alone."

Callie sat back in her seat, studying this person who talked about a group of prostitutes as if they were a respectable ladies' organization come to town to sell their crocheting. Hell, why didn't they just set up a table at the Wednesday Bay Creek Market?

Why the hell had she not heard of them before now?

She struggled not to appear totally flummoxed. Zeller had spoken of prostitutes, but this sounded structured. They almost sounded acceptable.

"But you don't know their names?" she asked. Surely Beverly had a first name... something to go on.

"I never wanted to know," she said. "Why would it matter to me? My husband had his own private *fille de joie.*" She released a lazy chuckle. "Ought to ask Sarah, don't you think? She might have a better feel for women who bed married men."

Oh no she didn't.

"Stop right there, Mother, and back your royal ass up. You agreed to Daddy continuing to see Sarah because she gave me to y'all to raise. She is my biological mother. You aren't allowed to criticize her after, one, you removed me from being raised by her, and two, you gave Daddy permission to see her as long as you remained in the queen-bee seat politically in Middleton. The fact all of you—equally—hid my lineage until I was forty makes you no better and no worse than Sarah Rosewood and does not give you the right in any shape or form to look down your patrician nose at her. Sort of buys you a pass from being hated, in my book, so don't muck it up by thinking you are so high and mighty and in any way higher on the social strata than Sarah."

"Enough, dear," Beverly said, a bit taciturn.

Callie obliged by lowering her voice more. "Were my words clear?"

"Yes, yes, dear. And you are correct. The plans were put in place by all three of us, and we were united in that effort. Every bit of it was for your best benefit, though. You know that. Being raised by a family of privilege, with a husband and a wife, made more sense than living in that household. You're old enough for that not to bother you much, don't you think?"

The woman apologized but still pulled it off with arrogance and the upper hand.

This... just this... this style of communication was how they'd lived for decades. Rubbing between her eyes, Callie fought to get a grip. She understood this behavior. She could almost write the script, yet she let herself become far too riled at those moments. This was old news, water-under-the-bridge stuff. Why couldn't she learn?

And Beverly had deflected talking about the ladies.

"You can't identify any of these *Summer Ladies*?" she asked instead. "I can't see you not being curious enough to snoop once you knew about this."

"I don't snoop. And I didn't care. Let it be."

The funny part was that Beverly hadn't even asked why Callie asked these questions. She didn't care because it didn't affect her. Either that or Beverly wanted to appear that way. Callie ought to know which but didn't. Her mother was just that good.

They'd both pushed their plates back, and the time inched up on eleven. "I've got to go, Mother. Appointment in Walterboro. But I have one more topic to discuss, and we don't have to dwell on it."

The waitress came by, and Beverly held a hand over her cup, indicating she was done. The girl took their plates and left.

"When are you coming to Edisto?"

"No idea. When the mood suits me. When Jeb is there, if possible."

Callie mentally shook her head. Beverly couldn't come just to see her daughter even though Callie had dropped everything to make the hospital trip. This hospital incident hadn't been a complete waste of time, though. Beverly had informed her of *The Summer Ladies*, which was worth pursuing. Lydia Barron piqued Callie's interest even more so now having such a legacy that Beverly seemed to be unwilling to discuss. Maddy, a woman who might be a fledgling member of this call-girl sorority, wasn't meant to be disposable, either.

The craziness of last night also had Callie thinking about Beverly's future. She made a note to dig into her mother's wishes, health insurance, retirement plans, and will.

But all of it... the scare, the reality of her mother's age, her Edisto knowledge, her fear of returning to the beach, all of it, led to Callie asking something she never thought she would.

"Seriously, would you like to come stay with me a while?"

Beverly stared at her as though she hadn't heard when she most assuredly had. *For goodness' sake.* Callie had finally made her mother speechless.

Chapter 17

SEATED ACROSS from Beverly in Sweetwater diner, their brunch dishes down to empty coffee cups, silverware and glass noise amping up as the early lunch crowd began piling in, Callie's phone rang. Thomas. Noting his caller ID made her glance at the time. Five after eleven. God, she had to get to Walterboro and be there when Nolan Brown identified Elizabeth Brown's body. He shouldn't be doing that alone, and she needed to see his reaction when he did.

Thank God for the interruption, too.

She had just now, out of the blue, asked her mother to come and stay with her in Edisto, an offer that had stunned the both of them. Beverly hadn't figured out how to answer. Callie was afraid to say anything else. Beverly never got taken by surprise, which had paralyzed Callie.

The ring came again, an elderly woman at the table next to theirs looking over at the interruption. A waiter stared as well at the call not being taken right away. Beverly leaned back, as if she'd just gained a reprieve.

Damn it, if the caller hadn't been Thomas, Callie would've let it go to voicemail, but her officer should be finishing up the search of Elizabeth's car and condo. He wouldn't be calling if it weren't important.

"What's up, Thomas?"

"Hate to bother you with your mother and all, Chief. Is she okay?" He halted then added, "Have you got a sec?"

"She's fine and go ahead. What's up?" She'd had to catch herself before she asked *what's wrong.* Not with her being in uniform. Not in front of people perfectly aware she dined with the mayor. Ears would be dialed in.

"There's a Nolan Brown here, raising hell that we won't give him the keys to his wife's car. Literally, I had to cuff him, and he's in the back of my cruiser. We're standing outside the Pavilion right now with the whole world watching. What do you want me to do with him?"

Well, so much for being late to Walterboro. "What state of mind is he in?"

"Yelling, then crying. Acting a complete fool, but he was about to muck up our search of the vehicle. He didn't want us touching the car. Said he wanted it just like it was. Wanted it to smell like her, feel like her, and we were messing that up, he said."

"Is he a danger to you, himself, or anyone else?"

"He isn't armed, and he isn't much of a physical threat. I mean, I'm not seeing much brawn to this guy."

She wished she were there to take measure, and she wasn't in a proper venue to talk someone down off his wound-up bout of grief. She lowered her voice. "He's upset, Thomas. He was supposed to meet me in Walterboro in about forty-five minutes to identify his wife's body. Sounds like he's struggling to cope with that."

Thomas spoke to someone in the background, saying he'd be with them in a minute, then he told someone else to step away from the car. "Yeah, I can see that. But do you think he's capable of driving an hour on these two-lane roads to meet you?"

Again, this was not the place, and Thomas was trained to handle the disgruntled. "Talk to him. I still plan to meet him. You're good with people. Put those skills to use. Assess his ability to drive once you've calmed him down. Just text me when he's on his way so I can be looking for him and know when to start worrying if he doesn't show."

"Ten four, Chief."

She disconnected and sat there, envisioning what was going on back at Edisto.

"No," Beverly said.

Callie couldn't collect her wits for a moment before remembering where she and Beverly had left off.

"No?" Callie asked.

"I can't come stay with you. I have to run Middleton, and I'd prefer to stay with my things..." Beverly looked around and lowered her tone. "Not recuperate like some feeble old woman who can't remember when to take her meds."

Callie almost whispered for her mother's sake. "Are you on meds?"

"Cholesterol."

"What about the gout?"

"No med for that. Just prednisone or an anti-inflammatory when it flares. I just ignored it too much this time. All under control, dear."

Never would Callie trust her mother to tell the truth. Her mother was a control freak, especially when it came to her own life, and that control freak would control Callie's life if she moved in, so in a way, she'd gained a reprieve. That admission flashed a pang of guilt through her.

"Hate to rush you, Mother, but I have to hit the road. Let me get you home." She pushed her way to the edge of the booth.

"I hate riding in that car of yours. People will wonder."

Humor had crept back into the day. "Not anyone who matters, plus, you're the mayor. You oversee the police. Not unusual in the least."

"No, dear," she said, moving past Callie to the exit. "Police ride with me, not the other way around."

NOLAN HAVING detoured to Edisto bought Callie enough time to take her mother home and comfortably situate her in a recliner with a glass of tea and the shortbread cookies she had delivered from the local bakery run by a British woman on Richardson Street, coincidentally two doors down from Sweetwater. A grand habit of Beverly's was that she supported her locals.

Callie's trip to Walterboro was fifteen miles less than Nolan's, and she waited to leave until receiving the text from Thomas that Nolan was able to drive and on his way.

People identified bodies at the county medical center. Nobody ever thought about the where and how of such a business, and even people who visited the hospital weren't readily aware such an area existed. The various directories around the facility didn't openly give directions, but Callie had been there a couple of times, once for an officer of her own, and she'd given Nolan proper directions. Regardless, she waited at the hospital entrance. He arrived ten minutes after she did, and she escorted him down to the morgue.

The process was quick, the only time-consuming part being to allow Nolan to collect himself before being taken to see Elizabeth. Callie stood at his elbow, just in case. Nobody could predict how a person reacted to seeing the love of their life cold, pale, and empty.

He gasped, nodded, then turned away, leaning on the wall in lieu of Callie having to catch him, breathing deep. She waited until his breaths caught up with him then took him down the hall to a family area and sat him down in front of the glass of water already waiting.

The room wasn't unpleasant—soft beige paint, flowers on a table in the corner, and chairs deep blue, upholstered with fake leather, and ergonomic with arms. On one hand the chair was comfortably appealing. On the other hand, also easy to clean when someone peed, crapped, or threw up after identifying a loved one, with arms to help keep them from fainting and toppling to the floor. The smell wasn't bad, but it wasn't good either. It was clean yet memorable, a too-sanitized scent one wouldn't find anywhere else but in a hospital morgue.

It was what it was... a place for people to talk death.

She got him settled. They'd made Elizabeth rather presentable, if there was such a descriptor for the dead. Callie praised the heavens the bump on Elizabeth's head wasn't obvious anymore, and the shark bites had remained under the sheet. No one had told him about that part yet.

"How did she die?" he asked, the shakiness in his voice almost gone. She'd told him at home, but she had no problem telling him again.

"In layman's terms, she died from being hit on the head... or her head hitting something in a fall."

His breath sucked in. "She might've been murdered?"

"That's what we're trying to determine."

Nobody ever believed they'd experience murder. It was one of those things that never happened except to others.

"How was she found?"

Here we go. Here was as good a place as any to reveal details. "She washed up on the beach."

"Maybe she drowned." His voice leaped to a new level. "I kept telling her not to swim at night." He thumped the table with the butt of a hand. "I should've stayed, goddamnit."

"She didn't drown, Nolan."

"How would you know?"

"No water in her lungs."

Dazed, he mentally tried to argue with that. Callie could tell.

"Could... could somebody have made a mistake?" he asked, pleading. "She took care of sick babies, for God's sake! Who in their right mind would kill a pediatric nurse who held dying babies so they'd pass into heaven being loved!"

The room was made to absorb sound, too.

She understood the mixture of feelings roiling in his gut. It was the not knowing. The not knowing whether his wife had been viciously stolen from him by some other human being or she'd been slipped away by accident. The latter felt more like God's decree, and who could stay mad for long with the Almighty?

"No. She didn't drown. That fact is clear."

He looked down, accepting. "What about...?" But he couldn't think of anything else to speculate about.

"Did she have any enemies at work?"

He shook his head, despair deep around his eyes.

"Any relatives she didn't get along with?"

He looked at her as if she were insane. "She's the family's problem solver. There's her mother, her sister, and a niece, and a couple cousins she exchanges cards with, and they all think she walks on water."

Only the good die young kept playing in Callie's head. "You need to know one more thing, Nolan."

He froze, scared to death to hear anything else.

"She has shark bites on her hand and leg. Just so you know when you—"

His voice bounced off the walls. "A shark killed her?"

"No, Nolan." Callie kept using his name, to make him focus on her. "The head wound killed her. The shark bites were after she was already gone, before she washed up."

That was a lot of visual to absorb, so Callie hushed to let him. No doubt, after having gone to Edisto to retrieve his wife, after having left her there on her own to wander the beach at night, he blamed himself for not staying with her. Whether to deter a culprit or to be with her when she died, he blamed himself. Regret deeply etched his face. Callie had read this story chapter by chapter too many times before.

She left him to his thoughts and rose to fix herself a coffee from the far corner, asking him if he wished for one as well. He barely answered. She fixed it anyway, with ample sugar, an age-old prescription for high times of stress. He needed it.

Callie would be talking to Assistant Coroner Smith after Nolan left. While the Walterboro coroner's office wasn't some big-city CSI with gadgets and technology that almost flew people to the moon, they could read whether a hit on the head was from in front, behind, the side, or above.

But for now, her job was to tend to Nolan, see him through this, and gather shreds of intel to aid in solving the case. Personally, she didn't see him doing in his wife, but facts would be the final determinants. Marie would find the car tag on the causeway cam. The employer would confirm when he arrived at work. The trip was long enough that he may have had to gas up the car and, therefore, leave a paper trail. The neighbors might have spoken with him or seen him leave or come home or head to work. She'd retrieve those names and numbers before Nolan left the hospital.

Back at the table, Nolan finally sat in silence, thinking, having fallen deep within himself. Callie set his coffee before him and backed away, giving him that privacy and mental distance for a moment more.

Instead, he pushed back from the table. "I can account for my whereabouts. I told the Nortons I was going to Edisto, and asked if a package arrived, would they take it in. I saw them the next morning before I left for work, because the wife works at Boeing like I do, in HR. I stopped at a Waffle House on Savannah Highway on the way back, the second one. There are three, but you probably know that already."

She didn't but good to know.

"It's the one right before you get on the Mark Clark Expressway which brings me north to home."

He wasn't just missing Elizabeth. He was fearful of being a suspect. The husband is always the suspect per every movie, tv show, and streaming mini-series. It was almost a cliché, but like most clichés, at some time or another, they were grounded in fact. With nobody else to suspect, of course anyone would consider Nolan. He was giving her the material to rule him out.

"I appreciate that, Nolan. If you don't mind, write down the names, addresses, and phone numbers of the neighbors on all sides of you, so we can tie this up nice and tight."

He looked around the room, and she knew enough to go into a drawer back near the coffee pot to find pads and pencils. She put him to work, walked out in the hall, and called Stan.

"How's it going?" she asked. "And don't let him know I'm talking to you."

"Oh, I'm not with him this morning," he said. "But first, how's your mother?"

God, that almost seemed like days ago. "She's fine. She and her hoity-toity drama talked herself into believing gout was a heart problem because gout sounded too common. That and she liked having Jeb around."

"Could've been both, Chicklet. Even as surrounded as she is by that town and its people, she lives in a house alone, pretending that's what she wants. Sooner or later anyone gets lonely, and grandmothers love their grands."

Stan was approaching sixty, and he'd divorced his wife of thirty years only three years ago. They'd had no children, therefore, no grands. He'd moved to Edisto because Callie did. His best friend was Mark.

Yeah, he could talk living solo

She didn't tell him that Beverly wasn't pining away for her, because it couldn't be said without sounding childish. "Well, our family doctor blistered her fanny about taking up everyone's time. I took her to breakfast then home. Sent Jeb to Edisto to get some decent sleep."

She couldn't decide whether to be furious at Beverly or worry about how desperate her whole charade felt.

"Why aren't you with Thomas?" she asked, going back to the probable murder because, *surprise,* it was a more comfortable topic.

Stan gave a *humph.* "Raysor took over managing Thomas with his county forensic team, and from what I saw, they didn't need me. Should actually be done by now."

"So, nothing in the condo, huh?"

"Not a thing. Her prints were everywhere. A couple others on obvious surfaces like doorknobs. We expect to identify the husband's, and any of a number of assorted cleaning people. No sign of this being a crime scene, though."

"No sign of a crime scene, period," she replied. "I'm with the husband in Walterboro. He's putting on paper who can vouch for him at home and work. Marie's identifying his coming and going to the beach. Unless I'm horribly wrong and he's incredibly savvy in his movements, he's not our guy."

"I'd hate to think..."

"Yeah," she completed for him. "I do, too. Someone willing to kill a lone woman on a whim."

"On Edisto Beach."

"I'd rather someone be specific and focused on their vengeance."

"Ditto, Chicklet. I'm here if you need me. Good luck."

They hung up with Stan promising to check on things here and there, and Callie asking him to update Mark in detail at his leisure. In the meantime, she kept Mark aware of her whereabouts via texts. But she still let her mind play her conversation with Stan about violence on the beach.

People had died on Edisto. Drownings, a hot tub death, anaphylaxis from seafood. And there had been the smattering of intentional deaths, but they had been caused by a personally motivated individual going after a specific person. None of this *see what I can find and kill it* behavior. None of this *let's go to Edisto Beach and hunt.*

Even what appeared random at first glance often wasn't as random as most people thought. Because odds were that killers knew their prey, and the prey knew why they'd been targeted. She hesitated to label this death as one stranger accidentally killing another. She'd have to talk to those nurses again, and others that hadn't been on duty last night, in order to better learn who just might be an adversary to Elizabeth. The neighbors both at Edisto and outside Middleton as well.

Her thoughts came back to Nolan... then to what he said. *Could somebody have made a mistake?*

It had been dark, during a time Edistonians slept. What if the killer had indeed mistaken Elizabeth for someone else? What were the chances a killer had insomnia at the same time Elizabeth swam in the night? A killer out with a purpose made more sense.

She pushed back into the family room where Nolan sat at the table with his head in his hands, his paper of names and numbers shoved across the table to where Callie had been seated. "Nolan, have you ever heard of a group on Edisto called *The Summer Ladies?*"

He peered up, eyes moist, the alone time having called upon his tears. "What?"

"You've owned a condo for several years. Ever heard of some regulars on Edisto called *The Summer Ladies?* A group that comes and stays several weeks each summer?"

He slowly shook his head, peering back down. She could tell his mind wasn't exactly open to Q&A now.

Sliding a box of tissues to him, she reclaimed her seat across the table, tucking the paper in her breast pocket. "Do y'all know anyone on Edisto? Surely after five years—"

As if in a spasm, he started to slam his palms on the table then caught himself, a man too civilized to get lost in emotion. "Don't you get it? The condo was for her. I can count on one hand the number of times I've gone with her. The place was hers to get away and collect herself. I bought it for her. I'm a goddamn engineer, for Christ's sake, so I don't get how she even wants to take care of sick babies. She does it... did it, then when it was about to eat her alive, she ran off to Edisto to fix herself. I never could figure out how I fit into that... process." His cheeks were wet with his misery. "I couldn't tell you anything about anyone who lived out there." He buried his face in crossed arms on the table. "I just never knew what to do." And he wept.

No, Nolan Brown probably knew nothing about his wife's Edisto behaviors, and understood little about the personal hell his wife endured in order to do good. That disconnect, that chasm between them, had led to her also dying alone without him, and it would continue to be his personal hell to live with for many years to come.

She decided to leave him alone at that point. Telling him to take his time and make sure he was calm and focused enough to drive safely, she left the room to hunt for the assistant coroner. She couldn't find him and made a note to call later. For now, she felt an urgent need to head back to Middleton in attempt to catch the neighbors unaware, to ask them about Nolan's and Elizabeth's comings and goings, and their relationship. She'd call Boeing. Then she'd head home.

Nolan might not be familiar with Edisto, but Callie knew of others who were old-time residents who kept their ear to the ground. Sarah and Sophie. Then once she'd spoken to them, picked their brains, she would go back to Beverly to supplement or validate what they said. Or maybe that was an excuse to check on her mother. Either way, the extra call wouldn't hurt.

Then somewhere in between she'd corner Deputy Don Raysor with his fifty years of island knowledge.

Then she'd bring everything around with a one-on-one with the person who knew anything about everyone... Marie.

The plan would take her through tomorrow if she ran at a clipped pace. At first blush, her efforts at learning about *The Summer Ladies* had nothing to do with Elizabeth, but a niggle in the back of her brain whispered a theory that she couldn't dispel just yet. What if Elizabeth had been mistaken for Maddy? For sure they looked alike. Same age. Same build. Same coloring, as if that mattered in the pitch of night.

But without a killer, without even a crime scene, there was no putting this puzzle together by just focusing on Elizabeth.

Chapter 18

CALLIE'D SPENT two extra hours back in Middleton speaking to Nolan's neighbors, which took her into the afternoon. Between hers and Marie's work on Nolan's alibi, his timeline was falling into place, verbatim to what he'd professed. Back in the car, she parked in a McDonald's parking lot to call Boeing, praying someone remained at four forty-five in the afternoon. Their HR answered and tried to give her a hard time, but in the end said they'd release the information once Nolan told them they could. She called Nolan, who eagerly agreed to accommodate, and it wasn't five minutes before Boeing called her back, allowing her to tick that box off her list. Marie had already found his tag crossing the causeway on the town cam. Nolan was looking cleaner and cleaner.

Finally, she headed home, thinking more and more that Elizabeth had been in the wrong place at the wrong time, which only raised her level of apprehension. No clues. No damn friggin' clues in any direction, of any kind as to what happened to this woman. The delay of learning who she was hadn't helped. The culprit could be long gone by now. The problem with a tourist town was that people didn't hang around long enough to be suspected.

What a friggin' day. Once her cruiser reached the Big Bridge spanning the Dawhoo River, Callie let the sight of a dolphin below deliver some calm. Egrets tiptoed snow white along the edge of vegetation touching the water.

There, better. But also, not better.

The only slightest potential of a clue was Elizabeth's resemblance to Maddy, whom nobody could find. The coincidence of Maddy's disappearance and someone looking like her washing up was all Callie had—the thinnest thread of a possible connection to a possible murder.

The chance that this was an unsolvable case sent a deep creepiness through her bones. Anyone who got away with murder held the emboldened potential of doing it again.

For a second, she thanked the heavens that she policed a tourist town. The killer would likely be some other town's problem by the end of the week.

But as safety and protection for Edisto Beach, her duty pushed her to fix this—now—for Edisto and so that it wouldn't become some other town's problem. The frustrating part was not having any idea what direction to pursue.

She put in a call to her other mother. The call dropped. She dialed again. Phone signal had its temperamental patches on the island, and she huffed at her failure the second time, trying again. She caught a signal, but only long enough to ask Sarah if she could come by. She got a positive reply, then lost the call.

Sarah Rosewood's affair with Lawton Cantrell hadn't been much of a secret to many of the established residents on Edisto, and Sarah had attempted an explanation a half-dozen different ways, each time apologizing for not having been more proactive in Callie's upbringing. She had loved Lawton before he met Beverly, but somehow, she and Lawton hadn't been able to abandon the relationship. Lawton had his love on Edisto, and his partner in Middleton, and he was perfectly fine with that.

They resumed their trysts in a random manner, with no particular plans, but the need for a plan reared its head when Callie came into the picture.

They agreed to hide her DNA for a while, which crept into forty years, yet they all three agreed that Lawton could see Sarah, and Beverly could see whomever she wished at the same time—which had been none other than Brice LeGrand, who'd courted Beverly before Beverly joined forces with the well-connected Lawton. But Beverly had remained loyal to Lawton.

Callie felt she was spawned by irresponsible teenagers.

But it wasn't as if she'd been mistreated, forgotten, or left to her own devices.

Like dear Marie, for instance. Her mother had left Marie with her grandmother when Marie was a toddler. Her grandmother then died— after a rough life of poverty and hate of men—when Marie was in high school. Yet having practically raised herself, Marie was a damn fine woman, conscientious, and loyal to all things Edisto.

Nurture or nature. Callie didn't give a damn. She just wanted someone she could call Mom, whom she could run to for advice and a hug. Beverly colored outside those lines.

But she was shrewd and had taught Callie good and bad ways to live. The gin... not so good; however, she'd been encouraged to develop and use her intelligence and keen cleverness, which had taken her far. While she hadn't learned quite as much or in the manner in which Beverly probably wanted, Callie had learned how to study, read, dodge, and interrogate people along with a few other political tricks practiced by the tough woman she'd known as her mother for most of her life.

But this hospital affair had seemed to crack that tough Beverly façade, giving a sense to observers who knew her intimately that her game might be slipping. Regardless of their feuding, that pained Callie. As much as she might dislike Beverly's ways, seeing her lose a tight grip on herself was uncomfortably sad.

Like the passing of an era.

She went by the Presbyterian Church and its cemetery on her left, along with Mike Seabrook's grave, the twinge not as acute these days. Time had a way of healing, scarring, or simply dulling the discomfort of events. And with the passing of such people, those left behind lost historical knowledge.

Beverly had suggested, in her astringent manner, that the seniors on the island might know more about *The Summer Ladies*, talking as if that cadre of folk didn't include herself. So at Beverly's suggestion, Callie was headed to Sarah's for a history lesson as well as a taste of that motherly love.

But before she reached the beach, she placed another call to Thomas.

"A travel cup in the cup holder held dregs of dry coffee, the only prints on it hers. We interviewed folks in the Pavilion. No one had seen her, but someone in Coots said she came in alone the night before we found her. Met a girl her age. They got along, and they left sober, laughing even. Nobody saw where they went."

"Video?" she asked.

"Nope."

"Description of the other girl?"

"Similar age and similar hair is all. Left together, either in the other girl's car or on foot since Elizabeth's car stayed put. No one else left with them."

"You showed them both Maddy's picture as well as Elizabeth's?"

"I did, but they said they couldn't be sure it was Maddy, but they couldn't say it wasn't, either. They hadn't seen her before and haven't seen her since. Some had seen Elizabeth from other visits."

Such an innocent scenario played out all the time. Locals and visitors pour into a place, make friends, invite each other to another place or someone's house, even just out for a walk on the beach. Especially the singles.

"What time did they leave?" she asked.

"Sometime after eleven that night. Maybe midnight."

In the dark, too. Who'd see them and remember any semblance of details in the night?

They had a new suspect now, but was it Maddy? This type of movement wasn't in line with what Lydia and even uptight Chiara had described as the last-known intention or location for Maddy. She'd had a date in the middle of the day. She hadn't called and didn't come back. This leaving with Elizabeth was practically a half day later, after her ladies' group had been frantically texting and calling for her to check in.

But then, Maddy had disappeared for reasons unknown. Her possible presence in Coots so late sort of supported her distancing herself from the group.

But Elizabeth washing up on the beach and Maddy nowhere around piled on more questions. Did Maddy kill Elizabeth and bolt? Did someone else kill both of them with only Elizabeth's body brought in with the tide and marine creatures and happenstance taking Maddy's to the depths? Or was Maddy taken and Elizabeth cast aside, one being less able to fend off a lethal blow? Or had someone killed Elizabeth by mistake, instead of Maddy?

Her mind raced, alert with the fresh what-ifs.

If Maddy wasn't a victim, she could be a witness... or the killer.

"Chief?"

"Just a second," she said, the causeway leading back to her beach only a mile ahead.

This was Thursday. Check-ins were usually Saturday afternoon or Sunday. Check-outs were the same with about six hours in between. Each week meant turnover, so a person could enter Edisto with bad intentions or even just pull an impromptu criminal stunt and be gone before they could be identified.

She had no choice. Time to text the residents a community emergency notice to be on the lookout for Maddy. Regrettably, also time to put an all-hands-out to hunt for Maddy, whether her lady friend group wanted to find her or not. Whether they wanted the publicity or not. Nobody had filed a missing persons complaint, but she felt strongly enough after Thomas's findings to proceed.

With the car parked at the Pavilion, the condo on Wyndham at the far end, and the body washing up even further around the sound, that could mean one to two hundred houses, or more. Add to that the fact that most of these people were transient, and seeing a girl in a bathing suit walking at night wasn't unusual. Unless the coroner found something critical on his end, there wasn't much to go on other than the hope some random person had seen two random women sometime late Tuesday or early Wednesday.

She told Thomas to get started. Trained on the grid of Edisto Beach, her officers would understand where and how to start once they had the updated particulars about the two women. She called Marie to call in the officers, to include Raysor. Callie would call Stan and Mark as well, ever her backups.

She hadn't spoken to Mark in ages. What she wouldn't give to go home with him right now, this very minute, and sleep for two days.

"We're knocking on doors tonight," she said, informing him herself. "Any chance you are up for it?"

"You have a tip on the dead girl's killer?"

"Yes and no." She explained the sighting of the two women walking the beach. "If there's a chance Maddy has been seen since, or if anyone saw what happened to them that night, we need to chase the lead. We aren't sure if she's the killer or a victim, alive or dead, but we've reached a dead end with Elizabeth. To have these two worlds cross makes me worried we're running out of time. It's been over forty-eight hours since Elizabeth died, and almost as long since Maddy was reported missing. We've lost too much time as it is."

"Sure. I pair with Stan as usual?"

"Yes, sir."

"We're on it." He didn't hang up, so she didn't either. "How's your mother?" he asked.

"For the first time I got a little scared, honestly. I'll tell you the long version later, but bottom line is she's fine. But it gave me insight into how quickly she won't be fine."

"Not sure I follow."

"Yeah, I know. Too much to tell you on the phone. But she is home and back to normal." Speaking of Beverly made her think of *The Summer Ladies*. Callie had about decided that at every path she crossed from this point forward, she'd be asking if anyone had heard of them. To include Mark.

"Have you ever heard of a group of women called *The Summer Ladies*?"

"Maybe."

"Maybe?"

"I mean, I've heard the term used. At first I just thought it was a catch-all for girls in bikinis on Edisto in the summer. You know, the summer ladies. Guys wink and such. I didn't give it much thought. Why?"

"They might be an annual group of ladies of the evening, so to speak."

"No joke!" he said and chuckled. "Guess that shouldn't be a surprise."

"No," she agreed, chagrined at not having known before now. "But when you knock on your doors, can you also ask if they've heard of such a group?"

"Like someone is going to talk about knowing prostitutes?"

"They might talk rumor and gossip, Mark. But I appreciate it. And I really appreciate you helping us."

"You'd do the same for me, Sunshine."

"Huh?"

"You know, if I was down a waitress or cook."

She let that sink in, picturing herself in uniform waitressing in a Mexican restaurant.

"I was joking," he said.

"And here I was trying to decide if I was waitress material," she said.

"Let me go line up the staff so I can start that door-knocking. You called Stan?"

"Not yet."

"I'll do it. Go to work, Chief. Love you."

"Love you back."

She hung up, one part grateful for him and one part disgusted at the fact she had to use him, as well as Stan, to step in when she was shorthanded. Town council had agreed to take her last meeting's report *under advisement* when she'd asked for two more officers, which meant no more than noted for the record.

Callie's grid involved Jungle Road, where she lived, and she better get on it.

She happened to be right there and turned onto Jungle, aiming to start at Sarah's house, then Sophie's, then she'd visit each resident up and down her assigned blocks.

But then she remembered she hadn't heard from Chiara, who was supposed to send her Maddy's sister's phone number. She needed it even more now. Callie would bet a week's pay that Lydia had told Chiara to ignore the request. Maddy could become a serious person of interest now, and in a quick second thought, she realized she didn't want anyone other than her to knock on the door of *Time in a Bottle*. Nobody but she needed to speak to Chiara Hamilton or Lydia Barron.

Weird. Lydia was falling into the same category as Beverly, someone who thought herself too smart to adhere to everyone else's rules.

She passed Jungle Road where Sarah resided, slowed, then made a command decision. She turned left and drove several blocks to where she could shoot down Palmetto to *Time in a Bottle*. A little voice told her not to announce her arrival. It was late afternoon, early evening, and she'd better rush to catch them home before their *dates* began.

En route she called Nolan to say the car was his to collect, and they'd be moving it to the police station for safekeeping until he arrived. He didn't answer, so the voicemail had to do.

Hanging up, she regretted having arranged to meet Sarah, but a dead girl trumped Callie needing her mother, even if she was also going to ask about *The Summer Ladies*. While she'd originally wanted to ask Sarah about Lydia's group out of curiosity, now they had a loose connection between Elizabeth and Maddy, making the question essential. But first she had to talk to Lydia and the crew.

She reached *Time in a Bottle* and parked in the drive, texting Sarah that she'd be late, and she should let her know if they needed to reschedule tomorrow. Not waiting for her response, Callie left her cruiser and headed to the front door. Mid-step, Sarah's answer texted back, *Take your time. I'll wait up for you.*

Yeah, that's how a mother was supposed to be.

Someone flipped the light on as she reached the last few steps, and Lydia answered the door before Callie had a chance to knock.

Bare footed and drink in hand, Lydia filled the threshold wrapped in that handsome shawl of red embroidery against velvet stitched atop an antique sepia background, the same shawl as when Lydia had come out to the beach to inspect Elizabeth's body.

"Evening, Chief."

"Evening, Ms. Barron."

She gave a crooked smile. "Lydia works. It's not like we haven't gotten to know each other of late."

Callie didn't reciprocate the offer to the woman to call her other than Chief. "Is Chiara home?"

"Out with friends," came the reply, still with no invitation to come inside.

"Mind if I still come in?" Callie asked, not the least bit social.

Lydia pulled her shawl together one-handed, near the throat. "Told you, Chiara isn't here. Neither is Robin."

Nothing was said about Vivien, and Callie tilted her head to show she waited for an accounting of the others.

"Vivien is on the porch, if that matters."

The question begged to be asked. "And Maddy?"

"She says she's coming home."

Stunned at that revelation, Callie hesitated, having expected the household to still tout the girl gone. "Here? Today?"

"Yes. Tonight." Still no invitation inside.

Even having seen the attitude, Callie still had no idea how to take the *laissez-faire* demeanor. "May I speak to you and Vivien then? We may have had a sighting."

The shift in posture, the slight expression around her eyes showed that Lydia hadn't expected that.

Callie waited silently.

"I guess, come on in," Lydia said, stepping back inside the house. "Drink?"

Callie grinned slightly at the offer and said she remained on duty. Lydia continued without a break in step to the back porch where Vivien was indeed relaxed in a rattan chair, feet resting atop an old woven ottoman. She didn't show surprise and held up a wine glass containing a red with fruit split and positioned around the rim. "Welcome to paradise, Chief."

"I was headed to the powder room then going to refresh my drink. Be right back," Lydia said, then paused in leaving. "Offer still stands on a drink. Water? I'm sure there's orange juice."

Callie shook her head, and Lydia disappeared inside.

The house faced west, meaning that after seven, going on eight, color painted the horizon orange and pink, the shreds of clouds showing lavender undersides. The sound caught no breeze, the water tranquil. The dune grass, however, looked as if the tips were on fire, the seed heads and fluff vivid instead of their usual beige.

Callie turned away. She hated dusk. Hated the pretense of fire, a personal phobia she'd yet to shed. Taking one of the wicker chairs by the back, she slid it around such that she could see the ladies instead of being distracted by the scene. The sun still gave Vivien's complexion a hint of a glow, but that Callie could handle. They sat silent, waiting for

Lydia, Vivien fixated on the sunset, clearly not engaging until her partner's return.

Didn't take long for Lydia to show, and the two women clearly exchanged looks, trying not to appear affected that their visitor came unannounced, with purpose, and unwilling to be relaxed by the glory of the evening water.

Lydia rearranged her shawl around her and eased into her chair an arm's length from her bestie. "The chief says Maddy may have been sighted around the island, Viv."

"Really?" Vivien seemed legitimately surprised, then her expression slid into puzzlement. "What does *may have been sighted* mean? If she was seen, when and where?" She stopped herself. "Did Lydia tell you? Maddy's coming home tonight? Trust me, whatever you tell us will be incorporated into our discussions with her. She's been way more baggage than expected. Not the best impression on her maiden voyage with us."

"Where do you assume she's been?" Callie asked.

"A new friend is our guess. As we've tried to explain, we are not familiar with many of her ways, chief. We relied on Chiara, and even she's disappointed with how this week has played out."

Lydia waited for Vivian to stop. "Explain this sighting you mention. I'd like to have a feel for why she felt more comfortable with a stranger than us... or Chiara, even. Someone might've even put ideas into her head. *Rude* is a word that comes to mind. And she still owes a share of this rental. We're not letting her walk away from that obligation. No, ma'am."

Callie heard Lydia but watched Vivian. Her expression shifted from a slight frown to observation, then understanding. She was clearly Lydia's right hand and loyal compatriot and following the woman's lead. If Lydia said Maddy vanished in a puff of smoke, Vivien would let that sink in and agree. A friend to the end.

"She was possibly spotted walking the beach at night with another woman she met at Coots," Callie said.

"Possibly?" Vivien asked.

"The description fits, but since nobody knows Maddy, we can't necessarily confirm."

"So talk to the other woman," Lydia said.

"We can't," Callie said. "She's the dead one found out there." She thumbed over her shoulder toward the water.

"Oh!" Vivien's drink slipped in her hand, sloshing wine across her lap. "Oh, shit!" she said, leaping up.

Callie just let the behavior play out. Lydia didn't exclaim nor offer to run inside and grab a towel. Instead, Vivien scampered inside, a trail of *shits* heard into the kitchen.

That left Callie alone with Lydia. And Callie recognized the new pillow on the rattan settee beside Lydia. It was the spitting likeness of those in Brice's window seats. It hadn't been there before.

And Lydia watched her studying it.

Callie made eye contact, trying to see her as the woman who bedded Brice.

"I hope you don't think Maddy killed the girl found on the beach," Lydia said.

Callie hid any reaction. "The girl's name was Elizabeth Brown. A pediatric nurse from Middleton, not far up the road. She was married to an engineer."

The personal about the dead girl seemed to stun Lydia a little. "I'm familiar with Middleton."

If she'd been coming here for decades, she would naturally be familiar with Middleton. But that wasn't the point.

When Callie didn't say more, Lydia continued. "Shame. She was pretty."

No concern that Maddy may have wound up the same way. No talk about how that event may have chased Maddy into hiding. No asking if Maddy was a person of interest.

Callie had an open crime on the books, and this woman kept drifting around the edges of it tightlipped and cold as a damn iceberg, drawing even more attention to herself, in her opinion.

"So, Chief," Lydia said. "We'll have Maddy herself call you when she gets in, as we promised. And since Chiara isn't here for your other questions, how about letting us fix you a drink? Surely, you're off for the day now."

"No thanks." She never told people she abstained for any reason other than she was in uniform.

"I assume you wanted to talk to Chiara about Maddy. We can get Maddy to give you that. She can text or call, your choice."

What Callie wanted wasn't anything secretive. "We'd like a list of Maddy's friends, the boyfriend, of course, her employer, and the sister and any other relatives. Her home address and phone number. I've collected some of this information but would like to validate it."

"But if she returns, she's no longer missing."

"I need the information whether she's missing or not. Someone looking like her was seen with Elizabeth Brown. It's no longer a matter of her bee-bopping around the beach any longer."

Lydia seemed to need to rethink that. "We'll have her get in touch."

Callie wouldn't hold her breath.

"I know we haven't gotten along, Chief," Lydia started, but Callie stopped her with an open palm.

"The point is to help me now."

Lydia recrossed her legs, repositioning the shawl. "I wish Chiara hadn't come to see you. She's blown this all out of proportion."

"On the contrary, Ms. Barron. It helped us. Knowing about Maddy made us look harder at the sighting of Elizabeth Brown. She could be connected to Elizabeth Brown's death. She's on my radar whether y'all wanted her found or not, whether she wanted to come home or not. At least now I'm not looking for another body, someone kidnapped, or an accident. She's safe and sound and coming home."

Vivien came back in, still dabbing at the wet spot on her pastel palazzo pants. That spill would leave a stain, for sure.

"While I have you both, I'd like to ask you a question I've been asking others," Callie said.

That stopped Vivien from dabbing. Lydia just stared, muscles still.

"Y'all wouldn't happen to be *The Summer Ladies*, would you?"

Chapter 19

Lydia

LYDIA'S BLOOD RAN chilled all of a sudden. "Pardon?" she said.

The police chief sat poised, still, and focused in a deck chair across from her and Vivien on the back porch. She'd dropped in without announcement, very inappropriately, and had made herself at home across from Lydia and her friend. She scolded herself for being surprised, then to top it off, she caught the chief noting Brice's pillow. She willed her pulse back to normal, but not without effort.

Chief Morgan was astute, but Lydia didn't have the time to admire her talents. She'd deduced who the ladies were, and, thanks to a weak moment in grabbing a memento, had guessed Lydia broke into Brice's house.

The trick was, which ones would she capitalize on?

And no doubt she'd attempt to dig at them, to break tongues loose about things they didn't need revealed.

But these women, particularly Lydia and her buddy, weren't novices.

"Have you heard of a group called *The Summer Ladies?*" Chief Morgan asked again.

Lydia blessed the stars above that Robin and Chiara were not home.

"We're ladies," and Lydia looked at Vivien who nodded in agreement. "And we return every summer." She followed with a dip of her chin, putting a period on the end.

Oh, how lame that sounded. Canned, and it almost came across like a cover-up, but admittedly, she'd been caught off guard. Nobody used that nickname openly. The ladies sure as hell didn't, and they hadn't been the ones to make it up to start with and didn't know who did.

The chief turned to Vivien for her next tactic. Viv was solid, but she was often too genuine for her own good. There was a reason she practiced paper instead of courtroom law.

Lydia had to hand it to this Morgan woman. She took her time with her words, adept at confronting people not wanting to be confronted. From what she'd heard of Callie Jean Morgan, she had quite a few solid years' experience in law enforcement, and she enjoyed being good at her job. Lydia'd met her mother and liked her, giving her more knowledge about Chief Morgan than the chief realized. Actually, Lydia had appreciated her reputation and given the woman a high degree of respect... until the group had become her pet project.

"A group of women is rumored to come back each year to meet friends and stay a few weeks, with a long track record of doing it. Like you ladies. What do you say, Viv?" the chief asked, using the nickname she'd heard Lydia use.

"I... I think it's a good name," she said.

Good heavens, Lydia thought. *Vivien answered worse than I had.* Lydia clung tight to a grimace, keeping her feelings to herself. Bless her, Viv usually responded better under pressure than this, but, frankly, so did Lydia.

"Any chance that is your group's name?" the chief asked, lasering in on her, sensing the easier target.

"What? No," Viv replied. "Why would we need a name? We're friends, not some organization. But it sounds like a perfectly good name for a group meeting each summer. It has a rather refreshing sound to it, too. Like the cover of a beach read."

Much better.

My turn. "You sure someone isn't just using those words on a more informal basis, with it not being a name? Like, *those summertime ladies,* meaning they're only seen during vacation time each year? Part of why we repeatedly return is to see others who do the same, like any other group."

"They seem to have a regular... clientele."

That was a pleasant way of saying hookers. But the chief wasn't about to call them prostitutes. She knew who they were and what they did, skirting the edge of formal society, but it wasn't really pertinent to Maddy's disappearance and Elizabeth's death. Until she made that connection, she couldn't afford to throw hard accusations about whoring around this beach. Not with their clientele list.

So Lydia shrugged. She hated the gesture, honestly. It reeked of lying, and in their experience, they'd learned to read people. Like she was reading the police chief right now. She'd pieced enough thoughts together to suck them into the dead woman's case and was intent on whittling at them until she was satisfied, one way or the other. Not good.

Lydia's earlier thoughts at Brice's place came racing to the forefront, and a thought she'd realized there suddenly became something they needed to do, immediately upon the chief's departure. Lydia stemmed the urge to knead the braid on the nautical pillow she'd taken from there, but the chief read her.

"Lovely pillow. Reminds me of those at the house of a friend of mine. He was killed not long ago."

Their gazes met, and Lydia had to force herself to maintain hers. *Yeah.*

"Where are the other two ladies?" the chief asked, taking a sharp turn from needling Lydia. "Robin and Chiara, I believe?"

She damn well remembered their names. "On dates," Lydia said.

"Dates," she repeated.

"Two girls out with two guys. Not sure what else you call it."

The dare was on the table, but Lydia didn't think the chief could say the word.

Chief Morgan lifted her head a bit, eyed her, then shifted her gaze to Vivien. Thank God, Viv donned her innocent look as if waiting to be asked another question, expecting to be too naïve and ignorant to answer. She was good at that.

"Officers are knocking on doors tonight, ladies," the chief said. "Hunting for Maddy."

"But we told you she was due in tonight," Vivien said. "Why waste—"

"They are also hunting for people who can identify either Elizabeth or Maddy. They are canvassing the beach in hopes someone saw them and can shed light on what may have happened the other night. Please cooperate if they call on you."

Lydia craved to ask if she was scouting them out in advance, reading them, then siccing her officers on them with a line of questioning designed to piggyback on this one. She wanted to ask if their household was the only one being treated that way. Likewise, Lydia craved to learn if the chief suspected they had anything to do with that woman's death.

Such questions, however, sounded like defensive queries from guilty parties.

The long game was Lydia's forte, so she kept quiet.

Not that any of them was guilty of Elizabeth Brown's death. But still, Lydia sat playing phrases in her head, wondering if she was second-guessing herself into being some sort of suspect.

She'd spent thirty damn years flying under most people's radar, to avoid people interfering into her business, past and present. She could be a friend. She could be a lover. But she never spilled her life to anyone. She learned a long time ago that personal space was important if you didn't want to get hurt.

Each person was their own best advocate.

"We'll have Maddy call you," she said.

Chief Morgan's stare narrowed.

Lydia tried not to squint back in return.

"She'll have to talk to me in detail about her whereabouts since the night of Elizabeth's death."

"Goes without saying."

"A lot is going without saying, I think." Morgan stood. She headed through the sliding doors to the inside, a direct line to the front door.

Lydia started to just let her let herself out, but rudeness and inappropriate manners only made them more memorable, more adversarial, and would only make matters worse. She rose and hurried to catch up, making all the right noises about thanks for coming, and how much they appreciated her being concerned for Maddy, but the chief didn't miss a step continuing to the door.

In the threshold, she turned, noted Viv remained on the porch, and whispered, "I'm not sure why you're holding out on me, Ms. Barron, but I will get to the bottom of it."

No, she wouldn't, Lydia thought.

She'd never learn, not even if Lydia's life depended on it, because once upon a time, she learned that police did very little for a woman in a crisis, even less in a chronic situation. Your life rested in your own hands if you wanted to have any kind of life at all.

The chief had been trying to read her mind, and while she hadn't, she wasn't giving up.

Finally, the chief turned and left, taking the stairs slowly as if she had a great weight on her. Maybe she did, but not their problem.

Lydia had realized a long time ago that you selectively chose your fights, and that discretion carried you a lot further than fighting. This woman wasn't fighting them, though. She was doing her job, but that didn't mean she couldn't wreck their lives in doing so.

In a lot of cases, people don't know what hurts them... until it does.

Lydia waited until the chief pulled out of the drive, then waited another minute to ensure she didn't come back.

"Viv," she said loud enough to be heard on the porch, but her friend had slipped up behind her.

"Go get Maddy?" Vivien said.

"Yes," Lydia replied. "No telling when she has to address these people, and it's time she got her shit together."

Chapter 20

CALLIE SAT BEHIND the wheel of her car for a minute or two with a couple of glances up at the backlit doorway. Lydia peered down for a little while then disappeared. Callie sensed the match of wills. Not just right now, but forthcoming.

She had no justification for a warrant to go through the house. She did expect, however, to hear from Maddy as promised. Those two ladies had sense enough to realize Callie'd be back straight away if she didn't.

She had Chiara's cell number, though. While Lydia and Vivien appeared to be old pros at diversion, Callie bet Chiara was not.

The call rolled to voicemail. Callie left a message, asking her to get in touch ASAP, day or night. There'd been a Maddy spotting on the beach, and Callie still needed the personal information she'd requested before, and more. Chiara wouldn't know Callie had already been by the house.

Hanging up, she bet that Chiara would still ask Lydia for guidance before calling. Lydia's hold on these women was potent.

Now she needed to canvas houses and see Sarah. Unfortunately, the decision to knock on doors had been made late in the day, once they'd learned about the possibility that Elizabeth had been seen with Maddy. That meant eventually interrupting people around bedtime, but sometimes you did what needed doing. That didn't give her much time.

She took the back way to Jungle Road, down Dock Site Road. At the west end of Jungle, she began knocking on her assigned doors. Mark had his set of blocks. Stan had his. Each officer had theirs. It also meant spending overtime for some of these officers, something the budget didn't have much of, and she even started making excuses to use for when Brice would come fuming and fussing about the town's coffers... only to remember those times were gone. Made her wonder who would hold her accountable now.

Edisto Beach had an emergency notice system used for such events as riptides, missing seniors, even the sightings of Mary Lee, a 16-foot,

3,500-pound female great white shark whose territory up and down the Atlantic included Edisto waters. The simple notification system went far in making Edisto residents feel safe.

Lydia stated Maddy was due back to *Time in a Bottle* this evening. Maybe she was. Or maybe they wanted her to stop looking for her. But Maddy hadn't appeared yet. She hadn't called. How was she supposed to believe for sure that Maddy would show up and divulge where she'd been and who she'd been with?

She'd already put out a text notice of a missing girl named Maddy Gillespie and some statistics, the defining characteristics being the two-inch gold hoops on her ears and a necklace with a gold circle carrying two diamonds, per what Chiara had described. In conversation with the people they canvassed tonight, they would likewise see if anyone had seen Elizabeth, but she didn't want to activate the system for a text on Elizabeth. The point was to avoid people wondering if this was the dead girl.

In conversation with these people, the two women were missing, and the families were concerned. No more, no less.

The Charleston television reporter who handled the Edisto beat—whose grandmother happened to live on Jungle Road and made the best chocolate chip cookies on the planet—had called Callie on the way home from Walterboro, querying whether or not a name could be released yet. Alex Hanson kept her relationship with Callie civil and professional, without tricks, because the entire journalism community along the coast understood Callie's dislike for the profession. Piss her off and you got nothing... forever.

But with Nolan having been notified about his wife and Elizabeth formally identified, Callie went ahead and told Alex, with the standard proviso not to embellish or throw out the *what-if* fabrications that her ilk were noted for spewing. Callie hoped that meant only one television station airing the name as a point of news and not speculation. Since Elizabeth was not someone exceptionally notable beyond her circle of friends and family, the press would move on quickly.

She also prayed that few Edisto folks caught the news tonight. Visitors usually tuned out the news while vacationing. Realistically, however, her hope of the story blowing over was a slim hope. That death certificate would only open the door to more questions. Somebody would think murder, then others would want to know the how, when, and why. Callie began to accept she had little time to function without people breathing down her neck for answers. The press would call the mayor who would require updates while telling her to keep things on the downlow. No one wanted Edistonians worrying about a killer on the loose.

Honestly, she didn't expect anyone in the houses she canvassed to have seen much since they were four and five blocks in from the sand. The two women had met at night and left at night, and Edisto wasn't exactly lit up. But there was the slim possibility they'd been seen enough to be remembered clearly in Coots, Whaley's, McConkey's, the Sea Cow, or the Waterfront. Pressley's or the Marina. Enough people hunted for loggerhead nests in the middle of the night these days to stroll the water's edge, but again, it was dark, and it's rude to shine a flashlight in someone's face to see who they might be. The odds just weren't good, but Callie and her crew had to try.

No way they'd hit everyone tonight, though.

Thomas and Annie, bless them, had already covered Wyndham as part of their search in and around the Brown condo, at least about Elizabeth. Now they had to repeat their tracks to inquire about Maddy.

Having spoken to residents along the driving path from the front gate to the condo, and everyone in view of her building, Thomas reported that nobody saw anything abnormal about Elizabeth. Only two saw her drive away due to her odd, upside-down hours. Nobody saw her return, again due to her backwards-activity agenda of staying out at night and returning early dawn. Someone said they may have seen her car the next day. No assurances. People checked in and out of properties all the time. The best place in the world to hide out was in plain sight in a tourist town. You were invisible.

Callie covered house to house until ten thirty, when the lights started going out, but because she knew most of these people, she continued, telling herself she'd stop at Sarah's and call it a night. At eleven, she radioed her crew to do the same.

Nobody had seen either woman. Same for all her officers. They would begin anew tomorrow. To wait longer would mean running out of the week, and the people in the houses would rotate through. She would personally talk to the workers at Coots again tomorrow, not that Thomas hadn't done his job. There might be someone new there, or the ones he spoke with thought about things after he'd left and realized how important their input was. Maybe they'd remember a detail to share.

But this day was about done.

Sighing with relief and exhaustion, last night having given her nothing but snatches of naps at the hospital, she pulled her cruiser into her own drive at *Chelsea Morning*. Mark's car wasn't there. He wasn't home yet from canvassing residents, so she texted him where she'd be and walked the two houses down to Sarah Rosewood's home. She told him not to wait up.

This would now be the second night since they moved in that she didn't welcome him when he came to bed. Felt weird.

The night was a dark one, and it was late enough that the crickets and frogs had gone to bed. A raccoon scurried twenty feet to her right, checking trash can lids. Hearing the snap of twigs, she flashed her pocket light around Sophie's house to spot two deer strolling down Jungle Shores.

Creatures came out en masse on this beach after dark, the deer being the most sought-after encounter, the most photographed. Strangers oohed and aahed at them, thinking them wildlife when in fact they were practically domesticated and highly inbred due to their isolation on the town's island-like perimeter. Albino and piebald deer walked the golf course, venturing out to stroll the streets at night. She'd seen the well-known "stunted buck' on the west end twice. His ten-point rack showed broad and impressive from his perch on the ground, but when he stood, it seemed far too large for his body. The Department of Natural Resources thinned the herd out every year or so, but of course none of that was advertised.

The lateness coupled with the inky night pushed in on her fatigue, and she purposely allowed her footfalls to sound on the stairs to announce her arrival. The porch lamp flipped on, and her mother appeared at the door.

Dressed in a chenille robe, in her mid-sixties, chin-length hair full of natural blond and gray curls, she looked every inch the sweet, elderly mother type. Callie's heart filled as her mother reached an arm around her, rubbing her back.

"You look tired," Sarah said, escorting Callie in and locking the door behind them. Nobody had to tell Sarah Rosewood to lock a door. Now a widow living alone, she'd seen enough and more through Callie's work to understand the meaning of security. "Coffee?"

"I'd love some," Callie said. "Mind if I...?" and she ran a hand over her utility belt that added fifteen to twenty pounds to her hundred-and-ten-pound frame.

"Not a bit, honey. Go sit in the recliner. I'll be right in."

The Rosewood house was not the typical beach house. Resident's homes weren't necessarily decorated of driftwood and wicker furniture like the rentals, and the styles inside could be anything from early American to New York modern. Homespun to art deco. Sarah's home flaunted whites and beiges and lighter wood. Her husband had done well for himself before he died a block over on Dolphin Road thanks to a slow trickling brain bleed from a fall. As the man's best friend, Brice had been a prime suspect at the time. Sarah had been suspected for a little while. Took her some time to recuperate from the shock, and she'd lived in Atlanta for the better part of a year after. Callie tried to make up for it all when she'd come back to the beach. They'd gotten quite close of late.

Families didn't get much more dysfunctional than theirs, but the two women had worked hard to make up for lost time.

The coffee came with a brownie that Callie accepted with relish, and she'd eaten half before Sarah settled with her robe around her on one end of the white leather sofa across from the recliner. "Long day?" she asked.

"In more ways than one. I spent the night at the hospital in Middleton."

That sat Sarah upright. "Are you all right?"

"Oh," Callie said, correcting herself in the miscommunication. "I'm fine. It was Mother... Beverly. Jeb took her to the ER, and both of us sat with her through the night. They released her this morning, and I took her to breakfast before taking her home."

"What in the world?"

Sarah didn't dislike Beverly as much as some would expect. Bless her, she appreciated all that Lawton and Beverly had done for Callie—that appreciation making her the crème de la crème of the parents in Callie's opinion.

Callie explained the gout, the misrepresentation, and the doctor's enjoyment in calling out Beverly. Sarah exclaimed, smiled, and chuckled before the story was through.

"I hope you can help me keep an eye on her, Sarah." While Callie had become accustomed to the two-tier mother structure, the name thing remained what it had always been. "I sensed a neediness there I hadn't seen before."

Her discussion of Beverly had morphed from her humorous recounting of her mother's dramatization of nothing, to concern at Beverly's overcompensating to prove she wasn't vulnerable, to her recognition that something might actually be wrong, if not now... all too soon. "Guess I'm a little concerned," she tacked on.

"As you should be."

Jeb, however, was the more difficult subject amongst them. He still saw Beverly as his grandmother and out of an odd sense of loyalty, wasn't willing to sacrifice one iota of love for her, purposely leaving little room for the newer model. They'd met several times, but the bonding wasn't happening. Maybe over time, Callie kept telling herself.

Callie explained to Sarah how she'd semi-confirmed the fact Beverly was indeed grooming him for politics. Guess she sought advice, maybe validation.

Sarah listened, undisturbed, then softly smiled. "He's a smart boy. Let him figure things out. I used to worry about the same for you. There was certainly no lack of trying on Beverly's part to reel you in to be molded in her likeness, but look at you. You figured it out. He will, too."

That helped. Yeah. That helped more than expected. Hell, why hadn't Callie seen that herself?

She'd long polished off the brownie, and the coffee had gone lukewarm. Her shoes had come off some time ago when she'd lifted the footrest, and weariness melted her into the leather.

"Want to stay?" Sarah asked. "You know I have the room."

She'd really love to. The thought of sleeping in and waking to a mother cooking breakfast felt like a hug in itself. "Wish I could," she said, meaning it to her heart. "But Mark's due home any minute." Still she didn't move. Sarah noticed and grinned knowingly, as though Callie would doze off any time.

But begrudgingly, Callie put down the foot and sat up. "Truth is as much as I'd like to say this was just a personal visit, I need to query you about a couple more things," she said, pulling out the photos of Maddy and Elizabeth. "Have you seen either of these women? In the stores, on the beach, anywhere out here."

Sarah studied the pictures, no recognition in her expression. "Sorry, hon, but I've never seen them. Those girls are a generation I might not pay attention to."

Sarah wouldn't be around the bars or eating in the restaurants alone. When she did eat out, she collected Mrs. Hanson across the street or came to El Marko's. Usually, eating out was a matter of coming over to Callie's for informal Lowcountry stew. More often, Sarah cooked. She was a lovely cook, which was part of how she'd hit it off with Ms. Hanson, the cookie queen.

"I saw the missing-person notice on my phone," she said, handing the pictures back. "Either one of these could fit the description. Who's the other one? Are they both missing?"

"No, ma'am," Callie replied, glad she was finally speaking to someone she could be honest with. "This one was the missing girl," she said, motioning with her phone to show the picture of Maddy, realizing Maddy hadn't called as was promised. She flipped to the next photo. "This one is the dead girl we found on the sound this week. We learned who she was last night. A woman named Elizabeth Brown who owned a condo in Wyndham. Came to it every six weeks or more per her husband. Usually alone. Stayed inside in the day and walked the beach at night because she was a night nurse. It was just her nature."

A hand went over Sarah's mouth. "Oh dear. Killed? Drowned? Accident?"

All the usual questions. "We're suspecting killed."

"Jesus," the mother exclaimed. "Who did it?" Reality set in. "Are they still loose?"

"We have no idea who, so we have no idea where. We're querying houses. We're also running with an observation by someone at Coots who saw them together the night Elizabeth died."

"So Maddy is probably hiding out after she killed Elizabeth?"

That first impression had occurred to Callie. But if the two girls just met—which was the probability since this was Maddy's first trip to Edisto—then had they really known each other long enough for them to fall out enough to warrant murder? One from Tampa and the other from Middleton? Was Maddy the type of girl to stalk another, and for what?

"I'm not leaning that way," she said. "The other one broke up with a bad boyfriend, but he's supposedly down in Florida. If he was going to kill someone, why not Maddy rather than a stranger?"

"Jealousy?" Sarah offered.

Maybe.

Sarah looked worried. "Not sure I want to go out and about much until you catch whoever it is." She waited for more. "That it? You look tired, honey."

"One more thing. This may sound totally out of the blue, but I have to ask. Have you ever heard of *The Summer Ladies*?"

Sarah gave three clipped laughs while rearing back to sink into her sofa, relieved at the switch from doom and gloom to something of a joke. "Of course I have." She laughed some more, then spotted Callie's seriousness. "You haven't?"

Not expecting laughter, Callie had to smile at Sarah's reaction so at ease and silly. "Afraid not. I'm beginning to think everyone's heard but me. Beverly told me about them, only she didn't tell me much. What do you know?"

Sarah downright giggled. "Not that I've met them, mind you. I wouldn't dream of it."

"No, of course not," Callie obliged.

"Honestly, I can laugh about it now with Ben gone." Then she sobered a little bit. "And Brice." Then she sobered even more. "And I guess Lawton, to be honest."

Sarah's husband with a prostitute? Yeah, Callie could see that. Brice? Without a doubt. But *son of a bitch*, Callie's father?

Chapter 21

PART OF CALLIE wanted answers to more questions; the other part just wanted to hang with her mom and not have to ponder the thought of her father with a prostitute. The recliner fit her backside perfectly, the leather warm under her to just the right temperature. The lighting took on a nice, soft evening glow.

She was exhausted but pressed to solve her cases. She might catch some shut-eye after this stop, though... if she didn't fall asleep in this chair first.

Her phone rang, jolting her out of her seat. Caller ID Unknown.

Damn it! Her heart jumped, bruising itself fast-timing against her ribs. She'd been settled, ready for her mother to elaborate on *The Summer Ladies*, but calls had to be answered. She'd told too many people to call her day or night if they remembered seeing Maddy or Elizabeth.

"Let me take this," she said, making moves to get up. Her mother motioned her to stay, instead taking the cups and napkins to the kitchen to give Callie whatever privacy she needed.

How nice... and a damn sweet change to have a mother who accommodated you and was proud of what you did. But then guilt rolled in. It wasn't that she hated Beverly. It was just that the exaggerated contrasts couldn't help but pit one versus the other in her mind.

"Chief Morgan," Callie answered, reaching to her breast pocket for a notepad, just in case.

"Oh," came a surprised voice Callie didn't immediately recognize. "I thought I'd get voicemail this late."

"Who is this?" She first thought Chiara, but the voice was different.

"It's Maddy. Did I wake you?"

"No, not at all." Callie was wide awake now.

Lydia followed through after all. "Where are you, Maddy?"

"At the beach house."

"Which beach house?"

"You know. *Time in a Bottle.* When I got in, Lydia told me to call. I wanted to wait till morning, but she said you would want to be notified whenever... so, here I am."

So many questions in her head, but this was not the place to ask them. Callie wanted to see the woman and take her time strategically pushing this way and that. "Are you okay?"

"Sure. I mean, I wanted to be alone, and I might've cried a little bit, but I'm good."

She sounded like a fifteen-year-old.

"Where have you been?"

"Honestly? Walking, napping on the beach. Two of Chiara's friends let me bunk with them."

Callie didn't ask the degree of what bunking meant, and frankly didn't care. She would, however, want those names. "Mind giving me those addresses? To confirm your whereabouts?"

There was some delay, and Callie quickly guessed the girl was being schooled. "Are we on speaker?" she asked.

"Um, no, Chief Morgan. I thought I heard someone, and I didn't want them listening in."

"Thought you ladies were close."

"I'm the new one. The trust isn't quite there, and after me staying gone a couple nights, they aren't too pleased with me."

Callie wasn't feeling much truth here. "The addresses?"

"They'd rather me not give those out," Maddy said.

"They being...?"

"The two gentlemen," she said, when Callie knew good and well Vivien and/or Lydia were guiding her in the background.

This was going nowhere on the phone. "We need to meet tomorrow, Maddy. My office is private, and—"

"I'd rather meet here, at the house," she replied.

"With others listening?"

"With my friends around me," she corrected.

Callie wasn't convinced that anyone other than Chiara was Maddy's friend, but she wasn't quibbling that in the middle of the night on a cell phone.

"Nine tomorrow morning, then," Callie said.

"Tomorrow afternoon at four... please."

This had Lydia's fingerprints all over it. If Maddy had indeed just returned, they'd want to groom her for the interview. Callie wasn't sure what the hell was going on, but she wasn't going to expect this interview to be truthful. Not by a long shot.

"Fine. See you at four," Callie said, and Maddy hung up.

Replaying the chat, she had to admit she hadn't been able to read much outside of it feeling somewhat orchestrated. She'd said just the minimum. In fact, she was surprised Maddy mentioned she'd been with two gentlemen, but if she didn't divulge the addresses, what difference did it make?

And meeting at the house was genius. Surround yourself with allies and witnesses and friends who could assist with interruptions, eyebrows, and pre-rehearsed gestures.

No. Not suspicious at all.

Victim, witness, or killer? Callie'd once wondered if Maddy was even involved. Now she was fairly convinced Maddy was one of the three, though if she were indeed the killer, she was pretty damn cool on the phone.

"Callie?" Sarah called lightly, poking her head out the kitchen entrance to see if the coast was clear.

The phone rang again, no caller ID. Again, she had to take it in case the canvassing had stirred someone's memory. "Edisto Beach PD, Chief Callie Morgan."

"Before, you said if nobody cared she was missing you wouldn't really... anyway, what's changed? Tonight about scared me to death."

"Chiara? Didn't Lydia talk to you?" Callie couldn't believe she hadn't. "I've left you messages to call."

"No, I was on a date, I don't interrupt dates, and I haven't gone back to the house yet. I just happened to be at a residence one of your people came to."

Callie sat straighter, reaching for a pen. "So, you talked to an officer?" She'd go to said house right now and query Chiara in more depth.

"No, sorry. Let me explain that better. My date spoke to her."

Her. Officer Annie. That meant Chiara had been somewhere on Wyndham unless Annie made good time interviewing people door to door, which could then mean somewhere on Dock Site Road. She recalled the women in *Time in a Bottle* came in two cars to Edisto. She could run down tags.... "Why didn't you meet with the officer? For goodness' sake, Chiara, you're Maddy's friend."

"Of course I didn't talk to her. Not my residence. My date didn't want the cop to see me, and just wanted to be rid of her. I can talk to you whenever I like without tangling others up in it."

It took embarrassing a john to make her call? Callie could've done that sooner. "What's your date's name?" she asked.

"I'd rather not say."

Not surprising. "Remind me again why you called?"

Chiara hesitated. "Just hoping for an update. I'm angry at Lydia so I don't talk to her any more than I have to. What's happened? I'm sorry about your meeting yesterday with Lydia, and I'm sorry about being half asleep, but I'm sick of just about everyone. I stay away from the house as much as possible. But y'all are still hunting for Maddy?"

She'd been far from half asleep when Callie came by. "Maddy called, supposedly from your group's beach house. She's supposed to be there now. I'm surprised Lydia didn't call you."

"So why are y'all hunting Maddy if she's back?"

Where was *any* excitement that her friend was back finally? Callie bet whatever Chiara charged for an evening that she already knew her friend had shown. Why the cops were involved was probably more the question.

"We're not on the best terms right now," Chiara said, "but I'll definitely call her as soon as I get off this call."

"Do you have the information I asked you for? Address, boyfriend, sister, employer? Did you get ahold of HR for the sister's contact like I asked?"

"Um, Lydia told me not to bother, and now that Maddy's back, you can ask her."

Callie would give up her vacation leave to have Chiara across the table. The call went quiet, but Callie still heard what sounded like palmetto fronds scratching a screen. She used to have that noise on her own porch, before her former house burned to the ground.

"Chiara, what's going on? Time to quit playing around. One life has already been taken."

"What's that got to do with any of us?"

"You recall the woman who washed up behind *Time in a Bottle* this week?"

Tentative, Chiara's voice quivered. "Um, yes. Why?"

Sure she did. The officer would've shown pictures of both women. "We think Maddy was seen with her walking the beach the night she died."

"Oh, God." Some breaths went by. "She isn't a suspect, is she?"

"Not yet," was all Callie felt right to say. Of course, Maddy was a person of interest, but nobody needed to hear that at this point. Maybe there was a reason Lydia had her out of the house when Maddy returned... assuming Maddy had returned.

"Work with me. Confirm her employer, at least? Same as yours, right?"

"Pinellas County School District, Tampa."

"Who's her sister?"

"Heidi... Wharton, I think. I don't know her address or have her phone. I've never met her. She's the younger of the two. Maddy called her about once a week. Their parents are dead. Tragic story. They died in a boating accident in Kissimmee when the girls were in their late teens."

Callie scribbled, letting Chiara tell her anything, meaningless or not. Callie was just grateful she'd bothered to call. Annie must've made a serious impression on the date for Chiara to want to call this late at night.

Callie flipped a page. "The boyfriend's name?"

The gush of intelligence ceased. "I don't want to talk about him."

"You have to talk about him. I thought he was the bad boy Maddy was avoiding. The main reason she needed this little getaway."

"She hasn't spoken to him in a month, so let it be."

Callie could hear the fear in her voice. "Okay, so you're scared of him. Lydia says Maddy is getting over a bad relationship, which I assume is this guy. What's his name?" Callie asked, each word powered up.

"He'll get angry if I give his name to the cops."

"How will he find out?"

"You'll call him, or you'll go hunting him."

"Is he angry enough to be... dangerous?"

No reply.

"Has he physically assaulted Maddy before?" Callie asked.

"Yes."

"Has she filed charges against him?" Those files she could get her hands onto.

"She started to but changed her mind. After the last time, she left him and moved in with me."

"You give me no choice then," Callie said, letting the dramatic pause fall a second. "After Maddy, I've got to pull in Lydia and you right behind her. Y'all are obstructing justice."

"Don't, please."

Callie put the words in order, knowing full well whatever was said here would go straight back to everyone in *Time in a Bottle*. "Yes, and you're smart enough to know why. Lydia's in charge. She's withheld information from an investigation. She's told you to withhold information, which you have, and that's just what I can prove at the moment. The entire police force is on this case, and y'all's secrets won't stay secret for long." She paused. "We'll find you out."

A whimper came over the line.

"Chiara, have you talked to Maddy?"

"No, only Lydia has," came the reply, mixed with what could be tears. "It's why I'm so upset. I'm supposed to be her best friend, but she doesn't call me. She doesn't confide in me."

"Is she in trouble?" Callie asked.

The quick curtailment of a cry told Callie the woman was trying not to be heard. The frond scraping had ceased, and Callie tried to hear her location. "Where are you?"

"Um, just got into my car."

"Come to my place," Callie said.

"No."

"Come to the station then."

"No."

"Don't make things worse than they are. I can always run you down. Your car's a giveaway."

"Then I'll walk."

This tit for tat was going nowhere. "Please, let's chat, Chiara."

"The only way to make things worse, Chief Morgan, is for me to keep talking to you."

The call dropped.

With a hard breath, Callie tucked away the pad.

What did Chiara fear so much? Was this about the boyfriend? How were Lydia and Vivien involved? Where the hell has Maddy been throughout all of this... and what the hell was *this*?

If it weren't the middle of the night....

These women acted more and more weird.

Callie'd been keeping their prostitution separate from the murder, but could one of them have killed Elizabeth? What if Maddy, in her novice ways, had upset a john who worried about being outed. He followed her and mistakenly killed Elizabeth in the dark?

Look at her.... God, she was really groping for ideas.

Sarah returned, studying her daughter. "That didn't sound like a good call."

"Two calls, and no, they weren't," Callie said. "I wish I could go home, honestly, but I'm not sure I don't have another stop to make before I sleep tonight."

She'd had cases like this before, where sleep got swept off the agenda for two, sometimes three days, but you followed the leads as they happened. Mark had texted a half hour ago saying he was home, and by now had likely showered off the restaurant's grease and spices. He waited for her in bed by now; he'd want her to wake him. The thought and visual were enticing.

"We weren't done talking about *The Summer Ladies*," her mother said. "You got time, or should we put this off?"

Callie didn't have a ton of time, but this could prove fruitful. Honestly, it was downright timely. "Go ahead. Brief me. Are they real, a myth, or a nickname that means something I don't understand?"

On the sofa, snuggling down into her robe, Sarah began again. "I learned about them via Brice. He wasn't one for secrets, though he called himself only telling *certain people*. You know how this island is."

Callie listened, attentive, not wanting to interrupt to save time. She had to admit that Brice, for being dead, sure seemed applicable in all her comings and goings these days.

"Well, we couldn't have been more than, what..." and Sarah had to think a moment. "Forty?"

Callie always did the math. In this case, she would have been high school age. She'd been rebellious. She would not have paid one iota of attention to anything any of these people were doing. All she cared about was going off to college and leaving Middleton with its sticky politics and public scrutiny. As the mayor's daughter, she was forever in the limelight, and she'd hated it.

"Ben had been out of town with clients, at the peak of his career, and was expected back on a Friday flight, but he called and said he'd been forced to have drinks with a client in hopes of clinching a deal. He'd catch a midday flight out of LaGuardia on Saturday. Nothing unusual, and, at the time, I was grateful for the solitude." Sarah sighed. "I don't know why we stayed married."

Callie stopped to absorb that memory, her comment a reminder of what Beverly said... how some wives used to be happy on Edisto that their husbands were socially occupied.

These people and their love triangles, quadrangles, whatever angles they played.

Callie thought of Mark, immediately discarding the thought of him chasing a skirt behind her back. Times were different now, or she'd like to think. Divorces were less scandalous, wives less patient with straying husbands. She realized she was thinking as if she were his wife.

"You knew Ben," Sarah said, rhetorically, pulling Callie back to the present.

Callie nodded.

While Callie wasn't fond of spouses stepping out on their partners, nobody understood a marriage better than the couple themselves, so she wouldn't ask why Sarah never left the man. Sarah's husband Ben had been abusive, mostly mentally, but occasionally the abuse turned physical. She'd had been a wreck when Callie first got to know her... before Ben died. Callie had felt his verbal wrath firsthand a time or two. Yet most of Edisto thought Sarah and Ben were a decent couple because they stayed together.

"Brice came over," Sarah continued. "Jovial and full of himself. Even pinched me once."

As if that were normal. Yeah, times had changed.

"He said he'd been with a friend who'd returned for the summer, and he wanted to let Ben know when to meet that night so they could all go get a beer together. In his zeal, he didn't even realize he'd let the word *she* slip out. I went to his wife Aberdeen, and she said *The Summer Ladies* were back in town. I felt rather naïve, listening to her brag about having time to herself for a few weeks without worrying about her husband's plans conflicting. She told me I ought to be doing the same... since Ben was likely following in Brice's footsteps. I was floored, took a harder look around me, and realized how right she was. Then like her, I learned to see these times with the ladies as a blessing in disguise." The memories weren't good ones, and she wilted a bit. "It meant less of his attitude because they genuinely made him happier. Try not to judge me, honey."

Callie rushed out of the recliner to beside her mother. "Never. Not my place to judge. I wasn't there." She gave her mother a hug, released her, and sat back. "Before you mentioned... Lawton?"

Sarah held up a hand. "Sorry, let me explain. Lawton knew *of* them. I'm not saying he spent time *with* them. You knew your father. He ran in way better circles than that."

Um, her father had kept the mistress sitting across from her for forty years. No, she would never be sure she really knew her father. And if Sarah could miss seeing Ben's dalliances, how could she not miss Lawton's?

"Who exactly are we talking about? Who are the ladies?" Callie asked.

"Friendly women who spent time with men here on the beach. That's all."

Oh, for Christ's sake, call them what they really were. "Prostitutes?"

But Sarah shook her head. "I cannot say for sure they went that far."

"Seriously, Sarah? Come on. You are not that naïve."

Sarah just shrugged. "Never witnessed the deed. Never heard anyone profess."

Had to be some reason that Brice and Ben got so chipper when those ladies came to town, and Callie was guessing it wasn't their choices of music and liquor. "Did you ever hear names for these ladies?" Callie asked. "First, was it the same lady or several?"

Sarah's brows shrugged this time. "Never heard the names, and while I can't exactly explain, I got the sense there was a collection of them."

"Ever hear of Lydia Barron?"

Sarah tried to recall such a name. "Sorry. No."

Beverly kept saying the older residents would know these ladies, yet Sarah knew *of* them but no details. Someone like Sophie, however, would be more curious and hopefully knew more.

And what about Deputy Raysor? For a quick second, she wondered just how much he knew, and how well he knew it. Again, not judging, but she almost wished he had infiltrated the group... so to speak.

Like an owl, where the hoot far outweighed the magnitude of the bird, an old-fashioned square brass clock chimed midnight over the fireplace, sounding twice its size. Callie waited for the resonance to fade away. "I need to go." She rose, reluctantly, feeling the creaks in her bones, and gave her mother a hug. "Thanks for staying up. Not many people would do that." The unspoken specific person, of course, being Beverly.

"Any time," came the reply, and she walked Callie to the door.

Callie made her way across Sarah's lot, past Sophie's to her own drive. She craved so damn bad to climb her own steps to *Chelsea Morning* and fall into bed with Mark. Even his car looked lonely parked in the dark as she pulled away in her cruiser.

She had texted him that she had one more stop to make on Palmetto before coming home. Then she explained specifically what she missed of him and signed off with a set of red lips.

With so much police presence at people's doors tonight, the police department's expectation was less crime, less family squabble, and minimal drinking and driving. As a result, she only had Officer Russell

Wiley on duty, and as odds would have it, he passed her as she headed west on Palmetto. He waved in passing, probably wondering where she was headed this time of night. Unlike Thomas, who'd radio her and ask if she needed assistance, Russell would merely wait until beckoned. There was a reason she preferred him on the night shift, and he had his own for accepting this type of assignment.

It was one in the morning, the roads dead of activity, feeling even deader under the barest sliver of a moon and almost no stars. Window down, she couldn't even hear the tide. Edisto Beach was like a tomb, which hopefully meant nothing bad at play in her town tonight.

She passed nobody else all the way down Palmetto then around the curve to the sound side of the road. She pulled up in front of *Time in a Bottle.*

The windows were dark. Pure pitch. No porch lights, no interior lights, not even the first sign of a nightlight.

But there were no cars in the drive.

The ladies had come in two cars, in what Callie assumed was Lydia's Mercedes and Chiara's Ford Explorer. Chiara had said she was in her car during the earlier call, probably at a date's residence, and if Callie wanted, she could patrol the roads until she found the girl. The same with Lydia's. But it was awful late to start that chase.

Somebody could still be home. Callie turned off the engine and climbed the stairs to see if she could awaken one of the other girls, catch one of them off guard without Lydia's strict oversight.

Nobody had turned on the light by the time she reached the porch. Nobody came to the door when she knocked, nor when she pounded. Peering in the windows, she hunted for signs of life, and finding none, she moved to the back. The door to the screen porch wasn't locked, probably hadn't been for years. She ventured in and amongst the rattan and wicker and peeked through disheveled blinds into two of the bedrooms, finding the beds empty.

Which probably meant beds elsewhere were full.

She came down the stairs, walking around the other side of the storage facility on the ground level, just to say she'd checked out the whole place. She slowed, then she stopped. The door to the ten-by-fifteen room stood a foot open.

She peered inside. The scent of stale salt air, old wood, and rust wafted to her as she took a step in and felt for a switch. Light consisted of two bulbs in an old ceiling fan that didn't work. Like all the others so common on the beach, the room held an extra grill, extra beach chairs, and hurricane shutters hanging on hooks embedded in bare studs, the bare necessities for owning a house on the coast. Other storage rooms might hold a freezer for shrimp and fish, a refrigerator for ample cases of beer and soft drinks, cots for overflow visitors, and surplus furniture too good to toss, too used to sell.

This one had bedding tossed against the north wall.

Chapter 22

BECAUSE THE storage room door had been left open, Callie took the liberty of letting herself in. She snapped a few pictures while being careful to avoid leaving a sign she'd been there.

A makeshift mattress of a blanket atop a chaise-lounge cushion had been someone's temporary bed. With pen in hand, she moved the material around, hunting for signs of blood or stains of any kind. She didn't hope for anything identifying like a driver's license or wallet, and her expectations were founded.

Easing down, she touched the blanket. The loose, makeshift bedroll wasn't warm, but this was June, and one couldn't necessarily tell. A bit of a sour scent in the bedding, and Callie didn't smell closer. Body odor or old urine.

Callie wondered what type of vagrant stayed in this house, right under Lydia's nose. Though not common, there was history on Edisto of individuals shacking up in the storage rooms of empty rentals, bathing in the outdoor showers designed to remove sand from people before they went inside, snaring food outside the kitchens of several restaurants. But the old Edistonians kept watch on the situations, and before long, one of them would find the person a job, then a place to stay, and the vagrancy stopped before it turned into theft or worse. Callie wasn't aware of any notable vagrants of late.

This didn't look like a vagrant situation though. Not even an empty water bottle, coke can, or paper cup in sight.

She pushed the door closed so nobody else was drawn to enter and disturb the scene, then got back to her cruiser.

Something wasn't right in this house, and she'd instinctively thought so from the beginning. Call it gut sense, a metaphysical feel, or years of experience reading people's vibes, she had to know more about these women as individuals. If she went home and crawled into bed, even as tired as she was, her mind would mull over, toss, and dissect thoughts, giving her minimal sleep, and nothing of value.

Inside her car, still in the drive, Callie researched Lydia's driver's license. Time to dissect this woman's life. And when she was done with hers, she'd launch into Vivien's then Maddy's. The others in due time.

Callie's intuition screamed that these women were up to something more than offering themselves as evening escorts. Way more. The creepy feel of something conniving crawled strong through her bones, and for a short time, before Maddy's call, Callie had even wondered if they'd disposed of the girl. She'd feel better laying eyes on the woman.

Diving into the database of driver's licenses, Callie found no one named Lydia Barron in Tampa, Florida. At least anyone who looked like Lydia Barron. There was one twenty years younger with blond hair and chunky cheeks. Sweet smile. Callie widened the search to the entire state of Florida. A couple more Lydias, not a one resembling the queen of this group.

Lydia operated under an alias. *Big surprise.* Did the others as well? Was that why Chiara was so hesitant about identifying information on Maddy? Was Maddy even her real name? Was Chiara hers?

She could tail them. She could conveniently knock on the doors of their dates each time they visited and make all their lives uncomfortable enough to cramp their arrangements and whittle their guest list down by a dozen or two names, but that could also cost Edisto some long-term summer visitors. The embarrassment could spread God knew how far since she wasn't sure who these women counted as long-term friends.

Town hall, the first responders, business owners.... She'd already heard that Brice and Ben had been members of the club. They'd been long-established residents.

No, she had to handle this deftly. She wasn't into throwing johns in jail. She really wasn't into throwing the ladies in there either. At least not just for their leisure fun.

A light-colored Mercedes slowed. Lydia's car. The Mercedes started to move on, but Callie jumped out of her cruiser, waving at the driver to pull in, the gravelly area wide enough for the driver to go around. The car had to back up ten feet to make the turn, but did as directed. As they drove in, Callie spotted Lydia at the wheel and Vivien beside her. Walking behind the creeping car, Callie waited for them to park and exit.

Lydia sighed. "What now, Chief Morgan?" The words sounded weary, matching her stance. She wore the shawl she'd worn every time they'd met, and Callie almost wondered what her physique really was like since she hadn't been seen in anything but clothes disguised by that wrap. Lydia seemed to consider it a part of her image.

"I heard from Chiara," Callie said. "Thanks for telling her to call me."

Lydia's head did a little hitch to the side, knowing full well she hadn't told Chiara to do a damn thing. One raised brow at the chief said both of them knew it, too.

"It's late," Callie said.

"Yes, it is," Lydia replied.

Lydia reminded Callie of Beverly and, therefore, brought out the worst in her. A woman a generation older who'd found her confidence and solid footing in the world, now toyed with the younger pup, giving her the chance to compete but unwilling to let her win.

"Out late with friends?" Callie tried.

The condescension dripped off Lydia's answer, laced with feigned injury. "As a matter of fact, yes."

Minimal talk. Smart. "Wouldn't you have Maddy with you?"

"She's on a date."

"After being scared, and missing, and driving everyone crazy, she goes on a date?"

Lydia allowed the silence to collect around them, letting what she thought was a sufficient accounting of their time sink in. "Why did you come this time of night? Sorry we weren't here to welcome you, but we had no idea you were coming."

"I spoke to Maddy, by the way."

"She told us," Lydia said. "Tomorrow afternoon... here, right? That's the time of y'all's meeting?"

"Correct. Mind telling me where she is? Where you've been?"

"No, we don't broadcast our activities and don't feel the need to now. We're very private ladies, Chief." She gave a second's dramatic pause.

Then her stance straightened as if she realized something. "Why are you even here?" She waved with a hand, the shawl's fringe dancing.

This woman was strong. "I was hoping y'all were up late and we could cut to the chase of this mess," Callie replied, recognizing how smoothly Lydia had shifted the weight of things. "I spoke with Chiara who provided some of the long-awaited details I'd asked for about Maddy's life. Not all, mind you. Maddy put me off. Assuming that was Maddy."

Vivien had come around the car, sidling up against Lydia, unconsciously fingering the shawl's trim.

"Chief," Lydia said, as if so tired of explaining the elementary. "We're not required to do your job for you. Just because you're not happy with our responses to your questions isn't breaking the law."

"Obstructing—" Callie started.

"Sorry, but may I interrupt?" Vivien said, releasing hold of Lydia. "As an attorney I might have a better grip on all this. Nobody is obstructing justice. You have every avenue of investigation open to you within law enforcement to get Maddy's details. You just don't like our behavior. There's nothing illegal in anything we've done. We've let you in the house. We've spoken to you whenever asked to do so. We've contacted you ourselves, if you count Chiara and now Maddy."

Remaining stoic, Callie had to admit Vivien had knocked the wind out of her sail. Time to shift gears. "On another subject, when I arrived, I knocked on the front door. With no answer, I looked on the back porch since y'all congregate on your porch."

The two ladies waited, listening for the rest, volunteering nothing.

"While going underneath the house, I noticed your storage room door open. Were you aware? There was a makeshift bedroll in there. Someone's been sleeping beneath your bedrooms."

Lydia's gaze gave nothing away, but Vivien's eyes darted to her cohort, then back forward. But they registered no shock, no concern, no bother about a stranger on the property. Some would be concerned said trespasser would try doors, attempt thievery, or worse. Not these women. Either they were tough as nails, or they knew more than they were saying.

Vivien took the reins. "Did you have a warrant, Chief? Were there any exigent circumstances? Unless you had specific information about someone being in peril on this property, you really had no right to enter, did you?"

Not a normal response to a vagrant on site, but Callie said nothing.

"You could've waited until we got home and asked permission to examine the storage room," Viv added.

"I had no idea when or if you were coming home, and I have a dead girl I'm concerned about who died right outside your house. Who says the killer hadn't been holed up beneath your rental? Who says that bedroll wasn't theirs? Besides, the owners would prefer their storage room not be left open, and I have a big responsibility to homeowners on this beach. On occasion we get homeless who seek opportunity just like this to take up temporary residence. I'd think you'd worry about that happening during your stay, particularly after a death. Especially the way Maddy pulled her little stunt."

Vivien, however, wasn't daunted. "In reality, we don't know what's down there. Could be teens messing around. I can definitely see the attraction if I were that age with no place else to go. I assume you locked it back?"

"The door is pushed to. Please look it over and lock it."

Pushing off the car, Lydia turned and held out her hand for Vivien to take. "Well, it's late. I feel a lumpy bed and cheap blankets calling me upstairs. How about you, Viv?"

"Right behind you, lady."

They turned and sauntered to the stairs, sashaying their way up to the top landing. Without a wave, they let themselves inside, turned on lights, and disappeared.

They'd shut the door on the conversation, and Callie had no choice but to leave. She'd allowed these women to get under her skin for no other reason than she was too tired to be on her toes. What the hell was she not seeing? Probably something obvious. Served her right coming so late and not a hundred percent on her game.

All of them, she included, danced around the fact they were prostitutes. Not something she appreciated in her town, but she wasn't eager to become the prude police. Beach towns weren't exactly ruled by etiquette, which meant enforcing the letter of the law to the nth degree could do more damage than good for a town depending on happy, returning tourists.

The occasional joint, for instance. Acceptable as long as nobody tried to drive or distribute. Sophie and her personal pot stash under the bathroom sink upstairs was the perfect case in point. No harm done.

Same with someone wanting to slip several hundred to a lady for providing a wonderful evening. Who cared when the ladies disappeared for the other eleven months of the year.

At a quarter to two, she eased her cruiser under *Chelsea Morning*. She sat there in the quiet dark, a bit annoyed at Lydia and Vivien's treatment of her, and how she'd taken it. That's what she got for running over there in the middle of the night without a solid plan, without sound questions in mind, already spent from a long damn day. An investigator wasted time being unprepared, and the result often showed too much of their hand.

But not in this case. Callie didn't have much of a hand to show.

Callie had fallen into bed as soon as she went inside and had slipped straight into a dream. In what seemed like minutes, she heard words mumbled in her ear. "What's this?" She was half asleep, and she desired to stay that way. However, not with the hand traveling down her arm to her ribs... and further.

"Got in late," Callie managed to utter. "Give me an hour." Then she realized that Mark had awoken before she had, meaning she'd overslept. "What time is it?" she managed to say, then gave a light groan as Mark found a way to keep her awake.

"Quarter after eight," he whispered. "Time to rise, Sunshine." And he continued his searching.

She rarely said no, and because he woke her way before she was ready, she let him do the lion's share of the lovemaking, not that she didn't enjoy the ride.

"You *are* tired," he said afterward, rolling over to one elbow. "Did I see you come in at two?"

Lying on her back, arms sprawled out on the pillows, legs out, almost like a body shot down in the street, she cleared her throat, really not wanting to talk. "Yes, two. And I have a full day." The night came back to her, and she opened her eyes. "We have hookers on Edisto Beach."

"For sure?"

"I'd bet big money on it."

"Anyone I ought to know?" he asked.

That made her think. "Hmmm, you flashed a picture of one of them in your door-to-door last night. Ring a bell?"

"Never seen her before the picture."

She rolled over to grab her phone off the nightstand, a quick glance at the screen telling her the day would be a bright one, most likely on the warm side. Beat rain, for sure. She glanced at texts, nothing urgent.

Mark patted her on the thigh and got up. "You sleeping some more?"

"No," she sighed. "Got places to be and people to see." She sat up. "But you've made me need a shower now."

"Shame," he called from the bathroom, the water going on. "Seems I need one, too."

He got under the water first, and she soon followed.

"Tell me something," she said, trying not to get cold while he sudsed up.

"You'd get it out of me one way or another with this interrogation tactic." Then blindly he reached to find her, hoping for a feel.

"No," she said, chuckling. "Listen. If I weren't in the picture, would you entertain something like *The Summer Ladies*?"

His eyes opened, instantly stung from shampoo, and he closed them to rinse. "No. I'm twenty-plus years of state law enforcement, Sunshine. Sort of not in our job description. When you get into the habit of not dabbling in the wares of anything illegal, that habit sticks, whether you're talking prostitutes or weed, pills or drinking and driving. It's not an option in my world. Make sense?"

She was a cop. Sure, it did.

"What about Stan?" She couldn't see him taking a taste either, but she wasn't a man.

"He'd be like me. I can hear him saying, *'I'm not paying for that.'*"

He changed places with her, kissing her on the hand when he did.

"What about Thomas?" she asked, eyes closed, hot water saturating her hair.

He laughed. "That boy is a chick magnet given the way he fills that uniform and flashes that smile. He can get all he needs without paying for it." His grin remained; the thought having amused him. "Are we covering everyone on the beach? We'll run out of hot water."

"One more," she said. "What about Raysor?"

Mark wasn't as jocular about this one. "Not sure I want to guess. I'd like to say no because he's law enforcement, but he's Carolina country first and foremost. And he's a single man."

Callie kept waiting.

"My guess is no, but he'd be the one most inclined to know who they are and where they hang out."

She tucked that away.

Ten minutes later, she toweled herself when her phone went off. Mark ran to grab it, handing it to her. She didn't immediately recognize the number, but the voice threw her headfirst into her day.

Nolan Brown. His weariness came through, sounding as if he hadn't slept at all last night. "Have you determined who or what killed my wife?" he asked without a salutation.

"No, sir. These things can take time." She didn't want to tell him she hadn't even found the crime scene yet and had serious doubts she would. She considered Maddy's resurgence a step forward, and in that meeting this afternoon, she hoped to put more together in the investigation.

But he didn't need to hear that.

"They won't let me have her yet."

"No, sir. Please give us a few more days." She wanted to give him a date, really she did, but his need for consolation couldn't trump the need to find who took down his wife and who might still be out there, thinking about a repeat performance.

"Well," he said, dragging the word out so long, ending it with only air. Then he sighed. "Please do what you can. I have a funeral to plan. People are asking."

Family and friends needed closure. Nobody understood that until they needed it themselves.

"I certainly will, Mr. Brown." She ended the call.

Mark wrapped sleeved arms around her nakedness. "You're good at your job, Callie Jean Morgan, but that has to be one of the hardest parts, especially for you."

It was. Wrapping her arms over and across his, she tilted to rest her cheek on his forearm. She'd been a widow. She'd lost a lover. She'd lost a father. All three violently. From her experience on both sides of the equation, cops never knew how to handle the ones left behind well enough. Informing the family was awkward each and every time.

She pulled away. "I've got calls to make, and I think I'll make them here."

"Look at you telecommute." Mark handed her back her towel. "I'll whip up breakfast. You setting up at the table?"

She nodded and hurried to dry her hair and get dressed. She chose cargos and a polo sporting the EBPD emblem. She left the tack belt off until it was time to leave the house. The shrimp and eggs arrived as she reached the table, coffee with it.

She checked in with Marie, relaying her morning plans. The two officers on duty today—

Officer Russell Wiley and Deputy-on-loan-from-the-county Don Raysor—continued the canvassing. Her old boss Stan volunteered to continue as well. The others were allowed to sleep in since they had worked until eleven last night, but a couple of them would continue later. Mark, however, had to run his restaurant. As soon as she finished with her phone calls, she might return to her door-knocking as well.

She'd practically ruled out Nolan, Elizabeth's other half, but what about Maddy's boyfriend? He was prone to attacking women from the little she'd learned from Chiara last night. However, best start at the beginning with Maddy. Chiara's help had been practically worthless. Callie would ferret out the facts herself.

After a quick search, she found four different school districts in the Tampa area, and she had to stop and think which one. She flipped back through her notes, but upon seeing Pinellas School District on her screen, the bell of recognition rang. From there she found the district's human resources department, but no names. As generic and bureaucratic a page as one could get, not revealing who was who. And there were... what...

two hundred schools? Seriously?

What had Chiara said about where they worked? Specifically. She scrolled down the list. So many schools... so many derivations. What happened to elementary, middle, and high school? There were technical, magnet, intermediate, exceptional, education schools, which she couldn't imagine as any different than regular schools, and more. Wait, Chiara said middle school, and something about honors. She went with magnet schools, scrolling, remembering the title being something beach related. Orange, Sunset, Sandy, Sawgrass... then she stopped on what she thought rang the bell—Seagull Middle School. A magnet school. Worth a shot.

She called the school who acted afraid to talk to her, redirecting her to the district. It took some holding time, twice the person coming back to ask questions. Her police chief moniker barely grabbed attention the first time or scared them off, but the second time she introduced herself more fully, adding she called regarding a murder. She didn't have to wait long. She expected an authoritative voice to answer, honcho to honcho, so to speak, but the man who answered sounded unsure of himself. He wasn't the head of HR, he said, but he assured Callie he could help.

"Did I hear right? There's a murder?" he said. "And you are who?"

She repeated her identity, pleasant as punch. "Unfortunately, we've experienced a murder, and your employee was with the victim around the time she died."

Close enough to get attention without mislaying the truth.

"Hmm," the man groaned, more like *how the hell should I handle this* versus any noise of concern for Maddy.

"We're trying to determine if she met with any abuse or threats lately. She might've reported them to HR, seeking assistance in case that threat followed her to the job."

"Hmm," he said again, but in the background, she thought she heard his fingers pecking on keys. "I'll be limited in what I can tell you absent a warrant for the information."

"Anything would be of assistance." She told him he could find her posted on the Edisto Beach's website and would be happy to Facetime him so he could confirm he was speaking with that individual.

"Maddy Gillespie," she repeated. "Teaches accelerated math at Seagull Middle. Roughly age thirty-five. Middle height. Blond. Pretty. She would have changed her address not long ago, rooming with another teacher in the same school who teaches honors English. She's down here for four weeks, but you might not necessarily be aware of that if she wasn't teaching in the summer."

"I can't tell you much," he said, still pecking. "Sorry," he came back. "No Maddy Gillespie."

Had Chiara told her wrong? Or had she point-blank lied? "How about Chiara Hamilton? Dark hair. Same age. Works on the same hall and teaches honors English. They are tight friends."

More pecking. "No such person."

"Okay, let me say this. Maddy has a stalker. Surely, she informed HR, or at least the school principal and Resource Officer on site to be on the lookout."

Silence on the other end.

"We have someone like that, but we have strict requirements on revealing anything about our staff without a warrant, and we most certainly cannot get into a law-enforcement situation."

He spoke the lingo, but she thought she heard a desire in his voice to say something.

"Why do you need to know?" he asked, his voice suddenly much lower.

"We're ruling out suspects."

"She's a suspect?"

"I sincerely hope not, but I would like to hear more about the stalker."

She could practically hear the man playing out all the privacy workshops he'd attended, shuffling the shoulds, coulds, and nevers drilled into their heads.

"I'm trying to keep her, her teacher friend, and my beach residents safe, sir," she said, with a small nudge. "She's afraid to talk. Both women are, honestly."

Bureaucracies, particularly the small ones like school districts and town halls, were incredibly narrow-minded, unable to get past the rules to see the need. The litigious nature of people made everyone afraid to say anything. Made law enforcement's position difficult at best.

"Then I definitely don't want to say too much. Need a warrant," he said.

"We could certainly use your help."

"Warrant," he repeated.

Like Mr. HR, she had restrictions on how much she could say, too. She'd almost said too much, and if she said much more, she'd compromise Maddy's and Chiara's employment. Just like this guy probably thought from his end.

She was more than half sure she'd made the right call, to the right place, which could only mean one thing.

Chiara Hamilton and Maddy Gillespie weren't their real names.

That's why she couldn't find Lydia Barron's name anywhere, too. She expected the same for Vivien Holden and Robin Nilsson. Only made sense that hookers donned fake names while on the job. Flesh professionals had been doing that since the dawn of time. These women just weren't named Cherry, Angel, or Candy.

Chapter 23

"HIT A WALL?" Mark asked. He still had an hour before he needed to be at the restaurant and had been piddling, cleaning, staying out of Callie's way.

"Yeah," she said, pondering angles. "If this weren't summer, I'd call the actual school back where two of those women say they work. This time of year, however, there'd be no more than a skeleton crew."

"Assuming the school's name is real," he said, peering over her shoulder at the school district's website. Callie pointed to a list on the left. There it was. Seagull Middle School. He scratched his ear.

"I hear what you're thinking," she said. "Why give me an alias then tell me where you work?"

Mark blew out a laugh through his nose and turned away, head shaking with wonder. People did dumb things. Criminals could be pure idiots and all but leave you breadcrumbs to who they were and where they operated.

But these women weren't criminals, if you didn't count the prostitute part. Lydia was another story, most definitely a deeper well. If she'd been in the room when Chiara started down the who-I-am road with Callie, she'd have seized the conversation and whisked Chiara away.

But not everyone was like Lydia, drawing lines. Not everyone was the district HR person, demanding warrants. There were a lot of people like Chiara out there, and Callie decided to roll the dice and give those odds a go.

She called the school again. She introduced herself to, it turned out, the same person she'd spoken to before, a Mrs. Patterson, the one who'd referred her to the district.

"Couldn't the district help?" the lady asked, and Callie tried not to envision a grandmotherly type in a summer shift and sandals, barrettes on either temple holding strands of gray out of her eyes... downplaying the dress code in the name of Florida heat. Real or not, visuals often helped when restricted to a phone.

"Okay," Callie started. "I have the names wrong, apparently. Rather embarrassing, honestly. Instead of calling him back and sounding like a complete idiot, I thought I'd call you since that is where they worked. Can you humor me a second?"

"Not sure," she said, and Callie decided she liked the visual she'd painted of Mrs. Patterson and went with it.

"Okay, here goes. The two teachers work there. They are about the same height. One blond with chin-length hair, the other brunette, a little shorter haircut. One teaches honors English, eighth grade, I believe she said. The other accelerated math. They work, coincidentally, on the same hall, a couple rooms apart. That stuck with me when she said it, because I imagined English and math on separate wings." Callie paused. "I'm sorry. Was that too fast? Didn't mean to run on like that."

"You described them to a tee," Mrs. Patterson said.

"They are roommates here and seem close."

"Oh, they are," the receptionist said. "So what's the problem you're calling about?"

"A murder," Callie replied.

The gasp came through loud and clear. "Oh, good, Lord."

"Oh," Callie said. "Neither of them. Didn't mean to give you that impression."

The release of air came through loud across the phone. "So how are they involved?"

"Oh, they're witnesses, or sort of. It was dark. They may have seen something but aren't sure. That kind of thing. I'm doing the legwork of confirming they are who they say they are. Have to do this for several people."

"Oh," Mrs. Patterson said, disappointed.

"Thank God they weren't involved," Callie tacked on. "Wouldn't want someone coming after them. One of them said she just got out of a bad relationship, but I imagine that's nothing compared to a murderer."

Callie waited... hoping... praying she'd played this woman right.

Some silence made her wonder if the woman was asking someone else what she was supposed to do.

She came back. "Nobody's available I can talk to, so I'll just tell you. The English teacher is Bristol Blake. The math teacher is Grace Ackerman. Poor Grace is the one with the psycho boyfriend. We've all been shown a picture of him in case he comes to the school."

Hallelujah. "Have you ever seen him?" Callie asked, feeding the woman's effort.

"Thank heavens, no. I believe the police talked to him. Maybe that's why he's never been seen here."

"Sounds like the Tampa police are on the job," Callie said.

"Humph," came a response Callie didn't expect. "If they did their job, he'd be off the streets, wouldn't he? These girls shouldn't have to deal with this shit."

Callie's image of sweet Mrs. Patterson popped, replaced with someone with more edges in their face, hair longer, needing a wash.

"You wouldn't be familiar with his name, would you?"

"No. Don't care to. If he'd been here, I'd have known more about him, maybe his name. Sorry."

"That's all right," Callie said. "You've been a joy to talk with. Do you enjoy working at the school?"

"Been doing it for forty years, so whether I love it or not really doesn't matter."

Mrs. Patterson had turned rather feisty.

"But if I didn't love it, I'd be stupid staying here that long. Of course I do. What's your name and number?"

Callie had no problem giving it to her. "Call me if you see or hear anything abnormal about these two ladies and this..."

"Lunatic?"

"That works. Again, thanks."

Didn't take long for Callie to connect with the Tampa Police Department after that, but it took three times on hold to get transferred to the right party, someone most familiar with that area and, hopefully, with the *lunatic*.

An officer listened to Callie's issues and tapped on keys. Tampa was large and several suspects came up, but when Callie asked for a repeat offender who went after a schoolteacher named Grace Ackerman who lived in the area of Seagull Middle School, the list narrowed to one.

"Yep, got him right here. I can send you a picture of both him and her," the officer said.

Didn't take a minute for the photos to appear on Callie's phone. Yep... that was Maddy. The guy? Callie had never seen him before.

His name was Kent Trevino.

Callie wasn't sure if the officer being a woman helped, but she'd take it if it did. The story got deeper, too. "Three reports of abuse, every case dropped when the woman wouldn't press charges."

"Damn, I hate that," she said, her curse a whisper of breath into the phone. "Three different women?"

"Yes, ma'am."

"Do you mind telling me the names of the three victims?"

"Not at all. Grace Ackerman, Khloe McPherson, and Bristol Blake."

"Yep," she said. "Send me the reports on the two others?"

Didn't take long for the reports and photos to pop up on her work laptop.

"Hunh," she said.

Bristol Blake was indeed the Chiara Hamilton on Edisto.

No wonder Maddy had been scared, and Chiara, aka Bristol, scared for her due to her own firsthand experience of the man's ability to abuse. Callie understood bullies well enough to appreciate how they reacted when scorned. In this case, Kent would have gone after either woman, particularly hating that they'd rallied together against him.

Callie had to get a grip on where this man was, and instinct said not to bet he remained in Tampa. Still, she had to confirm. "Any chance someone can do a check at his address for me? Work and home? Don't want to waste time hunting for a man stalking women on my beach when he's kicked back with a beer watching Netflix in Tampa."

"Be glad to."

Flipping through the attachments the officer had already delivered via email, Callie now had Kent Trevino's address, employer, phone number, car, tag, even email. She wasn't sure she'd ever be in Tampa, but if she did, she'd drop by with a thank-you for the Tampa officers. This sort of cooperation was worth its weight in gold. Some departments readily accepted such requests for outside jurisdictions, knowing the help would be reciprocated in turn. Other cities...? Well, they felt themselves too busy to bother, too caught up in their own bubble. The bigger the city, the less the chance they'd liaise. She'd lucked up with a city as large as Tampa. Sort of made her think more highly of Florida.

She called Marie and gave her Kent Trevino's description of him and his car and told her to pass it on. Marie started asking questions, but a hyper banging on the front door drew her attention. Mark had just finished washing the breakfast dishes and went to see who was so up-and-at-'em this time of the morning.

Sophie.

"Marie, gotta go. I'll check in later. Call me... you know."

Since Callie and Mark had moved back into *Chelsea Morning*, once again next door to the yoga maven, she'd come over at least every other day. Sometimes to borrow something, sometimes because she was bored, other days to ask questions about the latest hubbub like when a long-time resident ran into the water station in front of the town's government complex. There'd been a whole kerfuffle about whether the man should lose his driver's license, as if it were a community decision.

Mark barely had time to open the door fully before Sophie blew in. "Aren't you ever home?" she exclaimed. "I've been taking care of your son, you know. He was worried about Beverly. What is the deal? Is she serious or not? For the life of me, I couldn't read him well enough to know."

Mark shut the door. "Sure, come on in, Sophie."

"Oh, hey, Mark," she said then launched straight back into her questioning of Callie.

"Coffee?" he asked. "Sort of afraid to feed caffeine to you, but hey, I'm a nice guy."

"No thanks. Have a yoga class in forty minutes."

Callie looked at the kitchen clock. "Thought you taught yoga earlier than this?"

"Private session," she said. "Over at *Time in a Bottle*. They hired me back this week." She shrugged. "That's what happens when you're good."

Callie wondered if this was why Maddy had put her interview off until this afternoon. "Oh, honey, we've got to talk." She opened a new page to her notepad.

Sophie pulled out a chair and perched on its edge. "We sure do. Fill me in on Beverly."

First things first, Callie guessed. While embellishment wasn't Jeb's forte, he was adept at not telling the whole truth if it wasn't pretty.

"Beverly had pains in her arm, and she panicked," Callie said. "Since she had Jeb there, and this next part is my perception, mind you, she took advantage of the attention and read more into the pain than necessary. Not being versed in heart issues, that's what Jeb feared it was and took her to the emergency room."

"He's a sweet boy, you know that? I'll crucify Sprite if she ever dumps him. I see them making beautiful babies together."

Callie held up a hand. "Not something I want to think about quite yet, Grandma."

"Oh, I would never be called Grandma. That's so ancient sounding. I'd be something more like... Amala."

Callie had to ask. "Is that Granny in another language?"

Sophie giggled, a soft wave of her hand tapping lightly on Callie's. "No, silly. It is a Sanskrit word. Means *clean and most pure*. Also, it's the name of the Hindu goddess Lakshmi."

"Sort of explains your boyfriend calling you Goddess, I guess."

More giggling, only deeper, more devious. "Oh, that's another story, trust me."

Rabbit holes were common in Sophie's world, and Callie didn't have time for one of them right now. "Back to Beverly. She is home, probably at work today. She has gout, not a heart problem."

Sophie scrunched her nose. "Gout. Sounds... ugly, and common. Like something from old England that raggedy old men in alleys have."

Callie had to process that for a second. "Well, Google it. Jeb's more worried about her than he needs to be, but then I'm worried about how much Beverly hides from us, so I guess Jeb has somewhat of a right to be concerned. She'll lean on him more, and he doesn't need that. He needs to get on with his life. She wants him in Middleton politics. I don't. I've lived that life. It's not an enjoyable one."

"She seems to enjoy it. Who says Jeb can't?" Sophie asked. "Just because you don't doesn't mean it's bad for everyone."

Goodness gracious, I don't need this right now.

"Guess you're right there," Callie conceded, for no other reason than to move on. Then for a second, she saw the truth in her logic, which scared her. *Time to move on.* "Hey, since you brought up your yoga class with those ladies, I need to ask you something."

"Shoot," she said, elbows on the table, in a good mood since she'd been told she'd won a conversation with her police chief friend.

"Are they prostitutes?"

"Maybe."

"Why don't you know? You know everything."

"It's not a question you ask unless you're a cop."

Fair.

Sophie literally balled up on the kitchen chair, but then she was noted for her legs and their ability to make pretzel knots.

"How many classes have you taught since they've been here? One that I know of."

Sophie's brow arched up. "How would you know?"

"You told me. Plus you left your business card."

"Oh. Right. Well, today is my second time, but I've done yoga for them as long as I can remember."

Callie noted on her pad. "Was Maddy there the first time this summer?" She needed to be sure.

"Yes. And come to think of it, why do these women still want my yoga with Maddy missing?" Sophie asked.

"Well," Callie started, grateful for Sophie seeing things her way for a change. "They aren't and she isn't."

"Huh?"

"She showed back up. Said she was out and about on her own and decided to come home."

"I hate drama."

"You love drama, Soph."

Sophie stared out the window. Mark set a water before her, and she only eased a hand around the glass, without words. "Shame Brice isn't around. He was intimately familiar with them. Especially with Lydia."

Sighing, Callie had to agree. Chances were Lydia had nabbed that pillow from Brice's with a key he'd given her. "But he isn't. So, tell me what you know. More this time."

Giving a goofy smirk, a sort of shrug, Sophie at first acted as if she had little to offer... when Callie knew better. Once Sophie's brain kicked in, the mouth would follow.

"There are anywhere from three to four of them," Sophie said. "This year was different with five. Three are always the same, Lydia, Vivien, and Robin. At least as far back as I know, but Lydia and Vivien are tight. Probably in more ways than one."

Callie'd sensed the two were more than buddies, too.

"Chiara is recent years. Maddy is brand spanking new."

"She was last minute from what they told me," Callie said.

Sophie hugged the glass between her hands. Mark had disappeared into the bedroom. "They've had about ten or more come and go in their little clique over the years. All of them a decade younger than Lydia and Vivien. Maddy and Chiara are rather young, though. It's odd them being in their thirties. Anyway, they told me to reserve a lesson for five."

Were they getting back to normalcy? Or at least pointing out to the world that there was nothing askew in *Time in a Bottle*?

"I enjoy these ladies. One from years past even met a man out here and married him. He sold his beach house on Palmetto, down near White Cap Street. That's been seven or eight years ago. I still keep up with her. She took to yoga like nobody's business, honey." She seemed to take a trip down Memory Lane for a few seconds. "She thought it unwise for them to come back here as a couple, so they moved to another beach. St. Augustine, I think?"

A place where nobody would hear of their past.

"Do you know any of their aliases?" Callie asked.

That didn't set well with Sophie. "Don't you dare look down on them."

"I don't, Soph. I'm trying to solve a murder. I need to know everyone's real identity to help me piece this together. For instance, how do they pay you? Check? Venmo?"

She winked. "Cash, as do most of my clients."

Of course they paid in cash. And of course that's how Sophie ran her business.

"But I don't ask questions," Sophie added. "That's not how we operate out here on this beach, and you know it."

"Well, sometimes I'm the exception, and I need to ask such questions. It's the only way to keep you people safe."

And Callie didn't believe Sophie hadn't figured out who Lydia and the others were. That didn't mean she was astute at investigations, regardless of what she professed to everyone, but Sophie asked anyone anything and felt it her moral obligation to keep up with residents and travelers alike. In her humorous way, she'd poke and prod at you about yourself until she got what she felt was enough intel to trade. She was amazing at amassing social currency.

"The older ones, though," Callie continued. "Lydia and Vivian. Surely, you've gotten closer to them since they'd seen you since day one."

"Oh, yes, but they're shrewd. They have to be to have been in business this long, with as long a clientele list as they have. You would be amazed at who's on that list. And before you ask, I suspect a few people, but I can't say I can cough up proof. They don't freely chatter with me or anyone else. They have another life off the island. We've all got a history of that, don't we?" Her leaning query said Callie ought to know better.

This wasn't going far. Maybe Lydia was indeed that tight-lipped, even to someone as personable as Sophie. "How about doing something for me?"

Sophie looked skeptical. "I can't betray a student. For you or anybody. I have a responsibility!"

"Hear me out," Callie said. "You always say you want to be part of investigations."

Indeed she had, and as soon as she said it, Callie registered the temptation coming at her through Sophie's blue contacts. "Ask if Maddy's okay. Say you've seen the cops going around asking people about her."

Sophie didn't refuse, a pondering *what-if-I-do-this* in her expression.

"What if they don't want to say?"

"Then watch how they react, and how they say whatever it is they say. You can read people. Hell, you almost read minds."

"That I do," Sophie admitted.

Callie needed her friend to understand the seriousness of the situation, though. "I'm worried about Maddy. She was seen the night Elizabeth—the dead woman found on the sound—died. And we're thinking she might be afraid or involved."

"What if *she* killed Elizabeth?" Sophie asked. "What if Lydia helped her? Isn't that throwing me in danger?"

"Do you see them as the murdering type, Soph?" She'd just been singing their praises for goodness' sake.

Sophie thought. "I think not."

"I'm not seeing that either, Soph. And I wouldn't send you into a dangerous situation, would I?"

Sophie's expression relaxed. "Guess it can't hurt to ask."

"Thanks," Callie said. "I appreciate you doing this. Call me after. Or run me down. Nobody can do this like you can."

"True that," she replied, then glanced at the kitchen clock. "Oh wow, I've got to go." She held up a fist to bump, and Callie returned in kind. "I'd love to wear a badge someday doing this stuff."

"The badge gets in the way, Soph. It's the undercover people who make the biggest strides."

That puffed her up. "Then let me get to it." She carried her glass to the kitchen counter, turned, and gave a limp salute to Callie. And to respect her friend, she returned the gesture.

Once the door closed, Mark came out, dressed and ready for work. "You sure about doing that?"

"She only has to ask one question," she said. "How's Maddy? How can she mess that up?"

"Are we talking about the same person here?" he asked, then kissed her quickly and left. She thought she heard him chuckle as the door shut.

Funny how she'd diverted Sophie from talk of Beverly so easily. She wondered how long before Sophie realized it and came back to finish the conversation.

Her phone rang.

Beverly.

Dog gone it. It was as if thinking of Sophie and Beverly at the same time had opened some sort of portal.

"Hey, Mother. How are you feeling?"

"Tip top, dear. Yesterday was a total fluke. I relaxed half the day then went in to work."

Callie didn't ask what she told her staff about the absence, because the response wouldn't be the truth.

"What's your day like?" her mother asked.

Her guard went up. "I'm working that death case. Why""

"Sounds... I don't know... busy? Are you under a time clock with that?"

Say what?

Her age-old wretched ill feelings rocketed to the surface, happening every time Beverly entered the picture. "Just the usual time crunch of investigations. The husband of a murdered woman wants his wife's body which he can't have until I finish following leads and the forensics are done. Not sure we can put time clocks on that, though time is of the essence, I'd say."

Plus, she was to meet Maddy at four this afternoon.

"Regardless," her mother went on, "whatever you have, reschedule it. We need to meet."

Not pleasant to hear something like that from one's mother. "When and where?"

"Today. Edingsville Grocery. Two o'clock."

Edingsville hadn't been open more than a few years—a restaurant on the island, still on Highway 174, but not all the way to the beach, and about six miles short of the water. It had grown in popularity, with brothers Russell and Robert Hughes having outdone themselves with their Lowcountry cuisine and personalities. Clearly, Beverly had been gnawing on this offer. She would normally prefer Ella and Ollie's, or Pressley's, but this could be her way of easing herself back onto the island without coming all the way to the water to where Brice had lived.

"Can't it wait a few days?" Callie hated having to ask. Sort of made her the bad guy. She always felt like the bad guy with her family.

"No, it can't."

Short. Terse. Her mother's abruptness sent a chill up Callie's spine until she reminded herself she'd felt one of these chills the other night, too. Before she learned that gout wasn't a heart attack.

But this could be something more than physical ailments. This might be Beverly coming clean about the needs in her life, a topic that hung in transparent shreds between all of them throughout the hospital stay. This could be her actually noticing the family dynamics the other night and wanting to make amends.

Callie instantly thought, *what would Sarah do*, and hardly finished the thought before she knew the answer. Sarah—a genuinely kind woman—would meet with Beverly.

The time was going on noon. She still wanted to pick the brains of Deputy Don Raysor and real estate broker Janet Wainwright, who managed the lease agreement of *Time in a Bottle*. She wanted time with Marie. In all of this busyness, she hadn't had time for Marie, and that's who she normally probed for all things Edisto, and a thirty-year prostitute ring seemed to qualify.

"Yes, I'll change some things and meet you there." She held her breath for Beverly to tell her to bring Jeb, but she didn't.

"Good. Will you be in uniform? I'd rather you weren't."

Beverly never liked Callie in uniform. "I'll dress it down, Mother. And leave off the belt."

"Good. See you then." She hung up.

No ending with *I look forward to seeing you, dear.* Nor *I love you, dear.* Just an appointment confirmation with a dress code.

But look at the bright side.

Beverly reached out to her.

Second, she hadn't asked Jeb to come along.

Third, Beverly was daring to set foot on Edisto Island. It wasn't the beach, but it was a start. How was Callie supposed to decline the order, um, invitation her mother was making in what could be a quasi-attempt to overcome her fears of returning since Brice died?

And lastly... what was so important? Her backbone still held onto that chill.

The meeting could take an hour or a major chunk of her day. There was no point in making an appointment after the late lunch for fear of having to miss it. There was a point in defining what she did with the next hour and a half, though, because that was about as much time as she had.

So, Deputy Raysor, Janet Wainwright, or Marie?

Her gut told her to go with Don. Janet wouldn't necessarily be available due to clients and showings. Marie would be better first thing in the morning or last thing in the evening, when they'd be interrupted less.

Yeah, she could catch up to Don pretty quickly.

Edingsville. *Nice choice, Mother.* Now Callie looked forward to the meal. Appetizer fried chicken livers. Main course whatever the special was; it was all good. And cake. There was always cake made from scratch.

She called Marie first.

"Hey, my mother wants to meet this afternoon. Just letting you know."

Marie hesitated. "Is she okay?" She understood the complicated mother-daughter relationship. She'd watched it silently from a distance for three years.

"I believe so, but when a mother calls and says it's important you dine with her that day, well..."

"You do as told," Marie finished.

"But I called to also say we need to chat. Meaning you and me."

"Sounds ominous." Marie did a marvelous dry, tongue-in-cheek thing.

"I'll tell you some of it now, just so there isn't anything *ominous* hanging. I need you to search your data banks and your cadre of intel providers for a group called *The Summer Ladies*. They're at *Time in a Bottle*. Don't know where they've stayed before. I'll get that from Janet. There's a strong rumor they may be prostitutes, and the ladies themselves admit to a thirty-plus-year legacy out here. I'm embarrassed to say I've never heard of them, and everyone I've spoken to seems to be equally embarrassed for me. The women's working names are Lydia Barron, Vivien Holden, Robin Nilsson, Chiara Hamilton, and Maddy Gillespie. Maddy's the one—"

"That was missing," Marie said. "Working names?"

Callie explained the real names.

"Seen Maddy to confirm she's reappeared?"

"This afternoon. I have, however, learned of an abusive boyfriend. She was a last-minute addition to the ladies' group, too, so she might be running from him. I'll send you what Tampa PD sent me on the three abuse claims. You'll note that two of them belong to two of our ladies, so it seems we have another angle to scope. The stalker's name is Kent Trevino. They're going by his home to see if he's in Florida before I worry too hard about him being here, but we still need to keep our eyes open here."

"You've been busy. How much sleep did you get after the hospital fiasco?"

"Five hours. Enough to keep me going." Marie could be quite motherly for having never been a mother. "By the way, if you want to research the other two ladies for their real names, knock yourself out. I take it we've seen nothing on Trevino's automobile."

"No, sorry." Marie adored research. "I'll jump on this stuff, though.

Nothing else pressing today. Even with Wiley," she tacked on, mentioning the officer who exerted the least effort of all her uniforms. "Nobody canvassed recognizes Maddy Gillespie or Elizabeth Nolan yet, either."

It was as if these two women had moved invisibly around the beach. "Well, you know how to reach me."

"Ten four," came the routine sign-off.

Marie had asked about Beverly without hesitation, genuinely inquiring because she cared. She asked everyone how their momma was, preserving a generations-old Southern tradition, and if they had no mother, she asked about their family... or the individual, like Thomas. She was naturally maternal, and it was a crying damn shame she lived alone, but Marie lived the life she chose and dared anyone to feel sorry for her.

In all her years since graduating high school, there'd never been an eligible officer that Marie could pair up with. Already married, usually. The singles were too young or too old, because for the most part, officers came to Edisto to get started in their career or to wind it down. She didn't make enough money or have the pedigree to be acceptable to some of the old Edisto clans, and she had no desire to latch ahold of most of the families anyway, knowing all their skeletons.

However, she made family of those she worked with, cheered everyone on in the government complex, ever the one to bring in a birthday cake for an officer and put up the tree at Christmas. She was always the first to put presents under the branches, string the lights, and set the tone.

Everyone invited her to their place for Christmas, but she declined. They managed to drag her to a birthday lunch every March, but that was about it in terms of her celebratory ways.

Callie felt guilty for having talked about the controversy of having two mothers, when Marie didn't have a mother, a father, or any siblings that she knew of.

She would invite Marie to lunch with Beverly, but her mother had called this sudden meeting for a purpose, and with a third wheel at the table, she'd cause a scene or drop the subject. Not timely.

Next call, and this one she hated. The call to Maddy's phone went to voicemail. She asked to push back their meeting to the evening, yet she expected that to be postponed as well with what the ladies did. Whenever she left her meeting with Beverly, she'd call and cross her fingers she could catch Maddy before she got obligated.

Speaking of lunch, Callie had to hustle, so she called Don Raysor, the quickest to get ahold of, and the one who'd be the most succinct in answering her questions. As touchy as they might be.

During her chat with Sophie, she almost asked if Raysor would be familiar with such ladies, and then thought better of it. That would only set Sophie's mind to pondering, which could lead to more harm than good.

Nope, he wouldn't welcome being discussed with the island's primary information gatherer, sometimes disseminator, and often times mis-interpreter. She'd have him trolling with *The Summer Ladies* on a routine basis just because he was a single, middle-aged guy from Walterboro in need of a date.

"How's it going, Doll?" he answered after one ring. "Heard you found the missing woman."

"She called, but I haven't met up with her yet. Hopefully this afternoon."

"Well, I can't find a soul who saw either one. If the dead one hadn't washed up, I'd have thought this a damn joke, you know?"

She loved the nickname he used for her, one that had morphed from intentionally caustic when they first met to endearing once they'd come to appreciate each other. "Listen, I want to talk to you about these women. Can you take a break and come by the house?"

"Um, why the house?"

She hadn't had him over since she'd taken her sabbatical and had him come in civvies to help solve a murder behind the scenes.

"Want me to come in a plain wrapper?" he asked.

"Your patrol car is fine. There's nothing secretive. I just happen to be here, and in a little over an hour I have to book it to an appointment. Need to pick your glorious brain."

"Be there before you can count to a hundred," he said.

She didn't get to fifty before he knocked on the door. He had to have been no more than a block away.

Quicker than expected. Not quite enough time to figure out how to ask him just how familiar he might have ever been with these ladies.

Chapter 24

Lydia

WITH SOPHIE BIANCHI not able to work their private yoga session into her schedule until ten, the weather was a tad hot to be doing stretches outdoors, so Lydia made the command decision to move the furniture and use the living room. Robin was the one who desired to hear the ocean while they held their triangle poses and stiffened warrior positions, but *Time in a Bottle* was on the sound, where the water was more docile, without waves. So the living room it was... with the door open for Robin, the air conditioner on for Lydia.

Personally, she wasn't keen on a woman of her age sweating on the sand for passing tourists to ogle. Professionally, their local *friends* didn't need to see them in such disarray.

But Lydia had contacted Sophie to do this last-minute session in an attempt to make everyone calm down and give Maddy some stability. The evening before, once Lydia had gone to Griffin's place, Vivien roused Maddy, pumped her full of a breakfast dinner and coffee, and sat her down to get her head straight as to what happened, what couldn't be said, and how to function without casting suspicion. In hindsight, Lydia decided Vivien was the best personality to do that. Not her, being the boss, and not Chiara because she was too easily upset and too close. Robin... was just Robin. A woman who preferred not to think too deeply.

It had actually been Vivien's idea to call a class. When the yoga instructor arrived, Vivien was unplugging the lamp cords.

"Brought extra mats," Sophie exclaimed. Once that instrumental music began, however, Lydia liked how she fell into her calm instructor mode, voice mellow and pleasing. Lydia found Sophie's talents wasted in small Edisto Beach, her style beating anything in Tampa.

Sophie glanced around the room, taking measure of how this would work. The group had held a morning session on the beach earlier in the week, two of them on beach towels, because the two youngest, Chiara and Maddy, had forgotten mats in their hurry to get packed for the trip. Sophie had brought extras this time.

Lydia had pushed back an appointment for Robin until two, but for the good of the group and the sanity of most of them, this morning's yoga had to happen. It wouldn't cure Maddy, but it would set the stage for her recuperation.

While Sophie set up her music and chimes, Vivien set a pitcher of lemon water on the bar. Didn't take Sophie long to chime her little bell and direct students to their places.

"Where's Maddy?" she asked.

"She's coming," Vivien said.

Lydia reminded herself that this woman lived next door to the chief of police. Not a problem before, but now.... She also worked for the police chief's boyfriend. Sophie was a sweet woman, and nobody disliked her, but she wasn't bright enough to send undercover, in her opinion. But then, she would be someone quite unexpected to be undercover, wouldn't she?

The other three looked to Lydia.

"Maddy?" Sophie asked again.

This was Maddy's first appearance in front of, say, *civilians*? People who had no idea where she'd been and why.

Lydia held up a hand and made a slight face indicating she had this and glided into Maddy's room as if to urge the girl to finish dressing. Maddy, however, was already dressed in her leggings sitting cross-legged on her bed. Chiara had done her hair and face with lip gloss and a hint of mascara to be presentable. A touch of color on her cheeks which had gotten quite pale of late.

"Time to show yourself," Lydia said, and held out her hand, wiggling a finger for her to come.

Maddy's gaze was pleading. "I don't think..."

"Sure you can." She reached over, took Maddy's hand, and brought her to her feet. "Life goes on. You did nothing wrong. *We* did nothing wrong. And we are walking into the future chin high and thankful."

"Thankful? How can you say thankful?"

"You're not dead like Elizabeth Brown, are you?"

Maddy's shoulders loosened, barely.

"Exactly," Lydia said. "That *is* a blessing, so embrace it. Acknowledge the gift God gave you and live your life... starting with a good dose of yoga to put your mind in sync with your body. What do you say, my dear?"

The girl's shoulders relaxed more. "You make it sound so... noble."

"Noble. I like that. Park that in your brain and remind yourself of it each and every morning. Now, come. They're waiting in the living room."

She escorted Maddy in, who did a fair job smiling at the instructor.

"Good," Sophie said. "Everyone on a mat." She dinged her chime again, and the lesson began.

Lydia hadn't realized how badly she needed this, and went through the moves, each one taking her to a better place. She could only assume equal beneficial properties for Maddy. For them all.

While she had more reason than Maddy to be worried about the other night, she possessed more internal fortitude groomed from childhood. She was positive Chief Morgan had informed her police cadre of who they were, but if they'd learned the names of only a handful of the old clients, like Brice Legrand, they would look the other way like the chief's predecessors. The older chiefs had never minded them. With this one being a woman, though... a hint of uncertainty had taken up residence in Lydia, maybe chipping at her confidence.

Lydia tried to let those thoughts drift off so she could focus on strengthening her body and her inner self.

But damn it, if the chief had put her yoga friend up to something, Lydia would be mighty pissed.

The hour session passed in fits and spurts for her, but in the end, she had to admit she was glad they'd made the effort. She felt better. Maddy looked remarkably more stable.

They rolled up mats, put furniture back, and helped themselves to the lemon water, some seated at the bar, the others in the living room.

"So," Sophie said, having chosen to sit at the big table, so she could see them all. "How's tricks?"

Chiara choked on her drink, making Robin stand and pat her on the back.

"Tricks?" Vivien asked, with a side eye at Lydia.

"What makes you think we're that way?" Lydia asked point blank, as serious as a nun at vespers.

Sophie's brain short circuited, and her gazes darted off each one. She took another sip, then cleared her throat. "But I thought... I mean, after all these years of me holding class with you ladies... I just assumed... good heavens... I mean, you ladies have a way about you. Some of the men drool over themselves knowing you're coming to town. Trust me, I've dated some of those men. You girls got skills."

Vivien tried to hide a half grin, but Lydia almost let herself laugh.

Kudos to Sophie. She'd owned her words. That Lydia liked. Frankly, she'd always liked her. She just wasn't happy about having befriended the chief these last couple of years.

Not that they disliked all cops. They'd been known to love a few of them more than others over the years.

"Sophie, I've been meaning to ask you something," Lydia said. "Never got around to it last year, but I told myself to make a point to do so this summer. Or do you have a class we'd be holding you from? If so, we can put this off."

But Sophie was baited. "No, nothing else today. I just have to go to work at El Marko's around three. My time is your time, honey."

"How would you like to join our group?" Lydia asked.

Robin's brows almost disappeared into her bangs. Vivien didn't make any odd or sudden moves, but the *WTF* in her eyes spoke loud enough.

Chiara did a head-tilt thing, her gaze covering Vivien and Robin, as if she'd missed something while gone last night. Nobody looked at Maddy. Nobody wanted to put Maddy on the spot, but everyone silently waited for Sophie's answer.

Sophie's blush matched her painted nails, a coral color perfect for her skin tone. But she quickly recovered. "I'd be good at it, you know."

That revelation cut the tension in the room, and the entire lot of them burst out laughing. "Yes, you would," Vivien said.

"But I sort of have a steady guy right now," Sophie continued, her smile wide and stuck there.

She was genuinely flattered, which, in afterthought, made Lydia halfway consider the offer legitimate. She could be such an asset as a beach resident, an advance-notice person who could find the right house for them. She even owned a house, but being next door to the chief wouldn't cut it.

"You never keep a man very long, Miss Sophie, if my memory serves me right," Lydia said, giving her a sultry side look. "What do you think, ladies?"

"Oh, I'm all for this," Viv said.

"She'd be a hoot," Robin replied.

Chiara shrugged when the others waited for her response. "Have to admit she'd fit in." Such a double meaning coming from the one no longer fitting in.

Maddy had never had to vote on anything, so nobody put her on the spot, but Lydia caught the small grin on her face at the humor of it all.

The vote clinched it if Sophie wanted the gig.

"Sophie, let's talk about this."

Sophie basked being the center of attention, seated there so prim and proper, her posture to die for, as if she were on an interview for *American Idol*, waiting to perform something ad lib.

While Lydia had shot from the hip on the question, to throw Sophie off whatever game she might be playing, just in case, Lydia also knew Sophie had played the field and played it hard over the years they'd been coming there. She had indeed dated whatever was worth dating, and the man she dated now had tasted their wares a time or two. Buck Newell was an incredibly decent guy, and if they were an item, they'd be good for each other, but from what Lydia had seen of the man, he wouldn't be so keen on his lovely selling her flesh.

"Um, I have a house," Sophie said, a tad stumbling with the realization of how this could work. "But I don't think that would fly being next door to the police chief."

Vivien rolled her eyes. "Amen to that."

"No," Lydia admitted. "No cop is going to look the other way when you rub their noses in... us."

Robin gave one of her alto laughs at that one.

"Would I have to come up with a working name?" Sophie asked, not sensing the joke. Not sensing she'd been played at all.

Robin clipped off her chuckling, all but telegraphing the suspect nature of the question.

Lydia had to air the subject now. "Why do you ask, Sophie?"

"Seriously?" Her voice held a hint of a squeak. A nervous trait one might read as deceptive. "Are you really using your legal names? You're ladies of the evening, for goodness' sake." She pointed to each of them. "Are you really Lydia, Vivien, Robin, Chiara... and Maddy?"

Maddy's face reddened.

Sophie noted. "An alias is insurance, if you ask me."

Nobody spoke.

"I would pick something Hindu, but I think that would be a giveaway, don't you think? And I could stick with the guys who are visitors, not residents, so I don't get found out."

Everyone smiled at her naïveté. It wasn't a matter of *if* someone found out. She'd be the staked flag on Edisto Beach.

"Ooh, I know," Sophie went on. "Gypsy. Does that suit me or

what!" She tittered, so proud of herself, while the ladies watched, each wondering how in the world she'd stumbled upon their having aliases.

Lydia returned to pondering if Sophie had been sent to snoop.

"Well, think about it," Lydia said, closing the conversation. "Oh gracious, look at the time! You'll have to charge us double at this rate if we keep on talking. Discuss it with Buck. See what he has to say."

Sophie's smile dimmed to half strength at the mention of her beau.

Lydia rose. "The day is getting old, ladies. We have places to be. "

"Wait," Sophie said. "Maddy. I wanted to ask how she is. I saw officers going around everywhere, hunting for her. Thought you'd found a substitute when you made the appointment for five, but here she is." She beamed at Maddy, waiting for a reaction.

"I... I just had to be alone. Sorry I scared everyone. Totally innocent," Maddy said.

"Where were you?" Sophie asked.

Lydia saw clear through the pretense.

"With a gentleman who shall remain nameless," Lydia said, in all seriousness.

To that, Sophie reddened, reached for her lemon water, and finished it. "Well, time for me to go. Enjoyed it, ladies. You know how to reach me for your next session. Always love working with you."

"I hope we can continue," Lydia said, and from Sophie's fallen expression, she seemed to realize discretion was wise for job security.

Chapter 25

FUNNY HOW FEW people asked why Deputy Don Raysor wore beige instead of Edisto officers' uniforms of dark blue. The lighter color shirt made him appear larger than he was, but he was his own man, every inch of him. His manner was gruff with a redneck swagger; his complexion, even the back of his hands, was rough. Not the first sign of cosmopolitan flair whatsoever in Raysor, but those whom he respected were guaranteed loyalty in spades.

He'd lived in Colleton County his entire life, related to ten percent of the population, which meant he had reach, connection, and loads of information on the past and present.

Callie offered him coffee. He declined then changed his mind, one bushy brow propped up high in anticipation of what this unique meeting would require of him. He wasn't a genius, but he was keenly aware of people and how they functioned.

If Callie had an entire force of Dons and Thomases, she'd be the luckiest police chief in the country.

She set a cup of coffee at a place at the kitchen table, indicating he should take a seat. He lowered himself with a heavy breath, his utility belt creaking and clanking as sundry items on it hit the wood. "What's this about, Doll?"

"Keep on with the queries about Maddy Gillespie and Elizabeth Nolan," she said. "But Maddy has supposedly come back."

"Supposedly?" He waited.

"The two women connected, as I told you. Seen leaving Coots together."

He waited.

Okay. That was enough prelude. "Have you heard of *The Summer Ladies*, Don?"

His other questioning bushy brow went up, but he delayed answering, instead lifting his coffee, blowing on it, testing with a small, first taste, then taking a swig. In other words, in no rush to answer.

Propping elbows on the table, Callie rested chin atop her collected hands and waited. From his behavior, yes, he had awareness of the ladies, and while she was curious as to why he delayed answering, she wanted him to do so in his own time.

He set his cup down and let out a breathy groan. "Yes, I've heard of them."

"You make that appear rather difficult to say," she said.

"Why do you ask about them?" he asked instead of following her lead.

"Maddy was a member," she explained. "She was reported missing by Chiara Hamilton, another member, who has since caught grief from her cohorts for doing so. I've been talking to Lydia Barron, the leader, and she writes off Maddy to flighty behavior. I'm attempting to interview her since she arrived home yesterday but haven't been able to meet up with her yet."

He waited some more. She explained further.

"My mother Beverly said all the older, entrenched Edistonians were aware of the group, but nothing more, like she'd only heard of them, without involvement. Sarah, my other mother, said her husband and Brice were *friends* of theirs." She used air quotes for emphasis. "Sophie teaches them yoga each year but has no firsthand experience, says some of the ladies return like clockwork and others rotate. Guess I could ask Buck Newell. He's been flying solo long enough to maybe have checked them out."

She paused, hoping Don would chime in. Instead, he was draining her of all she knew to give. "Talk to me, Don."

"You can't seem to ask the right question," he said. "Have I used their services. That's it, isn't it?"

Yes, but no. "Just what are you aware of when it comes to *The Summer Ladies*? No judging."

His scowl made her heart drop. The last thing she wanted to do was insult this man, but because these women were who they were, and did what they did, how did she ask these questions without slipping across a personal line?

"I used them once in their second or third year in operation," he said.

In his thirties. Very understandable.

Callie held off showing any sort of reaction. Honestly, she didn't care. The women seemed discrete enough, smart enough, which meant safe enough. Here sat Don Raysor, none the lesser for the experience.

"Remember their names? Or her name, anyway."

"Vivien," he said. "Nice lady. Smart. She was beautiful, too."

"She still is," Callie said. "She's an attorney. Did you realize that?"

"Yeah. I seem to recall." His expression had softened, his memories mellowing his countenance. "In those days we came to their beach house. They glammed it up with scarves and soft lights, and an array of foods. You were bound to meet someone else coming or going, also with an appointment, and it didn't matter. In those days the police chief welcomed them... and they gave him a mighty thankful welcome in return, if you get my meaning."

Callie nodded. Since the beginning of law enforcement anywhere, a number of police chiefs and sheriffs held unspoken understandings with such ladies. Don had such a sweet look to him in his reminiscing, and it brought a smile to her lips.

"Was it just the two of them then?" she asked.

"Yeah, for the first few years. Again, I just visited the one time. I'm telling you, if I'd lived on Edisto instead of Walterboro..." He faded out with an *umm, um, um*.

"What'd you think of Lydia?" she asked.

"Oh, I had a choice, Doll. I just didn't want anything to do with Lydia," he said.

"Why's that?" What would be the difference to a thirty-something young man with no obligations?

"Just didn't," he said. "She was nice enough, just Vivien caught my eye."

Well, that was vague yet intriguing at the same time.

"Have you seen them since?" she asked.

"On occasion," he said. "And a dozen times give or take over the years. Driving past. Maybe at a restaurant. Never on a call. They keep their heads down, allow no trouble, and offer a decent service. I hear they're pricier than they used to be, which is surprising given their ages, but then, I understand much of their clientele goes way back to the younger days, and the ladies embrace those memories."

"Because they've aged together," she said. "They're safe."

He dipped his head, liking the word choices. "Yeah. Kinda nice in a lot of ways."

Don did make a ring of prostitutes sound like a reunion of high school friends.

She began to liken it to a movie she once saw, where a girl and a guy held an affair once a year at a favorite locale, each year seeing each other become grayer, move slower. The affair was wrong, but there was a sweetness to it that tugged at the heart. These women seemed to offer such a service, giving men something to look forward to each year.

But it was time to come down to earth, and if she had to be the anchor, so be it.

"Don, I've got feelers out for Maddy's old boyfriend, a chronic abuser, whom she was escaping from by piggybacking on this vacation with *The Summer Ladies*. Lydia seems to feel they made a mistake inviting her."

"Yeah, I bet. Lydia ran a smooth machine. I could name you a dozen gentlemen right now who relish these women because of the discrete professionalism, and you'd be shocked at their names. But these guys live for those four weeks of the year, I'm telling ya'."

He'd drunk the Kool-Aid.

"You think these people have a good thing going and hurt nobody in doing it."

"Yes."

"Sorry, but I'm not as big a fan."

He waited for the rest of the thought.

"Maddy's vague disappearance then being seen, we're pretty sure, with a girl that shows up dead, is suspect. Lydia and your Vivien get by with the minimal of cooperation with me on the case. Enough that I can't do much about it. I'm hoping Maddy's interview reveals something. Can't stop thinking she's flighty because of guilt, or fear."

He'd finished his coffee. "I think they have nothing to do with anything criminal. Just happen to be on the periphery. Not everybody's cut out to be a lady of the evening. Maddy maybe took off, embarrassed by the reality of her commitment, escaping the rental cost she realized she couldn't afford. Maybe the ladies aren't worried because they genuinely believe in their version of what's going on. This type of woman can usually read people, Doll. Give them some credit."

What kind of magic dust did these women throw over people to make others see them as a legitimate, if not a benevolent, humanitarian mission group?

"Don..." She was almost disappointed.

He stood. "I know what you're going to say. Can I still do my job knowing they might be involved? Can I still hunt for anyone who may have seen Elizabeth? I'm disappointed you might think anything but."

"Never said that, Don."

"Well, I'm also not ready to throw these other ladies to the dogs just yet."

He made moves to leave, but she wasn't ready to cut him loose yet. "Any idea where Lydia and Vivien came from?"

"Lydia is from the island. Vivien from Florida."

Good memory for only having one rendezvous. "Tell me about Lydia."

"Left here as practically a child. Hard-luck story with parents." He seemed to cut things short.

"What kind of hard luck?" she asked.

"Basically abandoned. Was abused. Got pregnant and left due to the stigma."

Callie admittedly was a little stunned at that. "Then you know her name? I mean, besides Lydia Barron. I've already unearthed the fact they operate with aliases."

He seemed to have to think hard. If he knew this much, he knew the rest. "Come on, Don."

"Bonnie something or other," he said, this time coming to his feet. He went to the kitchen and put his cup in the sink. "Anything else? I need to get back to canvassing these houses."

She wasn't up to alienating him, and if she needed to query him more, she'd do it when he was in better spirits... once she had more to go on. Also, so he wouldn't be in such a spotlight.

But he'd given her a name. Bonnie. In her early to mid-sixties. Left in her teens or twenties. Surely some old-timer would be able to latch ahold of that and fill in the rest.

CALLIE HAD THIRTY minutes to reach Edingsville Grocery, which was plenty of time. Raysor's visit, and his quiet disappointment in her, stuck in her head like a bad date. *What if* and *why did I* tunneled through her brain. The questions had to be asked, but how much had she gained by the asking? His memories of them were gentle and pleasing. His feelings protective.

Honest to God, she wished for the umpteenth time that Brice was here. The banter would be prickly, but he'd talk. He'd brag. But mostly, he'd tell her the real history. Sarah and Beverly recalled only secondhand information, sugar-coated by others to present the ladies as sweethearts. Maybe this lunch with her mother would open up an opportunity to dig deeper. Beverly had her own reasons for lunch. Maybe Callie had hers.

Her phone rang halfway to the restaurant. Sophie.

"What's up?" Callie asked. "I'm headed to lunch with my mother, and I'm not far from pulling in. Can it wait?"

Sophie came across breathless. "They asked me to join them."

Callie could only think of one set of *they*. "Join them to do what?" Dinner? A party at their place?

"Be a hooker," she said.

The laugh came from a deep place, and she regretted discounting Sophie when she did it, but who'd have thought? "When do you start?" she asked.

"I'd have to ask Buck, and I don't think he'd be happy with it."

"You think? Come on. What man would?" She wondered how a yoga session had diverted so far as to even reach that stage of a conversation. Then she figured it out. "Did you see Maddy?"

"I did. She worked out with us."

Great. She was indeed back. "What did she look like?"

"Pale, not sad but not happy. After we got through, however, she looked way better."

Callie hoped she finished with Beverly in time to get back to Maddy, and that Maddy still had that off-base feeling Sophie mentioned for Callie to tap.

"Well, update me on what Buck says."

"Oh, I can't tell him about this."

Callie'd love to be a fly on the wall for that discussion. "Smart move, girlfriend."

"Did I do good?"

"You did great, Soph. Thanks for being discrete."

"My middle name."

Callie almost choked holding back that guffaw. "Gotta go. I'm here."

"Kiss Beverly for me." Sophie laughed at the ridiculousness of the request and hung up.

Callie pulled into the gravel parking lot, her mother's Lexus already there, the car empty. At the door, however, she almost slapped her forehead. The posted hours said they closed at two thirty, reopening at five for dinner. It was just after two. Now what? She didn't want to impose on the owners, but Beverly would expect to be accommodated.

Inside, the stained-wood walls, floors, and ceiling gave the venue a cozy, humble feel. Beverly already sat at a table further inside, behind the enclosed front porch area, Russell already talked her ear off, her talking his off in return. He was quite the personable individual and half of a two-brother duo that owned the venue.

The mixture of aromas set her stomach growling.

"Oh, have a seat, dear," Beverly said, her smile bright. "Russell said he'd have them make us *crème brûlée*."

Russell beamed, happy to thrill his patrons. "Is that good for you?" he recalled.

"I never turn that down," Callie replied, grateful her mother still knew her tastes.

He skirted off to the kitchen to deliver their order and let his brother know they needed a different dessert for some special guests.

Beverly leaned in. "I asked if we could meet through their closed time, so we'd be alone."

Seems she was fully aware of her imposition then, and she'd snowed Russell into tending to her every need. He adored playing host so he wasn't put out, but Callie never enjoyed watching her mother play her games and get her way.

Callie received her chicken liver appetizer and Beverly her martini, and suddenly the room seemed incredibly big, empty, and silent. Callie tried not to look disappointed at how quickly Beverly had gone back to her old dietary ways.

But now was not the time. Callie had been summoned. She waited for what.

Reaching down beside the table, Beverly pulled out a tote bag with a bow on it. "For you, dear." She handed it around the end of the table to avoid bumping the dishes.

Speechless, Callie took the gift. "What's this?"

"A thank-you for taking so much time from your work to tend to me. Especially for it being a false alarm."

Callie couldn't remember the last time her mother... *oh, my, don't tear up*.

Instead of getting lost in words, she scooted back from the table and set the tote in her lap, reaching in. She pulled out a vintage Neil Diamond album, *And the Singer Sings His Songs*. 1976. Autographed.

"Oh, Mother," Callie whispered, running fingers over the cover.

She'd lost her Neil Diamond collection in the fire a year ago. The artist served as one of the few unspoken bonds mother and daughter held. As much as Callie had fought becoming fond of the singer who was also her mother's favorite, she couldn't help it. His songs rebirthed memories of being at Edisto as a child. Those were good memories.

"Here, dear." Her mother handed her a tissue.

"This was sincerely sweet, Mother. Thank you."

"I can be surprising some days," came the haughty tone, still wrapped, however, in a motherly sort of voice.

Until the meal arrived, Beverly prattled on about Middleton politics while Callie dipped her appetizer in catsup, the crispiness of the livers fried to perfection. Politics was Beverly's go-to subject, and since Callie knew most of the players from her growing up in the town, she understood enough to comment appropriately.

During the meal, Beverly spoke of Jeb, and how impressed she was of him, and how she wasn't pushing him into politics unless he had a serious taste for it. Half-hearted politics was a failure waiting to happen, she said.

So far so good. Callie listened more than spoke, lulled almost into believing this was a normal mother and daughter *tête-à-tête*. Other than bringing the food, the staff gave them space, soft music playing in the background. She wondered if Beverly had rented the entire place, the possibility telling Callie to hear her mother out.

It was once they brought the *crème brûlée* that the tone changed.

Just in a small way, at first. A whisp of caution blew through Callie about the time Beverly said, "Let's chat about Lydia Barron."

"I'm listening," Callie said, gently sliding her spoon along the crusty edge of her dessert, finally cracking through to the smooth custard middle. She had worried this lunch might be too good to be true, but she'd hear out her mother before forming an opinion. Maybe she had remembered history about Lydia that she wanted to share, to help the case. Maybe her health scare made her feel she should be more cooperative and nicer to her daughter.

No matter the reason, Callie was eager... wary, but eager to listen, her hopes up.

"Lydia and her ladies are not bad people," Beverly started.

Sounded like Raysor. "I'm trying not to pass judgment. I just need facts to help piece together a case."

Beverly broke through her sugar crust atop her dessert and took a first taste. "Umm, their desserts are delectable, aren't they?" She took another quick sample then pointed with her spoon. "I consider the ladies more of a service industry. No drugs, no pimp, no unsavory characters."

"The new one might have a connection to the murder," Callie said. "She's avoiding me, not wanting to talk. That borders on unsavory in my book."

Beverly's forehead—in spite of a smidge of Botoxing Callie was sure took place now and then—wrinkled. "That would be a first then. Why is that you think?"

"Maddy's a new member. Rather last minute. Unvetted, so to speak."

The wrinkles eased out. "That explains it. Had to be something altruistic on Lydia's part to allow a last-minute addition to the group. She's noted for properly vetting her ladies."

"How would you know this?"

"Irrelevant," Beverly said, sliding in another bite of dessert.

"What's her real name, Mother?"

"Sorry, I'm not willing to give you that."

A stunning revelation. "You know it?"

"I do."

"It's Bonnie, isn't it?"

The look on her face told Callie she was correct.

"You've met her?"

"I have."

"How many times?"

"A few."

Callie set down her spoon, her dessert over half eaten, anxious to move on to facts. "Tell me about those times." She waved to the waitress who periodically peered around the corner from the kitchen, and Callie asked if she'd bring two coffees. Otherwise, Beverly would go for a second martini. Her mother had to drive herself back, and Callie wanted the liquor off her breath.

Beverly waited for the waitress to leave, taking the dessert dishes with her, finally, leaving them to do nothing but talk.

"As kids, we met on the beach sometimes." She gazed over Callie's shoulder at nothing, recalling the time.

Bonnie-slash-Lydia had really been from Edisto.

"Nothing planned," she continued. My family came to Edisto every three months or so. As you're aware, they had a house on the two hundred block on the water."

Callie was aware. Wind Song went by a different name now, but while the three bedroom had been rather small, it was where Beverly had gained her love for Edisto. A hurricane had damaged it beyond repair after her parents died, and Beverly sold the land and repositioned the family homestead a few blocks back off the sand on Jungle Road. Callie lived on that site now.

"She... she wasn't around all the time, limited to when her

grandmother brought her to town. We had... fun," she said.

"Until?" Callie asked, sensing a shift in her mother's remembrance by her slight change in expression.

"Until the boy."

"Who was he?"

But Beverly shook her head. "I don't know. Didn't want to know. Her interest swung to him, and I was only worth seeing if he wasn't around. And when we did get together, all she talked about was him... until she didn't want to anymore. She was in and out of high school, for some reason. I got older. She got older. And we just didn't go to the beach anymore looking for each other. About the time I found Lawton, she was gone from here."

That sounded like too short of a story.

"Surely you saw her in the thirty years she's been coming in the summer, Mother. You cannot tell me you didn't try to meet up with your childhood friend." Having already heard from Sarah how much the men in Beverly's life were aware of The Summer Ladies, Callie couldn't believe Beverly hadn't attempted to see the beach girl-turned-madam.

Her mother held back, and Callie could sense the shuffling in Beverly's head of which memories to reveal.

"Her third or fourth year in the business, I don't rightly recall, I caught her walking the beach wearing a wrap that caught my attention. The day was warm, and I asked myself why anyone would wear such a thing in the sun. The closer I got, the richer it appeared, until I was quite taken by it, so I approached her." She hesitated to say more, as if she wanted to replay it in her head a time or two first. "We recognized each other immediately."

"Did you ask why she left?" Callie asked.

Beverly's brow pinched. "Never dreamed of it, Callie. The whole island had painted her leaving as some sort of scandal. Maybe the boy. I really didn't want some ugly gossipy tale to ruin what I wanted to recall as a childhood friendship."

Callie wanted to believe her. Beverly sounded so soft and vulnerable in her introspection. This was a side of her mother she couldn't recall having seen in... forever. If ever. Instead, she basked in that softness, wishing this had been the mother she'd lived with for all those eighteen years before college.

Beverly came around, resetting her gaze on her daughter. "I was frustrated that day. The conversation slid from her shawl to men." She gave a lighthearted scoff. "Those were the early days of our arrangement, and I was rather put out by your father at the time. I honestly never expected him to take Sarah seriously once we had you. Bonnie listened, though. I mean, without judgement. With a sympathy I just drank up."

"I thought..." Callie started.

Her mother finished the thought for her. "Agreeing to such a unique marital arrangement is one thing. Watching it thrive is quite another. Anyway, we walked from Access 6, if I remember, all the way around to the sound and back. Of course, she'd already heard my story, and she knew who Sarah was."

Because Lydia already knew Ben, Sarah's husband, no doubt.

Beverly's smile held a soft grace to it. "She professed to have a decent read of men, and by the end of the conversation, she proved herself pretty darn true to the claim. We talked about the only way to keep Lawton was to keep him on a long and very loose leash. Just enough to remind him how to come home. I'd agreed to the arrangement and built a quality life as a result of it, and to dismantle it this late in the game was to lose him altogether. In the process, I might've lost you."

Callie's stunned expression stopped her mother's story. "What is it, dear?"

"I... I'm just trying to take this in." This was as open as her mother had ever been with her, a vulnerability Callie'd never seen. Her mother not only pined for her deceased husband, but also pined for the side of him she'd given away to Sarah in order to keep Callie. In Lydia she'd found a kindred soul. A lump formed in Callie's throat.

"And we both understood Brice," her mother added.

"Brice?"

"Yes, dear. We both... liked him. Me in the past. Her in the present. The second time I saw her was when she was with Brice. Aberdeen had to have been out of town, and I spotted them at the liquor store. I reached out to Bonnie, gave her a hug, and Brice about fainted." She grinned at the recollection.

Sarah had mentioned Brice and a woman with the group, but not specifically a relationship between Brice and Lydia. "How serious were they?" she asked.

"Until he died," her mother said, her voice declining on each word. "Not sure who called her, but I believe she went to the funeral." That last sentence dwindled to a whisper.

"Oh, my." Callie's adversarial stance against Lydia softened. She hadn't seen Lydia at Brice's funeral, but Callie had been seated near the front, greeted just whom she had to at the reception, and left as quickly as she could. That had been a sad time for the entire community, in spite of Brice's caustic character.

"She lost someone who was special to her," Beverly said. "And since she listened to me all those years ago, I'm protecting her now."

"You know more?"

"Yes."

"Which you'd keep even from me?"

"Especially from you. You're a cop."

Wow. "I have a dead girl, Mother. Any kind of information might be incredibly important."

"Whether it is or isn't, I'm not telling you the personal secrets of her past. She had a traumatic life, Callie, and had to call upon a hell of a lot of strength to make the sacrifice she did. She left when she was very young, staying away for years." Beverly shook her head. "A sad tale that doesn't bear repeating. It would hurt people still here, so back off, please."

Callie wasn't sure what that meant. "Only the older Edistonians know of her, right?"

"Right. And I see her as a successful female entrepreneur. Kudos to her. Now leave her alone."

"Who else is aware of her past?"

"Callie..." She sighed. "A few people my age, mostly. If I didn't respect her so much, I would've stayed quiet. I just felt with you being my daughter, I could persuade you to let the woman live in peace."

Callie wasn't believing this. Her mother admired a madam and was going to the mat for her amidst a murder investigation. Why was Lydia considered so noble to another woman, especially one as high up as Beverly? Come to think of it, to Sarah, Sophie, and Raysor as well.

She was from the island, her mother said. People from the area referred to the beach or the island. Beverly had referenced the island.

So what had turned her into a prostitute?

In her experience in law enforcement, prostitutes became such due to financial need, trafficking, or abuse. Trauma. Somehow in their personal experience, the concept got pounded into their DNA, or they got cornered into having no other choice.

They ran toward something, or away from something. Few women decided, hey, let's try being hookers and see how we like it.

"Don't try to figure her out, Callie."

"I have to, Mother."

"God, why did you have to become a cop, and of all places, Edisto Beach?" Beverly said, the sweeter temperament she'd shown so sincerely vanished in a flash of snark. Her edge had returned. The guarded, old Beverly was back, wanting her way. "Let the woman be."

"What else?" Callie asked.

"Nothing you need to hear. Honestly, child, I gave you more credit than this. This woman..." Then Beverly reined herself in, remembering waitstaff remained in the wings. "I can see I made a mistake trusting you."

Suddenly the album, the lunch, the kind thank-you, and the idea that mother and daughter would share a lovely moment, withered into something more methodically orchestrated. A plan. The meal was to divert Callie off Lydia's trail, when all it did was make her want to pursue the woman harder.

When she spoke, she hated the sound of her own voice. "This was a charade, wasn't it?"

"No. I wanted to thank you for the hospital issue the other night. And I shared history with you."

Callie scratched her head. Her mother had been genuine to a point, but not to another. "I don't know what to take from this, Mother." The words built up, and an alternate side of her said to eat the words not say them. "I'm not sure what the truth is anymore when we talk."

Beverly said nothing, just watching her daughter.

"I wouldn't be surprised if you told me Brice was my father, and you were my real mother after all."

But Beverly didn't miss a beat. "I almost wish that were so, my dear. No, I believe that would have been a really good thing."

Callie thought she had been facetious enough, but her mistake. The remark only triggered Beverly to speak her mind, trumping her daughter by taking things to another level.

Touché, Mother. Touché.

Chapter 26

CALLIE SAW HER mother to her car, deciding enough time had passed with enough food and coffee in her system to dilute the martini. No point in Beverly landing a ticket on the way back to Middleton.

She belted herself in, blew a kiss to her daughter, and eased out of the gravel lot, acting totally normal. Callie watched the Lexus disappear north on Highway 174, shellshocked.

She'd been played.

And so the cycle went.

Every time she had critical thoughts about her mother, she managed to talk herself out of them, making excuses, and then next time running to her beck and call. Things would go smoothly for about five damn minutes, then everything crumbled at an ill word. Beverly would hide a condemning tone in words that on the surface sounded innocent. Then they wound up in a face-off about a topic of Beverly's choosing with Beverly usually nailing the win because she'd planned the whole damn discussion in advance.

Why did it have to be a win-or-lose situation?

Damn her!

Admittedly, however, in this case Beverly's agenda was not all her own. She'd gone out of her way for Lydia. Way out of her way.

"*. . . hurt people still here,*" she'd said. Lydia used to be connected to people on Edisto and, if she read her mother correctly, still was.

In her own car, Callie headed back toward the beach, searching through their conversation for new material, for maybe even something Beverly didn't mean to say. Then she thought about the album. So many mixed feelings about that album.

She reminded herself that Nolan Brown waited to hear about his wife, so he could bury her. Which meant she needed to talk to Maddy.

And Lydia was key.

And Lydia was the information Beverly had fed Callie.

Lydia apparently was an old Edistonian turned scarlet woman who left under questionable circumstances a long time ago.

Do the math, Callie.

Thirty years kept coming up in everyone's conversation, to include Lydia's. That's how long *The Summer Ladies* had existed. When had she left Edisto and moved to Florida, and how many places had she lived in between leaving and coming back to Edisto?

Callie didn't have her full birth name, but Bonnie was a start.

And what was the sacrifice Lydia had supposedly made? There was a boy. Maybe a child, but that child would be close to her age and gone with the mother, raised elsewhere and off on their own. Would it have been enough to make the news? Police reports? The beach was in Colleton County, the island in Charleston County. She hoped the news had been made in Colleton, since she had firsthand access to those files. If not, the research she faced in Charleston County was massive. *The Post & Courier*, then back to the *Charleston News & Courier* then *The Evening Post*. Their records were excellent online if you were going back twenty years, but she needed more.

A big problem was that thirty years ago, Edisto Island had a more rural feel, less vacationers, roads narrower, and bridges harder to cross. Edisto was considered stuck way out there, on the end of Charleston County. The people were fewer, the crime easier to get away with, some of which outsiders and news media weren't even aware of. Edisto had barely been considered part of the county which meant county law enforcement went out of their way not to go there.

While the lunch with Beverly had been taxing, it hadn't been long with all that tension packed in barely more an hour and a half. If she hurried, she could still meet Maddy, narrowly keeping to their original time of four.

She placed the call, again going to voicemail. No, she wasn't allowing Maddy to perpetually stall her. Callie started to call Lydia, then decided Chiara might be the better choice. She'd be afraid not to answer after all that had gone down to date... or at least Callie could hope.

She didn't answer either. Callie tried Lydia's number, leaving the same message as she had in the other mailboxes. Have Maddy call. They needed to talk tonight.

She smacked the steering wheel. What now? She'd love to hear from Tampa about Kent Trevino, but it was too soon to expect them to have done the favor she asked. Tomorrow, hopefully.

Four o'clock. She had another thought. She'd have to pass Wainwright Realty on the way to the station, and Janet Wainwright should still be on call at her real estate office. Janet's history went way back as well.

She drove back across the causeway and into the beach town limits. Less than half a mile in, she pulled into the parking lot containing three other vehicles, one of them the famous gold Hummer, which said Janet wasn't paying attention to quitting time.

Inside, a couple was about to leave, with a single gentleman waiting to ask questions.

Janet escorted the couple out, then the minute they were through the door, she turned to the other. He wanted a small house, on the beach, as soon as possible, just for his fiancé and himself. Janet burst his bubble quickly with the prices and the minimum size available being four bedrooms. Had to be on the beach, he said. Surely there was a run-down something in his price range. They didn't care about the quality. They were in love and just wanted to be on the friggin' beach.

He had no grasp of reality. Callie felt sorry for the guy, because he was about to gain a piece of it at the hand of Janet who wasn't known for stroking clients. It was what it was, price not negotiable, any inventory booked for a minimum of six months out. *No can do, fella.*

Janet truly sat in the catbird seat when it came to seasonal rentals. Her prowess, however, shined when she listed the houses and sold them, over and over. Callie wondered where the nephew was, with his small pickup, for-sale signs and posts in the rear. Despite his business degree, he did hard-core sweat labor for the real estate agency, sometimes filling in as agent when his aunt was too busy. The kid worked hard for the inheritance she perpetually held over his head.

Deflated, the young man left. Janet turned on her heel. "Now, what is it, Chief?"

"I need some history from you, if you don't mind."

Walking back to her office, the buzzed, white-haired senior Marine resumed her throne behind the massive mahogany desk, figuring Callie didn't need an invitation to find her way. The broker wasn't the most congenial realtor doing business on the island, but as the biggest listing agent, she could get away with less finesse. Great if she was selling your place. Your loss if she represented the other side.

Callie assumed her normal seat, still a little warm from the couple. "*The Summer Ladies,*" she began, "how long have you been leasing to them?"

"I only deal with one of them. Lydia Barron," she replied.

"That's not her name." Callie tended to get just as blunt when dealing with Janet. It's the language the Marine spoke best, making her less prone to eat you alive. Mealy-mouthed ones got the most taken advantage of.

"It's all the name I need," Janet said.

"She has to pay with a legal name, Janet. Four weeks is a major outlay of cash if you're attempting to be clandestine."

"Which she pulls off nicely," Janet said, slick and quick.

"Legal documents? Don't you ask for identification? She has to sign something which means she's falsified documents."

"Chief," Janet said, as if she hunted for a simple enough way to explain. "When I ask a rental owner if they are willing to rent their property for four straight weeks in the middle of summer, and that the tenant wants to pay cash and not disclose their identity, and that I've rented homes to this person every summer for years, what do you think they say?"

"Is that legal?"

"You're the police. You tell me."

"I would want to know if it were my house," Callie said.

"And I wouldn't be offering your property as an option. I know my people. It's more than about the rent. The owner doesn't have to pay for weekly cleaning between tenants or the extra repairs that appear because of the roughness of so many different people coming and going. Just mature women who want a quiet time at the beach. What's to turn down?"

Callie pushed on. "How many years have you rented to her? Or does she use other property managers?"

"Just me."

"You sure?"

"I make it such she doesn't desire to go anywhere else."

"Like?"

"Rent from me and see."

Damn this smart-ass woman, but if you asked her the right questions, she gave great answers. She and Sophie were as opposite as fire and water, but Callie plumbed both of them for information. What one wasn't aware of, the other likely was.

Out of the blue, Janet said, "I love that Lydia, though. She's my kind of lady."

"Do you realize what they do?"

She gave a bony shrug. "I've heard. I've seen Brice with her. Holding her hand, for God's sake. Damn, makes you wonder how that slug managed to pair up with someone that attractive. What the hell did he have in common with a hot, intelligent woman?"

"We never tried to date him, Janet."

She reared back like a stunned chicken. "Pardon?"

"Each of us is one person in private and another in public," Callie said, wanting to believe what she was saying. She too had trouble envisioning the town pain-in-the-butt with someone with such smooth airs.

"Well, I asked him," Janet said.

Of course you did.

"He said his wife left a bit to be desired. Then he gave this nasty, guttural chuckle, and said his talents might surprise me. Thought I'd vomit on the spot."

"Shift gears," Callie said, casting aside all those visuals. She uncrossed her legs and sat more on the edge of her chair. "Have you rented to anyone named Kent Trevino?"

"No."

"Don't you have to look?"

"No. Not unless you're talking decades ago."

"Now. I mean right now."

"Answer's still no."

Callie had Tampa checking his residence and place of employment. If only they'd call.... "What about Good Earth Realty?"

Trevino's employer. Janet would take note of a real estate company. No response.

Bingo. He was on the island. Maybe even on the beach.

"This guy works for Good Earth Realty, Janet. He's on my radar. Serious radar."

Putting on her readers, Janet turned to her desktop. "Like, is he along the lines of I-should-be-armed serious?"

The Marine would jump at the chance to arm herself, as she'd proven once in the past. Callie's gaze strayed to the closet to Janet's left, a closet where one assumed filing cabinets and office supplies were housed. Instead, Callie'd learned once upon a dangerous time that between the gun safe in that closet and Janet's arsenal at home, she owned more weapons than the police force plus half the beach... in a state that loved its guns.

"Where is he renting, Janet? And what was he driving?"

"First, what's he done?"

"Don't need you involved if I tell you, do you understand?"

"If he's a criminal, I damn sure need to know," she said, voice hard, as if that would impact the police chief seated before her.

"Maybe that's why you should get people's real identities when you do business with them," Callie said.

But Janet remained fixed on her fellow community leader, a slight glance to her screen telling Callie that she had the rental pulled up but debated whether to release it.

"He abused three women in Tampa, charges dropped because he coerced them into doing so. Two of those women are here."

Janet soured. "The dead one?"

"The one that went missing for a while. I really need to pay him a visit."

Janet thought harder.

"For God's sake, Janet, he's not a repeat customer, and I doubt he'll be coming back. The rent's been paid, and you have nothing to lose. In the meantime, he could be stalking someone. Give me his damn address."

Janet spun the screen around. "*Isle Be Back.*"

Callie thought she could recite all the house names, but this one drew a blank. Definitely not on the main drag, which made sense if he didn't want to be noticed.

"Fort Street," Janet clarified. "The owners have almost lost the place twice in as many years. Upkeep sucks. The hot water heater goes out twice a month. The rental goes empty half the summer because of the past complaints. I'd about decided not to list it anymore, but I hold onto it, in reserve, for times when someone can't afford squat and just wants to say they've been to Edisto."

Made sense. A place nobody gave a second look at when driving by, because the house sat on a street that nobody drove by. If you wanted to hide on Edisto, as small as it was, that street would be at the top of the list.

Callie tapped up the driver's license photo on her phone and flashed it at the broker.

"Yep. That's him. Want me to—"

"Do absolutely nothing," Callie repeated and stood to leave.

"Be happy to come with you, Chief."

"Appreciate the offer, but I'm good."

"Take somebody with you."

Callie hadn't decided about that yet. "One more thing. Your nephew, Arthur. Has he met any of these people? Trevino or the ladies?"

"No." Spoken just as snipped as you please. "I handled Trevino."

"You might not be aware if he's seen the ladies. I wouldn't tell you if I were him."

"One of the conditions of renting from me, Chief. Steer clear of my kin. Boy might be a college graduate, but his common sense goes on vacation too often for my liking. Boys that age..." and she stopped. "I'd hate to have to disown the little bastard. Nothing smears the reputation of Wainwright Realty. Including a Wainwright."

Callie rose to leave but turned with another question. "What's he driving?"

"My nephew?"

"Kent Trevino."

"Didn't see it, but he mentioned a rental."

Probably not a Florida tag, either.

Giving a thumbs-up, Callie left. She had a mission now. Finally, something shaking loose in this quagmire of a case. She called Raysor, to see if he'd gone home yet.

He answered. "What's up?"

He didn't say "Doll" this time, maybe still miffed about the earlier conversation regarding Lydia and his rendezvous with the beautiful Vivien.

"Got a lead on Kent Trevino, Maddy's old boyfriend. He's rented here on Edisto. Checking it out. Care to come?"

"Would love to," he said. "Where are you?"

"Wainwright's. You?"

"Lybrand, near Palmetto. Where're we going?"

"*Isle Be Back*," she said. "Like i-s-l-e."

Silence. He was trying to place it, too.

"Fort Street," she added.

"Meet you there." He signed off.

When even Don Raysor couldn't instantly place an address, one had to realize how secluded a house this was... and what a good place to take someone you might not want to be seen with.

Raysor was already in the drive when she pulled up. The house was an older one-story, still on stilts like most of Edisto's residences but not substantial enough a structure for one to feel comfortable riding out a storm in. The wood siding needed another coat of white paint, after hard pressure washing. With half the house in shade under palmettos that hadn't been pruned in five years, mold grew unchecked, creating an even dingier appearance, enough to make one wonder if mold penetrated to the interior.

Wainwright's yellow-and-red for-rent sign popped louder and brighter than the house, an odd juxtaposition of the professional (Janet) and the not (the owner). No car in the drive.

"You sure this is it?" Raysor asked as she got out of the cruiser. "I doubt they've rented this place in a year."

"Janet was positive. Come on." Callie strode toward the stairs, testing the railing before venturing up to the front door.

There was no overhang on the porch, which meant weathered planks, with some making Callie question their stability. They peered inside, the blinds mostly drawn except where they were busted from age and use, but even then, they couldn't tell if someone stayed there. The screen door creaked, its hinges more rust than not, but the wooden door held fast.

"I could kick that thing in with no effort at all," Raysor said.

"I could, too," Callie said, making the man look down at her and laugh.

Down and around back, they took stairs to a narrow but long porch, only in slightly better shape. They couldn't reach a bedroom window to see inside, but from the back they did spot signs of life through a broken blind. Beer, chips, and a pizza box. Some bags that might be carry out.

Raysor tried the back door, and, miracle upon miracles, it opened. He played with the handle and studied the lock. "Doesn't even lock. Surprised he didn't complain to Janet."

"He didn't want to be remembered, Don."

Not asking Callie for permission, Raysor stuck his head inside and in his best police voice shouted, "Mr. Trevino? Edisto Beach Police Department."

Nothing. The lights were off. No noise short of a faint buzz of a fly over the dried-out pizza.

Raysor took the bedrooms, Callie the living room. They met back in the kitchen. The search didn't take long.

"Find where someone lays their head and you're supposed to get all sorts of information," Raysor said, opening the refrigerator. "Leftovers from assorted deliveries. I'm seeing maybe three days' worth of ordering out? No sign of him being here for the last day or two, though. What does that mean?"

"Means he's somewhere else," she said. "Any Mexican?" Maybe Mark or Sophie had seen Trevino sometime during the week.

"Not seeing it."

"What's in the bedrooms?"

He shut the fridge door. "Only one's been disturbed. Saw his clothes strewn on the bed and across a suitcase on the floor. Didn't even unpack. Toiletries are still in the bathroom. Toothbrush, sink, and shower are dry."

"Living room's hardly touched," she said, peering over the food on the counter. "And this pizza is rock hard and two days old."

They stood in place, reinspecting their surroundings, finding nothing that said anyone had been there that day.

"It doesn't appear he's had anyone here with him either," she said.

Raysor opened the cabinets and studied the dirty glass and silverware in the sink. Not a drop of moisture on any of it. "There's no wallet or keys. No car."

"Go over the place again, slower," she said. "We need to be meticulous. This isn't *Law and Order*."

They did, crisscrossing each other's inspection, finding nothing exceptional.

Callie led them outside, her taking the south neighbor, him the north. One was a renter who spent more time on the beach than in the house and had seen nothing; the other was a long-time older resident who said he paid no attention to who was in the house next door, happy that a tall border of bamboo shielded his view and put the place totally out of his mind.

Now Kent Trevino was missing, too.

Chapter 27

Lydia

VIVIEN SHOWED UP, rubbing a hand down Lydia's back. "Robin's worried. What do I tell her?"

Lydia had moved to the porch, then having grown impatient, walked to the beach. The sound barely whispered as the tide went out, taking with it a part of her soul she was positive she had protected. This summer had become what she'd hoped would never be... the past invading the present.

She was sad, she was angry, but most of all she was unmoored.

The day had slid into late afternoon, but night was never quick to fall in June, taking its time as if to give people a second chance to remember the worth of living in such a paradise. Comfortably warm, she had wrapped herself in the shawl and sat cross-legged beneath it. Closing her eyes, she willed herself back to before this visit, when all was in order. She hungered for that place.

"Lydia?"

"Déjà vu, Viv. Déjà vu."

She'd had too much on her mind to want dinner. One decision had led to another, and here she was. On this visit, her past continually tapped her shoulder, versus the earlier summer visits when she could almost forget anything.

"I know," and Vivien went from a stoop to seating herself. "Don't fall into that place, Lydia. Just don't. There's no good in it." For a few minutes, they let nature speak to them.

"Tell Robin..." Lydia started, but this time she had no excuse she could stomach. Robin was a good woman. To lie wouldn't treat her right. Lydia had lied for so long and tired of it.

"Just let me sit here," she said instead, in barely more than a breath. The world weighed heavy.

Viv wrapped both arms around her, and they leaned into each other. "You're a good, beautiful woman, Lydia. Never lose sight of that."

Then she turned her friend's head with a finger and gave her a light kiss on the lips, before looking into her eyes. "I believe in you. Never lose sight of that." Then after another peck and a readjustment of the shawl, she rose gently, a svelte wave of movement to standing, earned from years of yoga.

Bless her. Without her Lydia would've fallen off the earth years ago.

Lowering head to her knees, she sank into herself, replaying choices. Recent ones and old.

She'd been Maddy once. She'd been Maddy ten times over, but her time was during an era when those on the outside looking in defined the used-up girl as the flawed one and women didn't stand a chance against an abuser.

All Lydia had known growing up was Edisto. The early years were the ones to remember and look forward to each June. The barefoot wanderings along creeks, the marsh lined with egrets and herons. Her family lived off fish, a garden in the backyard, and staples from the beach grocery store. Occasionally, when Grandmother made her monthly trip to that store, she left Lydia to wander the sand, the only time she got to enjoy the big water, even living only ten miles from it.

"Always stay within sight of the Pavilion," Grandmother would order, so she didn't have to hunt for the child after. A simpler time when Lydia wasn't old enough to understand poverty. She was just a kid doing what her grandmother told her in order to grow up right.

That's where the boy first showed, her twelve, him fourteen... him hiding behind pier columns where the sea washed in and around his feet, while overhead the young adults danced to live bands. He was new to the area. A straightforward opening to a coming-of-age story.

Tanned and shoeless, not so unusual in Edisto around the beach, he attached himself to Lydia that afternoon. That fall they found each other walking the same hall in school. They met on the beach when the grandmother needed groceries, and they passed notes on the way to class. He was someone to look forward to, and to a young, friendless girl who lived indigently with her mother and grandmother in the jungled marsh of the island, those moments were everything.

Wasn't until age sixteen, when he borrowed his uncle's old truck, that he came down Lydia's road and hung on the woods' edge, smoking, hoping for a chance the young girl could get away, saying at school that they could see each other outside of parental oversight if they really wanted to. Exciting and scary at the same time.

Didn't take long during those waiting, measuring moments, for him to learn who her mother was, though. A drunk, a whore, an addict who'd have Lydia turning tricks if the grandmother wasn't standing guard. A loose sort of guard, however, because her idea of teaching Lydia was to tell her to hide when Lydia's mother had dates, hoping to line her child up with whatever man came calling for the evening... for only twenty extra dollars.

Wasn't until Grandma came down sick with the flu, her eagle-eye watch lost in a haze of fever, did the mother get her way. Her latest lived toward the Dawhoo River, a tomato farmer, back when tomatoes made money, before Florida broke South Carolina's back in the market. When drugs were hauled up and down I-95 hidden in tomato boxes.

He raped her three times that night while the young boyfriend watched through the window.

Her heart had shattered.

Pausing, taking note of a gull overhead that scouted for morsels, Lydia pulled her shawl tighter. That memory had lost little of its ache, regardless of the years, and never failed to make her feel small and insignificant. No matter how hard she fought to be big, to be *noble* as Maddy put it so well, to be independently distant from such people anymore, like broken glass, the memories slid in and still cut.

But the memories never vanished at her whim and choosing. Once resurfacing, they played out.

The boy... he'd been cute and safe before that night with his shaggy brown hair, jeans and Rolling Stones tee. He had to have perched on the gas meter outside the window. Not appalled, not angry, not interrupting... just watching.

It took until the third time the man came down on her to realize said boyfriend wasn't going to save the day. The fact that he might barge in and interrupt, bring the police, or just make noise, changed to the realization that he didn't want to.

To him, she soon learned, that night was his interpretation of entry into manhood... and permission to screw the prostitute's daughter.

He'd been a poor soul like Lydia, who had moved to Edisto when his parents died, had been thrown to live in his uncle's house amongst people that didn't want him. They were both alone yet united against the world... or so she thought until that night.

Truth was, he'd been sent from Orangeburg to rural Edisto Island to live with an uncle, all right, but in hopes the uncle could beat sense into him in lieu of being housed in a juvenile detention center for abusing his younger sister.

Yet even ashamed and hurt, that next trip to the beach she still ran to him. He'd hold her, she told herself. He'd explain why he was only a kid and couldn't tackle a man so much larger than he. Maybe he would still help go to the police.

Instead, he threatened to tell the whole beach, the whole school, that she spread her legs like her mother... unless she met him in his truck after school.

To the world he pretended to be the cute, country beau.

The truck meetings turned into an old twin mattress he dragged into the woods a quarter mile out behind the house. Not able to fathom telling Grandma, when there was nothing she could do, she caved in on herself like a wet cardboard box in the rain.

Then her mother overdosed.

Would her courtesans come hunting for Lydia? She took to sleeping under her bed, with the naïve hope that nobody would see through the window or would open her door and note her gone.

Social Services didn't even check.

Soon the boy reappeared. Said he'd hurt the grandmother if she didn't....

Grandmother was all Lydia had left.

The grandmother who eventually spoke to the sheriff's office, but all they saw was a hooker's daughter picking up where her mother left off, and a poverty-stricken grandmother who surely must've looked the other way if not taught both of them the business.

The pregnancy was little more than another blip on the radar. Grandmother couldn't afford an abortion, but a Gullah woman took pity. Didn't take three months before she was puking again, this time to the point of dehydration, unable to afford a doctor. She begged the boy to get her one, pleading. Told him this wasn't the first time.

He punched her in the gut, leaving her writhing in a ball on the ground, him laughing about no charge for taking care of things.

After a week in bed, she approached the sheriff's office herself, then the Edisto Beach police, then anyone who might listen. Reputation be damned at this point, but nobody would listen much less act. It was so rural back then. People came to the beach and left, oblivious to those living down the dirt roads. Desolate country. Blocked from the mainland by a drawbridge, the island residents were so isolated and destitute that the few owning cars charged others twenty dollars a trip to go to Charleston.

The third pregnancy, the girl decided something had to change, and she had to be the one to change it.

SO LONG AGO, yet it felt like yesterday. A gull ventured within six feet of Lydia as she sat there outside the rental. He flew off when she peered up, her head having been tucked between her knees for God knew how long. Straightening stiff legs, she stretched her neck left then right.

She'd escaped the boy all those years ago, and she more than understood what Maddy went through as an abused woman. They'd all had a taste of that nastiness at some time. Spouses, boyfriends, a couple of them with other relatives. They should not have allowed Maddy to come to Edisto as last minute as she had approached them, but they had. Lydia had. Which made the young woman Lydia's responsibility.

Maddy's night could've gone so wrong in so many ways, but instead, Lydia had ensured it hadn't. By the time Lydia showed, Elizabeth Brown couldn't be helped, but Maddy could be.

She gave a low growl of frustration. These current times were more informed times, even more dangerous times, one might say. Things weren't over yet.

Chapter 28

CALLIE PUT OUT a BOLO for Kent Trevino to include his rental car, the tag unknown. Then she caught up with Marie by phone before she left for the day.

"What the heck?" Marie asked, once Callie had briefed her.

"I said—"

"No," Marie interrupted. "I mean, this group of women has been in the shadows for three decades, and suddenly they're harbingers of doom? How have we not been aware?"

The flash of concern took Callie aback. She stood outside next to her cruiser, Raysor standing outside his. If they'd been on Myrtle or Palmetto Streets, traffic would've slowed to catch sight of the reason for two police cars on site, but this was Fort Street.

"Marie," Callie said, feeling something she couldn't put her finger on coming across the call. "I've been struggling with finding time to meet with you. I wanted to ask—"

"Why? I've been right here."

What was with Marie?

This was odd behavior, then Callie put two and two together. *The Summer Ladies* were a side of Edisto that Marie wasn't familiar with. She felt she maintained a finger on the pulse of all things on this beach... on this island, for goodness' sake. Callie'd been in the dark and surprised she hadn't heard of *The Summer Ladies*, and she'd been in all the inner circles of Edisto for the three years she'd been in office. But Marie had lived there forever and sounded disappointed with herself for being ignorant. Marie didn't fluster.

"I know your knowledge of Edisto is unmatched, but honestly, you can't know everybody," Callie said.

Marie backed down. "Sorry. I sounded rather childish there, didn't I? It's been a day. With the canvassing everyone did yesterday and today, people have started calling my ear off this afternoon. They've had time to think, and some may have seen Maddy, some Elizabeth, but nothing concrete or confirmed. Some are asking if there's imminent danger for visitors. What were the police doing about the dead body? Were we hiring someone to shoot the shark? Shoot the shark, for God's sake, Chief."

This wasn't her Marie. The Edisto PD office manager ruled the island, and Callie's three-plus years of working alongside the woman, she'd never flinched, never blanched, never reacted other than straightforward and professionally whether a death or a stolen bicycle. If Marie's world shook, Callie's did.

"I just don't get this one," she said, on a much humbler note. "This Kent Trevino guy sounds scary, Callie."

Callie glanced at Raysor who had strolled over to see what was wrong. He scowled, registering an issue. Callie continued talking. "You go on home, hon. You're tired. You've worked late as it is." She added, "This Trevino guy is after two particular women, we believe. No serious concern. Just, as always, be aware when walking to your car."

"Maybe I should hang around here," Marie said instead. "A BOLO at this hour on a new missing person. I don't know..."

"No need, I assure you."

"If you think I'm not needed..."

"Oh, you're always needed, Marie. Just don't want to wear out the most important resource I have."

That drew a soft laugh. "Appreciate it, Chief. See you tomorrow."

Raysor's brows asked his question for him.

"Marie," Callie said, once she'd hung up. "The new BOLO has her nervous. She's a little disturbed about Trevino running loose and us having no idea on who killed Elizabeth Brown. She's inundated with the public's nonsense and it's wearing on her today."

Raysor nodded, understanding, then raised a lone brow as if to ask what now.

"Hunt for the car," she said. "Start with Palmetto since that's where Maddy met Elizabeth. Both sides, all the way around the sound. The BOLO covers the two counties and the island, but my gut tells me nothing left the beach. I don't like Elizabeth's body being found outside the house rented by two of his past victims."

He gave a half shrug, half tip of his head. "Not sure what we're hunting in terms of a car, but we'll keep eyes out for him and maybe Florida plates. What'll you be doing?" he asked, because he understood she wasn't going home.

"I have two ladies to talk to," she said. "Maddy hasn't been forthcoming, and Chiara ought to be afraid enough to spill if I've read her right thus far. I need to see their expressions when I query them about Kent Trevino. At a minimum, I need to warn them he is on the beach and advise them accordingly. Cruise their street more often than usual, if you don't mind."

Raysor squinted, sucking on the inside of his bottom lip before speaking. "Not so sure you don't need to be accompanied, Doll."

"Do *you* need to be accompanied, Don?"

That just drew bluster out of him. "Damn it, don't go getting all feminist on me. Just trying to say... hell, don't know how to say it now."

She brushed a hand jokingly down his sleeve. "You go do your thing and I'll do mine. We find that car, we hopefully find him. My time, however, is better spent interviewing these women. Right now we aren't sure what is most important, so we have to cover it all."

"Well, be safe, Doll," and Raysor left.

With the deputy gone, she sat in her car and dialed Chiara's number. She already had history with these women, and she damn sure wasn't putting an unknown uniform onto interviewing them at this juncture, especially someone new and male.

No answer.

She had to talk to Chiara. How had Maddy gotten to Coots? She could have walked, but the odds were against the three- to four-mile distance, and Chiara had a car.

Or had Kent Trevino taken her?

Callie called twice more, letting each roll to voicemail, without leaving a message. Chiara called back as Callie was beginning to dial a fourth.

"I'm on a date," she said, without greeting or question.

"We need to meet. Now. Or I'll find you and your *date* and interview you both on the spot."

"You can't do that."

"I can... *Bristol.*"

Silence. "I'm not—"

"Don't even try it, Chiara. I spoke to your employer. I have your driver's license. Meet me at *Time in a Bottle.*"

Chiara hung up and headed to the ladies' beach house. If Maddy wasn't there, Callie'd retrieve her just like she threatened to retrieve Chiara.

She called Maddy, in the hope of catching her before she disappeared on one of their many so-called dates. Voicemail, like Chiara.

Then, also like Chiara, Callie called again, then again, and on the fourth, Maddy answered.

She didn't answer angry at the incessant calls. Instead, she sounded nervous, as if she'd been caught. "I had my phone silenced. Didn't hear your calls."

"Doesn't matter. Don't care. I'm coming over to the beach house, Maddy, and we're finally having that talk. In all transparency, I'm going to inquire about Elizabeth Brown, where you've been, the truth this time, and the fact that Kent Trevino has been on this beach." Callie wasn't sure Chiara knew about Trevino, but she was pretty sure Maddy did. Her behavior reeked of it.

Dead silence on the other end rather confirmed such.

"Did you hear me?" Callie said.

"Yes, ma'am."

"Am I on speaker?" Callie asked.

"Um, yes, ma'am."

"Good. Then I don't have to call everyone else. Chiara is on her way. I'll see y'all in, say fifteen minutes. Any questions?"

A gap of more silence, which Callie assumed was Maddy seeking direction from Lydia, maybe Vivien. "Um, no ma'am. I'll be here."

Callie was pissed at all the unsaid and misdirection, but she had to go into this as cool and contained as she'd ever done anything, because she'd only have one good chance of gaining the truth. After this, they'd regroup, and acquire legal counsel more lethal than Vivien. Maybe even disappear and never be seen again.

Nolan Brown deserved better. Elizabeth deserved better. Those babies in Middleton Memorial Hospital on the fifth floor deserved better; therefore, Callie had to do her best tonight.

As insurance, Callie took a quick chance to call Tampa PD, hoping the number took her to someone still on duty and familiar enough with her request for an update. The voice told her she'd lucked up.

"Was going to call you tomorrow during duty hours, but now's good," the officer said. "Nobody's seen Kent Trevino for several days."

No surprise. "How many days?"

"At least five."

Timeline worked. "What's his employer say? Was his absence planned?"

"Funny you ask. The guy said Trevino was approved to be off this week, but he was still supposed to take calls from clients with pending sales. His mailbox is full, however, and nobody can get hold of him. His neighbors haven't seen him or his car."

Janet had said the man had mentioned a rental. The man had either parked it at the airport and flown in, getting a rental in Charleston, or he'd left his car in Florida and rented down there and drove up. Any kind of tag could be on the car. She bet he flew up, faster on a last-minute notice, which was likely the case since Maddy's trip was last minute, too.

She thanked the officer, promising future assistance if needed, as if Edisto Beach would ever be a blip on Tampa radar.

Elizabeth killed. Maddy shaken. Trevino missing.

Callie sat there a few more minutes thinking deeply, sorting and re-sorting, pondering what the hell she might've missed, what was within her power to do, but mostly what to ask Maddy and Chiara when she arrived.

When her phone rang, she about jumped out of her skin. No caller ID. A strange area code.

"Chief Morgan?"

Callie recognized Lydia's haughty voice right off the bat. "Yes, ma'am." She started to continue into her routine with the typical, *how may I help you*, but it felt fruitless with this woman who had seen Callie's help as nothing but a nuisance from the moment they met.

"We're ready for you at the house. Any idea how long? Some of us have places to be."

"As long as it takes, Ms. Barron. I'm right around the corner."

Leave it to Lydia to show a little power and try for control.

After texts to Mark about missing dinner, and a call to Raysor who hated texts, updating him on where she'd be, she left Fort Street, turned west on Mikell, and right on Palmetto, only a couple blocks from *Time in a Bottle.*

She'd never been quite as stymied over a woman such as this. The old-time Edistonians treated Lydia as a folk hero. Others relished her troupe of courtesans each summer. Lydia's cadre of ladies saw her as their savior.

Callie was the only one seeing her as a threat, but even that initial hatred for the woman was ebbing after hearing so many Edisto people describe her in a different light. Lydia infused purpose in her words and decisions on how to take care of *The Summer Ladies*. One could admire that... to a degree.

The porch lights had been flipped on, dusk falling since the hour was approaching eight. Vivien met her at the top of the stairs. Even in her early sixties, she indeed remained a beauty, the soft light and night shadows making her appear all the more lovely. Callie tried to envision her with her deputy once upon a time.

She wondered if Raysor had been back to see her more than he professed, honestly. He deserved somebody.

She hated doubting everyone on this case... on this beach, frankly. Something about these women made people hold fast to secrets and dance around details of the truth. Callie felt there was still a history she didn't know... that others did and were unwilling to say. And she wasn't sure what entitled one to know it.

"They're on the back porch," Vivien said, leading the way, her straight white hair down her back.

Callie walked through the rental toward the back. She continued through the sliding door to the now familiar porch, sliding a chair around like before, her back to the sea such that she could face the women and not see the sunset. She sat. "Glad to see you're alive and well, Maddy."

Other than the trepidation in her eyes, Maddy looked healthy. No marks on her hands, wrists, ankles, neck. Her hair was clean and recently blown dry, and she wore a light dose of makeup. Her youth showed in the smoothness of her complexion, but the lack of confidence was clear in her posture.

As though by design, Maddy sat across from and to Callie's left. She returned a weak smile, behaving much like Chiara had before, when Maddy wasn't accounted for. As the minor two women in the five, Callie expected them to be somewhat shackled to what the others let them say. Time and Callie's talent would determine how tight those shackles held before the evening was through.

The two timid ones appeared a contrast versus the three with poise and confidence. Chiara sat farthest away, Robin beside her as if she needed emotional support... or was being contained.

Callie tired of the game, but she'd play it as long as she had to.

The stronger women watched with interest, drinks in hand. A fresh charcuterie board sat on the long glass table in front of the rattan sofa, and in front of Callie. They'd fixed her a water with lemon, making this as social a moment as possible.

Well, she wasn't interested.

Lydia posed front and center, the closest to Callie, bare legged in shorts and a tank with that shawl having fallen behind her, puddled onto the cushion, its ends still draped over the crook of each arm. Vivien relaxed in a chair between Maddy and Lydia, leaning forward, her glass resting in one hand, her arms crossed over her knees.

"Chief Morgan," Vivien began. "What's your interest in interviewing my client?"

"Depends," Callie said. "Which one is your client?"

Vivien and Lydia exchanged knowing glances, while Maddy and Chiara stiffened, as though wondering which of them wouldn't be represented.

"Anyone sitting here is my client at present," Vivien replied.

If this wasn't scripted, nothing was.

"Let me introduce myself, Maddy," and Callie did. "Or shall I call you Grace?"

That revelation garnered little more than a slight brow raise from Lydia.

"Let's use my Edisto name," Maddy replied.

"Let's all use our Edisto names," Vivien clarified. "Easier for everyone. Especially you."

Callie mentally waved aside that discussion. She still hadn't nailed down Vivien and Robin's identities, and all she had on Lydia's was her given name of Bonnie.

"I assume you mostly need to talk to Maddy, and as my client she is not compelled to give you any information," Vivien said.

"True. But if anyone says they killed someone, you might have conflicting interests, counselor. You'd have to choose."

"Killed?" Maddy exclaimed, as Callie had expected.

"Yes," Callie said, her attention hard on Maddy. "It's why most attorneys don't ask if their client if they did it."

Maddy looked about to faint. Chiara's eyes had shot wide and round, Robin's hand moving to take hers. Robin looked clueless and puzzled, but not a sign of guilt, knowledge, anything. Her role was clearly to keep a grip on her charge.

Lydia, however, sat like a rock, attention frontal and spot on Callie.

Callie returned her focus to Maddy, her main interest. "I've been hunting for you, as have my team of officers. We need details. When and where you were the day you met Elizabeth. Where and when you traveled with Elizabeth. And where and when you two parted ways. What did y'all do. Why was it you seemed nowhere to be found for a while. Honestly, I never would've known a thing if Chiara hadn't come to me for help."

Chiara's stare went wide, and Maddy glanced over as if to facetiously say *thanks for nothing*.

A lot of questions to ask Maddy at one time, but the essence of the questions was to inform Maddy and her attorney that Callie needed details and a timeline. Elizabeth was dead, and Maddy had been a key player in the dead woman's universe during that time.

"You don't have to answer here, in front of this audience," Callie said. "We can go someplace more private, like my station. Chiara's familiar with where that is."

Callie sent another glance toward Chiara, still trying to weigh her limited role. Chiara couldn't maintain a gaze and turned to look south at the water line.

Callie half expected Lydia to step up and tell the story secondhand, to avoid Maddy getting the story wrong, but she didn't. The head mistress studied Callie instead.

"Maddy," Lydia said, her stare still on Callie. "You aren't alone. Answer the chief's questions, and when you don't feel you can answer one, turn to Vivien. We'll all help best we can, but Vivien will run interference on questions the chief isn't necessarily entitled to. If Vivien says do not answer, don't."

Callie's guess was that this meeting was a steam release. They agreed to meet to get Callie off their collective ass. They knew as well as she did that Callie had nothing on them, and their guess was Callie was fishing. They weren't far wrong.

Maddy hadn't replied to the questions. Time to make this simple. "Where were you Monday?" Callie asked. "Your first day as a lady of the evening."

"Ignore that second comment," Vivien said, as if in a courtroom.

Maddy looked between Callie and Vivien, already feeling pressed. "I... I went on a date."

"What time?"

"Noon."

"Where?"

"Don't answer that," Vivien said.

Callie hadn't expected to get that answer anyway. At least not now. "When did you leave there, wherever there was?" she asked instead.

"Around two."

Callie watched Chiara, who didn't seem moved by any of this. She knew. "Where did you go?"

"Walking. All over the beach. Got tired and just sat for a long time. Then I called Bristol... Chiara."

"To do what?"

"I was tired," Maddy said. "I was afraid to come back to the house and tell Lydia that I'd dumped my date, not feeling comfortable with the whole... anyway, I was getting hungry and didn't know where to find something to eat." She waited a second. "I also wanted a drink and asked Chiara to get one with me. She said she had appointments, but she slipped away to pick me up in her car and take me to Coots."

"She stay there with you?" Callie asked.

Maddy shook her head. "No, just dropped me off."

Callie turned toward Chiara, who again couldn't make eye contact. "Is that accurate, Chiara? Is the timeline right?"

Chiara nodded, her blush showing even under the porch lights, returning to watching the shoreline. She'd been told to keep her mouth shut, for sure.

"How long were you at Coots, Maddy?" she asked.

"I don't really know. I'd had three rum and cokes, sitting there dwelling on things. Wishing maybe I hadn't come... but I didn't think I had any other choice."

Callie didn't prompt her to explain but didn't have to. Maddy volunteered. "I had broken up two months ago with an abusive boyfriend, and he'd been harassing me back in Tampa. That's why Chiara suggested I come with them to Edisto." She reached for a glass of something dark, and Callie hoped it wasn't the same rum and coke she'd spoken of in her story.

"Kent Trevino," Maddy continued, her voice higher. "Surely you've researched him."

"Should I have?" Callie asked, just as patient as you please. "Nobody's asked me to."

Maddy gave a pleading look at Lydia, not Vivien. "She should have, right?"

"Moving on," Callie said. "You were at Coots. You'd had a few..."

"I might've been sniffling a little. My seat faced the water, and I was looking out the window into the dark when a woman my age showed. She leaned down and asked if I was okay, took a seat, and we got to talking."

"Name?"

"Elizabeth Brown," she said, the mention of the name forcing her to stare down into her glass. "She was a children's nurse in a hospital." She took a drink. "I really liked her... except..."

"Except for what?" Callie asked.

"Except for the... fact... she was killed." She blurted out a sob. "She was killed because of me." A couple more sobs.

"You're doing great, hon," Vivien said, and Lydia reached over to stroke Maddy's shoulder. Maddy reined herself in enough to continue talking.

Reaching down and taking her own glass, Callie took a strong whiff of its contents, finding it non-alcoholic, and took her own sip. Maddy had indeed been coached. So far, however, so good.

She set the glass back down. Nobody touched the snacks on the tray. "Now we're getting somewhere, Maddy. Vivien's right. You're doing great. When did you leave Coots, and did you leave with Elizabeth?"

Lydia reached out with a box of tissues that appeared from the side of her chair. "Go on, dear."

The *dear* reference threw Callie into a visual of Beverly, and she quickly shoved it away.

Maddy sniffled. "We didn't leave until Coots was about to close," she said. "I can't tell you the time, because I'd had five drinks. Elizabeth'd had three. She was afraid to drive in the state she was in, so we decided to walk on the beach, telling stories. So innocent." She refolded the tissues in her hand and wiped her eyes again. "We meant to walk to her place. She said she had a condo, but before we knew it, we'd gone down the beach and around the point, towards where this house is. We got about two houses from here before we realized where we were."

Tears rolled down her cheeks, and she kept dabbing at them. The memories prompted sadness but hadn't prevented her telling the tale.

Until now.

She was stalling or collecting her wits to get to the bad part, either of major interest to the police chief. It was up to Maddy whether she spilled facts or bullshit, and Callie was willing to give her all the rope she needed to hang herself while sipping on her lemon water.

"You parted ways," Callie said. "Then what?"

But Maddy shook her head, tissue over her mouth.

"You walked one way and she walked another. What's so hard about that?" Callie asked.

"I was drunk," she said. "I don't remember."

Amazing how stoically the supporting women sat there, mouths shut.

"Yes, you do," Callie said.

"I remember running," she said.

"Running where?"

"Someplace safe."

Callie let a slow five seconds pass. "Why did you need to be someplace safe, Maddy?"

Chapter 29

MADDY DIDN'T directly answer Callie's question about needing a place to hide. "I believe you're aware of the man who's been harassing me?"

Callie didn't confirm nor deny. "Tell me about him." This was Maddy's story, and it wasn't traveling in a straight line. Callie refused to support the script with affirmations, but she'd listen to it in its asides and shifts, forwards and backwards. Frankly, she was glad Maddy was here, healthy, and seemingly well, but the resources expended to search for this woman, who'd been somewhere right under their noses—not dead or kidnapped, steamed her under the collar a bit. It wasn't that Maddy hadn't gone through something. More like the rest of the women had strung Callie along, not wanting anyone in their business. The trouble was, Elizabeth stumbled into their business, which made their business Callie's.

Callie waited, giving Maddy a lot of silence. People longed to fill in silence.

"Um," Maddy said with a throat clearing. "I came to Edisto with these women because I was in a bad place. A man was hounding me in Tampa, so I escaped here for a reprieve."

She'd already said as such, but the nervous tended to repeat themselves, and Callie let her.

"His name?"

"Kent Trevino."

"When was the first time you saw him on Edisto?"

"Just the once," Maddy said, then caught herself.

"That's right," Callie said. "He was here. Explain where and when you saw him."

Vivien spoke up. "You don't have to answer—"

Chiara spun on them. "What the hell? Y'all never told me he was here." Then to Maddy, "Honest to God, *Grace*, you keep that asshole a secret from me? As I'm going out visiting people? When he could be stalking me, too?" She jumped up, snatching her hand away from Robin's. "What the hell else don't I know?"

"Sit down, Chiara," Vivien said.

Her cheeks had reddened, her core shaking. "I'm sick of all this. You," and she pointed to Lydia, then quickly at Vivien, "do not get to run my life. He beat me up and you don't think I need to know he's walking free hunting for us? Where's he been hiding?" She thought harder, her breath seething. "For all we know, he slept right under us in the storage room, waiting for one of us to come out alone. He could've fucked any one of us right here." She pointed at the floor, meaning the storage room beneath. "He could've beat the shit out of me, you, her. Hell, he could've killed us all."

She was on a roll, her whole body quivering. "All this sanctimonious talk about rules and accountability. I'm done with you people." Didn't take three hard strides for her to make it to the screen door that led off the porch. However, she paused, everyone there reading her thoughts. What if Kent Trevino was watching the house right now? What if he followed her out into the dark?

As though weighing what kind of woman she was as she drew an imaginary line in front of her used-to-be friends, she turned to Maddy, mouthed *fuck you*, and marched out onto the boardwalk leading to the water.

Funny how nobody sitting there spoke up, the least bit worried he might be there.

Callie returned interest to Maddy. "You parted ways with Elizabeth…"

"I was tired, but she wasn't because she sleeps days and works nights. My phone had died. The stress of the afternoon and the long, emotional sharing of our stories had drained me dry. I hugged her and came back here."

Way too simple. Way too convenient.

"Maddy, but you weren't here when Elizabeth washed up, nor when my officers came to interview the others about you being, supposedly, missing. Your story isn't quite jiving, honey. Try again."

"They told me later about y'all finding Elizabeth's body."

"Doesn't fill in the blanks. Try again."

"You don't have to tell her," Vivien warned.

Callie raised her brows. "Oh, so she has secrets to protect. Is that right, Maddy?" Then before Maddy could respond, Callie added, "Were you or weren't you missing?"

"I wasn't missing," she said.

"Yet earlier you said you needed someplace safe to hide," Callie reminded.

Maddy stiffened.

"You don't have to say anything," Vivien reminded.

"Don't say anything at all," Lydia interjected. "This meeting is done."

Maddy watched one lady, then another, then Callie, becoming more uncertain with each remark said.

"If this meeting is over, then I have no choice but to label Maddy a person of interest in Elizabeth Brown's death."

Maddy flinched. "What? I didn't kill Elizabeth."

"Then who did?" Callie asked.

"Don't answer," Vivien said.

Callie rose, slowly and easily. "Then you remain a contender for the title, Maddy. I have to ask you don't leave this beach for the time being."

"No!" she yelled.

"Stop it, Chief," Vivien said, voice hardened.

But Callie hushed, not moving to leave, waiting for someone else to make the next move.

Lydia leaned over for the tray of food. "Party's over."

Maddy went to the screen, staring into the night, maybe hunting for Chiara who surely hadn't gone far.

Callie went to her. Before Vivien had a chance to navigate around the coffee table and chairs, Callie spoke low into Maddy's ear. "We can go outside to help you remember. We probably need to go lay eyes on Chiara anyway with Trevino unaccounted for."

From Maddy's other side, Vivien said, "This is over."

"I'll go with you," Callie offered. "Hopefully, we can remove you from our list."

"Maddy," Vivien warned.

Maddy pushed the screen door and exited, without a word to either Vivien or Callie, the angel and the devil on her shoulders.

Callie loved it when people went off script. Lydia had to be thinking *oh shit* behind them in the house. By the time Maddy hit the boardwalk outside, Callie on her heels, Vivien had retrieved Lydia and followed.

The sun gone, the moon barely a sliver, light was little more than pricks in the darkness from houses up and down the sound. Callie would've ordinarily wished for a flashlight, to avoid wildlife and surprises that happened in the pitch out here, but this time she relished the blacks and grays, putting everyone at a disadvantage.

Callie caught up to Maddy, who'd unsurprisingly caught up to Chiara. "Let's go back to that night," Callie said. "You left Elizabeth about there, right?" and she pointed south, parallel to the water's edge. There was no exactness to the location, but Callie expected Maddy's gaze would home in on the exact spot.

Turning, scouting the area where they stood, Callie did more generalizing. "You had arrived right around... here? Headed home?"

Maddy nodded.

Chiara had moved to within reach of her friend, listening hard.

"You looked back," Callie said.

Another nod.

"What did you see?"

With a side glance at Vivien, Callie halfway expected an interruption, but the counselor didn't object, which told Callie this school of thought was close to the truth. Legit and likely unimpeachable. Lydia stood silent against her buddy, shawl wrapped tight thought the temperature still hadn't dipped below eighty.

"I..." Maddy said, then let her thoughts gel more. "I wanted to see that Elizabeth could walk okay, that she was safe to return alone. But..."

"But she wasn't?"

Maddy shook her head.

"Why? Who made it unsafe?"

There wasn't enough moonlight to confirm, but Callie heard tears in Maddy's voice. "A man grabbed her."

When she paused, Callie said nothing.

"He... he wrestled with her. She fought back." Another pause. "I just froze." Then she shook her head. "No, I didn't. I hid." With her chin, she motioned toward the end of the boardwalk, surrounded by dune grasses. "He dragged her toward the water. She was too drunk to fight hard, and he was so much bigger." She choked on the last sentence.

"Then what did he do?"

"He hit her in the head with something. Too far to tell. She fell into the water. They were about knee deep at the time."

Of course Maddy had remained hidden. It would've been her against a man who'd already demonstrated he could overwhelm a woman her size.

"What did he do once she was down?" Callie asked.

"He dragged her into the water until she floated. Then... I couldn't rightly see. He stayed gone a long time. I was too afraid to stand for fear he'd see me and realize he'd killed the wrong..."

"The wrong woman?" Callie finished. "Who was the man, Maddy?"

"It was Kent," she said. "I'm sure of it. He has these broad shoulders from the gym. He has a hurt knee he favors..."

Chiara moved closer, slipping her arm around her friend's waist. "He wrenched it during a 10K run in Clearwater."

". . . three or four hundred yards away," Maddy began again, repeating some of the facts. "He came back to dry land without her. I ducked behind the dune grass, behind the boardwalk, debating whether to go back. What could I do if I went back? What if Kent came after me?"

She spoke faster, her eyes pleading to be believed. "I waited, thinking he'd see his mistake. I waited for her to scream. I waited for anything. I was too afraid to come out of hiding, Chief Morgan."

She was pleading to be believed, but Callie only listened, leaving her wanting enough to keep talking.

"I waited for what felt like forever. Then I got afraid he was sneaking around, circling back. What if he'd stalked us from Coots, waiting to take one of us without the other? I got seriously freaked out when I realized Kent might've been stalking me. Elizabeth and I looked alike. People said so at Coots."

"How long did you wait?"

"No idea."

"What did you finally do?"

"Slipped up through the grass and ran to the house and got—" But she seemed to catch herself.

"Got who? Got what?"

Lydia stepped over. "She came and got me, Chief Morgan."

"Lydia," Vivien said. "That's enough."

But Lydia acted as if she hadn't heard her counselor. "She retrieved me."

"To do what?" Callie said. "One would think you'd call the police."

Lydia looked to Maddy, an unspoken agreement between them. Who knows, maybe they'd rehearsed this before, but Callie was willing to hear whatever was said, by whomever. She'd sort the truth later.

Lydia nodded and Maddy spoke. "I left out a part," she said.

Vivien raised arms wide. "I advise you not to do this!"

"What part?" Callie asked, as if Vivien hadn't said a word.

"He came hunting me. Kent. He was fully aware there were two of us, and when he attacked the wrong one, he came hunting me. He'd seen me stop here. I crouched under the boardwalk, mired in the sand, reaching around me for anything to defend myself, because he wasn't leaving a witness."

Chiara hugged her tighter.

"I watched his feet, moving around me. Then he reached under the walkway and dragged me out." Odd how she wasn't crying anymore. A hardness had set in. "My hand grazed along the wood, filling my hand with splinters, but about the time he lifted me to stand, I grasped a rock. I recall it being smooth and it almost slipping through my fingers. When he righted me on my feet, lifting me like I was a doll or something, I smacked him upside the head with it. As hard as I could." She lost her gazey look and turned to stare straight on into Callie's eyes. "I hit him. Then I went in the house."

"Why didn't you call me?" Callie asked.

Lydia inserted herself into the circle. "Because she retrieved me, as she was supposed to." She turned to Chiara. "You and Robin go back to the house."

Chiara hugged Maddy and did as she was told. Once they were out of hearing range, Lydia resumed the conversation. Vivien kept a hand on her elbow, as though to offer silent guidance.

"So," Callie said, "Maddy hit Kent, incapacitated him, then ran to retrieve you in order to decide what to do?"

Nodding, Lydia didn't seem moved at all. "She pointed him out to me. I directed her back to the house."

Interesting place to stop. "Have to admit you've intrigued me, Lydia. On the edge of my seat grabbed my attention. I'll go ahead and ask... and then what happened?"

Looking at Vivien, then Maddy, Lydia took a cleansing breath. "I dragged him to the water's edge. You can check. It was close to high tide. Not an easy feat, but I didn't have to drag him far. I splashed water in his face, in hope that Maddy hadn't killed him."

Maddy gasped, the only one affected by the visual.

"He woke," Lydia said. "With a headache, mind you, from the way he held his temple, but he could speak."

"Dying to hear this conversation," Callie said, trying to envision the distance from the boardwalk to the water and Lydia's ability to drag a hundred-eighty-five-pound man if his driver's license was correct.

"I got in his face, Chief. Nothing I haven't done before. Ask Vivien's ex. Ask one or two of mine."

Callie waited for her to get past the braggadocio. "And the

message?"

"Disappear now or disappear later. Leave my ladies alone."

Interesting. "And he took you seriously?"

But Lydia wasn't daunted. "Maddy just saw him drag someone into the ocean. He made the mistake of coming after her, identifying himself. What else was he going to do?"

Walking the distance from the dune grass to the surf, Callie estimated the distance with a higher tide. Twenty feet maybe? Glancing back over her shoulder, she estimated Lydia's strength. Her story would've been better if she'd, say, run back and forth from the soft ebb and flow of a high tide with water cupped in her hands, but the sand was smooth without obstacles. Possible. Maybe.

"You watched him leave?"

"Yes."

"He could've killed you," Callie offered.

"The reason I sent Maddy in the house, to protect the witness."

A chill went up Callie's back, the kind like when Beverly said one thing and meant another. A foreboding of something not right.

"Hiding her out in the storage room was your mistake," Callie said, as if she'd accepted the story as told.

"I fully concede that. She was a complete mess, as you can imagine. I didn't want to upset Robin or Chiara." The omission meaning she'd told Vivien. Who wouldn't tell the attorney in their fold?

"Honestly, I found her in the storage room, balled up in a knot against the wall. It was all I could do to keep her quiet and calm. Gave her a couple of my Valium then kept her somewhat sedated for the next day and part of the next. When Chiara," and Lydia lifted her hands in vexation, "kept on questioning us about Maddy, we had to tell her what happened. It's why the storage room was unlocked when you found it. We'd taken Maddy to bed, which took some doing getting her up the stairs, and worked to clean her up and calm her down, and completely forgotten to relock the downstairs room."

Callie stepped back toward the water, looking over the sound toward where Pine and Otter Islands would be seen during the day.

She had an accounting; how real remained questionable. She had a reported killer, who remained at large himself. She had a witness who was drunk and an emotional wreck. And the last person who saw the killer simply told him to go away and never bother anyone again.

"What else can we offer?" Vivien asked, daring to step closer.

"Formal statements," Callie said. "Now. In my office. If you call yourself assisting a murder investigation, that's how you do it. Whether it takes all night and all day tomorrow, that's what you can do. Are you that willing to cooperate? Or will this be like everything thus far, a cat-and-mouse game?"

Vivien gave a soft tip of her head. "We'll do it. Who would you like first?"

Callie looked at Lydia. "Maddy. Then Lydia. Then you, Counselor. The others tomorrow."

"Agreed," she said, and after the awkwardness of who returned inside first, they walked to the house.

When Callie went to leave, telling Maddy and Lydia she'd see them in thirty minutes, Lydia's expression hung as stoic and solid as ever. What was it about her that everyone protected, from Beverly to Raysor? What was her secret?

And here she was, protecting Maddy, a girl she proclaimed three days ago was a nuisance and not a real member of the team.

No doubt Lydia was impressive.

Callie drove to the office, making calls to Raysor and Mark about how her night was about to play out. Both offered to check in on her periodically. Mark said he'd drop off food.

Taking a quick moment to jot notes and set up her office, she replayed everything said, outlining how Elizabeth's final night supposedly occurred.

These women, each of them, proved to be a different breed than how she first read them. Instead of being women flitting around the beach once a year playing escort service, they were women fighting to be strong, refusing to let the world hurt them, chastise them, or take them down. They'd fought back from being victim to being firm and staunch, each possibly more than once.

She had at least narrowed down where Elizabeth was attacked on the beach and could talk to the residents or tenants of those houses about what they'd seen, but at three or four in the morning, what were the chances?

Almost made Callie wonder how many times Lydia and her ladies had gotten even elsewhere in their worlds.

Chapter 30

Three Weeks Later

EARLY MORNING, on her way to the office, Callie took a detour to cruise by *Time in a Bottle*, a habit she'd developed these past three weeks. The ladies had remained discreet, she'd give them that. She and her officers had kept an eye out for them and hadn't seen one of them in public, though occasionally one or the other of their two vehicles were spotted in a beach house drive.

Elizabeth's funeral had come and gone, and Callie had attended it out of some strange sense of guilt for not finding the killer. Nolan blamed himself more than anyone else, and he seemed more accepting of the case going cold than Callie.

Edisto Beach PD found Kent Trevino's rental in the driveway of the two hundred block of Palmetto Street the day Callie finished interviewing the ladies. The residence's owner filed a complaint, thinking a tourist had wanted to park closer to their spot on the beach than the main public lot.

The BOLO for Trevino landed nothing, with nobody having a clue where to look past what had already been canvassed. He never reappeared at his Fort Street rental. Janet Wainwright had to clear out his things and put them in storage, pending notification of what should be done with them. He never showed up to work or his home. The employer told his next of kin, a brother in Massachusetts, about his disappearance.

Callie wasn't happy having no conclusion about Elizabeth's murder and wasn't comfortable with Trevino's whereabouts remaining a mystery.

Trevino killed Elizabeth. That part was almost certain. Fearful of what he'd done, he disappeared, people said. Law enforcement would continue seeking him, but each day passing and nobody waiting at home for him sort of diluted the effort.

A missing person nobody cared about.

Having risen earlier than usual, unable to sleep, she'd cruised the beach this sunny and rather hot day, and this was her second time driving by the house. No cars in the drive either time, but if they'd had dates, they might not be home yet.

She parked at the station. Upon approaching the front door, she noted a bag hanging from the handle. Nobody else had arrived yet, and judging by the lack of dew on the bag, it hadn't been there long. Someone had worked a hole in it and slipped it over the knob, a note inside.

Found this on the beach. Asked around the houses nearby and nobody knew the name. Signed, Arthur Butler. His phone number followed.

The wallet and the items it had contained had been saturated with salt water, and while some Samaritan, probably Butler, had removed the items and attempted to dry them, they remained wrinkled, some fragile, the leather shriveled and ruined. The items no longer fit inside the wallet, and he'd left the driver's license, two credit cards, a medical card, and a laminated business card loose, unable to squeeze them back into their compartments. They all proclaimed the same owner. A licensed real estate agent named Kent Trevino.

Callie laid out the items on her desk then made her call. The Good Samaritan Arthur Butler answered on the second ring. Callie introduced herself, thanked him, then asked, "Sir, can you meet me where you found this wallet? Before the beach gets busy?"

"I just figured someone would've called in the missing wallet, and you would deliver it to him," the man said, nice enough, but leery of being questioned.

"The man's missing," she said.

"Oh, damn." Silence. "I don't want to get dragged into anything."

"No, sir. Just help us get our bearings on where the wallet was. That may help us in hunting for him."

After a little more coaxing, he agreed, and in ten minutes she met up with him on the 2900 block of Palmetto. At this locale, the sand spread wide and swung around to the quieter frontage, with fewer waves than the Atlantic but more than the sound.

"Found it half buried," he said, and he walked to a spot off from the Billow Street access, nowhere near the dunes, but way out closer to the water. "More than half buried, actually. About here. My wife stepped on it while wading. Lucky she found it."

"Y'all staying nearby?" Callie asked, wondering if maybe they'd actually seen Trevino. He might've changed residences, hiding in plain sight, but she wouldn't hang her hat on that one. There was no telling when the wallet got washed out into the water.

"No, we were just walking. We're staying back on Myrtle. Off Eddings? We try to walk three miles each day. I'm thinking if it hadn't been going on low tide, and we hadn't been there at the right time, that thing would've been lost forever."

He wasn't far from wrong.

"Any chance you recognize the guy?" she asked. "Ever seen him out here?"

The mouth scrunch clearly said no. "He's from Florida. We're from Michigan." Like that made a difference.

Truth was, if this wallet had been attached to a body, no telling how far it had traveled. The body would've eventually been repossessed by the ocean's creatures, but the wallet was light enough to have tumbled quite a way. People lost their wallets on the beach, sometimes the tide snatching them as it rose unexpectedly around dozing sunbathers, but Callie didn't see Trevino as a sunbather.

In her mind, today rather clinched the reality they weren't going to find this guy.

She drove back toward the station. A family of five went to cross the road, and she stopped for them. Their arms were full of rafts, boogie boards, and totes, the father tugging a wagon with a cooler, and the kids tripping over their precious water toys they'd use to dig to China. The day was brilliantly beautiful, one of those days Callie could hold a smile from sunup to sundown, happy to be assigned to a place so enticing, but she wasn't feeling it. The wallet had dredged up keener feelings about what had happened to Elizabeth and Maddy, and, of course, Lydia. She saw herself as a better detective than this. No, it wasn't that she wasn't sure what happened. She just couldn't prove it.

The lights were on inside the station. Marie had arrived, and per the county sheriff's office vehicle, Deputy Raysor was as well.

This time, however, there was a box at the door, tied with string. *To Marie* written on the outside.

She carried it inside. "What's with the gifts dropped at the door? First, I find Kent Trevino's wallet in a plastic bag, and then this. Next, we'll be finding babies in swaddling clothes."

Callie handed the package off to her office manager. Raysor loomed over Marie's shoulder. "Who's it from? Got a tag?"

"Secret admirer?" Callie asked, rummaging through phone notes Marie had taken from yesterday evening.

Marie didn't blush, so odds were not a boyfriend. Nobody in the station had seen Marie on a date or heard about a beau. She attended events alone or with an occasional resident. She led a secluded life, pleased with her life's choices.

"Probably a thanks from someone. We get things like this at least once a month," she said. "You forget I'm the face of Edisto Beach PD because you guys are always out and about. I'm the nice one." She winked once at Raysor.

A phone message in her hand caught Callie's attention. A domestic case she'd already spoken to three times. "These two ought to just get divorced," she said, thankful their bruhahas continued to be verbal and not physically abusive. Abuse made her think of *The Summer Ladies*.

The box fell and hit the desktop with a smack. Marie backed away with a hand over her mouth.

Callie dropped her messages and ran over to see what had shocked this unshockable woman, thinking threatening notes or body parts. "What is it?" What kind of damn joke had someone sent her?

Raysor peered in the box for something sinister, shrugging at Callie when he found nothing. Just a vintage red shawl neatly folded, not even the fringe much out of place.

"It's..." Callie started, then wasn't sure what to say. Of course she recognized the shawl. She'd seen Lydia arrange and rearrange the elegant fabric around her shoulders too many times.

"Hmm," Raysor said. "Was there a note?"

But Marie wasn't touching the box, a confusion of emotions in her face, in eyes that weren't sure whether to cry.

What was this? Marie didn't cry.

With Marie not responding, Raysor queried a look at Callie who draped an arm around Marie's shoulders. "What's wrong, honey?"

"That's my great-grandmother's shawl," she whispered.

Callie carefully removed the item, laying it gently on the desk, then studied the box inside and out, then both sides of the tissue paper. No message. No tag. Nothing but *To Marie* written on the lid.

"My mother left with it when I was a child so young I was barely talking. My great-grandmother used to describe it to me, claiming it was the most precious thing to her other than me. She compared me to that shawl to the day she died."

"Are you sure it's the same—"

Marie jerked out her phone, not wanting to explain herself, the cover on her phone a photo of a photo showing an elderly woman wrapped in the very same shawl.

"Is she back?" she asked, peering at Callie.

"Is who back, honey?"

Raysor stood behind Marie, out of her vision, as if he expected her to fall.

"My mother. She left under a cloud, and I haven't heard from or seen her since. Of all the Edisto secrets I know, of all the skeletons in so many Edistonian closets, my own is the one I know least about. And the older people get, the less chance I'll ever find out. My Nana said my mother left for my sake. That never made sense." She dared to finger the material. "Why now?" she asked. "It was hand delivered from the look of it." Now she teared up. "Why now? And why not just deliver it to me herself?"

She stared up at Callie, seeking answers Callie didn't have.

Or did she?

Marie turned to Raysor for guidance. He shrugged, but once she turned back around, he shook his head at Callie. *Don't tell her.*

He knew, too.

Callie thought through the luncheon conversation with Beverly about the woman who left Edisto years ago, who sacrificed for family, whose real identity had to remain anonymous. Callie had assumed she'd disappeared and taken the child with her.

Janet, Sarah, and Sophie showed no signs of being fluent in Lydia's past, yet they'd learned to hold onto some level of respect for her, probably conceived from the first-hand knowledge of Beverly, Raysor, and Brice.

"Well, now the shawl is yours," Callie said. "And it's exquisite. I want to see you wear it. The sender felt it was yours to have, so appreciate the gesture. Think of your mother and your great-grandmother when you hug it around you. Feel like their strengths have been passed down to you. That's what heirlooms are for."

Marie reached tentatively for the wrap, its folds falling out as she slowly lifted it.

Callie took its edges and loosely draped it over Marie's shoulders, understanding clearly that Lydia would know Callie recognized it. A farewell, maybe? An end to *The Summer Ladies* returning to Edisto?

For some reason all those years ago, Lydia had left the island in shame without her child. Leaving a baby behind wouldn't come easy for almost any sort of mother. There was a story there. A story Marie didn't know that others did, and those others had been asked to remain quiet, probably by the great-grandmother in order to protect the child from old rumor.

Callie asked the question that had gone unanswered by so many. "What was your mother's name?"

"Bonnie. Bonnie Gadson. My great-grandmother was Lillian Gadson. We go six generations back."

That was about as Edistonian as one could get.

Now that Callie had this much information, one day soon, maybe when Callie checked on Beverly's gout, she would pry the entire story from her mother.

"I assume there was a grandmother in between?" she asked.

"Ruby Gadson," Marie said. "She was not a good person. That's all I was told."

All Gadsons. No married names. Women who continued families most likely without husbands in the picture.

Callie was afraid to ask more questions.

Now she was part of the secret. The secret nobody would tell. Not Beverly, not Sarah, nor even Raysor. Callie didn't possess the whole story, but she garnered the secrecy was in the name of protecting Marie.

What had Lydia done to warrant abandoning her child, yet was worth risking coming back incognito once a year to be near Marie? Callie envisioned Lydia watching her daughter from afar, which had to be difficult considering how rare Marie's public appearances were. And painful being unable to approach her.

Callie reached up and brushed a tear off Marie's cheek with her thumb. "It looks beautiful on you. Now, only happy thoughts, okay? Someone sent this to you to enjoy not feel sad about."

Smiling through moist eyes, Marie nodded, then promptly wiped both palms across her face.

Lifting her pile of sticky notes warranting her attention as chief, Callie turned toward the door. "I need to check a couple of these. Be back in bit. Call if anything comes up." Business as usual, which helped Marie right herself and do the same. She started to take the shawl off, but on second thought, left it in place.

Callie exited. She'd reached her car when she heard the heavy trot of Raysor behind her.

"Where are you going?"

"To *Time in a Bottle*," she said.

"Don't put your nose in something that doesn't merit it," he warned.

"I just have to see for myself, Don. Give me some credit."

"Think about Marie."

"Always," she said, got in and left.

Took her two minutes to reach the beach house. Took her two seconds to see the ladies were gone. *Time in a Bottle* was being rented by a family of six from the hubbub of people unloading two vehicles packed with groceries, beach miscellany, and suitcases.

No more *Summer Ladies.*

And while Kent Trevino's case might remain active, it would quickly go cold... and remain that way.

Chapter 31

Lydia

THREE WEEKS SINCE the chief had asked each of them that pointed question. *What happened the night Elizabeth died?*

Whether they did it or not, they weren't helping the police put a name on the killer. Justice got lost in the justice system, the aftermath taking the shape of whatever its victims could make of themselves, an assortment of broken parts that no longer fit. Often times with the culprit continuing his path of destruction.

Selling their wares to selective customers put them in charge. They vetted others for their clientele list. They charged them what they thought a client was worth. They dictated who, when, where, and how they offered or received pleasure. They spent four weeks constructing a quality of life and deciding who was invited to share it with them.

They owned their own lives.

The practice had worked seamlessly for thirty years.

Lydia understood this day would eventually come but hadn't expected it. A day when her Eden ran out of perfection. All it took was one fucking snake.

It was amazing how Maddy had changed their last three weeks, putting into perspective real danger versus that of being a *Summer Lady*. She grasped how much they were in charge of their destinies, recognizing the wisdom and heftiness of personal empowerment. They'd protected her like no uniform had. They'd restored her confidence to a degree she hadn't experienced for years.

They made sacrifices to be who they were, and they did their damnedest to maintain the integrity of who they'd become.

They wouldn't be back next year, though. The decision pained Lydia to her core.

"Lydia?"

Vivien. Bless her. In their vote last night, she posed the most concerns. Where would they go next summer? How would they find a new clientele as loving and understanding as these? Could they tell the Edisto people where they'd be next year, in case they wanted to follow? Would they remain quiet?

Their whole circle wept at the loss of their customers whom they'd come to cherish.

Kent Trevino's case wasn't closed without a body. What if a body, or bones of it, appeared and anyone went so far as to reopen the case?

"We will forever be suspects in Chief Morgan's eyes," Lydia explained. "Our anonymity is gone. The magic of who we were is tarnished."

Surprisingly, Chiara cried hardest. "This is all my fault. I never should have talked to the police."

Lydia didn't tell her how true her words were, but Lydia should've brought her into the fold of what happened that night, and none of this confusion would've happened. Chiara as much as anyone understood who they were and what they stood for, and she'd be stronger in carrying on the mission elsewhere. There were enough beaches in Florida. They only came to Edisto because of Lydia's past, what little of it they knew.

If they only knew.

"Lydia," Vivien repeated. In spite of the rain, Lydia had removed herself to the back porch of *Time in a Bottle*, slinging her grandmother's shawl around her, staying far enough back not to let moisture ruin the velvet and silk. The wrap had been her mother's as well, and it was all she owned of family, other than memories, many of which she hated. The slide of the material, the faded reds, the simple endurance of age gave it wisdom. Not that she had unlocked its secrets. Each time she slung it around her shoulders, however, she felt... *noble*. Maddy's word.

But its strength belonged on Edisto.

"You want company?" Vivien asked.

Lydia stood and removed the shawl. "No. I was about to come in."

They went to the kitchen where a box rested on the bar. Lydia folded the shawl and gingerly wrapped it in tissue paper.

"We about ready?" she asked.

"Yes. They're outside. They might be a tad worried about you. As am I."

Lydia tied the string around the box. "I'm good. Change happens."

"Not like this."

"Just like this," she said. "This is when we learn the most about who we really are."

The words sounded noble indeed, but the pain in her core almost stole her breath.

"Let's go." She willed herself forward. "We have a quick stop then we're off this beach."

She hugged Vivien, who said, "This is growth. This is us practicing what we preach, that we are strong, in control, and do not let others rob us of our souls."

Vivien gave her that soft smile Lydia loved so much. Viv was good at these little preachings. Inside, however, the old cracks in Lydia's old heart had opened anew. She was leaving Edisto, and the reality she might never return was tearing her apart.

She would be buried out here though. She didn't care then who remembered her past and how. Who knew? By then those familiar might be dead, too.

Chapter 32

THE FOLLOWING Sunday, Callie officially and physically took off work to remain home and enjoy it. Mark chose to do the same, with a warning that he was on call due to it being late July and one of the busiest times of the year. They'd at least try to do nothing but vacuum, catch up on laundry, and eat dinner together on the porch. Plain and domestic. Braindead and relaxed.

In the days following the shawl delivery, Callie had looked up all she could on Ruby, Lillian, and Marie Gadson. In the Charleston newspaper archives, in the Edisto Beach paper archives, not that it went that far back. The only findings were those in the local paper accommodating Marie for her years in service.

Raysor wouldn't tell her any other parts he knew and whether or not they even existed. Why had Marie's mother left her, and why had she been raised by her great-grandmother instead of the grand? Callie had heard already how Marie had been living solo by the time she was seventeen, finishing school on her own, then going to work for the Edisto Police Department. A simple life history until you realized there was a hidden story there. Callie didn't do well leaving a puzzle incomplete. Not solving Trevino's case was hard enough.

"Some secrets need to remain secrets," Mark said, chopping the throw pillows back into place after vacuuming the living room. "Quit dwelling on it."

Barefooted in threadbare khaki shorts, Callie brushed by him, her arms filled with the last load of dried laundry. "Um, I'm dwelling on how you learned to stage pillows."

She'd relayed everything to the deepest detail to Mark. Half of her regretted telling the Gadson secret, the other half refused to harbor secrets from him. Their relationship was new enough to thwart but embedded enough to respect.

"When are you ready for the steaks to go on the grill?" he asked.

Sometimes you wanted protein other than seafood.

"Any time you are. Baked potatoes are about to go in the oven, but you haven't started the charcoal yet, so we still have time."

He nudged the vacuum into the closet. "Ample time for what?"

She'd slipped up behind him. "For whatever you think you can handle while the coals get hot."

He pivoted around to face her. "Sometimes things get hot fast."

They kissed. "Yes," she mumbled, kissing him through the words. "They do."

A knock sounded at the front door.

Heads touching, both sighed. "Sophie," they said in unison.

There was good and bad in Sophie being their next-door neighbor. Where was Buck? Shouldn't Sophie be having her own afternoon tryst?

Callie reached halfway to the door before she realized that the knock wasn't Sophie's. She rapped a door in triple time, like a hummingbird on speed. This was a casual, respectable knock. The silhouette behind the etched glass hinted at an all-too-familiar being.

Callie opened the door.

Beverly had actually crossed the causeway and set foot back on Edisto Beach.

"Mother? I... didn't..."

"I was afraid you'd say no if I called, so I didn't," her mother said, then tacked on, "May I come in?"

"Of course you may come in." Mark appeared as backup punter. "As timing would have it, we just finished cleaning. It's like an omen."

Beverly slid over the threshold in khaki slacks, making Callie take note they wore the same color, the same material... one fashionably styled for a casual tea, the other fitted up for tag football. She carried a tote in her hand, déjà vu their Edingsville lunch.

After an approving smile at Mark's etiquette, her mother took a moment to take in the surroundings. She hadn't seen the rebuilt home that had replaced the burned one. "You did keep the same floorplan."

"Yes," Callie said. "What do you think?"

"Looks more like you than me now," came the reply. She made her way to the living room, whereas most visitors cozied up to the kitchen bar.

Callie could do living room.

Mark disappeared into the kitchen, Callie hoping he was after refreshments, and for a second, she had a mind lapse as to what, if anything, was worthy of bringing out. Then she mentally kicked herself for falling into the old routine of feeling less than acceptable. "What made you come all the way out here?" she said, meaning what had enticed her across the bridge.

"Marie," she said.

Stunned, Callie looked up at Mark who peered back at her over the bar from the kitchen, equally surprised.

"Who...?" She let the question trail away, wondering who would contact Beverly about Marie.

"Need to know, dear, as you detective sorts are fond of saying."

Releasing an abrupt snort in the kitchen, Mark tried to cover up via ice in glasses and clearing his throat.

Beverly ran a hand over the sofa cushion, feeling the nub. "No doubt you've done research on Marie and her family once she received the shawl."

Okay, the tattler could be Raysor, but she'd be surprised if he'd made that call. "I have."

"And you found nothing."

"That's right."

"Let's keep it that way."

Finally, Callie had been brought into the fold, so couldn't they talk openly now about the subject? "Explain it to me, Mother. This means something to you, or you wouldn't have set foot on the beach. After Brice's funeral–"

"He was one of several who understood firsthand. We cannot afford for you to disturb what needs to remain buried. Do you understand me?"

Do you understand me? pinged through her head. Memories of Middleton rushed in. She hated those words. She'd fought not to say them to Jeb. There were so many other words to use rather than these four so routinely beaten over Callie's head growing up.

But Callie caught herself before arguing about something so frivolous. The topic Beverly crossed the bridge for held much more importance.

Mark handed them both a tonic and lime, sans gin. Cheese, crackers, and pickles were arranged in little towers on a plate. She loved his loving to fool with food. She loved even more making Beverly do without alcohol.

"Explain to me, Mother," Callie said, then downed a sip for what suddenly seemed to be a dry mouth.

"Marie grew up hard. She probably doesn't realize how hard. Her mother grew up harder. Her name—"

"Bonnie Gadson."

Beverly paused then nodded. "Yes, and her great-grandmother—"

"Lillian Gadson. Yes, I've learned the family tree. Marie told me."

". . . made some hard choices when Marie was a toddler. Bonnie was raped repeatedly by a boy a few years older. Her mother overdosed, leaving Bonnie to be raised by her grandmother. Invariably the rapes turned into pregnancies."

"Pregnancies? As in plural?"

"Yes. She chose to carry the third one."

"Marie?"

Beverly nodded.

"Bonnie..."

"AKA Lydia," Callie tacked on, keeping track. "Society was tighter back then, but leave her child? With four generations of Gadson, doesn't that say they didn't have many marriages in the family anyway? What happened with the father?"

"He disappeared." This time Beverly took time to sip her drink, eating an entire hors d'oeuvre before returning her gaze to her daughter.

Mark had made himself comfortable across the room, out of the conversation, but to this his brows raised. "Disappeared?"

Callie lifted her hand barely off the sofa, a motion for Mark to let her handle this. "How did he disappear, Mother?"

"Nobody knows."

Like Kent Trevino.

"Why did Lydia, um, Bonnie, leave if she didn't have anything to do with it?"

"Nobody knows."

To that they all sat silent. The fact that Callie had been made aware, and that only a handful of people were aware, culminated in the fact nothing could be proven. Not forty years later.

Like she couldn't prove anything about Trevino today.

The pieces weren't difficult to connect. The lack of a case. The community shutdown of shared information, which had been brilliantly handled. Suddenly the burden set heavy on Callie's back, and Beverly's overt effort to come to Edisto after the pain of Brice's demise gave it an even heavier weight.

"A new police chief came into town when Marie was about twelve years old, and he took the family on as a project, seeing to it that Marie had what she needed. Seeing the great-grandmother was buried a few years later."

Callie caught on. "And he hired her right out of high school to give her a decent start on life."

Marie's loyalty wasn't just a work ethic. It was repayment for keeping her from becoming her ancestors. A step up. Marie had worked over twenty years for nine different chiefs before Callie.

Suddenly the chief's job came with a new duty: to protect Marie.

"Let her mother decide what Marie knows and what she doesn't," Beverly said. "It's what the beach promised. There aren't many of us left, but those here still want to maintain that vow."

Callie set her glass down, with no words to say. Her mother had broken her vow to continue its protection by informing her daughter, the police chief now entrusted with the secret. Marie was Edisto Beach PD's to protect.

"Oh," Beverly said. "I brought you this." She set another tote in front of Callie.

Callie shifted attention to her mother's housewarming gift. Inside were two more Neil Diamond albums, again, autographed. Beverly had to have somebody on her staff scouring the Internet on auction sites for these.

Callie slid them onto her lap. This time, however, with a wary eye, she studied her mother.

"No strings," Beverly said.

"Just a promise," Callie added.

"Yes, ma'am," her mother replied. "Now, I hear this man of yours is a good cook. What are we having for dinner?"

Chapter 33

Lydia

VIVIEN BROUGHT them each a vodka tonic and joined Lydia on their shared Bayshore condo balcony, peering across the vast green area to the water beyond. Lydia studied once again the photo on her phone's screen saver and couldn't stop blessing over and over the Edistonian who'd forwarded it to her.

Vivien was fully aware of what kept her attention. "She's embracing the wrap. I'm so happy to see that. I was worried..."

Lydia released a deep sigh, telling her not to finish the thought. Moving the phone to her chest she closed her eyes, silently enjoying the community noises below.

"Thought about next summer?" Viv asked.

"Still thinking," Lydia said.

The options tossed about varied from Tybee Island, Georgia to Miami. Always on the water. It had to be on the water.

"We still don't have to rule out—"

"I'm thinking about it, Viv," Lydia said. "I'm right there on the edge of seriously thinking about it."

The End

Acknowledgment

My books take a lot of alone time, but I could not write them alone, if that makes sense. The following people make me want to stay in this business of writing mysteries, and I feel them worthy of mentioning.

First, always first, is Gary Wayne Clark, Sr. My other half is the best cheerleader in the world with the patience of Job. He listens while I edit aloud, noting technical errors or just words that don't "sound right." Hardly a day goes by that he doesn't ask if I need to work on a chapter, and if so, he'd be ready to hear one on the back porch.

The sons and grandsons, and a beautiful daughter-in-law, brag and stand by me, making me feel rather famous and special on occasion. Every few weeks, one particularly precocious grandson asks, "How famous are you now, Grandma? " My single son, Nanu, has somehow roped his girlfriend's entire extended family into being fans.

Thanks to Kingfisher Strength, my son Stephen, daughter-in-law Tara, and the family at their strength-training gym. The health regimen they've coaxed me to adopt has given me energy that has traveled not only into my days but into my keyboard. I didn't know life could feel this strong.

Bless The Coffee Shelf in Chapin for being my South Carolina Midlands headquarters for "the Chapin author." And a big hug to Karen Carter at The Edisto Bookstore for making sure every island visitor is familiar with The Edisto Island Mysteries, a twelve-year commitment thus far.

A big call out to Dee Stogdill as fan club leader in Chapin, where I live, and to Edisto's Deni Ashby, my resource for all things Sophie.

I can't speak highly enough about my former publisher, especially Debra Dixon. This time particularly merits mention. Her coaxing and gentle advice carried this book to a much higher level.

And a nod to Carrie Nelson Burch Leo, for reasons we'll keep between us... for the time being.

About the Author

C. HOPE CLARK has a fascination with the mystery genre and is author of the *Carolina Slade Mystery Series* , the *Craven County Mystery Series*, as well as the *Edisto Island Series*, all set in her home state of South Carolina. In her previous federal life, she performed administrative investigations and married the agent she met on a bribery investigation. She enjoys nothing more than editing her books on the back porch with him, overlooking the lake, with bourbons in hand. She can be found either on the banks of Lake Murray or Edisto Beach with one or two dachshunds in her lap. Hope is also editor of the award-winning FundsforWriters.com

C. Hope Clark

Facebook - facebook.com/chopeclark
Instagram - instagram.com/chopeclark
Author website www.chopeclark.com